HEADCASE

CHRIS K. JONES

THINK-STRONG PRODUCTIONS, LLC

Think-Strong Productions, LLC
www.think-strong.com & www.chriskjones.com

Cover design by Howard Grossman.

Headcase / Chris K. Jones —1st ed.
ISBN 978-1-7377154-1-2

This book is dedicated to Paul Buhtanic, my high school Creative Writing Teacher. Mr. Buhtanic, you were the spark that ignited a young man's dream to become a writer.

WORLD OF HEADCASE

Welcome to the World of Headcase.

The world that my protagonist, Dr. Andrew Beck, lives in is an alternative reality of the New York metro area in April 2019, a year before COVID-19 invaded our lives. Andrew is a sports psychologist who works with professional athletes, but there is no NFL, NBA, MLB, NHL, or PGA in the World of Headcase. Instead, there are the Professional Football League or PFL; the Basketball League of America or BLA; the Professional Baseball League or PBL; the North American Hockey League or NAHL; and the Professional Golfers League or PGL. In the World of Headcase I do use some familiar venues and sports figures. Most of the players are all athletes that competed pre-1990's but I use the players to make an emphatic point. For example, I refer to the Masters Tournament in Augusta, and to former champions Jack Nicklaus, and Arnold Palmer. This is because the impact of the conversation between Andrew and his former Masters Champion father, Ted, needed to be big, and using made-up players was not going to have the same impact as using these golfers whose names are synonymous with greatness.

It seemed daunting at first to have to create all the athletes, teams, and leagues in my alternate reality. But then, as I sat at my desk, I recalled my childhood in Rutherford, New Jersey, with my friends on Wood Street, and I realized we did this all the time. We used to pretend we were these three-sport superstar athletes back in the '70s and early '80s before Bo Jackson and Dion Sanders. The only twosporter was Danny Ainge, who played basketball for the Boston Celtics and baseball for the Toronto Blue Jays. Well, not to be outdone, we pretended to be guys talented enough to play three sports at an elite level: football, basketball, and baseball.

One of the best things about playing God in my own world is my ability to make all the New York Teams playoff contenders in their respective sports, proving that my writing is an utter work of fiction. The last time New York had contenders in every sport was 1969 when the Jets, Mets, and Knicks all took championships that year. The only exception in 1969 was that the Rangers went to the playoffs but lost to Boston Bruins in the first round. But not to worry—in *Headcase*, my hockey team, the New York Sentinels, gets their revenge against the Boston Freedom, almost ensuring them a birth in the playoffs. Sorry, not sorry, Boston!

As I began to recall the make-believe worlds we built as boys, the World of Headcase started to form. Although the players Andrew treats are all fictional, I didn't have to change much there, but I did have to come up with new team names and leagues and the names of opponents when they spoke about them. I also had a blast coming up with their uniforms, colors and fonts.

The New York Tides' baseball team comes from the old minor league affiliate of the New York Mets, the Tidewater Tides. The Tides colors are gray with blue pinstripes and lettering. In the book, there is a scene when Andrew is 12 and playing baseball with friends, which are the actual names of my childhood friends, and the Tides' uniforms that year were baby blue. I love Columbia University's colors and that's what I pictured the Tides uniforms were like in the 1990s of Andrew's youth.

The Tides also had a personal connection to my childhood. My big brother and the other older boys on the block would tease me when I struck out in Wiffle ball and say, "We're sending you down to Tidewater." Which meant I was relegated to the minors, and they wouldn't let me play until I got better. This demotion made me practice harder to earn my way back up. So the Tides had that place in my mind - scrappy players fighting for a shot at the big leagues. And now that I was in command as an author, I thought, why not let the

Tides finally make the majors?

The basketball team is the New York Black Knights. The Knights had been used in *The Natural* with Robert Redford, so I didn't want to use that. I liked the juxtaposition that a Black Knight is a winner and a good guy in the "World of Headcase." Finding their font was tricky and took the longest, but it was fun. I loved designing the black and gold uniforms. They are strong colors that go well together, and Pittsburgh doesn't own them! The Black Knights uniforms are my favorite ones. It was not until after I finished the novel that I realized that West Point's mascot was also the Black Knights, and their colors are a similar black and gold, but not exactly like mine. I decided to keep the Black Knights moniker, I like the uniforms I came up with better anyway.

The New York Sentinels are the hockey team in the World of Headcase, and their uniforms are like the Minnesota North Stars uniforms (they moved to Dallas in 1993). I came up with the Sentinels moniker because Vladimir Poplov is an enforcer, also known as an "ice guardian." As I looked for synonyms for "guard", one of the words was a sentinel. The Sentinels white, green, and gray uniforms projected the image of a steady, tough hockey team that no one messed with.

Once I had the players and teams, I needed to create the arenas and stadiums. Some of the most famous entertainment venues in the five boroughs are sports stadiums: Citi Field in Queens, Yankee Stadium in the Bronx, and Madison Square Garden in Manhattan. For *Headcase*, I had to create venues that could rival these real-world cathedrals of sport.

The Tides baseball team plays in Empire Stadium. It's still in Queens but much closer to Flushing Bay around College Point. The multi-use arena where the Black Knights and the Sentinels play is in Hudson Yards. I named it The Tomlin Insurance Sports and Entertainment Complex, affectionately called "The TISEC," pronounced as "tiZ-eck."

Tomlin Insurance is a real company in Barbados. The Tomlin family has been a big part of my life in the last few years, and I wanted to show my thanks and name an arena after them (See the Acknowledgements for the backstory). The reason why I put the "TISEC" in Hudson Yards goes back to 2012 when Mayor Bloomberg tried to get the Olympics hosted in NYC, which would have been a disaster, in my opinion. He also tried to lure the New York Jets back from the Meadowlands to Manhattan. They came up with the concept for the West Side Stadium. There were lots of drawings and renderings I was able to find that helped me picture the stadium in Hudson Yards. Hudson Yards also becomes important in *Headcase* as a dispute between one of the lead contractors and the local electrical union indirectly pulls Andrew and his wife Sandra into a mysterious murder.

The other stadium I mention in the book is in the Meadowlands in East Rutherford, NJ, the next town from my childhood home. I created a football team called the New Jersey Bulldogs. I chose the Bulldogs as the mascot because it is the same as my high school in Rutherford. I even used my school colors of navy blue and white for the team's colors. I changed the name from the current MetLife Stadium to Meadowlands Stadium, but I kept the same location.

Let me introduce you to Andrew's patients and the teams they play for. The players are: John Palmer, a second-year pitcher for the New York Tides; Lamar Hayes, a forward for the New York Black Knights; and Vladimir Poplov, a defenseman for the New York Sentinels You will get to know them intimately during the course of the book so that's all I'll tell you for now.

All my athletes are an amalgamation of my experience with pro athletes as a fan and other athletes I trained and competed against as a competitive athlete. I was a gold medal winner in Judo at the 1994 Nutmeg Games, and I also medaled tournaments in NY, NJ, CT, and RI.

My first face-to-face experience with pro athletes came when I was 17, when I worked in the locker rooms for the visiting teams playing the New Jersey Generals in the long-time defunct USFL. During the games I worked the sidelines handing out Gatorade to the players and helping the trainers with injured players getting whatever they needed. After the game and in the locker room I used to talk to the players about their lives outside of football. I was always interested

iv

in what kind of man they were, as a person. Most were kind and generous with their time even after playing a hard game. Glen Corano, the father of MMA fighter and actor Gina Corano, was a former quarterback with the Dallas Cowboys who was at the end of his career playing with the Pittsburgh Maulers. Mr. Corano spent a good half hour with me talking about life and he encouraged me to pursue my idea to become an accountant and help pro players manage their financial affairs. I had heard so many stories about players who made bad investments and managed their money poorly that by the time they were out of football they were penniless. Typical of a middle child, I thought it was so unfair to these men who were ill-equipped for life out of football. These stories and more of player off-field antics were verified by my older brother, who worked with the New York Giants in the 1980s as an equipment manager.

My dad also designed personalized athletic wear for pro athletes for the various New York teams. Players would call the house, and I would talk to them about their latest game and stats for a bit before my dad gave me a stare that would burn a hole through my head as I reluctantly handed over the phone.

I have spent a good portion of my life around athletes and understanding how they think. But in the end, I learned most that pro athletes are just like us, except they have a very particular set of skills that makes them perform amazing athletic feats. And those talents earn them millions, sometimes tens of millions of dollars a year, but for a very short time. Almost every athlete I researched experienced some kind of trauma growing up. Some were horrific. They struggle with certain parts of life, and they work in a profession where split-second decisions under extreme duress are ruthlessly analyzed. This scrutiny comes not only from their coaches, general managers, and team owners—but by journalists, fans, and even their own extended family whose existence depends on their ability to play and excel at a game.

Headcase is a novel about a troubled psychologist, who is treating professional athletes with real traumatic issues, and his own childhood traumas and gambling addiction get him in trouble along the way. But during the story, I am also trying to show the reader the plights of pro athletes. Although these are fictional characters, the problems of drug addiction, gambling addiction, rage issues, impulse control problems, and a deep-seated mistrust of others are common amongst athletes and people everywhere.

My primary goal is to entertain my readers with a world from my imagination. I hope they like the characters, feel empathy for them, and root for them. Secondly, if I could increase awareness that seeking help for mental health issues is an act of bravery and courage, that would make me very happy. Lastly, I wish to bring some awareness to the hyper-focused world of pro athletes and remind the most ardent of fans that athletes are people too, they suffer, and when they say they are experiencing mental health issues, we need to believe them, care for them, and support them. As Michael Phelps said in his 2020 HBO documentary Weight of Gold, "It's okay to say you're not okay."

If I can do all of the above, then I feel that the World of Headcase has done its job, and so have I.

HEADCASE

BOOK 1: SHOCK & DENIAL

PROLOGUE

1984

At the Greenwich Country Club in Greenwich, Connecticut, pro golfer Ted Beck was at the driving range with his two boys, Brandon, age seven, and Andrew, age five. Ted received a round of applause as he entered the range, managing waving to the crowd while also struggling to move his two boys along and carry some kid-sized clubs.

A week ago, Ted had just placed 18th in the Master's Tournament in Augusta, Georgia. He had been in third place at 5-under par going into the final round when he took some big risk shots that his caddy advised against, surprised his opponents, and gave his agent indigestion. His errant shots dropped him fifteen places on the leaderboard, but the fans loved him for it. Ted went for the flag, but often landed in the water or the sand. His purse dropped from $35,000 to $8,000.

Greenwich was his local club. Ted shook hands with some of the golfers and talked about his play. Andrew had wandered away into the nearby pine trees and found a nice sized stick. It was just the right thickness and length and with one small branch to hold onto as the pistol grip and it had a nice sized nub from a broken off branch to use as the trigger. It was the perfect stick machine gun, which he was happy to be shooting the monsters coming out of the towering pine trees that lined the driving range.

Ted was giving Brandon some early golf lessons and had a child-sized 9-iron for Brandon to swing. Ted set up the ball on the tee for his boy and crouched as Brandon approached the ball. Ted gave the 7-year-old instructions that were probably better suited for a 15-year-old. Brandon was confused, but he was so happy to get some attention from his famous dad that he nodded his head enthusiastically with each instruction and grinned ear to ear. Brandon took a swing, holding the club like a hockey stick, his hands far apart. He totally missed the ball. Hiding his frustration, Ted asked the over-excited Brandon to slow down his backswing and put his hands together.

Brandon nodded again, but he did not understand a word his father said. He swung again. His club thumped the ground two inches before the tee, taking out a massive divot. The reverberation in his hands stung, and he immediately dropped the club like it was electrocuting him.

Ted was embarrassed by the hole his son had just made and quickly stamped the ripped-up grass and dirt back in place. He tried going behind Brandon, and together they swung the club. With Ted's help, the ball went off the tee this time. Brandon almost cried because he was so excited. Ted then told him to try again on his own, now that he had shown him how to do it.

Once again, Ted took a crouched position, gave his boy some words of encouragement. Brandon had a determined look on his face. But he was more determined not to disappoint his father than he was determined to hit a little white ball off a small piece of wood sticking out of the ground.

Brandon swung and missed and then quickly swung again before Ted could say anything. But he missed again. His third attempt was so cautious, that he was able to tap the ball. The ball slowly rolled down the tee box into the grass just a few feet below. Ted grew frustrated and again gave technical directions to fix Brandon's swing.

Brandon's eyes watered as he didn't understand a thing his father was saying about "addressing the ball" or "having a fluid backswing." Brandon exclaimed in a flurry of questions, "How do I know what address to put on the ball? Our address where we live? And what is a backswing? I thought I had to hit the ball forward, not backward?"

A couple of the men nearby stifled their giggles at Brandon's questions and turned away so Ted could not see them. Ted covered his face and tried not to lose his temper in front of his fans. He looked down at his 7-year-old. Brandon's face was red and flustered, his eyes watering and chest heaving. His shallow breathing sounded like a hiccup. Ted looked around to see who was watching, but the men had gone back to hitting their balls. He quickly crouched down to Brandon's eye level, and Brandon calmed when his father's hand landed on his shoulder, in what he thought was going to be a reassuring pat. "C'mon Brandon, don't cry. You don't want everyone here to think you are a baby, do you?" The encouraging caress became a fierce, firm squeeze—painful. "Just take your time and swing through the ball."

Brandon swallowed hard, wiped his eyes so no tears could be seen, and then he pictured in his mind his club splitting the ball in two as he "swung through it." Brandon swung again. He hit the ball, and it skimmed along the ground about 10 yards. Brandon was just so happy that he didn't miss. He watched the ball roll on the ground until it came to a stop in the two-inch grass. Ted didn't share Brandon's happiness as he looked at the ball and shook his head from side to side. Brandon took another ball from the bucket and tried teeing it up on his own, but he couldn't get it to stay on the tee he had pushed over like the Leaning Tower of Pisa.

Ted smacked Brandon's small hand away and straightened out the tee. Huffing, he backed off and watched Brandon set up. As Ted watched, he kept hearing this spitting sound and then another high-pitched sound like a bird dying.

Ted looked around for the sound and saw Andrew running around happy as can be, shooting at all the other golfers with a stick.

Andrew had grown bored of shooting the imaginary monsters coming out of the pine trees—he wanted some live targets to shoot. Some of the men and older kids turned their clubs around and playfully shot back. "You missed me!" Andrew yelled.

Ted called, "Andrew, stop that! You're bothering these men!"

The men all said for Ted not to worry about it, but Ted was adamant. But so was Andrew at finishing his target practice. More machine gun and shooting sounds came out of his mouth as his spit left a big saliva stain on his blue Cookie Monster shirt.

Ted yelled out, "Andrew, I'm not going to tell you again, stop that crap right now. These men are trying to play golf!"

Andrew looked up at his father. He pursed his lips, his light and fluffy curly blonde hair flapping in the wind, and his crystal blue eyes squinting as he filled with little boy rage. He stopped shooting, then marched up to an empty driving range stall, took his stick/machine gun, and with the thickest bottom part, swung the stick as hard as he could at the little white ball while yelling out at the top of his lungs, "Poopy golf!"

The ball sailed off the tee. The other men stopped in amazement. He hit that ball 15 yards in the air with a stick! Ted watched as the other men all looked on, grinning and laughing. Ted looked at the ball, then at his angry 5-year-old. Without another thought or word or look, he took the club out of Brandon's hands and walked towards his youngest son. When he did, it was as if he ripped Brandon's heart out along with the club. The feeling of dejection struck Brandon at the deepest level. He burned from the rejection, embarrassment, and being outshone by his little brother.

Ted handed the club to Andrew. But Andrew didn't take it. His little arms were crossed right over Cookie Monster's neck, his cookie-munching mouth and googly eyes joined in Andrew's protest.

Ted ordered, "Andrew, take this club and hit the ball again! Now!"

Andrew let out a grunt and took the club. Ted set up another ball and Andrew swung and hit the ball again at least 25 yards. Ted moved Andrew's hands closer together and said, "Do it again." Andrew hit another and another, and the men stopped practicing and gathered around to watch this 5-year-old torque his body and smash a little white ball a little farther each time.

Brandon sat on a bench, head in his hands, tears dripping down, but he wiped them away as fast as they came. He saw his little brother through the gap in one of the grown-ups' legs and bit his lip hard enough for it to bleed. He spun around on the bench, sticking his legs out, dangling them in the air. He didn't want to see everyone standing around clapping for his little brother. Then he covered his ears with his hands so he wouldn't have to hear all the claps, the "amazing," and the "good job buddy" comments from Ted and the other men.

After a few more balls, Andrew turned to his father, "Dad, can I stop now? My hands hurt."

Ted looked at the other men before he answered his son. Their faces were beaming, and their chins nodded fervently, like they were witnessing the second coming—but of what it was too soon to say.

"You got quite a little golfer there!"

"Never seen a little boy hit a ball like that!"

"Chip off the old block."

There were other comments, but all Ted could see was a protégé in the making. He would bestow all the knowledge and experience he had on Andrew. Unlike his father, who cursed him for playing a "silly game for drunkards and playboys." Samuel Beck had forbidden Ted to play golf. Not only did Ted disobey his father as a boy, but golfing became his profession. Although he was just scraping by now, someday he'd be making the big bucks and show his father he'd become rich playing this game. And now, to top it all off, he had a son who could play golf. Ted swore to himself he would do everything in his power to make Andrew a champion. And together, they would show Samuel Beck what a real father and son relationship should be like! He would dedicate his life to making his son a winner. Just like himself!

The two boys sat in the back of Ted's 1979 red BMW 320i, with a football-sized dent by the rear wheel and an engine that sputtered at red lights. Andrew was strapped in a primitive child seat while Brandon sat a few feet away, seatbelt-free. As they drove to their modest two-bedroom home in Old Greenwich, Ted rambled on and on about golf swings and training and getting a set of clubs that would fit Andrew's pint-sized body. Brandon reached across and took Andrew's stuffed Curious George monkey away from him, and when Andrew let out a bellowing cry that would shake the paint off a wall, Ted yelled at Brandon to give it back. Brandon threw it, hitting Andrew in the face.

Andrew yelled at his brother, "Why you'd do that? I didn't do nothin' to you."

Brandon hissed, "You always ruin everything!"

Andrew stuck his tongue out at his brother and looked out the window, hugging Curious George and whispering, "I don't even like golf."

1

Dr. Andrew Beck never tired of the view of a baseball diamond from the owner's box at Empire Field in Queens, New York. Seated in an oversized plush leather chair overlooking the first base line from the mezzanine level, he had an unobstructed view of the entire field. The Empire Field engineers had constructed the box to be at the perfect angle to watch the pitcher, the catcher, and the batter. Andrew sat back and stared out at the fans finding their seats. He admired the dedicated fans in upper tiers wearing full jackets, some even with gloves and wool hats to fight the wet wind from the East River and Flushing Bay that slapped them in the face. Although the retracted plexiglass windows in the owner's box let the early April chill spill in, the heating vents' counterblow made the room temperature more than comfortable.

The hostess, dressed in tight New York Tides gray pinstriped apparel with navy lettering, put on the narrow granite table in front of Andrew a sampler plate of buffalo wings from Dan and John's, lamb skewers from Peter Luger Steakhouse, and some assorted rolls from Sushi Ishikawa. As scrumptious as it all looked, what Andrew really wanted was a hot, soft pretzel. But for that, he'd have to wait until the vendor came around.

He thanked the woman and asked, "What Scotch do we have back there?"

"Johnnie Walker Blue. Would you like a glass?" she asked with a smile.

Andrew returned the smile and said, "No, thank you. Just a ginger ale, please."

A deep raspy voice boomed, "What, Johnnie Walker Blue not good enough for you, Dr. Beck?"

Andrew pivoted his head and saw the Tides' General Manager and Head of Baseball Operations Seth Rothstein approach. Andrew stood up to shake his hand and said, "I'm partial to Macallan 18 my-self."

Rothstein was in his sixties, in good shape, steely eyed, sharp, and known as a tough but fair General Manager. They had a good work-ing relationship, but today the rubber would meet the road.

The men took their seats, surveying the Tides warming up. An-drew noticed Rothstein scanning his players and referring to a printout of the Tides' player performance charts and statistics. Roth-stein exhaled loudly and shook his head when he flipped to the page with the stats on 23-year-old pitcher John Palmer, Andrew's patient and a recovering drug addict. The Tides had invested significant money in John's treatment, Andrew being the principal beneficiary of the six-figure payments.

Andrew tried to make small talk about the team with Rothstein, but he was engrossed in his stats. He just nodded or gave a polite smile with little fanfare. The silence became deafening as if Rothstein was "icing" Andrew to keep him on edge.

The two men ate their food, watched the opening day ceremonies, and clapped as the stadium announcer called out the players' names one at a time as they took their positions on the field. Andrew listened closely to the fans' reaction to the announcement of the Tides' final player: "… And at pitcher, number 42, John Palmer." The announcer elongated "John" for effect.

John ran out onto the field to subdued applause and a scattering of boos. The fans felt betrayed by last year's late-season crumble and his confession that he had pitched all of his rookie season high on amphetamines. The only thing that had saved him from a suspension was the season was over when he came forward and he went immediately into a Tides-sponsored rehab program. The owner's box reception was as chilly as the weather: only a polite smattering of applause. Andrew hoped it was because the owner and team brass were busy getting their food and drinks and not because of their lack of enthusiasm for their opening-day pitcher.

Andrew had put John through six months of intensive therapy during the off-season. Treatment included a ninety-day stint at the upscale Wooded Willow's drug rehabilitation facility in the rolling hills and snow-covered mountains of the Catskills in upstate New York. Every week Andrew made the two-and-a-half-hour drive from Greenwich, Connecticut, to have four-hour sessions with John. By March, John had to be off the drugs and mentally and emotionally ready to report to Tides' spring training facility in Tampa Bay, Florida.

After John was released from Wooded Willows, Andrew followed him down to Tampa Bay to continue John's treatment and make sure he didn't fall off the wagon. When Andrew wasn't with him physically, they had nightly check-in FaceTime calls and John's curfew was 10:00 pm. This routine was not altogether different from the overprotective routine Craig Palmer had for his only son. John pitched well during spring training and the pre-season. But the pressure is not the same when the balls, strikes, and earned runs don't count. Every player, coach, sportswriter and fan knew this.

On opening day today, the Tides were playing their rivals, the Washington Warriors. Last season, the Warriors stole the Eastern Division Title away from the Tides after a late-September collapse sent them from first to third place and out of contention for a playoff berth. Many fans and the Tides management made the young drug addict pitcher their scapegoat. However, Andrew argued to anyone who would listen that John's record was 16 wins and 9 losses. He pitched, from what John confessed publicly, *all* his games under the influence of amphetamines, so what about the 16 games he won? But Andrew also knew, in professional sports, it's not always rationale that gets a second-year player cut, traded, or sent down to the minor leagues for "development." It's all about optics. Perception is reality.

Watching John pitch was a thing of beauty — the strength and technique, how the lefty threw his entire body behind every pitch. Andrew couldn't help but smile every time he heard the ball pop when it hit the catcher's mitt during his warm-up pitches. Andrew observed John's pitching motion and looked for any tightness in his shoulders or restrictive movements that might reflect abnormal levels of tension or anxiety. But John looked relaxed. Perhaps, in this case, being only a second-year pitcher and naïve for his age, he was clueless about how high the stakes were right now.

John had been a force last year. He was a shoo-in for Rookie of the Year until his tear-filled drug confession blew up the internet and his career. On Real Sports News, the over-the-top sportscasters argued about what it was that gave John his power and confidence on the mound. Was it solely the drugs? Or was it his raw ability channeled with the frenetic energy of an amphetamine high? They directed this talk at the Tides management, and Rothstein had to prove that their scouts and player development personnel had found a young pitcher with enormous talent who had a solvable problem. When it came to a pro franchise team's reputation, money was no object.

Rothstein's media response was consistent in that he claimed John's drug addiction did not differ from a pitcher going through Tommy John surgery. He was going from a potentially career-ending injury to a full recovery. Andrew cringed every time he read or saw Rothstein repeat the soundbite. Drug addiction and family trauma weren't the same as ulnar collateral ligament reconstruction. A tear in an elbow can heal a lot faster than a tear in the mind.

John wasn't the first athlete to succumb to drugs to deal with the pressures and anxiety of being a professional baseball player. However, all eyes were on him to prove that he didn't need the uppers to be a top-notch pitcher. Did he have the ability and fortitude to perform under pressure while sober? At the end of winter, Andrew assured Rothstein that John's recovery was successful and that for the first time in his young adult life, John was emotionally stable. Andrew would prove to the sporting world that his treatment plan and cognitive-behavioral therapy worked. He would change the optics around John from last season's rookie-sensation-turned-pariah to

4

this year's comeback kid hopeful who overcame addiction and family tragedy. Then, when John succeeded, Andrew imagined, other pro teams would come calling, filling up his schedule and bringing him to the top of his profession. It wasn't good enough for Andrew to be successful—he had to be great. In Andrew's mind, there was no prize for second place. It was greatness or nothing.

Andrew felt the butterflies in his stomach as the first batter came to the plate against John. It reminded him of the decade-plus years of amateur golf tournaments and stepping up to the tee for his first drive of the day. But after the whoosh the driver made during his vicious backswing, the melodious ping the ball made when titanium hit the Surlyn-covered ball, the butterflies would disappear. The golf prodigy blocked out the claps of the supportive parents, and he especially blocked out his coach and father Ted Beck's critical comments. Andrew didn't hear any of it. His world was his club, the ball, and the hole. He prepped John to focus the same way. Andrew would instruct, "Block out the fans, the noise, and even the batter and just throw 'your perfect pitch' to the catcher."

The stadium sound system boomed, "Now batting, for the Warriors, the center fielder, number nine, Warren Cromartie!" The hometown fans booed Cromartie, who batted from the left side of the plate. Rothstein flipped to another printout with the Warriors player stats and pushed the spreadsheet with a grimace to Andrew, tapping his finger on the line that showed that Cromartie had batted .333 against John last year. Cromartie was one of the few left-handed batters in the league who hit above their batting average when facing John.

Then Rothstein belted out as if the statistics spoke loud and clear, "Let's see if all that money we paid you was worth it."

The dig pissed off Andrew, but he politely smiled. He knew it was the pressure speaking more than his gruff demeanor. Rothstein was sharper than that, but it was his way of letting Andrew know they were *both* on the hook.

John's first pitch was a combination curve ball and fastball, known as a cutter. The ball looked like he aimed for Cromartie's right shoulder, but then the ball curved downward, right below the "Warriors" stenciled chest-height across his jersey. The ball hit catcher Leo Wilson's mitt with a loud pop. The umpire thrust his arm out and let out an exaggerated yell, "Stiii-rike!" Andrew heard the yell clearly from the box. It was opening day for the umpire, too.

On the next pitch, Wilson called for another cutter. This time the pitch broke more dramatically. Not knowing if a pitch will be inside or outside the strike zone, most professional baseball players will try to swing at the ball rather than take the chance the ball lands for a strike. Cromartie swung late at the ball and missed it. Strike two. The ump held up his fist silently to acknowledge the second strike. John then threw a 96-mile-per-hour fastball that zipped past Cromartie. The umpire leaped out to the side and let out a loud guttural yell, informing the entire stadium it was strike three. The batter struck out. The stadium organ music blared as the finicky Queens fans roared for their young pitcher.

Andrew pushed the stat sheet back to Rothstein and drew a "K" with his finger over Cromartie's batting average, baseball lingo for a strikeout, and gave Rothstein a self-satisfied smile. Rothstein tried to hold back his chuckle, sending his shoulders up and down several times. He acknowledged the touché.

The second Warrior was a right-handed batter. He swung on a rising fastball but only hit a small portion of the ball, resulting in a slow grounder to shortstop Orlando Velasquez for an easy second out. The next batter had a count of two balls and two strikes, and Andrew resisted the urge to jump to his feet and resorted to pulling at his wavy blonde hair in anticipation. John threw another cutter that started way outside-left, on the right-handed batter, but it curved in, just nipping the corner of the plate for a called third strike. The umpire screeched again, but this time the batter didn't agree with the call and shook his head, and he glared at the umpire before walking off slowly in defeat, cursing at himself.

Andrew clapped loudly and cheered. On the Jumbotron screen in center field, Andrew clinically observed the batter's face and body language as he walked off dejectedly back to the dugout. Andrew strained his neck to watch the slow-motion instant replay on the TVs inside the owner's box. He marveled at the surprising curve the pitch took and smiled like a proud papa.

John fist-pumped to himself to the dugout, where his teammates greeted him with a multitude of fist bumps, high fives, and chest bumps. The entire stadium was jumping.

Rothstein subtlety turned his head towards Andrew and gave him the slightest nod and wink, which was a glowing endorsement from Andrew's experience.

The Tides took an early lead in the first inning when after two singles, the catcher Leo Wilson hit a blast to left center that hit the wall and bounced away from Cromartie. The runners on first and second scored easily. Wilson reached second base with a stand-up double. The 2-0 early lead brought smiles to the owner's box. The knot in Andrew's stomach untied and had him thinking of seconds on the lamb skewers and buffalo wings. He checked his Rolex Submariner watch with a Tides logo, a gift from John when the Tides named him the starting pitcher on opening day two weeks ago. He figured he still had another 40 minutes before it was pretzel time.

John continued with his cutters, sliders, fastballs and even a changeup here and there, befuddling the Eastern champs for two more innings. After three innings of play, John was pitching a perfect game. No runs, no hits, no walks, and five strikeouts.

The score was still Tides 2 and Warriors 0 going into the top of the fourth inning, and the owner's box was much livelier. Andrew could feel the positivity shifting in the room. Rothstein stopped obsessing over the stats, and Andrew caught him pretending to wipe his mouth with a napkin, but Andrew observed his eyes and the squinting crow's feet around them, revealing that Rothstein was in a full smile behind that paper curtain.

The top of the Warrior's line up was up again, and Cromartie looked determined not to get fooled by John's curves and fastballs. He took his time as he dug into the left-hand side of the plate. John returned the favor, making the batter wait for John to be ready. Cromartie stepped out of the box, effectively calling a timeout, and the umpire directed both pitcher and batter to play ball. Andrew intently watched the first pitch. This time the fastball reached 98 miles per hour. Cromartie, probably expecting a curve ball, which would

7

have been much slower, watched helplessly as the ball zipped by him, hitting Wilson's catcher mitt with a loud pop. The ump yelled out for strike one.

The batter thrust his bat out to drag bunt on the next pitch, taking advantage of the extra two steps to first base. The ball rolled up the first base line, and John leaped off the mound and fielded it. The ball rode so close to the foul line that the runner collided with John, sending both players to the ground. Andrew leaped to his feet. His waist caught his plate and scattered the bones of his buffalo wings and wooden skewers everywhere. Rothstein used his napkin to chase off a half-eaten lamb skewer that landed in his lap and shot Andrew a nasty look.

Despite the bone-jarring collision, John had held onto the ball and tagged the batter out. Both players got off the ground. Neither seemed injured, but Andrew could tell the collision shook John up. The trainer came out of the dugout with catcher Wilson to check out John. Andrew remained standing with his hands clasped on top of his head. Andrew joined the supportive fans in clapping for John as he walked it off, rotating his left arm a few times.

John returned to the mound and asked the umpire to throw a few practice pitches to test his arm, but the commercial break must have been over because the umpire refused and said to play ball. Andrew saw John shake his head and Wilson throw up his shoulders and arms in resigned defeat. The next batter stepped into the box, a right-handed batter.

Andrew watched John closely. Something didn't look right. His shoulders tensed up and he was grinding his pitching hand into his glove. Wilson called for a cutter, but the pitch started high and left and stayed high, sailing out of reach of Wilson's extended glove. The umpire, crouched behind Wilson, bobbed his head to avoid being struck in the face. The fans in the seats 45 feet directly behind home plate instinctively ducked as the ball hit the safety netting in front of them. Wilson retrieved the fallen ball from the backstop, asked the umpire for a new ball, and walked out to the mound to chat with John.

Both players kept their mitts over their mouths so no one could read their lips and figure out what they were saying. When Wilson returned to home plate, John threw a fastball, but it was high and outside again. Ball two.

On the mound, John stood tall, but he was very fidgety and shook his shoulders. Then suddenly, he stopped moving. Andrew thought John regained his body control by using one of the calming exercises he had taught him to use during tense game situations. But then he saw John look over Wilson's head. He was looking at something in the seats behind home plate, and then he... dropped the ball. The fans gasped, and the umpire leaped from his crouched position and signaled for a balk. Since there was no one on base, the penalty was not detrimental to John or the Tides, but Andrew knew something was very wrong with John. Was it physical or psychological? Andrew felt a deep pang in his stomach, and though he hated to admit it, he hoped the trouble was with his arm rather than his emotional state.

John couldn't find the strike zone on the next two pitches. He was high and wide on both, walking the batter on four pitches, sending him to first base. Perfect game ruined. But he still had the no-hitter going and a shutout. Murmurs bounced around the owner's box to send the team doctor to check if John could physically pitch. Andrew walked away from his seat and stood at the top of the fourth and final row of seats in the box to get a different view and get away from the grunts Rothstein made after every errant pitch.

The next batter, a right-hander, smelled blood in the water and went aggressively after a high rising fastball. The bat connected with the ball, but the ball hit the top of the bat, sending the ball high in the air for an easy pop out to left field. Two outs.

John was wiping his face with his sleeve, but Andrew gathered he couldn't have been sweating. It was barely 50 degrees. John's shoulders were tight. He kept shaking them as if there was something on them he was trying to wiggle off. Again, he wiped his brow as the batter, Juan Martinez, last year's home run king, came to bat. Martinez had popped out to left field on his first at bat, but now he stood confidently in the batter's box. Andrew's thumbnail made its way to his mouth before he caught himself and crossed his arms. One more out and the inning would be over. He could breathe easy again.

Wilson called for a pitch, but John shook his head, meaning he didn't want to throw what Wilson was calling. It looked like Wilson insisted, but John shook him off once again. They came to an agreement as John nodded, went into his windup, and threw a fastball, another high rising one. Martinez got all of it. Andrew's eyes tried to follow the rocket that launched off Martinez's bat. He lost sight of the ball as the box's ceiling momentarily obstructed the arc of the ball, but then he saw it ricochet off a barren section of the left field "nosebleed" seats. The ball bounced like a pinball from empty seat to empty seat as rabid fans scrambled over each other to get an opening-day souvenir. Andrew figured Martinez hit that ball well over 550 feet. The left field wall was 380 feet from home plate.

Martinez's home run blast tied the score at 2 to 2. The fans did not hide their disappointment, yelling and booing at John. But there were some supporting chants from the crowd. Inside the owner's box, the mumbles became clearer. Rothstein turned around and glared at Andrew as if *he* had given up the home run instead of John. Other heads did the same.

Andrew tried to ward off the stares burning a hole in the side of his head and see what was going on with John. The next batter was a lefty. John struck him out the last time, but the Warriors, and everyone else in the stadium knew John was rattled.

John kept looking over Wilson's head into the stands, then shaking his head or wiping his sleeve across his face. These were not John's typical body tension reflexes when experiencing anxiety. His were tightening the shoulders, making excessive hand movements inside the glove, digging at the dirt in front of the mound, or his eyes leaving the mound and looking up to center field scoreboard. However, these new ones had him befuddled. What was going on in John's head?

The first pitch was a high fastball, ball one. John again shook off the initial call from Wilson, but Wilson insisted by emphatically thrusting his arm down. John conceded, but the pitch, a cutter, didn't curve in like it usually did and went completely behind the batter as he stepped across the plate to avoid being hit by the pitch. Ball two. The umpire was ready to give John a warning for intentionally throwing at the batter, which pitchers, in their anger, sometimes did after a big home run. But the veteran Wilson stopped the umpire, undoubtedly convincing him that the pitch got away from him and there was no intent to hit the batter on purpose. Wilson threw the ball back to John and motioned with his arms downward to say, "Settle down."

John followed with two more outside fastballs, clearly staying away from the batter to walk him on four pitches.

John left the mound, turned his back on the plate and stared into center field. He dropped his head down and looked like he was talking to himself. After a few moments, the umpire yelled out to play ball, and John walked slowly back to the mound. He started digging his right foot in the dirt in front of the pitcher's mound, and then looked up to face the next batter, a righty. The batter must have expected John's control was in the shitter, because when John's fastball stayed straight, it messed up the batter's timing just enough to hit a hard grounder towards the left side of second base. The shortstop Velasquez scooped up the grounder and tapped the base to end the inning.

John jogged off the field to the dugout. The owner's box smattering of applause matched the fans in its half-heartedness. Andrew replayed the last few minutes and tried to figure out John's sudden and strange movements. He watched on the TV as John entered the dugout and headed down a ramp connected to the Tides' locker room entrance. His exit was not something players did unless something was wrong. Andrew clenched his fists and took a deep breath. He was so lost in his thoughts and watching the TV that he didn't see Rothstein approach him.

"What the fuck just happened out there?" Rothstein said with a glare.

Andrew jerked his head at the apparition before him. He gasped but said, "He's fine. He pitched his way out of the inning. I'm sure the jar of the collision just took him out of his rhythm."

"Why was he shaking off Wilson so much? Why the fuck was he throwing the ball into the bleachers?"

"I honestly don't know, sir, but—"

"You sold us on John Palmer being ready for opening day. That by making him the starting pitcher, it would make him 'a new man.'"

"Yes, sir, I still believe—"

"Frankly, Doctor, I don't care what you believe. Get down there and fix this, or I'm done with the both of you. I'll trade his ass to god-damn Detroit if I have to."

"Yes, Mr. Rothstein, I got this."

Andrew made his way to the exit and tried not to look directly at the heads shaking and glaring at him as he left. The door opened before he could reach for the handle—and in strolled a man in Tides' garb with a tray full of steaming, soft, hot pretzels. Andrew watched helplessly and took a deep inhale of the salty-doughy goodness. He shook his head and let the door behind him slam closed.

2

Andrew left the owner's box and rode down in the VIP elevator with the security guard. As a boy, he loved opening day. The Tides' baseball season meant that spring had arrived after a long, cold Connecticut winter, even if the temperatures were still in the 50s. Every year he would burst with anticipation and hope that this was the year his team would go all the way! The Tides usually missed the playoffs, crushing his boyhood dream of a championship season, but anything was possible for those two weeks in April.

Andrew loved early April not only because it was the start of baseball season, but it also coincided with the Masters golf tournament. Andrew didn't care about the tournament, but like clockwork, his father would head down to Augusta, Georgia, to prepare to play in golf's most prestigious event. And while Ted Beck focused on his golf game, the frozen tightness Andrew carried around in his young body would, like Greenwich, begin to thaw. He didn't go near his golf clubs while his father was gone. Sometimes Ted would call to check in on his family and future golf champion. When he asked about Andrew's practice, his mom, Helena would give Andrew a wink and cover for him.

For those two weeks, Andrew would be up all hours of the night, studying the stats of every Tides player. He would shine a flashlight under his bed covers so he didn't wake up his older brother, Brandon. Andrew loved to impress his friends with his predictions of the starting lineup. When challenged by the other wealthy Greenwich boys at North Street School playground, Andrew would bet his lunch money that he could get the batting order right on opening day and predict who the starting pitcher would be. He seldom went hungry.

Andrew emerged from the elevator into the cool, damp concrete corridor. He passed an army of food vendors decorated in Tides colors, sending reinforcements to relieve the exhausted troops on the front lines of the stadium food concession stands. A group of smartly dressed young men and women passed him without a glance, their official Tides staff lanyards swinging uncontrollably in the wind. Golf carts whirred by carrying official looking people, and other carts rolled past loaded with toilet paper, towels, and cleaning supplies.

Between the wind and the roar of the crowd reverberating against the high concrete ceilings above him, it sounded like the jet planes that frequently flew over Empire Stadium on their way to LaGuardia and JFK. Normally those were the sounds that reminded Andrew of his success. He had made it to "The Show". But he couldn't take the time to revel in the years of effort, struggle, and the mercurial nature of professional sports. His only thought was *what the hell had gotten into John Palmer?*

For most psychologists, when their patients had a bad day, millions of people did not see it on live TV. Additionally, after a bad day, those patients didn't have to fight off an entire crew of reporters dissecting a few seconds of their work that missed the mark while wearing nothing but a towel.

Andrew was part of an elite group of about a hundred therapists retained by professional sports teams to treat their athletes. But there was another side to sports psychology. The side that justified why pro teams paid him big bucks to shrink the heads of their stars either after a major fuck-up or when their personal lives interfered with their performance. The "front office" thought themselves woke and compassionate for hiring a psychologist to help athletes deal with their performance issues. But most of the suits didn't care about their athlete's mental health as long as their stars' heads got fixed. Fixed so they could get back on the field, get back to their winning ways, and sell more tickets and merchandise.

It felt antithetical to his work how quickly a team could turn on him, lose patience, or even outright ignore his treatment plan, putting the player in a situation they were not ready for just because there was a big game coming up. It was disgusting, but it was part of the deal. The stakes were big and the money even bigger. He loved the work and the challenge, but he also loved the box seats, flying private, the requests for speaking engagements, and the money that came with being in such an elite club.

Outside the Tides' locker room stood Larry, a retired cop from the 112th precinct in Queens who now provided security for the team. It was like Andrew was seeing a favorite uncle, the one who always had a smile, handshake, and love for their favorite baseball team no matter how crappy of a season they had.

Andrew knew how to fit in with the finance guys and deal makers, many of whom he had grown up, like him, around the country clubs of Greenwich and Westchester, attending Ivy League Schools. But he hated the pretense, the one-upmanship, and the yacht-sized egos. When Andrew was around men like Larry, he admired them for their no bullshit attitudes and how they could find joy in simple pleasures like arguing who was the better slugger, Hank Aaron or Barry Bonds.

"Copy," Larry said into his walkie-talkie. "Yeah, I see him now. Over." He grinned. "Hey, Dr. Beck."

Andrew clasped Larry's hand with his in a warm and familiar greeting. "Hey, Larry, how we doing tonight? You keeping those goddamned reporters out of the locker room?"

As Larry shrugged his big, rounded shoulders, his yellow windbreaker made the distinctive sound of cheap nylon fabric rubbing together. Combined with Larry's Queens accent, it was a workingman's symphony. "Ah, you know, Dr. Beck, nobody gets past me."

Andrew chuckled as Larry added, "The Warriors got to JP pretty good. Is he okay?"

Andrew winked. "Yeah, he just needs a little pep talk. He'll be good as new."

Andrew opened the locker room door, and Larry, in a not-so-discreet whisper, asked, "Hey, Doc, he's not... you know?"

Andrew shook his head. "No, no, no, we kicked that habit over the winter. He's clean. He's a good kid. I'll straighten him out, don't

15

you worry, Larry."

Andrew reached for a fist bump, Larry's meaty hand hit his, and they gave each other a nod.

The Tides locker room was spacious, with forty open stalls along the two of the walls with gray Aeron chairs lined in front of them. The players' street clothes hung neatly and there were shelves for their shoes and various other footgear. About halfway down the row, John was pacing back and forth, his cleats scraping the carpet. "Stupid! Stupid! Served that one up on a fucking platter!"

John threw his baseball glove at a locker across the room. In an odd coincidence, it landed in the locker of Wilson, the catcher. It hit with a loud thump and knocked Wilson's street shoes to the ground.

Andrew spoke up. "Hey, John. How we doing, buddy?"

John turned, startled. "Dr. Beck? Oh, man. What, did they, uh, send you down to talk to me or something?"

Andrew smiled and stretched his arms out as if greeting a congregation of Sunday worshippers. "Are you kidding me? I haven't missed an opening day in thirty years! This is gonna be our year! The Tides are going to win a championship!"

John scowled. "The Tides haven't won a championship since before I was born."

"You know, when I was a kid, I used to predict who the starting pitcher was going to be. How amazing is it that *this* year... I *told* the Tides who the starting pitcher was gonna be?"

Andrew tapped John lightly on the shoulder a few times and gave him a big smile. Andrew could see the tension building.

John popped his left fist against his right hand as if putting a ball into his glove. A nervous gesture. "That fucking highlight-reel homer is going to be all over fucking Real Sports News tomorrow."

"John, whether it hits the upper deck or just barely clears the left field wall, they still get the same number of runs. Here, take a seat." Andrew pulled up two chairs, and John flopped down with one arm propped on the armrest to hold up his heavy head while his other tapped his leg. "What happened? Talk to me."

John's legs started bobbing up and down as the nervousness in his hands shifted downward. "I was rocking, Doc. I was mowing those fucking guys down. My fastball was working, and my cutter was dancing like a fucking Wiffle ball. You saw, right?"

"Yeah, you were amazing." Andrew paused. "Then right after the first wild pitch, you dropped the ball for the balk. What happened?"

John stopped bobbing his knees and broke eye contact. His voice got quieter. "I saw him."

"Saw who, John?"

John's voice cracked a bit. "He was there, right behind home plate. With his score pad and notes, critiquing my grip, my wind up, every damn pitch."

"JP, who was behind home plate?"

There was a brief silence. John's eyes began to glisten, shiny as polished glass. John's hands went limp over his now still legs. He barely choked out, "My dad."

"John, your father's been dead for two months."

The nervousness returned to John's legs with a vengeance. His knees bobbed, and he covered his head with both arms as if protecting himself from something falling from the sky. From the hiding place, his muffled voice said, "I know, I know, but I saw him!" John released his head and looked up. His expression oscillated between sadness and anger. "And then he gave me that look."

"What look?"

John paused and glanced up at the ceiling as he sniffed. "That look when I've disappointed him."

John was triggered. Intense negative emotions such as stress or grief could make people vulnerable to hallucinations—especially a recovering drug addict. The brain had difficulty controlling the memories and images that surfaced. How individuals reacted to their hallucinations also impacted how they felt about them. Andrew needed to know more.

"But you just pitched three innings of no-hit shutout ball. What's there to be disappointed about? Right?"

John stood, wiping his eyes with the dark blue sleeve that stuck out under his gray-and-blue pinstripe Tides jersey. He started pacing again. "I know, I know, but after that pitch got away from me, I don't know how to say it—but there he was. I saw him as clear as I see you,

Doc! Am I fucking crazy?"

Andrew stood up and put both his hands on John's shoulders. "No, JP, you're not crazy. You're a professional baseball pitcher who has gone through a lot. You have anxiety. Who wouldn't in your position, and with everything you've been through? The mind can create illusions when under stress."

Andrew felt John's shoulders relax as the pitcher looked down at his dirty cleats. He made an instinctual motion, digging his right foot into the carpet like he was on the pitcher's mound in front of the rubber. "Maybe I can get a little pick-me-up, and I'll be fine."

Andrew took his hands off John's shoulders and folded his arms. "You think that will help?"

John gave Andrew a well-practiced grin, the one he often used during his therapy sessions when he was trying to charm and deflect his way out of doing "the work."

"It always has in the past."

Andrew looked down. "I don't know, John." Andrew used his best poker face to hide his surprise. He needed to explore where John was taking this.

John stepped closer to Andrew. "Just this once. I promise. Then never again." After a pause, he added, "I mean, Skipper gave me the ball on opening day, for Christ's sake! They believe in me again! I gotta win! No matter what, right?"

Andrew looked up at John and nodded. "That's true; we need this win to keep the Tides happy. So *both* of us can keep our jobs." Andrew bluffed his way through a shared chuckle.

John pumped his fist a few times up and down, "Let's start the year with a victory, Doc! It will set up our entire season!"

"Yeah, good point. But, uh, John?" While patting his hands over his jacket and pants pockets, Andrew said, "I don't have any pills on me."

John took off his baseball cap, tussled his wavy brown hair, and said, "Well… um, I…"

"You have some uppers? Where?" Andrew asked.

John pointed over his shoulder. "In my locker. Behind my deodorant."

18

Andrew walked towards John's locker and pointed to where John threw his glove earlier. "Why don't you go get your glove out of Wilson's locker. I think you'll be needing it. I'll get your greenies."

John hustled over to Wilson's locker, retrieved his glove, and pinched it under his right armpit. "Thanks, Doc. I won't tell anyone, just this once. I promise."

"Sure thing, JP." Andrew reached into John's locker, his hands shaking and his stomach tight. He searched the top shelf, knocking over the deodorant. Just like John said, the pills were there.

"Got 'em," Andrew said as he huffed out a sigh of relief.

He shook the small translucent orange pill bottle, and they both heard the familiar maracas sound of small pills rattling in their container.

John walked towards Andrew and rubbed his hands together with a clap as if his prayers had been answered. "Great! All right! Let's get this party started!"

John extended his hand, expecting a few green pills to land in it, but Andrew ghosted him and headed into the bathroom where the heels of his dress shoes echoed on the tile of the empty room.

John's voice cracked like a boy whose friends had just ditched him. "Hey Doc, where you going?"

Andrew opened a stall door and lifted the toilet seat with his foot. The clack of the seat reverberated in the stall. He pressed down and turned to open the child safety cap—or in this case, knucklehead pitcher safety cap. He slowly turned the bottle over the toilet and tapped it with his index finger until the pills were dropping out one at a time. The plunking sound of each pill hitting the toilet water helped calm him while he thought about the difficult situation that John had just put them both in.

"Doc, Doc! What are you doing?!" John yelled out in horror from the empty locker room.

Andrew turned the entire bottle upside down, emptying its contents as the plunks turned into a splash. The splash echoed in his mind and then there was clarity. John was young, just a 23-year-old kid. Craig Palmer controlled everything in John's life, including his drug use. John was a man-child.

19

Andrew flushed the toilet with his foot. He rushed back into the locker room and got close enough to John to verify that his pupils were dilated. Then he pointed at him without touching him. It was as if Andrew was a manager arguing with an umpire over a bad call.

"What am *I* doing? What are *you* doing with these pills? Do you know that I'm supposed to report this to management?"

John looked confused. "Wait, but you're my doctor? What about all that patient confidentiality shit?"

"The Tides pay me. I'm treating you, but I work for *them!*"

John's blank face and open mouth made Andrew change tack. "John, I don't want to report this to Rothstein. We worked too goddamned hard to get us to this point. We aren't going to let a little thing like one tough inning ruin our work, right?" He paused, seeing the fear in John's eyes. "You're so much stronger than this!"

John covered his face in his baseball glove and choked up. "But I can't...I can't see his face anymore."

Andrew moved John's arm so the glove wasn't covering his face and asked, "Look at me. When did you first see him?"

John's face was flushed. He sighed several times and blinked his watery eyes. His voice was unsteady. "After that first wild pitch. It was a cutter. It didn't drop like it was supposed to. It just took off. It went straight over Wilson. Shit, I almost took off the ump's head."

Andrew positioned himself so they made eye contact. "Then you saw him?"

Andrew saw John's pupils get large. "I got so scared I dropped the fucking ball! I was seeing a fucking ghost, man!"

John put both his hands on the top of his head, but one hand still had his glove on it. He was also wearing his baseball cap, so with the way his triangular mitt sat on his cap, it looked like a platypus just joined the conversation. Andrew resisted the urge to smile and focused on John's face as he hard-swallowed and choked out, "Dad was shaking his head at me and writing notes. Then, every pitch after that, I saw him." John took a deep breath and sniffed. "And then Wilson called for another cutter against Martinez. But I was afraid I'd throw that fucker into the bleachers or something. So, I shook him off and threw a fastball, and then Martinez took me upstairs."

Andrew gave John a moment to steady himself. "Okay, JP, you lost your confidence and control of the ball. You are still dealing with repressed feelings about your father. You do one thing wrong, and your dad's critical nature shows up. It was just one curve ball that got away. It happened to Nolan Ryan all the time."

John jerked his head, his lip curled as he shifted on his back foot. "Nolan Ryan? Man, you're old."

The comment didn't bother Andrew as much as the deflection. It was John's favorite tactic when the work got hard. Andrew shifted to a firmer tone, closed the distance between them, and stood upright. "Please focus, JP. You're seeing your dad because you're disappointed in *yourself*. His memory and imagery get triggered by the guilt and shame felt when you found him dead in his La-Z-Boy not even sixty days ago. Add in that the last time you saw each other, you blamed him for giving you drugs and told him you never wanted to see him again." Andrew took a breath and lowered his tone. "There's still a lot of work we need to do to process that."

John's breath shuddered. Andrew moved closer and put his hand on John's shoulder and, in a quieter voice said, "Your dad's heart attack—it wasn't your fault."

As a single tear fell slowly down John's cheek, he broke eye contact and nodded. "I know, I know."

Andrew kept a steady, comforting hand on John's shoulder and repeated himself. "John, listen to me. It wasn't your fault."

John sniffed, tapped the tear with his glove, and let out an enormous sigh.

From the top of the short ramp that connected the dugout to the locker room, the pitching coach ducked his head in and shouted, "Hey, JP, you better get up here. There're two outs!"

John turned his head to acknowledge the coach's bark, but before he responded, Andrew grabbed John's shoulders with both hands, locked eyes, and set out the game plan. "Okay, we only have a few minutes, so listen up. When you are up on the mound, it's only you and Wilson playing catch. Block out the crowd, block out the bench, block out the fucking batter. Play catch. Just like the visualization exercises we practiced, remember?"

John sniffed as he said, "Yeah, I remember."

Andrew followed up with a firm command. "Recite your affirmation."

John broke away from Andrew. "Now?"

Andrew crossed his arms. "Yeah, now."

"Aw, come on, Doc. It's goofy."

Andrew uncrossed his arms and tapped his index finger on the face of his Rolex watch several times to make a point. "Tick-fucking-tock."

"Aw man, I'm getting the dreaded Doc Beck stare."

Andrew had a stare he used when he needed to show he was not budging.

"Do the work, JP."

John took a deep breath, exhaled and looked over Andrew's head, said in a monotone voice, "I am strong. I stand tall on my mound. I throw with all my might, power, and skill. I am unbeatable."

Andrew shook his head. "Again. Louder."

The second attempt had more enthusiasm, but not to the level of intensity Andrew wanted, so he got within six inches of John's face and increased the firmness of his tone and volume. "Look me in the eye! Say it!"

John embraced the moment as he pounded his left hand into the palm of his mitt, "I am strong! I stand tall on my mound! I throw with all my might, power and skill! I am un-fucking beatable! Yeah!!"

Andrew stayed with him, held back his self-satisfied grin and pointed with an extended right arm towards the dugout and the field, "Good! Now go beat those fucking Warriors! This is our house!"

Andrew gave John a supportive "at-a-boy" slap on the back as he headed towards the dugout.

John dug his left fist deeper into the mitt on his right hand. "Fucking-a-right!"

John touched the brim of his baseball cap and pulled it up and down in a time-honored baseball gesture of appreciation. He smiled and nodded. "Thanks, Doc."

The coach yelled down again, barking like a drill sergeant. "Palmer, let's go!! The inning's over. Get your fucking ass out here!

Now!!"

John replied in a sing-song way like kids do when answering their parent's call to dinner. "I'm coming, coach!"

But as John was jogging up the slight incline, he stopped, turned and said, "Hey Doc?"

"Yeah, JP?" Andrew was smiling with his hands on his hips, bursting with pride at the turnaround and progress he made with John in a matter of minutes.

John pointed at Andrew with his mitt hand and bobbed the mitt with the flow of his words, "You know, you're just like your dad, full of positivity and encouragement. You and Ted must have had some killer moments, huh?"

Andrew's smile dropped. He swallowed hard. The pride he felt just a moment ago had vanished, replaced with a Mike Tyson gut-punch. Andrew forced a grin and replied, "Yeah, we did. Now get out there!"

John pointed his left index finger at Andrew along with his outstretched glove hand, made a two-armed acknowledgment, "You got it, Doc. Thank you, Doc! Thank you!"

The pitching coach shouted, "Last fucking time, Palmer! If you don't get up here in two seconds, you'll be running the stadium steps all fucking day tomorrow."

John picked up the pace and ran up the incline shouting, "I'm coming, Coach, I'm coming!"

Andrew could hear the organs playing as the Tides took the field, and the fans roared. He stood alone in the locker room. The rush from his work with John turned into a pit of acid in his stomach.

John had asked Andrew a few times about his favorite pro golfer and Master's champion, Ted Beck. John idolized Ted's gutsiness. John didn't know, though, how as a boy, Andrew used to watch fan-favorite Ted interacting with his admirers, giving encouragement and free advice to grown men who gushed in his presence. Then that affable, lovable guy came home and ran the Beck household like a power-mad overlord, with an iron fist and a sharp tongue. Ted was a two-faced tyrant.

The hypocrisy of keeping his father's legacy unblemished took away Andrew's proud moment of getting John's confidence back. It was just one more time that Ted Beck had to be the center of attention, even when he wasn't in the fucking room.

Andrew wanted to scream. He pulled at his wavy blonde hair and crouched as if he was dodging a flying object. He mumbled to himself, "Fuck. Fuck, fucking, fuck! Yeah, killer moments."

Andrew stood up, took a deep breath, and tried to push down the rage that was building within him. He knew there was only one way to get this feeling out of his system. But it would have to wait. He had to get back upstairs to the owner's box and face Rothstein. Andrew pushed a ball of repressed anger and resentment deep into his gut. He rose from his crouch, fixed his jacket and headed out of the Tides' locker room.

Larry thrust his chin in the air and asked, "Everything all good in there, Dr. Beck?" He pointed with his thumb to inside the locker room.

"Good as new, Larry." Andrew forced out a smile.

"Way to go, Doc."

"I'm not the one who has to face Martinez again."

"Yeah, but *you* gotta swim with them sharks upstairs."

Andrew nodded in acknowledgment. He heard Larry's vinyl windbreaker rub as he waved. Andrew waved back as he walked to the VIP elevator.

He tried to put together what he would tell Rothstein about John, but the sound of his father laughing at him, happy with stealing his thunder, bounced around in his head. When he got in the elevator, he told the attendant he was heading back to the owner's box. As the elevator rose, he heard the crack of a bat and the fans cheer. The sound made him smile, and he thought about the last time he made that sound. The smile on his face quickly left as the full memory played out in his head.

3

1991

North Street Elementary School Playground. Andrew was playing baseball with his two best friends, John-John and Charlie. That morning, Andrew had finished his golf practice and afterward headed over to the baseball diamond for casual batting and fielding drills.

It felt amazing to Andrew to swing a bat instead of a golf club. He loved the *crack* sound the bat made when it hit a ball in just the right spot. That sound made him smile ear to ear. It even felt better than when he hit a golf ball perfectly. There was something to it, maybe it was the fact that someone else was throwing the ball at you, rather than hitting a stationary ball, but whatever it was, when he hit a baseball, he felt all warm inside.

Andrew stood at home plate, batting righty, back elbow up, firm grip on the bat, and not hogging the plate. His baby blue New York Tides hat, with a big capital T in gray on the front, shielded his eyes from the midday Connecticut summer sun. Charlie was on the pitching mound and John-John was in shallow left field. It was just the three of them, and they would each rotate after ten hits each.

Andrew was ready for his pitch. Charlie wound up and threw a straight fastball right over the plate. Andrew swung hard and connected with a loud crack! The ball hit an open spot in left field and John-John tried to chase it down, but it landed in the green grass and took off towards the trees separating the school from its nearest neighbor.

Charlie yelled out, "Nice hit! Extra bases on that one!" The boys were happy to acknowledge each other—it was only practice after all.

An all-smiles Andrew called out, "Pitch another! Faster this time!"

Charlie nodded, pulled at his Tides hat, and squinted his eyes. "Okay, here comes a Nolan Ryan fastball!"

Andrew called out, "Yeah! Give me the heater!"

Charlie's grin turned to determination as he wound up again and threw the baseball as hard as he could. The ball came in hissing, but Andrew swung hard and connected again, this time deep into left field over John-John's head, who was retrieving the previous ball. Now John-John raced back out to stop the ball from getting lost in the trees and underbrush.

"Wow, that one almost made the trees on a fly!" yelled Charlie.

A young Andrew fist pumped and shouted, "Yes!" This feeling of happiness and joy was something only a young boy knew. This moment was one of the most memorable of Andrew's childhood.

The moment was short-lived as a piercing yell called out to young Andrew and the sound shook him to his core.

"What the hell do you think you're doing?!"

Andrew turned over his shoulder to see his father marching onto the baseball diamond, and his face reddened. Andrew tried to explain himself, "I practiced this morning. Mom said I could play with John-John and Charlie."

Ted's long strides had him on top of Andrew in seconds as he yelled, "Mom doesn't count! I do! I tell you when you can play and when you can't. I know what it takes to be great. Do you think that these boys are going to be great at anything?" Ted jutted his thumb towards Andrew's friends.

Charlie responded, "My dad says I'm pretty good at—"

Ted cut the boy off, barking, "Your dad's an idiot!" Then he turned his attention back to Andrew. "To be a champion, Andrew, you need complete focus! You live, you breathe, you eat, you sleep, you dream...golf. Understand?!"

Andrew's embarrassment overtook him, and he yelled out something deep inside him that he had been dying to say: "Dad, it's just a game!"

Ted grabbed Andrew by the neck and squeezed. The pain ran through Andrew's body; he thought his head was going to pop off. The pain in his neck was nothing compared to the humiliation he felt. But what hurt the most was when Andrew turned and saw Charlie's face, as he waved goodbye. The boys knew right there and then, their body language told the entire story, that they would never play together again. A sadness took over Andrew as if the entire world went from color to black and white.

* * * *

The elevator stopped moving, but on the ding before the door opened, Andrew heard in his head Ted's disembodied voice yell, "Loser!"

Andrew tried to shake his boyhood memory and Ted's voice out of his head. He took a few deep breaths to calm himself before he entered the lion's den to offer an explanation to Rothstein.

The owner's box was bustling with the sights and sounds of the guests mingling with the Tides' top management. The game on the field had become background noise as they sat on the leather sofas and cushy seats eating and drinking, talking about summer plans in the Hamptons and Martha's Vineyard. A few young kids chased each other around the outside of the couches, occasionally bumping into an adult as they tried not to spill their food. Andrew noticed that there were still two hot pretzels in the tray. His body was magnetically pulled to the table, but Rothstein intercepted him, cutting him off from his golden-brown prize.

"So? What the hell happened?"

"Mr. Rothstein, there is something you need to understand—"

"Oh yeah? And what's that?"

"Well, if you would stop interrupting me, I'll tell you."

Rothstein gave Andrew a stern look, crossed his arms, but kept quiet.

"John got rattled after the collision. And then he threw that first wild pitch and lost confidence in his cutter. He wanted to stick to fastballs and curves. Which is why he was shaking off Wilson's signals so much."

"And the balk?" Rothstein asked in a professional tone.

"Yes, that was on him. He got anxious, started sweating a lot, and he lost his grip on the ball. He should have stopped and picked up the rosin bag to dry his hands. But the ump wasn't cutting him any slack."

A teenager wandered by the food table and picked up one pretzel, leaving a single vulnerable pretzel in the tray. Andrew had to get it.

"Oh, so we are blaming the umpire now, is that it? Very professional."

Andrew's head bobbed back to Rothstein, as if he had been slapped. "I am not blaming. It's an explanation of his state of mind. This isn't a sore elbow that you just put some ice on it, take a few Percocets, and you're good as new. You know, with all due respect, sir, your expectations around his recovery are unrealistic."

Rothstein's face reddened, and he pointed at Andrew. "What we paid you was unrealistic! We paid you $20,000 a week for five months. So *our expectations* are only meeting what *you* demanded in payments. Your patient is obviously still undergoing major issues. He's not ready like you said he would be. You lied to me!"

Andrew felt the ball of anger he forced deep in his gut, rising higher and higher.

"You want the big bucks; then you better produce big! Welcome to the big leagues, Dr. Beck!" Rothstein said with a smirk.

"I took a young man addicted to drugs and in four months counseled him through that. Then his father dies of a heart attack and is left in his La-Z-Boy for a month to rot! And I get him through that too!"

The talks of the beaches in South Hampton stopped as all heads turned to watch the best entertainment in the stadium.

Andrew continued, "I got him through spring training, he pitches three perfect innings against the division champions on opening day, and he has one tough inning and suddenly my therapy failed?"

"You said it, not me."

A woman passed by the food table and hovered over the remaining hot pretzel, looking long and hard at it. Andrew was tempted to push Rothstein aside and grab it before she did, but she shook her head at it as if to say "I shouldn't" and made her way to a huge Tides labeled blue salad bowl. For a moment, Andrew felt relief at the survival of the pretzel until he processed Rothstein's sarcastic comment and noticed his shit-eating grin.

"Well, sir, I can't work under delusional conditions like this. If the Tides don't believe in my cognitive-behavioral therapy treatment, then maybe John and I should work together privately."

Andrew felt a deep sense of relief as he uttered those words and the itch of his anger suddenly scratched. A portly man whose oxford shirt hem escaped his pants, made his way to the food table, piling his plate with something from every station. He zeroed in on the pretzel tray.

Rothstein's arms remained crossed as he looked down at his shoes and paused. When he picked up his head to speak, Andrew felt Rothstein's steely blue eyes become laser focused on his. He squinted, and his voice rasped. "Well, Dr. Beck, that works just fine for me. Let Palmer foot your outrageous bill."

Andrew knew his aggressive gamble faltered. Rothstein called his bluff. He didn't have the chips or the cards to stay in the game. The itch was now a burn, and his eyes widened as he thought, *What the fuck did I just do?*

Rothstein uncrossed his arms, walked calmly and confidently towards the door and opened it.

"The owner's box is for Tides employees and *our* guests. You can leave now."

Andrew, now unobstructed, strode to the food table. As the portly man was about to reach for the last remaining pretzel, Andrew swatted away his hand. The man recoiled, almost spilling his tower of goodies all over himself. Andrew grabbed the last pretzel and started chomping on it. He ignored the smirking Rothstein as he walked out the door, shoving the now cold pretzel in his mouth.

4

Andrew choked down the last bit of cold pretzel as he pressed the key fob to unlock and remote-start his Lexus LC 500. The purr of the engine brought some temporary relief from the burn in his gut, but he still needed to relieve the ache in his mind. When he sat in the car, he let out a sigh of relief. His car was his personal sanctuary. Some people go to yoga, some meditate, and some do CrossFit—Andrew drove.

The car had a Nightfall Mica exterior, a metallic deep blue, but not quite navy blue. The interior was tan leather with metallic trim. It had 5.0-liter V-8 engine, which was overkill for Connecticut suburban roads and, based on how Andrew drove, perilous on New York City's clogged arteries. What Andrew enjoyed most were the car's acceleration and handling. It was "race day" every time he got in his car.

He exited the players' parking lot at Empire Stadium and made his way onto I-495 West, also known as the Long Island Expressway. As the traffic piled up on the on-ramp he gritted his teeth, banged the steering wheel, and swerved onto the shoulder of the on-ramp. He drove past the line of cars to a cacophony of horns. Seeing space in the far left lane, he flattened the accelerator, gunning it to 75 mph, cutting across three lanes of traffic to find some open space, blasting the Mark Levinson sound system to the Record Company's "Off the Ground." The race was on.

In just a few minutes, at the speeds Andrew was driving, he could see the beginnings of Long Island City and the Manhattan skyline across the East River. He wove in and out of traffic using the shift paddles more than was necessary. The closer he got to Manhattan, the more the pangs inside him grew; but he knew that soon he would find relief from the anger, the frustration, and… the fear. He fucked up, and he knew it.

Andrew slowed up to the oncoming E-Z Pass booths for the Queens-Midtown tunnel, and his stereo cut out as his Apple Play lit up with the words "Sandra."

Sandra Wells was Andrew's wife of seven years. Nine years ago, Andrew met Sandra at the Greenwich Country Club, when she was twenty-eight. Both of their families had a long history with the club and Greenwich in general. Being five years apart, they didn't talk much in their youth. Sandra was strong, resilient, and whip-smart. So when they found each other, it was a natural fit. But to their surprise, they spoke a language that few in their circles understood: disdain for the elite.

Sandra had a slim build and long dark blonde hair that curled elegantly at the bottom and rested neatly on her shoulders. When photographed together at various events, they were frequently labeled one of Greenwich's "power couples." Sandra, a success in her own right, was Senior Vice President in her mother and CEO, Roxanne Wells' firm, Wells Public Relations. And while Roxanne was the social lynchpin, Sandra was the brains of the operation. She knew how to make the trains run on time and think outside the box. She also kept Andrew's personal life in order; she was the yin to Andrew's yang.

Andrew wasn't in the best of moods, so he took a few deep breaths and forced a smile. Andrew knew that body language could be interpreted through vocal patterns, and when a person smiles, their tone becomes more positive and friendly. If he were to keep his current negative posture, frowning face and defensive attitude, it would come across in his voice. The last thing he needed right now was his naturally curious wife questioning what he was doing and why.

He pushed the answer button on his wheel and chimed, "Hello, Sandra, my love."

Sandra answered him surprised, "Oh, I was just about to leave you a message. Aren't you at the Tides' game?"

"I'm heading back into the city for a meeting. It's going to be a late night, so don't wait up."

Sandra tried to engage Andrew and keep the connection. "I'm surprised they didn't pull John out after that rough inning he had."

"You're watching the game?" Andrew asked.

"No, I have the Real Sports News app running. I have alerts set up whenever John, Lamar or Robbie are playing. I saw a post that John ran into the locker room after the inning. Is he okay?"

Andrew paused as he made sure the green "thank you" light flashed as he went through the toll for the tunnel and returned to the conversation after a brief but distracted pause. "He's good. I talked to him. He'll finish strong."

Sandra pushed. "Must be an important meeting for you to leave while John's pitching."

"San-draaa?"

Sandra recanted, "I'm sorry, I'm sorry, confidentiality, I know."

"It's okay." His world became enclosed as the road narrowed to two heavily trafficked lanes. "I appreciate you tuning in to see how my patients are playing. What message were you going to leave me?"

"Your mom called. She wanted to have dinner with us on Saturday, but that's our date night and..."

Andrew, with all the charm he could muster said, "We don't fuck with date night."

"Exactly," she responded. Andrew could hear the tension in her voice drop. He could feel them reconnecting.

"Can I move her to Friday?" Sandra asked.

Andrew scanned his memory, trying to visualize his Google Calendar and remembered seeing an event in Tides' blue. "No, JP is pitching again on Friday, but we can watch the game at home together and order in?"

Sandra offered another option as she was scanning her brain for a date that worked because, unlike Andrew, Sandra could remember every appointment with immediate recall. "Okay, that would be nice. What about Thursday?"

Andrew was at a loss. He couldn't see it in his mind as he was following the claustrophobic Queens-Midtown Tunnel. His lane was separated by three-foot pylons and enclosed by monotonously tiled rows of royal blue, white and yellow. As many times he made the trip heading to Empire Stadium for John Palmer, or to Flushing Meadows Tennis Arena for Robbie Owen, his talented and volatile tennis star, he could never judge how long it was before the end of the tunnel. It always seemed to pop up on him.

He chose the left lane, but it was the "turtle lane," which annoyed him. Between the monotony of the tunnel, the frustration of not driving 70 mph, and being unable to visualize his calendar, Andrew's mind bottlenecked. "Uh…" he mumbled uncertainly.

"It's okay hon," Sandra said supportively, "I'll talk to Gina tomorrow. She'll put the appointment in your calendar."

Andrew let out a sigh of relief as the lights from the streets and buildings, which made the night Manhattan sky look gray, overtook the endless sea of tiles. A large green and white sign that read "Downtown" swept into view.

Andrew received a message from his brain, and he tried to relay it to Sandra. "Oh, yeah, we're going to the Greenwich Country Club for date night."

There was a pause and Sandra said, "What about Polpo? We haven't been there in a while. I'd like to avoid the club if possible."

"Sorry, darling, but I need to drop off my clubs to get them cleaned, polished and regripped. Ted and I are playing the club's annual first round of the season together on Sunday."

"You're playing golf with your father on Sunday? I thought we were going to meet with the decorator?" Sandra said, distressed.

"Yes, which is why I booked us an early tee-time, so I'm back and ready to go by one."

"Andrew, it has taken me weeks to get on Francois' calendar. If we are even five minutes late, he won't see us. You know how these Greenwich interior decorators are."

This was Sandra's and Andrew's dance. The one where Andrew put Sandra in a situation she had no control over, and she had to rely entirely on his calculations and logic to make something happen. Andrew would then forget a very important detail, which would result in a last-minute change that created tension.

"Sandra, I'll be on time. I promise. Please don't worry."

"I'm a PR exec, and I'm a professional worrier."

Andrew chuckled and chose to interpret her quip as humor. He then used a conversation reframing technique and adopted a counseling tone. "Seriously, babe, worry and anxiety will cause you to release adrenaline and cortisol unnecessarily, which will affect your sleep and energy levels. Is something else going on? You sound stressed."

Sandra paused. "Yeah, well, I fired Robbins today."

The mercurial Peter Robbins headed Robbins Publishing. Roxanne's oldest friend and client made him a perpetual thorn in Sandra's side.

"Holy crap. How did Roxanne take it?"

"She 'ah-uh-ed' me when I told her, which means she was multitasking and not paying attention. Then her office phone rang, which I assume was Peter, and then she hung up on me."

"She's a tough one that Roxanne Wells," Andrew said. "Babe," he said gently, "try to get some rest. You don't handle her too well when you're anxious and sleep deprived."

"I know," she said with a deep sigh. She took a pause and then said, "Drive safe, honey."

Andrew veered hard to his right to avoid a car double parked on the left side of Second Avenue. In the process, he cut off a black Honda with a New York Taxi and Limousine Commission plates, an Uber car, that blasted its horn and screeched its brakes. This created a chain-reaction of other cars braking and honking. Andrew accelerated through the traffic light on 23rd street, which was already yellow. Andrew smiled as he said, "I always do."

5

The burn of resentment and anger reappeared, but in a few more minutes, Andrew would breathe easy. He sped down 2nd Avenue, going 63 mph in a city-wide 25 mph zone. He cut down Houston Street, and he was the third in line in the narrow turn lane to make a left onto Mercer Street. The back end of his car didn't quite fit in the turn lane, to the horn honking displeasure of the drivers who had to go around him. The protected green left turn arrow flashed, but the first car didn't move—no doubt the driver was texting. The two cars in front of Andrew blared their horns, a 'New York poke'. Andrew piled on with his horn too and yelled, "Come on!"

His annoyance subsided as he focused on the soft bumpity-bump-bumpity-bump-bump that his car made as he rode over the cobblestone as he drove down Mercer Street, one of the few remaining cobblestone streets left in Manhattan. It would be just a few more minutes before he was in his secret sanctuary, The Five Iron, and he would sit at a card table, ready to unleash his talents and feel the rush of adrenaline course through his veins and he could be, "himself" again.

He turned left into the steep driveway that led to the underground parking garage just a short walk away from The Five Iron. At the attendant's station, he leaped out of the car like a superhero, separated his Lexus key fob from his other keys, and threw it to the twenty-something parking attendant.

"Hey Buddy, just a few hours. If you can keep her for easy access,

I'd appreciate it."

The young man approached him with the paper ticket. Andrew took the ticket, and in its place, he handed the attendant a $20 bill without breaking eye contact. The young man nodded and gave him a half-smile.

Andrew walked with purpose onto Mercer Street and headed south towards Grand Street. He diverted off the sidewalk to walk on the street. The only sound better than driving on cobblestones was walking on them—only forty more yards. The slight scraping sound caused by the friction between leather sole and stone, followed by the "clip-clop" of his heels, was rhythmic. It was like his very own entrance song, as if he was a professional wrestler. But tonight, was he the "baby face" or the "heel"?

A nondescript steel elevator sat in between a red building at 28 Mercer Street and the glass door of a boutique at number 30. The elevator looked harmless enough, but what awaited Andrew after that brief descent into a devil's playground called The Five Iron was freedom.

For Andrew, there was no feeling like sitting at the poker table. He longed for the dopamine, or "reward chemical," that coursed through his body when he read his opponents' tells and won a big hand. This liberation of this process, this game, was unmatched. At The Five Iron, he was free from the expectations of society and his profession. Only at The Five Iron was he truly off duty, no longer subject to the Hippocratic Oath, or any other standard, ethical or otherwise. Andrew went to The Five Iron to win—to win with *no apologies*.

When Andrew reached the steel elevator doors, he looked up at the camera so the military grade facial recognition software could scan him. The doors opened. The interior of the elevator had neither buttons nor controls. Everything was controlled from within the club.

The elevator descended rapidly, and a husky and familiar voice from a speaker greeted him. "Dr. Beck, good to see you again."

Andrew looked up at the camera and said, "Hey, George. Is that you? Working the door? Did Fergus demote you or something?"

The disembodied voice answered, "Nah, Mr. Mackenzie lets me

wander around on quiet nights when there are no collections."

"Well, with the arms on you, I hope you never have to collect from me."

Despite its descending speed, the elevator came to a soft, controlled stop. The doors opened silently. George was waiting. He was an imposing six foot five, 300-plus pounds, and most of that was muscle.

Andrew stepped out of the elevator and greeted George with a smile. George winked and leaned his massive frame into Andrew to whisper, "Same here. You're one of the few white people I can tolerate in this place. No offense."

"None taken. Glad I made the list."

George was the club "collector." If he visited you, it wasn't good. Maybe you escaped with a few bruises that you could explain to your boss or significant other—a nasty fall down the subway steps, perhaps. There weren't many rules at The Five Iron, but one rule was ruthlessly enforced: *All debts must be paid.*

Andrew turned over his shoulder and exclaimed, "Hey George, if you see Fergus, give him my regards, will you?"

George gave a two-finger salute. "Sure thing, Dr. Beck. Good luck tonight."

Andrew felt a sense of relief as he approached the check-in desk. It was the relief a person feels when they have to pee really bad and are fumbling for their keys to get in the house, and then they race to the bathroom before their bladder explodes. That kind of relief.

A young man, known only as "the concierge", dressed in a tuxedo, stood behind a black granite top counter. On the counter was a silver tray, with two handles at three o'clock and nine o'clock. The tray had the words "The Five Iron" in an Old English font engraved in the middle of the tray in between the two handles.

The concierge greeted Andrew formally but spoke to him as if it was his first time at The Five Iron, giving instructions, "Good evening, Dr. Beck. Please put your keys, wallet, cell phone and any valuables on the tray."

The formality of not addressing other members by their first name was a rule at The Five Iron. This rule was not so much about etiquette as anonymity. Guests were forbidden to reveal their first names or ask questions about where people were from, and details about their profession were discouraged. Andrew wanted to be addressed as Dr. Beck, so he openly told people he was a psychologist but never mentioned that he specialized in treating professional athletes.

As requested, Andrew turned off his cell phone and put his wallet, keys, and iPhone on the tray. The keys made a clanking sound as they hit the tray. When his iPhone's protective covering hit the tray, it sounded like those alphabet magnets when they get stuck to a refrigerator.

Andrew's leather wallet was slim, just a few credit cards, license, medical insurance, and a magnetic money clip on the outside held several hundred-dollar bills. Andrew put his wallet leather side down so the money clip did not clang on the metal tray. But before he did, Andrew took out his "marker card."

Everyone at The Five Iron had a marker card; this is what you used to gamble, drink, eat, and pay for other "special services" a patron might request.

The marker card, made of black graphite, was weighty, similar to the American Express Black Card, but it was nondescript except for the gold printed number on each card. Andrew's number was 69521. Its only other visual characteristic was an electronic chip that held all his transactions and the balance.

The concierge asked, "Would you like to see the balance?"

Andrew responded, "Yes, please." Andrew handed the concierge the card.

The concierge slid it into a machine that looked like a portable credit card reader but without the roll of paper and a bigger screen. He punched in a code, the machine beeped, and a number flashed on the screen. The concierge turned the screen and held the device with two hands as if he was presenting a bottle of fine wine. "Your balance, Dr. Beck, is $1,240,000. Does that look correct?"

Andrew nodded his head in the affirmative. "I believe so. Thank you."

With the check-in process complete, Andrew felt every breath as if he was in the mountain air. He was ready for a good night. He put his marker card in his jacket breast pocket, looked over his shoulder and saw he was being observed by Fergus Mackenzie's right-hand woman and protégé, Lorry James. She was hard to miss. The fiery red-haired Scottish lass was in her early thirties, five foot seven, and her mind moved as she did: quickly, silently, and with a mathematician's precision. Lorry had a steely veneer, and her emotions didn't betray her. Plain and simple: Lorry was a bad-ass.

Although she was a stunning beauty, the employees of The Five Iron feared her. Lorry ran a tight ship. The staff propagated the fear through several Five Iron legends. Most recently, a new security staffer from Staten Island landed a wayward hand on Lorry's shapely behind, with a flippant, "You got it… *Boss.*" Lorry landed a spinning wheel kick that sent the man, twice her size, crumpling to the floor. The beating didn't stop there; she mounted him and took him to "ground and pound" school as a flurry of hammer fists hit the mark every time, sending blood and teeth everywhere. It took three security staff to pull her off the guy, but not before she smashed the hand that touched her with the heel of her boots.

She was wearing a black pantsuit, but instead of heels or wedges, she had on a pair of black Dr. Martens Vondas lace up boots embroidered with red roses. She marched towards Andrew. When she came within ten feet of him, her confident march slowed to a controlled stroll and she called out to him in her professional Scottish accent, "Dr. Beck."

Andrew turned to his right, and a warm smile graced his face. "Miss Lorry James, how are you this evening?"

Lorry did not return the smile but offered a softer tone. "I'll take you to your table, Dr. Beck. This way, please." The two walked side by side.

"I've seated you with Mr. Davidson tonight."

"Great, he's pretty easy to figure out." Andrew said.

"So tell me, Doctor, do you use your psychology training to help you win at poker?" Andrew could feel her probing, sizing him up like two well-matched boxers looking for an opening.

"You play the man, not the cards. In poker, people reveal traits about themselves all the time. I act on them to my advantage."

"You think that's fair?"

Andrew looked her in the eyes and smiled, "All's fair in love and Texas Hold 'Em."

Lorry gave him a stare that looked like she just heard a dad joke and sped up her pace to get a few steps in front of him. He looked down at his shoes and tried to hide a broader smile, to no avail. Andrew focused on Lorry's thick red French braid. It moved from left to right as she walked, right step, right swing, left step, left swing. Lorry moved with no wasted movements.

Lorry was an enigma to Andrew, which was very unusual for him and an attractive trait. He loved his wife, Sandra. However, he always had a fascination with anyone he couldn't get a read on. His inability to get into Lorry's head, combined with the tenacity she exuded, made him inextricably attracted to her. He wouldn't do anything about it, but he had his moments of fantasy and enjoyed the sport of flirting with her, knowing she would never react. But she also did nothing to make him stop either.

After a few moments of him following and watching her red hair swing, he asked the back of Lorry's head, "Besides Mr. Davidson, who else will I be playing against?"

Lorry turned her head to her right, showing her earwig, and the swing of her head sent the braid over her left shoulder where it rested there as she said, "Ms. Park."

With some sarcasm Andrew said, "Oh, the Dragon Lady."

Lorry shot back, "Think you can handle her?"

Andrew didn't take the bait. "We'll see."

Lorry and Andrew walked with pace past the dining area and came to the open table area where tables of small groups of twos and fours with dealers and non-ranked players lined the floor. Only Lorry and Fergus knew how the players were ranked. But tonight, the tables were full, which was odd for a Monday. But the end of winter gave Manhattanites the irresistible urge to escape out of their cramped apartments and have a night out even if it meant losing a few thousand dollars.

The ranked players and high rollers gambled in an exclusive area called the Players' Tables. These were usually high-stakes games, a

$500,000 table stake, meaning everyone came to the table with $500,000 in chips, and the blinds (or forced bets) were $10,000 a hand.

Lorry and Andrew took a hard right down a Persian carpeted pathway past the Sports Book area. The area had two plush brown leather couches, U-shaped with an ornate but modern square coffee table with an assortment of salty snacks and patron drinks set upon it. Recliners bookended the couches, and each set of couches had giant 85-inch screen TVs flanked by two smaller 64-inch TVs on each side, giving viewers five screens to observe.

On both of the 85-inch screens, the Tides game was on and John Palmer was still pitching.

Andrew stopped short. "Oh, wait, can I watch the game for a minute? I want to see how my Tides are doing."

Lorry shrugged her shoulders, and her Scottish accent became more pronounced. "Be my guest. I'll come back for you in a bit, yeah?"

Andrew took a few steps inside the metal rails that went around the Sports Book area to get out of the foot traffic of patrons and wait staff hurrying by. Seated on the couches were mainly men, entranced by the various sporting events on all the screens and making bets on the games' outcomes. There were a few women who were chatting rather than watching the games. Andrew stood behind the couches, but the speakers were loud enough to hear the Tides announcers.

The TV showed the score Tides 3 and Warriors 2. There were two outs in the top of the sixth inning. The announcer added, "Washington has base runners on first after a lead-off single by Cromartie. John Palmer really settled down after that rough fourth inning."

The second announcer chimed in. "Yes, whatever happened in the locker room seems to have done the trick. Palmer has had some control problems tonight, but he's kept the Warriors to just a few base hits after that monstrous home run by Juan Martinez."

The two announcers continued their back and forth. "Speaking of the devil, look who is coming to the plate. It's Juan Martinez, who seems to have Palmer's number tonight."

A graphic showed on the TV as the massive frame of Martinez stepped into the right side of the batter box. The graphic showed that

Martinez was 1 for 2 with a monstrous home run, that ruined Palmer's no-hitter and shutout.

The announcer suggested, "Maybe Palmer should pitch away from him."

No JP, you pitch to him!

Andrew clutched his chin thoughtfully and reflexively made a fist to support John. A suited, stocky, bald man with a reddish goatee approached him. His meaty hands suggested a lifetime of contractor's work, and he walked with a certain discomfort in the clothes he was wearing. Although tailored, it looked like he overruled the tailor to make the suit fit his ego rather than his bulging body.

"Dr. Beck. Didn't make you for a Tides fan."

Andrew recognized the harsh Brooklyn accent and barely moved his head to acknowledge the man's presence. "Mr. Keegan. Yep, life-long."

"Wow, you really like to punish yourself."

"Maybe so. But we're gonna have a helluva year. Especially with that guy on the mound." Andrew pointed at the TV.

Mr. Keegan scoffed, "Ah, Palmer's gonna choke. You watch. That freaking drug addict gonna get crushed."

Andrew raised his voice a bit and clapped, "Let's go JP, you can get him!"

Some of the other men and even the women chimed in with some supportive clapping and a "woo hoo" from one heavily Queens-accented lady who added, "Yeah, you go Paameaa!" She missed the L and the R in Palmer.

Mr. Keegan sneered, "I bet you a hundred grand he chokes."

Andrew felt a deep pang in his stomach, a clear warning from his intuition as a quick skirmish battled between the synapses in his brain, one side begging him to take Mr. Keegan's bet and the other side knowing the consequences if he did. Andrew made eye contact with Mr. Keegan's dark gray eyes and scanned a face that had seen some hard times in life. "I don't bet on sports."

Mr. Keegan smirked, but before he could open his mouth, a deep Scottish accented voice boomed, "Good evening, gentlemen." A six-

42

foot, slim, but broad-shouldered man in his mid-fifties stepped in between the two men. Fergus was dressed sharply in a black shirt, white tie, and a red tie clip with an embossed monogram "TFI." "I hope you are enjoying yourselves tonight at The Five Iron."

Andrew greeted Fergus warmly, "Hello Fergus. Good to see you again."

Mr. Keegan gave Fergus a head nod and mumbled, "Hey."

Fergus stuffed his hands in his pockets, stood between the two men, and looked up at the big screen. "What do we have going on here?"

Mr. Keegan shot a finger at Andrew in disgust. "Ah, Beck is all talk, no action. I wanted to bet him a hundred thousand that Palmer will choke on this beast he has to pitch to."

Fergus paused as if he was carefully considering his next words and said, "Well, I don't really understand your baseball game. But Dr. Beck, you believe in this lad, do you? Palmer is his name?"

"Yes, John Palmer. And he'll get him out."

Andrew was looking at the screen, but he noticed Fergus staring at him as if searching for something out of his peripheral vision. "How are you so sure, Doctor?"

Andrew turned and looked Fergus in the eye. "Let's just say I have a good gut instinct on this kid."

Fergus nodded and joined Andrew in looking at the screen and then crossed his arms. "Fair enough, mate." He then turned to his left, "Mr. Keegan?"

"Yeah?"

"I'll take that bet."

Andrew winced, trying to hide his concern. "Are you sure you want to do that?"

Fergus leaned over into Andrew's personal space and quietly inquired, "Are you sure the lad will get him out?"

Andrew quickly regained his composure, locked eyes and confidently declared, "I'm sure."

"Well, that's all the assurance I need." Keeping his arms crossed, Fergus turned towards Mr. Keegan. "Do we have a bet then, Mr. Keegan?"

Mr. Keegan let out a sinister grin and chuckled, "Always happy to take the house's money, Fergus."

The three men then turned their attention to the TV. Mr. Keegan had his hands on his hips in a superman pose, his hands going under his suit jacket that was wrinkled and stretched across the back. Fergus stood stoically, and Andrew kept his hand on his chin, trying to look more confident than he was feeling.

The TV cameras showed a view from centerfield. It was a common angle to allow viewers to see the pitcher's full throwing motion and how the batter was standing. A real savvy viewer might even see the hand and finger signals the catcher was giving the pitcher, telling him which pitch to throw.

Andrew knew most of Wilson's signals because he and John had discussed them. So in many cases, Andrew knew what pitch was coming, which enabled him to study John's body movements on each type of pitch. It also gave him insight into John's physical tells and if he was self-assured in throwing a particular pitch.

Andrew observed that Martinez was looking very confident. He stood tall, waggled his bat and had a determination on his face when the camera zoomed in on the behemoth.

The camera panned out and Andrew could see the Cromartie first taking a good sized lead of first base but John checked the runner and focused on Martinez.

Wilson made a complex set of hand movements, ending with a tap to the inside of his right thigh, which Andrew read as Wilson's sign for a cutter, thrown inside. John indeed threw a cutter, but it broke too far to the right and Martinez watched it pass low and inside for ball one.

The announcer said, "Staying away from Martinez isn't a bad idea, but that one wasn't anywhere near the strike zone."

If Martinez hit another home run, the score would be 4-3 in favor of the Warriors, and not only would John get pulled out of the game and the Tides would probably lose. John would probably get traded too. Andrew could see John's shoulders tighten. He had good reason to be anxious, but he had to get this batter out. John's anxiety got the better of him, and he moved too quickly through his next pitching

44

motion, throwing a curve ball in the dirt, but a nice defensive play by Wilson throwing his body at the ball saved the wild pitch and the runner from advancing.

The cameras panned the Tides dugout as the first TV announcer resumed his call of the game. "That's ball two. Two and oh to Martinez. Palmer may have rushed that last pitch."

The camera focused on the Tides manager, Arnie Costas, who moved to the dugout's top step, a telltale sign the manager is concerned about the situation.

The second announcer blurted out, "Might be a good move to pull him now."

Mr. Keegan barked at Andrew, "They pull him out. I win."

Andrew didn't break eye contact with the screen and responded a bit annoyed with the obviousness, "I know, I know."

Fergus tilted towards Andrew. "Not to be daft, mate, but what's he going on about?"

Andrew took his hand off his chin and talked with his hands demonstratively, pointing to the screen where the manager Costas was. "The manager can substitute pitchers at any time. If the manager thinks the current pitcher can't get the batter out, he will put in another one. Even in the middle of the at-bat."

Fergus shook his head a little. "And?"

Andrew blinked and pursed his lips and crossed his arms, matching Fergus. "And if John gets pulled, we lose the bet."

Fergus leaned in even more. "Well mate, are *we* going to lose?"

Andrew replied reassuringly, "He'll be fine. Costas isn't ready yet. See, he's still clapping. When he stops clapping, then get worried."

Mr. Keegan antagonized, "Wow, a two-fer. I get Fergus' money and make you look like the quack you are, Beck. Psychology, what a bunch of horseshit."

Based on the signal Wilson gave John, Andrew believed it would be a fastball. John took his time on this pitch, and it blazed past Martinez at 98 mph for a called strike. Disagreeing, Martinez stepped out of the batter's box and said a few carefully chosen words to the umpire.

The announcer said, "Oh, Martinez is not happy with the umpire there. I think he was looking for a ball."

"The count is two balls and one strike. Palmer steps off the mound and picks up the rosin bag, trying to buy some time."

The rosin bag was a small canvas bag filled with rosin powder (a sticky substance extracted from the sap of fir trees) used by pitchers to improve their grip on the baseball and keep their hands dry. Andrew advised John to go to it whenever he needed a moment to center himself. This was one of those moments. The camera panned in on John's face, and Andrew could see John's lips moving, but he wasn't looking at his teammates or the batter.

The second announcer's voice pitched up. "Now it looks like he's talking to himself."

Incredulously, the first announcer replied, "Who can understand the mind of a pitcher?"

"You said it," said the second announcer.

Mr. Keegan scoffed, "Look at that; he's talking to himself. He must be having one of his cokehead relapses."

Andrew retorted, biting on the taunt, defending his patient, "He wasn't a coke addict."

Mr. Keegan shrugged, his Brooklyn accent getting more pronounced when he said, "Doesn't fucking matter. Once a drug addict, always a drug addict. C'mon you bum, throw him a meatball so I can have some pocket money."

Andrew felt his body stiffen. He tightened his crossed arms, bracing himself against the anticipation of disaster.

Come on, John, stand tall, throw like I know you can.

John took his time, checking Cromartie's lead on first, giving himself a few more precious seconds to find his center. He was still moving his lips when he went into a big windup and threw the ball so hard it took him two steps forward off the mound. Martinez took a massive swing missing the 99-mile-per-hour fastball. But Cromartie took off running during John's pitch and stole second base with ease. The count was now two balls and two strikes with a runner on second base.

The TV crowd went wild with applause as the people seated on the couches joined in, clapping loudly and yelling words of encouragement.

Andrew pumped his fist and joined in, "Yes! Count's even. Stay with him, JP!"

Fergus again tilted his body to Andrew and quizzically stated, "Oi mate, do you really think he can hear you? Never understood why grown men shout at the telly."

Andrew laughed out loud and cocked his head and grinned at Fergus. "It's a bit crazy, isn't it?" Andrew caught himself with his professional faux pas. "So to speak." This got an uncharacteristic chuckle out of Fergus, who recognized good wit.

John was back on the mound and Andrew saw him look over Wilson's head into the crowd. The cameras panned the Empire Field seats, showing the fans on their feet, cheering John Palmer on, but he stepped off the mound. Martinez stepped out of the batter's box, stopping play. Andrew could see from the camera closeup on John that he looked spooked. John shook his head as if he was trying to force his thoughts out of it.

Andrew squeezed his fist so tightly he could feel his nails dig into his palm. John's shoulders were almost to his ears as he began his windup. Andrew closed his eyes and muttered under his breath, "No, no, not now."

John wiped the sweat off his head and stepped back onto the mound and Martinez stepped back into the batter's box. John threw a cutter, but it didn't break right and instead went way outside left. But this time, the pitch got past Wilson and rolled to the backstop—another wild pitch. Cromartie advanced to third base. If Martinez got a hit, Cromartie would score and then the score would be tied.

Wilson recovered the ball and checked the runner. He motioned to Palmer to settle down as he tossed the ball back to Palmer.

Mr. Keegan gloated, "That's it, Beck! Costas will pull him for sure. Your money's as good as mine, Fergus."

Andrew pointed at the screen. "Not so fast."

The camera showed Costas looking at Palmer, but he was still clapping and shouting words of encouragement. His teammates in the dugout did the same, and they all climbed to the top of the dugout.

The announcer added some color, "The whole bench is up on their feet. They are really giving Palmer all their support. This is great to see!"

The second announcer added, "Wow, Costas is putting a lot of faith in the young pitcher, who's clearly in trouble."

"With first base open and a 3-2 count, the Tides will definitely put Martinez on base with an intentional walk."

"That would surely bring an end to Palmer's night."

Mr. Keegan shouted, "Hey Beck, if you're so sure about this bum, let's double it!"

Fergus didn't blink. "Done."

Andrew looked down and closed his eyes for a second.

JP, you better not blow a fucking gasket. Come on, now.

With three balls and two strikes, John took his time getting to the pitching rubber and digging in the dirt with his right foot, one of his signature anxiety moves. He was mumbling something to himself again too.

"Is he mad?" Fergus asked.

"No, no, it's part of the game. You step off the mound and delay the game a bit to make the batter wait. The batter gets impatient, and they swing at a bad pitch. John knows what he's doing."

"That's not what I meant. He's bloody talking to himself."

"Oh, that. Yeah, players do that all the time."

No, no, come on, JP. Not now, your dad's not there! Get out of your head. I should have stayed at the game. Fuck!

Mr. Keegan pointed at the TV and clapped. "Oh, oh, oh! Palmer's fucked. He's going to lose his shit right on TV."

Come on, John, get it together. You are strong. You stand tall on your mound! You throw with all your might, power and skill. You are unbeatable. Come on, John, say it with me.

Fergus asked Andrew, "You say something, mate?"

"No, why?"

Fergus shrugged, "Thought I heard you say something." He took a moment before straitening himself up. "No matter then."

The announcers were trying to make heads or tails of John's unusual actions and commentate on them. "Palmer again talking to himself. Maybe he's trying to channel Mark Fidrych?"

"Mark Fidrych? Well, that's going into the archives. Look, the pressure on this kid is enormous! I know it's only opening day, but the Tides clearly sent a message after Palmer spent the winter in rehab. But if he gives up a hit here, were tied, if Martinez hits another home run, it would put the Warriors in the lead. He's got to walk, the home run king now. He's just too dangerous."

"I agree they have to walk him."

"It would be crazy not to."

Mr. Keegan made one last shout at the screen, "C'mon walk him, you son of a bitch!"

John got the sign from Wilson and went into his motion again. With a big kick of his leg, he threw a blazing fastball. Martinez, probably looking for a curve ball, wasn't ready, and let it pass. The umpire screamed a called strike three! The batter was out, and John was out of the inning.

The announcers were jubilant. "I don't believe it! What a gutsy call by Wilson! Calling the fastball! Palmer had perfect placement, low and inside. Wow!"

"That one clocked at 101 miles per hour! Amazing pitch!"

The seated crowd on the couches rose to their feet, clapping and shouting to support John Palmer.

The second announcer cried out, "Unbelievable! Palmer is exorcising all sorts of demons tonight!"

Mr. Keegan shouted, "That drug-addicted lucky motherfucker."

Andrew bent over to see around Fergus looking at Mr. Keegan. "He's some kid that John Palmer, huh Mr. Keegan?"

Mr. Keegan retorted, albeit subdued. "Go fuck yourself, Beck. Bet me yourself next time, you big pussy."

Andrew's grin grew wider. "Sticks and stones, Mr. Keegan, sticks and stones. See you at the Players' Tables, and then *I'll* be the one taking your money."

Mr. Keegan turned his body square with Andrew and aggressively pointed at him, "Yeah, yeah, promises, promises, you fucking headshrinker quack."

Fergus stepped in between the two men like a schoolmaster stopping a fight before it started. "Mr. Keegan?"

Mr. Keegan reached in his suit jacket pocket, the motion straining the threads of his underarm to almost ripping. "I know, I know, here's my fucking marker card."

Fergus took the card. "Cheers, mate. I'm sure you'll make it back at the tables or our Sports Book. Please, have dinner on me. And I'll make sure whatever drinks you had tonight will be back in your account."

Mr. Keegan stumbled over his words, "Thanks. That's, uh, stand up of you Fergus."

Without missing a beat, Fergus turned 180 degrees around to Andrew and put out a hand to shake. "Well, Dr. Beck, I guess thanks are in order, eh?"

Andrew obliged as the two men shook with a firm but not overpowering grip. "You took all the risk. I had nothing to lose there."

Fergus, not letting go of the extended shake, raised an eyebrow. "Did you not? Come on, Doctor, level with me. He's a patient of yours, isn't he?"

Andrew let go of Fergus's hand, and in his best poker face said, "No. I'm just a big Tides fan. But congratulations on your win, Fergus."

The two men stared at each other in silence. Fergus' stoical look prevented Andrew from getting a proper read on him. Andrew did his best not to reveal the anxiety he felt just a few moments ago.

"I should go. I've held up my table long enough."

Fergus gave a nod as Andrew left the Sports Book area and headed for the Players' Tables. As he walked away, he felt his nervous system catch up with him.

Well. That was stupid. What the fuck am I doing getting involved with a bet like that? Fergus called me out on JP too. Gotta be more careful—that Fergus is a crafty one.

6

Two security guards in a secured area watched over the Players' Tables. Four small red-carpeted steps lead up to six tables on a large platform that extended 150 feet, surrounded by red velour ropes held by gold-colored stanchions—ruby red curtains tied with matching gold sashes enclosed each table. If the club was hosting a poker tournament, the curtains were open, but mostly they remained closed, giving the players privacy and the allure of exclusivity.

Andrew received a coordinated nod from both security guards and hopped up the steps. He separated the curtain and entered the room, pulled out a padded wooden chair, and took his seat. The chair wasn't the most comfortable in the world, but it suited its purpose. It looked aesthetically pleasing, but its back was quite rigid, and the ornate carvings of cranes were not suitable for long nights of poker. Andrew always thought Fergus did this on purpose to annoy the players subconsciously with a beautiful but impractical chair. Over time, the chairs would have a subtle effect of causing discomfort, leading to poor decision-making at the table. However, the chairs were not something the patrons would protest. At The Five Iron, everything was a test of one's will and wit. To counter the chair, Andrew would sit upright and engage his core, so he didn't rely upon the chair for support. After long nights at The Five Iron, sometimes he would wake up the next morning with sore abs, as if he had done a few hundred crunches.

There were only two other players seated at the table: Mr. Davidson and Ms. Park. Andrew thought it was unusual that there were only three players rather than the usual five, but the night was still young. All the players handed their marker cards over to the dealer, who deducted the buy-in. He would hold the marker cards until the game was over or the player finished playing for the evening.

Andrew was very familiar with Mr. Davidson. They had played together many times, but this was the first time he had ever played against Ms. Park. She wore a black Farah sequined bandage dress. It fit her slender Korean frame well, and the long sleeves left no skin exposed. She was mid-thirties, short hair, flawless skin, piercing jet-black eyes. She wore only one piece of jewelry, a large sapphire ring surrounded with small diamonds, on her right ring finger. Ms. Park was not monikered the Dragon Lady for nothing. She had the reputation of being a very strategic card player, but also for trash talking. She enjoyed rubbing it in when she beat the men. Emasculation was her go-to verbal weapon of choice. Andrew assessed that all that emasculation concealed an anger inside her that was always near boil, but she had the self-control never to let it bubble over. Andrew's goal was to find the trigger that would send her off-kilter and have her make a bad play at the wrong time, one that he could capitalize on and win her money.

Mr. Davidson, or "Mr. D" as Andrew liked to call him, was a pretty easy mark. His salt and pepper hair matched his beard, and he always dressed in black: black shirt, black jacket, black tie. Over a lifetime of card playing, he amassed skills, but there was the dark cloud that always seemed to arrive right as Mr. D was about to make a big score. Story of a card player's life.

He reminded Andrew of his maternal grandfather, "Big Papa" Hargrove. The irony was that Big Papa was only five foot five. But when a precocious 4-year-old Andrew tugged on the leg of his grandfather's work jeans, and he cried out "Big Papa," the scruffy, elderly man smiled ear-to-ear, lovingly picked up his grandson, and the name stuck.

Big Papa had the same salt and pepper hair like Mr. Davidson, but unlike Mr. Davidson's stately coif, Big Papa's hair perpetually looked like he just woke up. Andrew always loved Big Papa's practical and folksy wisdom, and Mr. Davidson, just like Big Papa, liked to expound as well.

Andrew knew the similarities caused Paternal Transference, which is when someone unconsciously transfers fatherly, or in Andrew's case, grandfatherly feelings, towards another person. He was in constant battle with these feelings with Mr. D. The safeguard was that Andrew hated losing. He relied on the dopamine release of winning to beat down the empathy he felt when he saw Mr. D's frustrated face after another enormous loss.

Ms. Park sat on his right and Mr. Davidson on his left. Andrew reached to shake hands with Mr. Davidson. "Hello, Mr. Davidson. How are you doing tonight?"

Mr. Davidson gave Andrew a firm handshake and in his throaty voice said, "Good, kid. But if it wasn't for bad luck, I wouldn't have any luck at all."

"Aw, come on now, you're a player."

"Well, in all my years in places like this, I've learned one very important thing. You want to know what it is?"

"Of course, I'm always one to listen to good advice."

Mr. Davidson gently pointed his index finger down at the green felted table at the spot he held his cards, tilted his head to the side and remarked, "We are all one bad hand away from humility, kid. You remember that."

Andrew nodded in agreement. "That's good advice, Mr. Davidson." He turned and gave a broad smile to Ms. Park. "Wouldn't you say so, Ms. Park?"

"Are we going to play poker or philosophize?" said Ms. Park. She shot daggers out of her eyes, directed at Mr. Davidson. "Personally, Mr. Davidson, if your bad luck continues, that's fine with me. And Dr. Beck, is it? Your sexy smile and charm won't work. I'm here to fuck you, but not in the way you fantasize about."

Andrew exaggerated his slide into the back of his chair and looked at Mr. Davidson in astonishment. "Wow." He nodded his head in the affirmative as he smiled his sexiest of smiles, "Hey, Mr. Davidson, did you hear that? She said I was sexy."

Mr. Davidson got in a laugh. Andrew quickly glanced at Ms. Park to gauge her reaction and body language. She was unamused. Her intimidation and stare down tactics had backfired. She scrambled to find a dominant position. Her lips pursed, eyes squinted a little, and she clenched her fist. She took out her frustration on the dealer. "Will you deal the fucking cards, please?"

The dealer, a young man—Andrew gathered in his late twenties—was professional and skilled. The Five Iron's dealers, male and female, all had a look: chiseled faces, physically fit, perfect hair, no emotion. Fergus was very particular about his staff.

Politely and calmly, the dealer responded, "Yes, Ms. Park. The game is No Limit Texas Hold 'Em. As you know, the table stakes are $500,000. The small blind is $5,000 and the big blind is $10,000. I've deducted the amount from your marker cards and you each have $500,000 of chips. Ms. Park, ladies first, you will be on the button."

"Lady? More like Dragon Lady." Mr. Davidson remarked, trying to "tilt" Ms. Park.

Ms. Park didn't lose her cool, but fired back, "Is that a racist remark because I'm Korean?"

"Nope, you'd have to have a soul to be Korean. You're just a fire-breathing dragon."

Ms. Park's face tightened, and she lowered her tone as she gritted out, "I'm going to bury you, old man."

The young dealer outstretched his hands towards Mr. Davidson and Ms. Park and weighed in before the confrontation got out of hand, "Players, please, The Five Iron has a code of conduct at the tables. Ms. Park and Mr. Davidson, you're both receiving a warning. The next incident will be a $25,000 fine. Next incident after that, you will lose your rank and your Players' Table privileges will be revoked.

Andrew could feel the anxiety of his day drifting away as he used his mental energy to focus on Ms. Park's and Mr. Davidson's body language, facial micro-expressions, and vocal tones. He was fully engaged in getting a baseline for their behavior to find vulnerabilities he could capitalize on. He was getting into his "flow," forgetting all about John, Rothstein, the Tides, Keegan, and even Sandra and the busy social calendar she had planned for him.

The dealer expertly shuffled and dealt the cards. The ubiquitous sound of the cards, along with Ms. Park and Mr. D playing with their chips, was Andrew's favorite symphony. Andrew was not a chip shuffler. It was perfunctory to control his body and not display any physical habits.

Andrew used the first few hands to get a readout on his opponents. He tested how his opponents did in different situations. It was not unusual for him to fold out of a decent hand to get an accurate baseline on his opponents' betting strategy.

It was getting the read on someone that was his real pot—the knowledge that he had someone completely pegged, and he could get in their head whenever he wanted to. He loved the focus, the patience, the subtle observation, and the mental notetaking it took to understand someone. He fed off how it made his mind and body feel to put a player's profile together and figure out their tells. Then use this information to predict what a poker player would do in key situations. His sixth sense kept him in many hands that he had no business staying in. His favorite tactic, used sparingly, was when he would predict what cards another player had. It was as if he had x-ray vision. This feeling was usually the breaking point when he knew he was totally in a player's head.

Whether someone tried to hide their eyes behind dark wrap-around sunglasses, or trash talk, or stay stoically still, Andrew would be relentless in his pursuit of cracking their personal code. If it meant losing $250,000 but getting a complete understanding of the player's tendencies and playing habits, it was a worthwhile investment because once he could get in the head of another player, that was permanent. People rarely change their habits and body movements. Repeated habits create consistency, and consistency creates situational patterns, which are predictable, especially in gamblers *and athletes*.

Over the next few hours, the chip lead passed from player to player, no one taking a dominant lead. Mr. D was fairly predictable in his plays. He would hold his own and then either win big and then slowly give away his chips with a series of overconfident plays or lose big and then scrap his way back, treating every hand as life-or-death. Andrew reckoned that Mr. D was a better player when he was down than when he was up, as he was tighter in his plays and his ego brought more in line with his abilities.

Ms. Park was a better player than Mr. D. She calmed down since her outburst and played strong. She played straight and didn't bluff a lot. Of course in poker, when everyone else folds, the winner doesn't have to show their hand, so you never truly know if a player was bluffing or not. Andrew observed that she bluffed now and again, but they weren't huge bluffs, more like semi-bluffs. It was more like she only had a pair, but tried to represent like she had two pair or a full house, which is a pair and three of a kind.

Ms. Park's fatal flaw was her temper. Although it was tough to get her fuse lit, and it couldn't be just any sexist remark that sent her flying off the handle, it had to be precise. It had to be subtle enough to make her feel as if she was worthless without her being conscious of the feeling. Not a simple thing to do, but Andrew believed everyone had an "operating system". In every operating system, there is a bug that reveals the weakness that can allow the system to be manipulated. Andrew would work tirelessly like a black hat hacker at 3 a.m. in a dank basement to find the decryption key that would lead him into the backdoor of his opponent's mind. And the ransomware installed yielded multiple rainbow colored $100,000 chips.

Being mindful of game time was another one of Andrew's skills he practiced relentlessly. People get fatigued, add in some alcohol, and the synapses in the mind, the small pocket of space between two cells where messages are passed, start to misfire. That microsecond of ill timing could lead to poor decision making under pressure and losing a $2,000,000 pot a player should have won.

He nonchalantly glanced at his watch. It was 12:36 a.m.; they had been playing for almost three hours. He was about even on his chip stack, but he needed to feel the rush one more time before the night was over. He was not immune to fatigue, and it was a long drive back to Greenwich, even with minimal traffic at this time of the night or morning. He had been nursing his second Macallan's 18. Taking a sip here and there, and he also had a glass of ice water. But even a small trace of alcohol could affect decision making when tired.

Andrew put in his $5,000 chip for the small blind, and Mr. D put his $10,000 chip in for the big blind. Andrew's hole cards were a jack of hearts and an eight of clubs.

Andrew deliberated his position. Based on his analysis of Ms. Park when she was on the button, she came out leaning, forcing him and Mr. D. to defend their blinds or fold and give them up.

Ms. Park counted five $5,000 chips and slid them in the pot without making eye contact with the other players. "Twenty-five thousand," she coldly said.

Although Andrew's face was blank, inside he was confidently smiling: *I love it when I'm right.*

Andrew exchanged his $5,000 chip for a $25,000 chip and called. Mr. Davidson followed, exchanging his $10,000 chip for a $25,000 chip that hit with a kerplunk as it landed on the other chips. "Call."

Ms. Park shifted her shoulders, leaned in, and stared Mr. Davidson in the eye. "Call? Weak play. You sure you took your dementia medicine tonight, old man?"

Mr. D. didn't budge. He kept his hands on his cards, gave her a toothless grin and said, "Well, we'll just see about that, won't we?"

Ms. Park then directed her ire at Andrew. "Hey, what kind of doctor are you, anyway?"

Andrew didn't make eye contact as he glanced at his cards, feigning as if he had forgotten what they were. "Psychologist."

Ms. Park made a short raspberry. "What a bunch of bullshit." She raised her voice several octaves, singing with childish innocence, "Oh, boo hoo, I got my feelings hurt because my daddy didn't hug me." Then in her normal voice: "Fucking snowflakes."

It pleased Andrew that Ms. Park addressed him personally and even started busting on his profession. It gave away her offensive techniques for trying to get in his head. Her tactic was a full-frontal attack, which Andrew found predictable and easy to counter. Andrew's next tactic was to divert the attention to the feud brewing all night between Ms. Park and Mr. Davidson.

The dealer took the top card and put it face down off the board, known as "burning a card." He then dealt three cards face up and next to each other in a row, "the flop." The flop cards showed:

K♣ Q♦ 9♣

Andrew held an eight of clubs and a jack of hearts.

The board gives me a king, queen, and a nine, that makes it, eight, nine, jack, queen, king. I got a backdoor flush draw and a gut shot straight draw. I have a 17% chance to get a 10 and make the straight and only a 4% chance to get two more clubs to make the flush. Neither is a high probability play. What the fuck! I'm going for it. I'll see if I can tilt Ms. Park a little further.

As Mr. D and Ms. Park checked their hole cards to consider their play, Andrew quietly put in a $25,000 chip and then turned his body perpendicular to hers as a show of aggression, "Would you like my professional diagnosis of you, Ms. Park?"

Ms. Park flicked her hand, rolled her eyes, let out a raspberry again. "Pfft."

Mr. Davidson saw an opportunity to get in on the action and said, "You tell her, Doc."

In a serious and unhesitating clinical voice Andrew said, "You didn't get the love you needed as a child, especially from your father, who I assume was a hard-working man who had little time for his family. And although you come from wealth, you won't take a penny of your father's money because you're smart, beautiful, and ambitious. But most of all, you want to show not only your father, but every man, that you can beat them. And that you don't need anything from them, especially their approval. But deep down inside, that's what you crave, Ms. Park. Approval. So you gamble and throw verbal daggers at Mr. Davidson and me just to prove to us how strong you are, and that you can beat us. But you know what? You're weak, Ms. Park. And you want—no, you *need* my approval."

Ms. Park stopped shuffling her chips for a moment, and Andrew let that moment pass before he broke the stone-faced professional look and said with his sexy smile and some bewilderment in his tone, "Either that or you're straight-up bat shit crazy. It's one or the other. I don't know which."

The punchline made Mr. Davidson laugh heartily, and Andrew grinned. They were like two guys at a bar exchanging jokes that may not have been too funny, but they enjoyed the camaraderie of a laugh together.

Ms. Park, to her credit, didn't take the bait; instead she stiffened, matched Andrew's body language, and retorted, "Okay Doctor. So what does that say about you? You're gambling at an illegal underground casino. I guess your life of listening to people cry about their pathetic bullshit problems has you so bored you need to risk all the meager money you make at this table just prove to yourself that you actually have a pair of balls and you're not a pathetic fucking loser like your patients."

Andrew's grin went away. He started nodding his head and turned back to Mr. Davidson, wagging his finger, "You know, Mr. D, she might have something there."

Mr. D stopped laughing and jutted his chin, "Oh yeah son, what's that?"

Andrew excitedly raised his tone, "I'm *not* making enough money. I should raise my rates! Great advice, Ms. Park, thank you."

Mr. D resumed his laughing as Andrew grabbed three $1,000 chips and tossed them gently at her stack, "Here's your fee."

Ms. Park was enraged. She picked up the chips and threw them at Andrew, one hitting him in the chest and the other two flying off the table. "Fuck you!" she grunted.

Andrew recoiled and looked to the dealer, arms extended, like he was appealing to the referee after someone committed a flagrant foul on a layup. "Whoa!"

"Hey now!" Mr. Davidson added his two cents.

Without skipping a beat, the dealer eyeballed Ms. Park and in a conversational tone said, "I warned you, Ms. Park. That will be a twenty-five thousand dollar fine."

Ms. Park protested, "Me!! What about those fucking guys! Just because I'm a woman you fine me?"

The dealer said firmly, "No, you threw chips at another player and—"

Ms. Park cut him off and tossed him a $25,000 chip. "Fuck it! Here! Take it!"

She then eyeballed the dealer as if she was trying to drill into his skull. "It was fucking worth it. That was your tip. Fucker."

Mr. Davidson picked up five $5,000 chips and said soberly, "$25,000, call."

Ms. Park quickly recovered from her outburst and deadpanned, "Raise, $50,000."

Andrew placed $25,000 more in chips into the pot.

Mr. Davidson responded immediately by throwing in two $25,000 chips to match Ms. Park. "Call," he said in an abrupt and gruff voice.

The dealer then flipped another card face up at the "turn," putting it next to the other cards. The pot was now $225,000 as the dealer announced, "Ten of clubs."

On the board there was now:

 K♣ Q♦ 9♣ 10♣

Andrew did not react outwardly to his good luck, but in his head he was ecstatic.

Holy shit, I got my straight. It's a sucker straight. If either of them has ace/jack, I lose the straight. If I come out hot here, I will bring the attention to me rather than stoking the fire between both of them. So I will make a small bet to see how they react.

Andrew looked down at his chips and purposely looked a little tentative as he grabbed two $5,000 chips and tossed them neatly into the pot, saying, "$10,000."

Ms. Park switched her wrath to Andrew. "If you are going to bet, Dr. Sheep, make a real bet."

Andrew zeroed in on her body language and in microseconds, his strategy played out in his mind.

Okay, her chip shuffling increased. And her nostrils just flared. She's pissed. Now, she could have pocket kings or queens, giving her three of a kind, which I still beat her. If she has ace/jack, then her straight beats mine and I'm fucked. But I think she's holding a queen and a nine, which would give her two pair. And my straight beats her two pair.

Mr. Davidson quickly threw in a $10,000 chip and called. He wanted to see how Ms. Park would react.

"Looks like both of you left your balls at home," Ms. Park said as she threw a $100,000 chip in the pot.

Mr. Davidson looked paternally at Andrew. "Hey son, don't let her goad you into giving your money away. I'll tell you what, if you fold and I win, I'll split the pot with you just for fun."

That kind of collusion would be a problem in most places, but at The Five Iron, considering the whole gambling operation was illegal, Fergus gave his crew leeway to let the players make side bets. A little bit of chaos made the game more exciting and part of the mystique of playing at The Five Iron.

Andrew responded, keeping his true emotions well hidden, "Wow, that's a generous offer, Mr. D, but I'm going to stick around a bit if you don't mind. I'll call."

Mr. D carefully grabbed one of his more colorful chips, a $100,000 along with two $25,000 chips. He carefully looked at Andrew first and then locked eyes with the intense woman across the table, "Raise to $150,000. Is that a real bet, Ms. Park?"

Andrew quickly glanced over to Mr. Davidson.

That's a powerful play from Mr. D. But based on his betting history. He doesn't have two pair. If he did, he would have come out stronger, earlier. He likes to show command of the table when he has a strong hand. So that would leave him holding maybe a queen and a ten or maybe a pair of nines which would give him three of a kind. I'm betting he's holding king ten, which would give him two pair. Which in that case, with my straight, I still win. With Mr. Davidson, his tells are all in his hands. All I need to do is read his hands. Right now he's got them on top of his cards, and he is playing with the chips on his cards. For him, that's a bit of confidence. Two pair it is.

Ms. Park looked at her cards, tilted her head, and pursed her lips. Mr. Davidson tried to reclaim some ground lost in their trash-talking and mind games and said, "Yeah, that's right, you take your time. But you don't have the sand, missy. You should just walk away."

Ms. Park didn't react to the goad and looked at her chip stack. She glared at Mr. D as she tossed two more $25,000 chips in front of her and stoically announced, "Call."

Andrew was looking at his chip stack, contemplating his move, when Mr. D warned, "That's a big bet, son. You sure you want to do that?"

"Sorry Mr. D, like you said, Ms. Park doesn't have the sand. I'm in for $150,000."

The dealer turned his final card of the hand.

Shit! A pair of kings on the board. If Ms. Park has a king/nine, then she will have a full house. If she only has a queen/nine, she will have two pair and I win. But I think if she had the king, she would have raised Mr. D. That would have been consistent with her play. It must be queen/nine. But if Mr. D has ace/jack, then his straight beats mine. If he has two other club cards, then he would have a flush. Fuck. There is $675,000 in this pot. I got a straight, but I could lose to either of them. Got to play my chances. If I lose to Mr. D, so be it.

Mr. Davidson snapped, "I'm in it to win it. $200,000."

But as Mr. Davidson threw his chips in, he extended his elbow, like making a stiff arm in football. Andrew detected false aggression here. Davidson was trying to scare everyone off. His hand wasn't as strong as he wanted the table to think.

He doesn't have ace/jack. And he definitely doesn't have the kings, because if he did, he would've gone all-in. Holy shit, he's only queen/nine or queen/ten. Two pair at best. But I'm in a tough position on the table. Does Ms. Park have a boat or not? If she had the full boat, she wouldn't have been talking so much smack. I think I'll make some flirty eye contact to see if she reveals anything.

Mr. Davidson tried the fatherly approach again. "Hey kid, my offer still stands. I don't want to take any more of your money."

The last call gave away his position. Andrew tried to sound appreciative and said, "Thank you, Mr. D."

Andrew turned to Ms. Park. He led with his sexy smile. "Say, what do you think I should do, Ms. Park? Should I take him up on his offer and let you two duel it out?"

Ms. Park lowered her tone and stared menacingly at Andrew.

"You think it's that easy, Doctor? Smile at me, look me in the eyes, and expect me to give myself away? Nice try. I'm not some flounder, you know."

Andrew looked down at his stack and made a pause for effect as he turned up the corners of his cards to break eye contact with Ms. Park. "Ah, well, you can't blame me for trying."

But then he gazed deep into her eyes and summoned all his charm, saying, "But I must say Ms. Park, you do have the most beautiful eyes I've ever seen. Just gorgeous."

He glanced back down, but out of his peripheral vision he was still looking at Ms. Park, looking for the micro-expression that would reveal her true feelings.

Ah ha! There it is! Just for an instant, she broke eye contact. She bit her lip to keep from smiling. Then she looked down and away from her stack. Well, it could be nothing, but if I threw her off, she will delay her bet.

Andrew noticed that Ms. Park slowed down her chip shuffling to slower than normal, and she gave out a quick chuff of her breath as she tried to maintain control.

She shot back at Andrew, "You don't have queen/jack suited, Doctor. You're trying to use some of that mental shit and bluff your way out of this. Well, fuck you. I'm all-in."

Ms. Park pushed all of her chips forward. It was an obvious play of trying to dominate, but Andrew maintained his confidence in his reads. He pushed all his chips into the pot as well.

Mr. Davidson chuckled. "Well, look at you. Good for you, son. I'm sorry, I'm going to have to take your money."

Andrew kept eye contact with Mr. Davidson and gave him a warm and genuine smile. "Couldn't give it to a better guy."

As he said that, Andrew noticed that Mr. Davidson looked down and pressed on his stack over his cards. His fingers turned red when he pressed down, which Andrew read he was feeling anxious.

He's only got two pair, and I'm sure of it now.

Ms. Park quickly recovered from the fluster and immediately went on the offensive, "You can suck each other's dicks later! You in or out, old man?"

She doesn't have it. I got her. Come on, Mr. D, fold! You can't win this one. Please fold.

But Mr. Davidson wanted to get in on the Nostradamus act too as he tilted his head to the right, closed one eye, and pointed a bent index finger Ms. Park's way. "No way you have queens or jacks. Best thing you have is two pair, missy."

He then sat back in his chair and turned, regarded Andrew. "As for you, my friend, as much as I hate to say it, I think Ms. Park has got you pegged. Maybe you're not bluffing, but you don't have a winning hand. I'm all in."

Mr. D pushed all his chips in and then flipped over his cards first. "Sevens and queens, two pair."

Ms. Park let out a gleeful squeal, "Ha ha! Got you, you son-of-a-bitch, two pair, nines and queens."

Ms. Park started reaching for the chips, but Andrew put a gentle hand out to stop her. The touch caused Ms. Park to recoil like someone spilled scalding water on her. "Ah, ah, ah, not so fast."

Andrew flipped over his cards but looked directly at the dealer and announced professionally, "King high straight."

The dealer acknowledged Andrew's hand and in a calm, neutral voice said, "Dr. Beck wins the pot, less the rake to $1,327,500. I will add it to your marker card."

Mr. Davidson sat back in his chair, clucked his tongue, and gave a half smile. "Well, I'll be damned."

Ms. Park's glee turned into frustration, and she let out an astounded, "Fuck."

The dealer returned the marker cards to Ms. Park and Mr. Davidson $500,000 less than they began the night.

"Well, you know what, it was worth a half mil to see you trounce that dragon," said Mr. Davidson, with a chuckle.

With the game over and Ms. Park scowling, she stuffed her marker card in her purse and let loose her ire. "Fuck you, old man. And fuck you too, you limp dick fucking shrink."

Ms. Park pushed the chair away, scraping the carpet and got up, but not without a parting shot from Andrew. "You kiss your father with that mouth? Oh, I forgot, he doesn't even know you exist."

Ms. Park's face turned white as her eyes rounded and jaw dropped. She turned hastily, bumping into a server who had just entered through the curtains. The silver tray with drinks he was carrying flew. Andrew athletically eluded the spilling liquids as Ms. Park pushed the man out of her way, bellowing, "Get the fuck out of my way! Clumsy fuck!"

Although clearly not his fault, the server tried to apologize, "I'm… I'm sorry, ma'am." The curtain flapped from Ms. Park's violent haste.

Andrew turned to Mr. Davidson. "Sorry about that, Mr. D. I'm sure your luck will turn around."

Mr. Davidson stood and shrugged his shoulders, "Ah, you played the hand well, kid."

At that moment, George the "collector" stuck his head into the room and thrust his chin out at Mr. Davidson. Andrew's head whipped around as he saw the voiceless communication taking place.

What's George doing? Oh shit!

George motioned to Mr. Davidson and softly worded, "Mr. Davidson, we need to talk."

Mr. Davidson looked down and tapped the green felt table gently. "Yeah, I know."

Andrew tried not to show panic in his voice. "Everything okay, Mr. Davidson?"

"Yeah, don't you worry about me, son. I'll be back."

As he took a few slow steps toward George, who was holding open the curtain for him as he could barely fit in the room, Mr. Davidson looked back at Andrew, winked and made a six-shooter with his finger. He sounded like an old western gambler as he grumbled, "You better watch out when my luck turns. I'm gonna get you."

The crimson and gold curtain flapped a few times in the air as the dealer cleaned up the spill on the felt table and called on the radio for a clean-up crew. Andrew stuck his marker card in his jacket pocket while staring at the flapping curtain.

Fuck. I hope he'll be all right.

7

Andrew felt the rush of his competitive itch thoroughly scratched as his heart pounded with an exuberance of winning the pot and getting a zinger on Ms. Park. But as he glanced over to Mr. D's empty seat, he conjured guilt-ridden images of George giving him a beatdown. The pang in his stomach told him that the rushing river of satisfaction had led to a waterfall, and he was going over it.

"Dr. Beck, will that be all?" asked the dealer.

"Uh, yes, thank you." Andrew used his brain power to focus on blocking out the violent images in his mind. But then his brain sent him a rapid message about etiquette, and he said, "Oh, no, wait! Take $10,000 for yourself."

Andrew gave back the marker card to the dealer, who cracked a slight smile, but only for a millisecond as he said, "Thank you, Dr. Beck."

Andrew nodded and pulled at his hair. The dealer inserted the card, pushed a few buttons, and then gave the card back to Andrew.

The curtain parted as he left the room, and the noise of the patrons and other card games filled his ears. He needed a drink. He walked with intention towards the bar, but when he saw the Sports Book area, he realized he needed to see how John and the Tides had made out.

Andrew flagged down a server and ordered a Macallan 18 neat. This one he would drink to enjoy. Real Sports News was blasting from the big screen, going through the day's scores. Andrew took a seat on the couch and watched as they covered the day's baseball results. Andrew politely thanked the server, who brought him his Scotch. He tasted the warm, smooth burn as he sipped it. It brought a smile back to his face as he blocked out the projected images of what George might be doing to Mr. D.

The Tides vs. the Warriors game eventually made it to the screen. The highlights from the game focused on John's meltdown in the fourth inning and then his strikeout against Martinez in the sixth, which brought a smile to Andrew's face. He took another self-satisfied sip and watched the rest of the highlights. Costas sent in a reliever for John after the sixth inning. The Tides added two insurance runs in the eighth, driving the score to 5-2. But in the top of the eighth, the Tides used three additional pitchers in the inning after giving up two walks, an infield singles and other "small ball" plays, which enabled the Warriors to manufacture two more runs to bring the score to 5-4. But the Tides held off the Warriors to start the season off with a victory.

John Palmer got the win, letting up two runs on six innings pitched, two hits, two walks, six strikeouts, and two wild pitches. Not a bad outing for John. Andrew watched the replay of the Tides players hugging and high-fiving each other at the end of the game. He reached for his phone to text Rothstein with an "I told you so" message. But instead of the protective phone covering, he felt the cold graphite of his marker card.

He chuckled at his own knee-jerk reaction to instinctively reach for his phone, something he and most people are never without. But at The Five Iron, no calls, no pictures, no emails, no devices of any kind that might confirm its existence are allowed. The Five Iron flew deep under the radar and Fergus and Lorry went through a great deal of trouble—and expense—to keep it that way.

Andrew took another sip of his Macallan 18. He closed his eyes as he let the flavor sit on his tongue and sized up his ledger for the night. He had won over $800,000 at poker. Andrew's impromptu therapy session in the locker room helped John win and might have saved John from being traded to Detroit. Finally, he won $200,000 for Fergus from Mr. Keegan after the bald-headed fucker ran at the mouth.

On the other side, the losses included getting fired from the Tides as a paying client. He now had to convince John to stay in therapy and pay the bills himself. John's contract was worth $5 million per year for the next three years, so money wasn't an issue. But it wouldn't be a no-brainer. Without team-sponsored therapy and no one "making" him go, John might just opt out. Andrew thought about his leverage points. He made a mental note to call John's "super-agent" Steve Gotski. They were golfing buddies and shared clients. Andrew would ask Steve to apply some pressure for John to stay in therapy if need be.

The post-game recap also showed some interviews in the locker room. The reporters crowded around John, but instead of them blasting the young pitcher like they did last year when the American Baseball League suspended him, they were praising his comeback and a new lease on life.

Andrew watched the reporters ask questions about his rehabilitation and how he kicked the habit. John and Andrew had painstakingly rehearsed answers to key questions that Andrew expected would come. Like any athlete, you perform a routine enough, and it becomes rote. However, it got a little tense when a notorious sensationalist reporter from Real Sports News rattled John, sticking his iPhone with a recording app running underneath John's chin.

"John! John! Thomas Underwood, Real Sports News. What happened after that rough fourth inning when you dashed into the locker room?"

"Yeah, I needed to shake off the inning, so I took a minute to go into the locker room to get refocused."

"A minute? You were in there the entire inning! Do you think you were mentally ready to pitch tonight?"

"Look, the home run shook me up. It happens. First game of the season and all. But Skipper Costas and Mr. Rothstein believed in me. I got the start tonight, and even when I got rattled, they kept me in the game. And we finished up strong. We got the W. In the end, that's all that matters."

Underwood persisted. "Yeah, but first you drop the ball, then you drop that homer to Martinez? He had to hit that ball 600 feet!"

John kept his cool. "Hey, you know, whether the guy hits the ball in the parking lot or barely clears the wall, you get the same number of runs."

The reporters from the other news outlets laughed, and Andrew chuckled to himself out loud, "He took my line."

Andrew saw out of his peripheral vision the man sitting a few cushions down from him look at him quizzically. Andrew tried to recover from his guffaw. "That's a great line. Kid handled that well! That Underwood's an asshole."

The man nodded. "Yeah, those reporters, always looking for cheap shots. That kid's gonna be all right."

Andrew glanced down at his Rolex. It was almost 1:30 a.m. Time to head back to Greenwich, where Andrew visualized Sandra passed out with all the lights on and her laptop occupying Andrew's side of the bed.

Andrew finished his Scotch, gave a polite good night to the man on the couch, and strolled to the concierge's desk. Andrew handed over his card as the concierge slipped it into the slot and waited for the reading. After a few beeps, the account flashed, and the concierge reviewed his take for the night. After the rake for the house and his $10,000 tip to the dealer, Andrew's account increased by $817,500 for the night. His marker card now held $2,057,500 in total.

The concierge handed Andrew his personal effects on the same silver tray. Andrew put them in their designated pockets and asked, "May I have another $10,000 chip, please?"

The concierge slid a colorful $10,000 chip to Andrew, who hid it in his hand as he could see Lorry's signature "all-business" gait heading towards him. He greeted her warmly with a smile, "Hello, Lorry."

"Have a good night?" she asked, but her facial expression did not match her words or tone. Her face was like the Vermeer painting, Girl with a Pearl Earring, and there was an uneasiness about her.

"Great night."

Lorry squinted and said, "Like all streaks, it'll end."

Andrew confidently turned on the charm and gave her a soft but direct smile. "But not tonight."

Andrew grabbed her right hand gently and handed her the chip. "Here, take this."

She grimaced at the chip. "$10,000 dollars? I told you, I don't work for tips."

Andrew walked to the elevator, where the guard pushed the request button, turning to Lorry. "You run the players list. Call it a fee."

Andrew gave Lorry one last charming smile as he stepped into the elevator. As the doors closed, Lorry slid the chip to the concierge and said, "Put it with the rest, please."

The elevator opened silently. The spring night in SoHo greeted Andrew with honking horns, sirens, and people getting where they needed to go.

Andrew headed back up Mercer Street to his car in the parking lot. There were no cars parked on the side of the street The Five Iron was on. Alternate side parking rules were in effect. He instinctively walked on the cobblestones in the street, not too far from the curb in case he had to avoid getting clipped by a wayward eco-friendly lime-green Prius cab. As he walked, he pulled out his iPhone and turned it on. After the Apple logo appeared, Andrew ignored the notifications that popped up and selected the Otter.ai voice recorder and transcription app. When it came up, he pushed Record.

"Client John Palmer. Patient Notes. John pulled out a victory today on opening day. Had to go to the locker room for a private session. Please charge the Tides for an emergency visit plus bridge tolls, parking, and milage expenses. Billing note: All future billings will go to John personally. The Tides are no longer subsidizing his therapy. Client Note continued. John continues to see images of his father. The trauma of finding his father dead still plagues his psyche. After a wild pitch, the shame and anxiety caused him to hallucinate, seeing his father in the stands critiquing him. If hallucinations continue every time he throws a bad pitch or lets up a home run, he will need more intensive therapy and probably go on the 60-day injured list. That might lead Rothstein to label him a 'headcase' and follow up on his threat to trade or cut him. Now that he's off drugs, we need to work on other trauma areas rising to the surface…fast. Stop."

Andrew stopped the recording. In less than a few seconds, Otter.ai processed the transcription. Andrew scanned it for gross inaccuracies while he waited for the light to turn at Grand Street and Mercer Street, then sent the file to his assistant Gina Perez's email. Andrew stuffed the phone in his sport coat's breast pocket. The notifications kept dinging and buzzing. But he was having a good night. They could wait until tomorrow.

Andrew stared up at the Manhattan sky. It looked like the entire city was under some huge gray dome. Andrew heard a computerized voice say, "Walk, walk, walk."

He looked at the flashing white walker and strolled across the white striped crosswalk. His thoughts wandered back to John and his triggers. Finding his father Craig dead after all John went through had to be a shock. *What would I do if I found Ted dead in a chair? Or if he has a heart attack like mom fears? But I keep telling her, Mom, Dad can't have a heart attack. First, he'd have to have a heart.*

The smile from his face vanished as his phone rang out with the caller ID flashing Lamar Hayes. *Oh fuck, what now?*

Three men stepped out in front of him from under an awning. When he turned around to avoid them, two more were behind him. He was surrounded. iPhone still ringing. The adrenaline of the fight-or-flight response was filling his body, and then he heard a rough Brooklyn accent yell out, "Hey Beck! We ain't done, me and you."

Andrew hit the green answer button and spoke calmly into his phone, "Lamar, I'll call you right back." He hung up.

Andrew pocketed his phone. "What do you want, Keegan?"

The men parted as Mr. Keegan appeared, his suit was strained to its limits and more wrinkled than when he saw him. The wrinkles of his bald head caught small beads of perspiration. His cheeks were flushed, his chipped front teeth ground as he spoke, pointing a finger at Andrew's chest, "I want my fucking two hundred K back, mother-fucker."

"Go ask Fergus. You lost the money to him, not me."

He moved closer, his hot whiskey breath slapping Andrew in the face. "You fucking cheated!"

Andrew's hands flew up and his tone peaked in a John McEnroe "You cannot be serious" moment and said, "How do you figure?!"

Mr. Keegan took a step back when Andrew's arms flew up, but he maintained his finger pointing and said, "I heard you talking into your phone. You're Palmer's fucking shrink. You didn't say that when Fergus and me made the bet. Was he in on it, too? You both set me up! You fucking cheaters!"

Andrew's arms fell lifelessly to his side and slid into his pockets. He lowered his tone. "No, Fergus doesn't know I treat Palmer. Look, there's no reason to involve him."

"Yeah, all right, this is between you and me."

"So what, I give you a check or something, and we're good?"

"No motherfucker, it ain't that easy. This is what you're gonna do."

Andrew shrugged his shoulders. "What's that?"

Mr. Keegan leaned into Andrew's ear, but he didn't exactly whisper. "You're going to lose to me on purpose at poker."

Andrew pushed Keegan away from him as his men tightened the circle.

"Are you a fucking idiot? Fergus will kill us both."

At that moment, Andrew heard several guns cock and felt one barrel stick in his left kidney and the other in the small of his back as the men surrounding him closed ranks.

Mr. Keegan's confidence surged, and his eyes got big and bulgy like someone on cocaine. "You think I'm fucking around? I wouldn't worry about Fergus if I were you. I'll make you disappear! I'll put you in the bottom of the East River, you pompous fuck!"

Andrew took the sleeve of his jacket and wiped some of the spittle that escaped from the isosceles triangle gap in Mr. Keegan's front teeth and splattered on his cheek. He took a moment, wiped his hands like he had dirt on them, and grinned, "Okay, so I lose to you, and if we don't get caught and get a bullet in the eye, then we're square?"

Mr. Keegan took a heavy, meaty hand and dropped it on Andrew's shoulder twice, then straightened out Andrew's jacket collar and calmly stated, "Yeah, then we're good, and this stays between you and me." He looked around at his crew, grinned, and held up his hand. "Scout's honor."

The chuckling men put their guns away. They all followed Mr. Keegan as he turned. One man spit at Andrew's shoes, missing, but not by much. Mr. Keegan turned in the middle of Grand Street and yelled, "I'll be back on Wednesday."

Andrew made a megaphone with his hands. "Can't wait!" Then under his breath said, "Asshole."

In the garage, he saw the same attendant with his car fob. Andrew pulled out a $100 bill and handed it to the boy in silence. He protested, but Andrew shook his head, putting up his hand and gently took the fob from him. He got into his car. The leather seats squeaked as he slid down them. Andrew pushed the start button to turn on the engine, pushed the gas pedal to let it rev for a few seconds. His heart pounded faster.

Through pure muscle memory, he connected his iPhone to the USB cord. Andrew's training as a doctor and an athlete allowed him to stay present and relatively calm in a moment of stress. However, a few minutes later, after the stress event was over, his body caught up with his mind with a vengeance. He couldn't tell if he was going to throw up or pass out. He felt his heart race. He took a couple of deep breaths, trying not to hyperventilate. His thoughts raced from how the fuck was Fergus not going to find out about this. Then to Sandra, and now that Keegan knows who he is, could he do enough research to find links to his "real life"? He being the son of Ted Beck, the Masters Champion? His work with other athletes? His thoughts moved to Sandra and all the charity and society events they'd been photographed at together. Would this animal go after her? He couldn't let this bald-headed fuck blow up his life. He had to do something. He felt the fear subside, and from a deep place in his stomach, he felt a burning anger rise through his chest. He punched the steering wheel several times, causing the horn to honk on a few of the strikes. "Fuck, fuck, fuck! I'm not going to let you fucking animals ruin my life! No! Not today! Not ever! I'm in control!"

Over the Apple Play system his phone ringer, set on high, blared. The jolt almost ejected him through his moonroof. The caller-ID showed "Lamar Hayes."

Andrew took three deep and quick breaths, hit the call answer button on the steering wheel, and tried to hide his freak out. "Lamar."

"Where you been? I been calling you all damn night! You gotta help me, DB. I'm in trouble."

Andrew glanced down at his phone and saw seven missed phone calls and six voicemail messages, and five text messages, all from Lamar. He mouthed to himself, "Fuck."

Andrew asked, "Where are you?"

"At the office, man."

"I'm on my way."

Andrew squealed out of the parking garage, made a hard left, and got the green light at Grand Street. He sped down Mercer, made an illegal right on red at Canal Street and sped at 57 miles an hour to the West Side Highway, heading north. The Talking Heads' "Take Me to the River" blared off his playlist. Andrew hit the Volume Up button on his steering wheel to an uncomfortable but not painful point. Anything to palate-cleanse his brain from the previous few minutes.

8

Andrew sped up the West Side Highway, weaving in and out of traffic like it was a slalom race. He used the paddles on the steering wheel to shift into manual to reach maximum torque in the car, which went from zero to 60 in less than four seconds. Andrew tested that theory at every light, screeching and moving lanes to make sure that if he was going to miss the light, he would be in the front row. Cars and cabs beeped long and hard as Andrew caught green lights from West Houston Street until traffic caught up with him at West 14th Street. Andrew looked to his left, catching the massive driving range at Chelsea Piers.

Andrew remembered the countless winter Saturday and Sunday mornings when he and Ted hit what seemed like thousands of balls into the flat Astroturf field, littered with little yellow flags simulating a golf course. As a boy, he didn't dare complain about the howling Hudson River wind that whipped his ball left and right or the frozen hands that hit it. Once when he was 14, the wind worked in his favor, and he hit the back of the net, 200 yards away. Ted pooh-poohed the drive as luck. But from then on, Andrew always tried to hit the ball over the netting and into the Hudson. As he got into his late teens and grew to Ted's height, he got close a few times, which was when Ted stopped taking him to Chelsea piers.

On a summer break back from Berkeley College, he and his buddies hit balls at Chelsea Piers, and the bet was always the same. Free drinks if Andrew hit the back of the netting ten times in a row — Andrew drank for free that whole summer.

An Uber driver disturbed the walk down memory lane when he rolled down the window at the light to yell at Andrew in accented English. "You modder focker crazy guy!" he shouted and flipped Andrew the bird for good measure.

Andrew hit the gas pedal full on at the flash of the green light, leaving the pissed-off cabbie in the dust. Andrew noticed three out of every four nondescript cars had Taxi and Limousine Commission plates, denoted by a "T&LC" on the bottom of the plate.

Is everyone a fucking cab driver in this city now?

Andrew could see the curved-cornered squared arena as he drew closer to the Tomlin Insurance Sports and Entertainment Complex (TISEC — "Tiz-eck") in Hudson Yards. He thought about blowing the light at West 33rd Street, but he knew there were always cop cars there. The service road was a great place for New York's finest to catch up with each other while also having a perfect view of moving violations on the West Side Highway. Andrew used his paddles to slow down and tapped the brakes for good measure, but he mistimed it and came to a hard stop halfway inside the crosswalk. At the red light, Andrew became deep in thought about Lamar, ignoring the harsh stare from a late-night runner who crossed the street and had to scuttle around his front bumper.

With Lamar Hayes, the star forward for the New York Black Knights of the Basketball League of America (BLA), Andrew never knew what he was walking into. If they were sitting at the poker table together, Lamar would be a hard man for Andrew to get a read on. Lamar would bluff when he had no business bluffing, and then go big and let everyone know he's going big, spoiling his pot, and then fold when he had a good hand because he got a "bad feeling" at the table. Andrew reckoned Lamar would be one of those guys wearing dark sunglasses at the table to hide his eyes, but his nervous hand actions and hard swallows would give his tells away. The man was unpredictable in many respects, except one. Andrew might be the

78

only person Lamar told the truth to, including himself.

Lamar was all ego, but he had a good heart and was incredibly loyal. He was also temperamental and sensitive to criticism. His antics drove the Black Knights' management crazy, but his teammates and fans loved him. He gave his all on the court, diving for every loose ball. He hated to lose. Every call against him was a bad call. Journalists who questioned his plays were idiots. His big mouth got him fined by the league all the time. As much as he hated receiving criticism, he doled out more than his fair share. In February, he was ejected for the seventh time this year against division rival the Philadelphia Storm after being called for a personal foul after a hard-fought layup. Lamar thought he was blocked, but the ref thought differently. Lamar spiked the ball, sending it into the crowd, for which he got a technical foul. His ejection came just a few minutes later when he went nose-to-nose with the ref and told him the only offensive foul committed was the *foul offense* of the ref's body odor.

The ejection, $100,000 fine, and three-game suspension that followed put the Black Knights Management in an uproar. Some of the execs wanted to trade him, but Lamar averaged over 28 points a game with 12 rebounds, and he put butts in seats. Trading Lamar was off the table, so management's plan B demanded Lamar see a sports psychologist. Lamar's super-agent, Steve Gotski, recommended Andrew to help Lamar reign in his impulsive tendencies. On and off the court.

Lamar had the reputation of being a womanizer. His social media and paparazzi pictures showed that Lamar lived "the life" of a pro athlete, all stereotypes included. However, Andrew hadn't seen real proof of it. Although there were hours of Instagram and TikTok videos staring Lamar alluding to that behavior, Lamar never had a paternity suit filed against him. No women ever tweeted about being used and abused, and no one had ever tried to blackmail Lamar. As far as Andrew could tell, it was all an act.

Andrew believed Lamar's posturing came from a deeper place. In the two months they had been working together, Andrew felt he was getting closer to uncovering the treasure of emotional gold that Lamar buried deep in his psyche. But Lamar was crafty. And he had an intellect that most people didn't see — or didn't want to see. Lamar was a challenge for Andrew as a therapist because he dodged his questions with a through-the-legs dribble spin move and usually got the shot off at the buzzer.

I wonder what trouble he's in now?

Andrew pulled up to the players' entrance, rolled down his window, and flashed his Black Knights ID. The guard leaned out from his guard shack, armed with a clipboard and a small radio velcroed to his shoulder with a curlicue wire down his broad frame. His finger dangled off the talk button as he thrust his chin at Andrew. "Dr. Beck, welcome back to the Tizeck." He looked down at his watch and asked, "Kinda late for a house call, ain't it?"

Andrew cocked his head to make eye contact, smiled, and said, "Nah, Lamar and I always play games of HORSE in the middle of the night. Kinda our thing."

The guard chuckled as he waved him in. "Well, he's waiting for you Doc, good luck!"

The sharp turns combined with the underground garage's concrete surface made his tires squeak at an almost deafening pitch. Andrew saw a lone seven-seater Cadillac Escalade in black and glossy gold trim, backed in. The yellow-gold and blue New York State front vanity plate on the Escalade read "L-Baller."

Double glass doors lead down a corridor into the locker room area, and then he saw lights from the wide opening that led to the basketball court. Andrew could hear the echo of a basketball dribbling and Rick Ross' "Stay Schemin" featuring Drake and French Montana from the speakers. Over the chill trap rhythms of the song, Andrew could hear the distinctive twang of a ball hitting the rim and bouncing away, followed by a shout, "Fuck!"

Another shot hit the rim. *Twang! Bomp, bomp, bomp, bomp.* Followed by a distinct and loud, "Fuck Me!" The music played on.

The next shot Andrew clearly heard hit off the back board and the rim. *Boom, twang, bomp, bomp, bomp.*

"Goddamn, motherfucker!"

Lamar was shooting from the free throw line. Andrew had his hands in his pockets as he strolled onto the court. Lamar glanced at

Andrew, then gazed downward as he dribbled and set up his foul shot.

The song's repetitive tempo fell in line with Lamar's movement. Each beat, Lamar dribbled in synch. Andrew wasn't sure if he was doing it consciously or unconsciously. "Stay Scheming's" snare drum: *tap, tap, tap, tap*, to Lamar's dribble: *bomp, bomp, bomp, bomp*.

Lamar's next shot hit the place where the rim and the backboard meet to a heavy clang as the ball bounced toward Andrew. Andrew recovered the ball and bounced-passed it back to Lamar.

"Where you been, motherfucker? I've been calling you all damn night!"

"It's two in the morning, Lamar. I'm here."

Lamar changed his tone and went right into the story, bouncing the ball. "Yeah, all right. You know Willy Cooper?"

"The actor?

"Yeah. He's fucking great. He can do drama, comedy, play a fucked-up superhero. Nothing my boy can't do, right? You feeling me on this?"

"Not really."

Lamar continued to dribble, shifting his feet at the foul line, heel to toe, heel to toe, as he looked up at the rim, made his shooting motion but held the ball and did not shoot. "Well, I was at this fundraiser for some shit, and I met his ex-wife, Janice. And we hit it off, right?"

Lamar shot and missed again as the ball twanged off the right part of the rim, ricocheting towards Andrew's face. Andrew reflexively caught the ball with two hands and steered the ball away from his face. He exhaled and shook his head, realizing he had just avoided a bloody nose.

Lamar continued his lament. "Normally I'd be all up in that. But Coop's my boy. I ain't feeling too right about that shit. It's got me all fucked up. You know what I'm saying?"

Andrew held the ball and wrapped his arms around it as if he had just recovered a defensive rebound. Lamar just grabbed another ball off the ball rack next to him. Andrew buried the ball in his chest. It felt comforting to Andrew at a deep level to hold a ball, any ball. But Andrew's tone intensified. "I'm sorry. Did I miss something? Are you friends with Willy?"

Lamar stopped dribbling, put the ball under his right arm, leaned forward, and emphatically gestured with his left. "I said he was 'my boy.' Are you listening to me, man?"

Andrew shot back, "'Your boy' can mean many things, Lamar. I'm just trying to figure out which one."

"Yeah." He took a quiet pause. "We're friends." He took two dribbles, stopped and added, "And now I'm all fucked up over his hot ass ex-wife."

As much as he loved being on a court with Lamar, his patience was wearing thin. His adrenal glands had been pumping high-octane cortisol all night. Andrew's mood was getting dark between Palmer, Keegan, Fergus, marathon poker, and his race up the West Side Highway.

Lamar shot again, but the ball again smacked the left part of the rim. This time, hard enough to put the ball way out of Andrew's reach in the paint. They both watched helplessly as the ball bounced towards the seats.

Lamar threw his arms in the air at the wayward ball and shouted, "See! Look at that weak ass shit, man. I can't think straight, and I got Lawrence Nelson from the LA Bears coming in here. You gotta fix me DB!"

Andrew's frustration peaked, and he snapped, "Are you serious? You drag me down here in the fucking middle of the night to discuss your love life?"

Lamar jabbed back, "That's what I pay you for, motherfucker."

"You don't pay me *that* much."

Andrew took the ball he was holding and punted it into the stands as he walked off the court. Lamar raced up to Andrew to block his way, extending his arms but not touching Andrew. "Hold up, hold up! All right, I'm sorry. C'mon man. I'm trying to do the right thing here."

Rick Ross filled in the silence between the two men as they locked eye to eye.

Something in Andrew's brain bypassed the exhaustion and annoyance, and he shifted to a calm place. He took a step into Lamar's personal space, locked eyes, and said, "Call her. Invite her to dinner at your house. Call your boy Fieri to cook for you. Go top shelf. She'll flip. Don't talk about Willy. Make it all about her. And most importantly, don't fuck her."

The two men maintained an eye-to-eye stare like two MMA fighters in the center of the octagon, getting the referee's instructions, each waiting for the other to blink.

Lamar broke out into a big smile, ran to the ball rack, grabbed a ball, took two quick dribbles, and yelled out, "That's what I'm talking about DB! Damn!"

Lamar's foul shot made the most satisfying sound to any baller. The "pffth" as the ball swished the hoop. Lamar kept his right shooting hand dangling in the air as he yelled out to a departing Andrew, "You the man, DB! You the man!"

The thunderous bass beat ushered Andrew out as he walked through the dark tunnel.

9

A wave of fatigue hit Andrew as he pulled up to the intersection of the West Side Highway. Greenwich was just too fucking far. The cops weren't at their favorite hangout on 33rd Street, so Andrew pulled an illegal U-turn, made a left on 8th Avenue, and headed uptown.

Just a few straggling Uber cars and yellow and green cabbies dotted the road. Andrew felt the heaviness of his eyes and lowered the driver's side window to get some cool fresh air. Andrew got more than he bargained for as a New York City Sanitation truck pulled up next to him. The whiff of the pungent combination of rotting food, stale beer, and garbage stung the inside of his nostrils. The odor worked more like smelling salts to wake up an unconscious quarterback after a blind-side hit. He blinked his eyes and shook his head. He was awake.

The office of Beck Sports Psychology was on the 28th floor of the Historic Hamilton Building at 135 Central Park West, overlooking Central Park. It was his fortress of solitude. His office was a place where he always felt confident and in control. It had an underground parking garage closed off by a large black gate and keypad coded entry. The elevator bank in the underground garage had two elevators. The one on the right went from the garage to the lobby, and then residents and visitors switched to the main elevator. A key card summoned the elevator on the left. This one made two stops, one to Andrew's office on the 28th Floor and the other to the penthouse.

Andrew had cut a special deal with the building and the billion-aire who owned the 10,000-square-foot penthouse to get direct elevator access. Fortunately, the hedge fund manager was a big sports fan and was sensitive to the private nature of Andrew's patient visits. In turn, Andrew would invite him and the building manager to games and bring them into the locker rooms. He would also get them VIP passes to charity events hosted by big name athletes and get them some face time with some of the world's biggest stars.

The elevator opened into the spacious lobby of Andrew's office. There was a circular blonde lacquered wood reception desk. It had multiple monitors on it, but they were strategically placed so Andrew's assistant could maintain eye contact with anyone seated on the couches.

The couches were comfortable leather. Andrew had the manufacturer customize the legs and skirt of the couch to make them six inches higher than normal. Most of Andrew's patients were much larger than the average human. Every step, every moment a patient experienced in Beck Sports Psychology was orchestrated to give them the feeling of safety, security, privacy, and comfort. Here, they were seen, understood, valued.

The elevator doors opened to a ding, and Andrew stepped into his office, which was cast in shadows from the lights over Central Park. Andrew didn't bother turning on the reception lights and made his way to his office door without incident.

Andrew's muscle memory kicked in as he turned on the first switch on the multi-switched light panel. The recessed LED lighting illuminated his desk, finding the right amount of light not to blind him while also enabling him to see the couch. He shed his jacket and kicked off his loafers.

Text Sandra, let her know I'm here.

Andrew took his phone out of his jacket pocket to text Sandra but then became distracted when he felt his Five Iron's Marker Card adhering to the back of his phone. Andrew separated the card from the phone, pulled out his billfold clip and credit card holder, and stuck it behind his American Express Platinum Card, which was heavy enough to be a weapon if in the right hands. He placed his phone, wallet, and keys on the coffee table in front of the couch. He threw his jacket on his Herman Miller Eames recliner and ottoman. The classic Eames was black leather with oiled palisander, wood paneling, and an ottoman to match. It was where Andrew sat when holding therapy sessions. The chair was for him, and for him only.

The jacket didn't hang neatly but crumpled into the seat of the chair. Andrew didn't bother to fix it. It was that time of the night. He sat down on the couch, exhaled, and ran his hands through his wavy blonde hair. Every time he closed his eyes, he saw a rotating montage of faces: Rothstein, Mr. Keegan, Fergus, Ted, John, Lamar, and Sandra. The circular movement of the montage gave him a drunken bedspin-like feeling. He thought he was going to vomit, but, he choked it down.

A wave of exhaustion overcame him as he thought, "Sandra, have to text Sandra." He reached for his phone. But his body responded as if he had just taken a fistful of Ambien. His eyes shuddered, his hand fell limply to the side of the couch, several inches short of reaching his phone, and he fell into a deep slumber.

10

The morning sounds of Manhattan are ubiquitous in every neighborhood. Even the exclusive Upper West Side was not immune to cars honking, sirens, and trucks rumbling down the streets, with their high-pitch hydraulic brakes screeching as they came to a red light. The sounds would be enough to make even an original New Amsterdamer like Peter Stuyvesant jump out of his skin, but Andrew slept soundly. He was snoring as his chest heaved and relaxed.

On the table, Andrew's iPhone vibrated and dinged the Apple "Calypso" tone as a text message hit the phone. Five seconds later, another text hit the phone. Another five seconds went by and a third rattled the phone to where it vibrated off the edge of the table onto the carpet. This happened without even a movement from Andrew. He was dead to the world, his chest rising up and down rhythmically with each breath.

Outside in the lobby, the elevator door dinged, and out of it came a Latinx woman in Lululemon black yoga pants and a gray "Run Briskly" half-zip top. She carried a garment bag, gym bag, and a navy-blue New Jersey Bulldogs freezer bag. The logo had a bulldog running on two legs, with one paw holding a football and the other paw out straight, in a stiff arm.

Within two steps out of the elevator, she could hear the snoring from the open office door and rolled her eyes and shook her head. Just then, the office phone rang, and with a grimace, she dumped the load on the couch, glanced at her Fitbit Versa, which showed 7:16

a.m., and raced behind the desk. As she reached for the phone, she watched the bulldog do somersaults as her lunch bag tumbled to the ground and rolled under the large, ridiculously high coffee table. She took a deep breath and hoped her girlfriend closed the Tupperware lids tightly when making her lunch. She picked up the phone on the fourth ring.

"Beck Sports Psychology. Gina Perez speaking."

The voice on the line was distressed, and even though the caller didn't tell Gina her name, she knew who it was.

"Oh, hi, Sandra. Yes, Andrew is here. He's sleeping on his couch."

Gina went immediately into damage control and spin mode, a familiar modality for her. "No, I don't think he was drunk. You want me to wake him?" Gina grabbed a pen to write any potential instructions but put the pen down as she noted a change in tone.

She contained the damage. Gina pursed her lips and nodded her head instinctively. "Okay, I'll have him call you as soon as he wakes up."

Gina's blue and fluorescent yellow Puma Evospeeds squeaked across the marble floor as she went into Andrew's office and stood over him. "Andrew, Andrew. Hey, wake up, Boss."

Andrew took the pillow from behind his head, put it on his face, holding it with both hands, and let out a muffled moan, "Mom, I don't wanna go to school today."

Gina laughed. "Get up, goofball. You didn't let Sandra know you were sleeping here."

Andrew immediately pulled the pillow down to his chest. His eyes were wide open. "Ah fuck." Andrew slowly sat up. "It was a late night. Lamar was a mess. I was with him until God knows what time."

Gina headed towards the kitchenette. "I'll get you some coffee. You hit the showers. You smell like my soccer cleats."

As Gina passed out of the room, Andrew belted out, "Is that what I pay you for? To insult me?"

Gina's voice came mixed with the clatter of cupboard doors. "No, you pay me because no one else will put up with your shit. And no one can keep your life organized like I can." Now a kitchen faucet ran.

Andrew nodded and scratched his head. "Oh yeah, right. Good point."

Andrew reflected on her comment. It was spot-on. Gina not only kept Beck Sport Psychology business affairs in order, but she could connect with Andrew's superstar athlete clients on a personal level while always being professional. Gina had been the co-captain of the US Women's National Team in 2015 when they beat Japan in the World Cup final, 5 to 2.

Gina was a beast on the field. She was afraid of nothing and no one. Even though she was considered too short and too slow to be a defender, her driving tenacity, all-in attitude, and aggressive play earned her the respect of her teammates and opponents alike. Gina's highlight reel on YouTube showed her throwing her body into every ball. Her slide tackles got "all ball" as well as the player. Her father, Francisco, nicknamed her "Chica Dinamita," because when Gina slide tackled, her trademark was to hit the ball first and then the player hard enough to launch them in the air as if they had been blown up by dynamite.

Gina took every shot on goal from a forward as a personal offense. And if an opponent was lucky enough to get a shot off, every time they touched the ball from then on, they were going to feel Number 4 knocking the crap out of them. Gina seldom got yellow cards despite her aggressive play, and that was her secret: "controlled-aggression" taken to the limit. She was never reckless on the field, but in her personal life, that was another story.

Andrew had learned of the roots of this aggression in many late-night conversations with Gina. It all came from her mother, Louisa Perez. Louisa could never accept her daughter's sexuality, and it caused an insurmountable rift between them. Andrew diagnosed that her mother's rejection created the toxic anger and shame that Gina exorcised on the field. The soccer pitch was a "safe place" for her to expel her resentments, and when she performed as she did, she was "seen" for who she was.

"Hey, Boss?" Gina asked, returning to the room carrying a steaming mug of black coffee.

"Yeah?"

"I read your transcription when I was on the treadmill. What's this about the Tides not paying for Palmer's therapy anymore?"

"Yeah, well, you know how that goes. He gets a W on opening day, so they figure he's cured."

"Yeah, but what about—"

"I know. That's what I told them."

"And when he—"

"Exactly! See you get it. But you know that bastard Rothstein. To him it's all dollars and cents."

"So John agreed to pay for therapy personally, like Lamar?"

Andrew squealed a little, "Well, not exactly." Picking up the mug before him, he blew over the rim. "I mean, not yet…"

"Oh shit."

"But he will." Andrew didn't sell it.

"Whatever you say, Boss." Gina left his office shaking her head.

Yeah, he will. Why won't he? I got him through opening day? Shit, I better practice my pitch some more.

Andrew headed for the shower, mumbling to himself, "John, the Tides are proud of the progress you made, and they encourage you to continue your therapy… John, you did great on Monday, and I know with more therapy, we can work through those triggers that are affecting your pitching… John, you need more fucking therapy bro, you're a goddamn mess…"

He laughed out loud at his last comment as he turned on the shower. Sometimes he wished he could say what was going through his mind.

11

Freshly showered and dressed, Andrew sat at his desk. He kept spare shirts, workout gear, and a go-bag in case of a patient emergency or if he had to fly out immediately to pitch a team. If a call from a pro team came in for a meeting, Andrew would do all he could to get the appointment within twenty-four hours. With access to private planes, he could be almost anywhere in just a few hours. Andrew picked up his iPhone to face the music with Sandra, but before he could, his interoffice phone rang.

"Did you call Sandra yet?" Gina asked.

"I was about to. How pissed was she when you spoke to her?"

"She's nice to me. She knows what I put up with all day," Gina snarked.

To prevent laughing, Andrew made an angry cat sound on the phone. "Raaeeer."

"You just better hope you only get a yellow card instead of a red card and a five-night-sleeping-your-ass-on-the-couch suspension."

Andrew did his best sensitive and romantic guy impression. "You should know, Gina, that Sandra's and my love knows no bounds."

"Um-hmm…"

"On second thought, book lunch at the Four Seasons for 1 o'clock."

"There you go, Boss. I'm on it. You call her and see if you can charm your way out this one." She hung up, and her cynical laugh echoed in the office.

"I heard that!"

Gina's cackle got louder.

Andrew shook his head and picked up his iPhone. "Siri, call Sandra, mobile."

Siri replied in her monotone, polite voice, "Calling Sandra, mobile."

The phone rang. Andrew took a deep breath and braced for impact.

A terse Sandra answered, "What happened last night?"

"I'm so sorry. Lamar was a goddamned mess. I was exhausted and just drove to the office. I should have texted you or something. I apologize."

Sandra took a beat. "I'm worried about you. You're out all hours of the night lately."

"Darling, baseball season just started. The Black Knights are on target for winning the division for the first time since 2005. Tennis is a twelve-month sport and Robbie is at the Barcelona Open this week. You remember the shit-storm she caused last year? And on top of all that, the football draft is in two weeks, and I have a new patient starting Wednesday. My first hockey player. So, yeah, it gets like this."

"I understand. I get busy too. Can you please let me know when you're not going to make it home so, like you said, my cortisol levels don't rise unnecessarily?"

Andrew appreciated her deference. "Touché. Gina is booking lunch for us at the Four Seasons at one. Can you make it?"

Andrew heard the springs of her office chair groan as if she'd just sat forward, revived. "Oh, lovely. I have to talk to Mom about the Robbins account in a few minutes."

Andrew moved instinctively into coach mode. "Okay, good luck. Be strong. Don't let her bully you."

"Thanks, I won't. See you soon, hon."

Andrew hung up, and as he did, his interoffice line rang. He picked up immediately, but before he could say anything, Gina teased, "You in the doghouse?"

Andrew grinned. "Referee said play on. Got all ball on that slide tackle. Woo hoo!"

"Luck-key. Hey, I got John Palmer on line two."

"Great, put him through."

Andrew heard Gina faintly through the door, "Great game, JP. Way to pull that one out. I knew you would do it." After a few seconds, Gina added, "You're going to have a great year. We'll see you soon."

The office phone rang, and Andrew answered it immediately, and with his endorphins firing due to not being in hot water with Sandra, Andrew jumped right into the call. "JP! Great game, buddy!"

"Hey, just wanted to call you and thank you for last night," John said humbly.

"No sweat, John, just doing my job."

John gave a brief pause, and his voice shook a little. "I was looking for you after the game…"

"Yeah, sorry about that. I had an emergency call last night."

"So, I'm not the only one that freaks out?"

"John, it's part of the process. It will happen, but I'm here for you. You know that, right?"

"I know, I know."

"Hey, John?"

"Yeah, Doc?"

Andrew altered his tone to be somber and emphatic. "If you ever take drugs, we're done. That's a nonstarter for me. You made a promise, and our relationship is built on trust."

John's voice cracked, and he cleared his throat. "Sorry about that, Doc. It's just when I was high, nothing ever got to me. Now that I'm sober, I'm scared, Doc. I'm scared all the fucking time."

"John, being sober *is* scary. It means you have to deal with your feelings. You have to take responsibility for your actions. Your father enabled your drug use and took care of everything in your life. Now that he's gone, and you don't have the drugs to numb you, you're vulnerable. I know how scared you feel, but you're stronger now. You have come so far. I believe in you. Skipper Costas believes in you, and Mr. Rothstein, he believes in you too."

"Really? Rothstein? I thought he was going to trade me."

Andrew bluffed. "No. He thinks you have a bright future. He told me so himself. You pitched opening day, right?"

"Yeah, you're right. Thanks, Doc." There was a pause. "You know, I'm, um, pitching on Friday in Miami."

"Yes, I know."

Andrew could hear him scraping his foot as if he was digging out the dirt with his cleats by the rubber on the pitcher's mound. It was one of his familiar responses to anxiety. His voice warbled like a teenage boy's who's just hit puberty.

"You, you, think maybe you can come down?"

"John, there's something we have to talk about."

"Okay."

"Mr. Rothstein said the Tides won't pay for your therapy anymore. Their position is that they got you to opening day, and now the team feels you can continue therapy on your own."

"*They* got me to opening day?"

"I know. It's infuriating, right?" Andrew didn't wait for a response. "You and I know how much work it took to make the progress we did in such a short time. You're responding well to therapy, but we still have a long road to travel." He let it sink in. Then added strategically, "We got through opening day, but it could have just as easily have gone sideways on us."

"I know."

Andrew took another pause. He could hear John fidgeting with the phone. He had to make some more points.

"Personally, as your doctor, and now that we have gotten past the addiction, I believe we are just scratching the surface on your emotional health. We need to understand the triggers that are causing your anxiety, and..." He paused for effect, "the hallucinations of Craig."

Andrew heard John take a deep breath and exhale. "Okay, so then you'll come down to Miami?"

"John, we agreed, no away games, remember?"

"I know, but I would feel better if you were there. I'll fly you down private. On me!"

Andrew felt the tide turn in his favor. "We can talk before you go out on the field."

John pleaded, "C'mon Doc, you can leave as soon as they put in a reliever."

Andrew let the moment sit.

John's voice spiked. "And, and, and I'll pay you fifty grand! Please!"

Andrew resisted while he continued to prop him up. "John, it's not about the money. You can do this. You don't need me there."

John panicked. "But, but what if, like you said, I see him again?!"

"You won't."

"How can you be so sure? If I start out the year at two and oh, I'll be able to settle in. The Tides won't be breathing down my neck anymore. What do you say?"

Andrew's strategy worked. John was on board. He quickly assessed the risk-rewards of alienating John in his moment of vulnerability and losing him as a patient or breaking Friday night plans with Sandra. It was a no-brainer.

"My wife's gonna kill me. But, okay. Text Gina your charter flight service info. I'll be there at first pitch."

"Thank you, Doc! I appreciate it!"

"Hey, we're a team. You and me."

"Absolutely."

There was a brief pause as Andrew waited for his moment and then made sure John wasn't getting away with this breach of Andrew's rules without some level of payback.

"John?"

"Yeah?"

"Say it."

"Really?"

"Say it. And you better mean it, too."

John recited his affirmation unenthusiastically. "I am strong. I stand tall on my mound. I throw with all my might, power, and skill. I am unbeatable."

"Yeah, it doesn't sound like you meant it; I'm hanging up now."

"No, no, no! Okay, okay!"

Andrew heard him take a deep breath and cleared his throat. "Ahem."

This time John responded like a young athlete used to being told what to do, where to go, and how to act by coaches, agents, media, his father, and his psychologist. "I am strong. I stand tall on my mound. I throw with all my might, power, and skill. I am unbeatable.

"I believe that. See you Friday."

Afterward, he told Gina he was flying down to Miami when John pitched on Friday.

"But Vladimir Poplov and the Sentinels play on Friday," Gina explained. "And besides, I thought you didn't—"

Andrew interrupted, "Well, sometimes you give a little to get a little. John is onboard. How much time do I need to get to Miami?"

"Hold on, let me do a search."

Andrew and Gina did this dance frequently and seamlessly. They could exchange roles like soccer players covering each other's position on a switch play. Sometimes they poked at each other like siblings, sometimes they spoke deep truths that only two close friends speak of, and sometimes, like now, they spoke professionally, each knowing their role and how to put a ball at the other's foot on the run and strike a one-timer to score a goal.

After a few audible mouse clicks and keyboard clacking, Gina had the data and reported it militarily with no pauses, "Okay, it's a two-and-a-half-hour charter flight from Teterboro to Miami and a 15-minute ride from the airport to the stadium. First pitch is 8:05 p.m. I know the people at Blade. I can get you a helicopter ride to Teterboro. If you leave here around 5:00, you'll easily be wheels up by 5:15 or 5:20. It'll be tight, but we can do it."

Andrew responded, "Book it. And also bill Palmer $50,000 plus expenses."

"Yeah?"

"His offer."

As they were about to hang up, Andrew remembered something. "Hey Gina, wait. When is Vladimir coming in for his patient intake meeting?"

"Tomorrow, Wednesday at 3 p.m."

"Okay, good. Hey, can you call Rafael, Darryl Jenkins' assistant, and see if I can sit with DJ? I don't want to sit with that asshole Roth-stein."

The position switch happened again as their tones changed. "That's messed up. Your patient is a Tide, and you're going to sit in the Miami Surf's box with *their* CEO?"

"Yep."

"So you two still stay in touch since your 'bro-cation' in Cooper-stown for his Hall of Fame induction?"

"Yeah, but not in a professional capacity… as far as you know."

Gina laughed. "Got it. I'm on it."

Andrew hung up, leaned back in his desk chair, and threw his hands behind his head. A smile graced his face as once again he snatched victory from the jaws of defeat. But the smile didn't last long as a flash of Mr. Keegan's face appeared in his mind. Keegan, that knuckle-dragging gorilla. He had to figure out how to lose at poker and not let Fergus' watchful eyes find out about it.

12

The Four Seasons on 57th Street between Park Avenue and Madison Avenue was Andrew and Sandra's go-to sanctuary when they needed a timeout from their hectic lives. It was a short walk for Sandra, whose office was on Madison Avenue. For Andrew it was a 10- to 15-minute Uber ride.

The casual dining restaurant called The Garden had tall windows that allowed natural light to fill up the restaurant on sunny days. Several strategically placed acacia trees reached toward the ceiling, giving privacy to patrons.

This NYC oasis of plush green velvet chairs, outstanding service, and wonderful food was where Sandra and Andrew talked through their work issues and business ideas. Sandra would talk about new client pitches and run through strategic visions for her big and small clients. Andrew would get her advice on what speaking engagements he should do to earn him more exposure to teams. Andrew couldn't talk about his patients' treatment, but he would dispel many of the rumors the press and the Twitterverse would chirp about his athletes in therapy. The Four Seasons offered a nice buffer and mind dump so that when they got home, Greenwich's power couple could leave their work at the front door.

It was a sparse Tuesday lunch crowd. They scored a table right under one of the acacias. Sandra had the kale salad and Andrew the cauliflower steak as both attempted a healthy lunch. Soft instrumental music played in the background as the two ate. Sumptuous violins, tinkling piano.

"So, how did the conversation with Roxanne go?" Andrew asked.

"We didn't have it." Sandra stabbed at her salad.

"What? Why?"

Sandra put her fork down and wiped her mouth delicately with her white cloth napkin. "She got another client call and never got back to me so, I don't know."

Andrew replied, "How do you feel about that?" It was an obvious question from a shrink, but still a genuine way for a man to engage conversationally with his wife. At least he hoped.

Sandra exhaled and put her hand on her forehead, supporting the arm by placing it on the table. "You know I'm getting a little tired...." At that moment, Sandra's phone rang. "Shit, that's her."

"Babe, let it go to voicemail so we can have a pleasant lunch."

"No, I better take it."

"Hi, Mom… Yeah, no problem. So I wanted to talk to you about…"

What Andrew knew of his mother-in-law was that Roxanne Wells, the founder and CEO of Wells Public Relations, was confident and unforgiving in every way. She had been a social staple and icon in both New York City and Greenwich.

Andrew assessed that Roxanne used belittling and dismissive language to control Sandra and keep her limited in her personal growth. This behavior frustrated Andrew to no end because Sandra was twice as smart as her mother and five times as strategic. However, sometimes it only took one word from Roxanne and Sandra would feel the years of harshness and gaslighting which put her on the defensive or in a state of quiet acquiescence.

Sandra tried to make her point on the termination of the Robbins account. "I know you two go way back, but Mom, Pete Robbins is argumentative, indecisive, and pays his bills late. He's not good for us."

Uh-oh, here we go. Come on, Sandra, don't fold. You have the stronger hand.

Sandra continued after a retort and raised her tone to be emphatic.

"Yes, Mom, that's exactly the problem. He's known me since I was a girl, and he doesn't take me seriously…"

That's it! Put your foot down!

"Mom, he said he wanted to reach a younger audience, then started talking about doing a direct mail campaign. His entire staff cringed. He's gotta go, Mom. He's bad for business. Well, it's my call—he's out." Sandra's eyes narrowed, and the carotid artery in her neck throbbed.

Yes, raise that shit! You got those pocket aces and a pair of tens on the board. Get her to fold, babe!

There was a long pause, and then Sandra closed both her eyes and clenched her fist. "I know, Mom."

Uh-oh.

Sandra subconsciously picked up her silver dinner knife, held it point down, and began twisting it into the tablecloth. "I know it's your business, but if you'd just listen…"

Oh shit, she doesn't have the chips to stay in the game.

Sandra dropped the knife and held her hand over her forehead again, bowing her head and lowering her volume. "Okay. Okay. I'll go to his office tomorrow."

Ah crap. She folded. She should have gone all-in and threatened to resign. She had the stronger hand. But that's the way it goes. If you can't bet the chips, you will always get beat.

Sandra hung up the phone, placed it face down on the table, and immediately began to cut her salad ferociously. "Shit, shit, shit," she whispered.

Okay, Andrew, be supportive, be supportive. "What happened, babe?"

"She… she overruled me."

"Oh no! I'm so sorry. I thought you made some good points."

She dropped the fork and knife, the latter clanking the China plate on the way down and bouncing into her food. "God, I'm so sick of her and her frigging cronies. I can't take too much more of this."

Andrew clutched her hand as she looked upward at the acacia tree, eyes glistening. "Well, you are the bigger person for it. I'm sure it'll work out."

Sandra pulled her hand back and fired a look at Andrew. "Oh

Christ, Andrew, just stop."

"What?"

"Patronizing me."

Sandra sat back and crossed her arms. "You knew she was going to do that, didn't you?"

Andrew shrugged, "Do what?"

"Pull rank."

Andrew wiped his mouth with his napkin to buy two seconds and sat up straight in his chair. "I don't have a crystal ball. But if you want my honest opinion, I'll tell you."

"Go ahead."

Andrew spoke with his hands. "You should have threatened to resign."

"What? Don't be ridiculous. I built this firm just as much as she did. She's going to retire soon, and I'll take over. I just have to be patient. I can wait it out."

"Without you, that place would fall apart in a week. Don't let her bully you. A threat says you're serious. When she plays the 'I'm the boss' or 'I'm the mommy' card, counter with a threat of resignation. Hell, you could start your own firm."

Exasperated, Sandra threw her hands up at shoulder height. "Why should I give up what I earned, what I built?"

"As long as Roxanne knows you'll never walk away, she'll walk all over you."

Sandra blinked. Before Sandra could reply, her phone rang again. "Oh shit, what now?"

"Wells Public Relations, Sandra Wells speaking...' She paused. "Hi Wendy, what can I do for you?"

A small smile eked out on Sandra's face. Andrew always marveled at how quickly she could emotionally shift gears. "That's great! My team and I would love to attend the ribbon-cutting with Senator Mann." After a pause she asked, "When is it?" Sandra's eyes widened. "Oh! That's in two hours!" She straightened up and spoke accommodatingly. "No, no, no. We'll be there. Great, thanks for the opportunity."

Sandra took a breath as Andrew delicately asked, "Everything okay?"

Sandra started packing up her things. "I gotta go back to the office and head up to Fairfield. A client has a ribbon cutting at their new community center. Senator Mann is going to be there. She's up for reelection in November. She's going to need a good PR firm."

"Ha ha. She'll need the best!"

Sandra quickly got up from the table, came to Andrew's side, and kissed him on the cheek. "I guess it's my turn for a late night."

Andrew received the kiss with a smile and softly responded, "No problem, darling."

It looks like I get to play poker at The Five Iron tonight. Yeah Baby!

"What are you smiling at?"

"I dig seeing you in work mode. You have so much drive. I admire that about you."

A guilty look came over Sandra's face. "Oh, thank you. Sorry about lunch."

Andrew gave her a reassuring smile. "Duty calls. We'll do it another time."

Sandra blew him a kiss and walked down the small stairs out of The Garden into the main lobby area. Andrew watched Sandra power walk as her heels click-clacked on the marble floor down the steps, clickity-clack, clickity-clack, clickity-clack to the doorman at the revolving door. With each clickity-clack sound, Andrew grinned ear to ear as in his mind he saw chips landing on each other in an ever-growing pile. He felt a warmth in his gut, and it wasn't from the cauliflower steak.

13

The poker game from less than 24 hours ago still had a lingering effect on Andrew. To clear his mind and boost his endorphins, Andrew hit the gym for an hour of cardio and another 45 minutes of kettle bells and weights.

He thought more about Mr. D as he drove downtown to The Five Iron. He liked Mr. Davidson, and he could feel the Paternal Transference kicking in. He looked at the mental association he created between Mr. D and "Big Papa" Hargrove. He self-counseled himself that such a transfer of affection could be very dangerous in high-stakes poker. It could cause him to make an error that would wipe out his marker card. Andrew was a "take no prisoners" poker player, so these feelings were unusual. But the thought of the old-timer taking a beatdown from George for over-extending his credit with Fergus was hard to stomach.

At the Players Table, Andrew was meticulous about watching for tells in every player. Tells were free information just waiting to be had, but only for those who paid close attention. Of course, Andrew tried to make his observations inconspicuous, and most players tried to do the same thing to him. Andrew not only excelled at it, but this mind game was the part he enjoyed most.

For Andrew, there was no feeling in the world like that last moment in a poker hand, "the showdown," the moment between winning and losing. He felt it in golf when making a winning putt, and he felt it when convincing a superstar athlete that his therapy and methodologies would cure them of all their issues affecting their performance. Even when Keegan's men stuck a Glock in his ribs, his adrenaline rush was triggered. This was the same rush he felt when the stakes were high. The higher the stakes, the deeper the rush, and if it was life or death, that rush was hard to beat.

Andrew was relieved to see Mr. Davidson at the table looking untouched. Andrew hid the smile and the laugh to himself that his projection of Mr. D getting a beatdown was only in his head. Surely, Fergus was not an animal, and you can't get your debts paid from a broken man?

The table stakes were the same as last night. Andrew enjoyed his reputation as a top poker player in The Five Iron, and tonight he was at a table with Mr. Davidson, a Mr. Van Winkle, a Ms. Luveaux, and a Mr. Chin. The player's table at The Five Iron is an exclusive but small group, so they had all played against each other at least once.

Andrew pulled up his mental player profiles of each opponent. He read them in his mind like he was reading the stats off the back of a baseball card.

Mr. Van Winkle, late thirties, sells medical devices for a Dutch company. He's fluent in German, Dutch and Italian. He was a steady and tight player, not a lot of bluffs from him.

Mr. Chin is in his mid-forties and a fun-loving joker. He drinks a lot and flirts with the female servers when he folds. He is not an attentive player.

Ms. Luveaux was Haitian and in her mid to late twenties. She was wearing a black Yankees hat with the Yankees NY logo, also in black as opposed to the typical white. She wore oversized round sunglasses with dark blue lenses and a bright yellow bomber jacket covering a sleeveless tee. She was braless, and the tee was low cut. Andrew figured Ms. Luveaux did it to distract players off their game. Andrew also pegged her as the table wildcard. She was fearless and a player in her own right. She kept the table banter to a minimum. Her only flaw, Andrew assessed, was her gum chewing and blowing bubbles. However, some of that was clearly to annoy the other players and distract them when the bubble made a big pop.

Last was Mr. D. Tonight, he had been playing well, and he was ahead of Andrew in chips but nowhere near recovering the half-million-dollar loss from the previous night.

Andrew wasn't playing Mr. Davidson in his usual way. He folded a few times when he surmised Mr. Davidson didn't have the cards to beat him.

I might hate myself tomorrow, but right now I don't mind carrying Mr. D. and letting him think he's earning back his money. I think Big Papa would be proud of me right now.

The table was set, and as usual, the small blinds were $5,000, which in this hand was to Mr. Davidson and the big blind of $10,000 was to Andrew. His two hole cards were a seven of clubs and six of clubs.

Okay, not great, but I can make do with this. As the big blind I'm already in for $10K, so let's see what everyone else does.

Mr. Van Winkle limped in with a $10,000 bet. Mr. Chin and Ms. Luveaux followed suit. Mr. Davidson threw in another $5,000 to complete at $10,000. Andrew checked it off, giving everyone a cheap look at a flop. The dealer scooped the chips to center, burned one face down, and turned over:

$$7 \diamondsuit \quad J \diamondsuit \quad 7 \heartsuit$$

Andrew tried not to react. His seven clubs and the two sevens on the board gave him a set at the flop. Now he had to see how he could get the table to build up a big pot.

Mr. D checked, and so did Andrew.

Andrew watched Van Winkle examine his cards. He made a frustrated face as if he was contemplating what to do with his hand against this raggedy board—but Andrew thought he was trying to fake out the table in believing his hand was weaker than it was.

Maybe king/jack or ace/jack?

Mr. Van Winkle looked over his chip stack and fiddled with some chips as he contemplated his bet. Then he led out with four $25,000 chips, putting them neatly in the pot.

Andrew turned his focus to Mr. Chin, as it was his turn next. He was playing with his chip stack as he contemplated his move. He then abruptly sat back in his chair and folded his arms. Andrew interpreted this play as he was going to fold. A mischievous grin arose on his face as he addressed Mr. Van Winkle, "Quite a bet, Mr. Van Winkle."

Mr. Chin's grin grew bigger. And accent became more pronounced as he added, "You don't say much. Maybe you are asleep like Rip Van Winkle? Is he a relative of yours?"

Mr. Van Winkle didn't react or reply. He kept his focus on his cards. Andrew noted that. Mr. Chin broke the tension with a laugh. "Ah, ha, ha, I'm just fucking with you. I'm going to fold and get another drink." He then waved his hand at the server and called out to her. "Come here, gorgeous!"

Ms. Luveaux, other than chomping on her gum a few times, gave no hints to her game play. She threw in four $25,000 chips, matching the bet of $100,000 and calling. Mr. D also called $100,000. Andrew added his $100,000 as if he had no hopes of improving. He still felt his three of a kind was the strongest hand, but now was not the time for a raise. He didn't want to scare away Van Winkle with his top pair.

As the dealer dealt the next card at the "Turn," Andrew calculated the pot to be $450,000.

The dealer turned a nine of diamonds and placed it next to the other cards.

Andrew was satisfied with his three of a kind. Yes, Mr. Van Winkle might have pocket jacks, giving him a full house, which would beat him, but it was more likely that he had ace/jack, or king/jack, then he would only have two pair and Andrew would win.

In a not too surprising play, the conservative Mr. Van Winkle checked, effectively passing his move to the next player. Ms. Luveaux didn't give away anything in her facial expressions and quickly followed Mr. Van Winkle's play with a check as well. Mr. Davidson smirked after rubbing his gray stubble on his chin.

Okay, Mr. D, what's your play? You got that smirk you get when things are going your way. Thanks to yours truly, of course. And you're tapping chips against your cards. A little different from the last game. But something to watch.

Mr. Davidson took two multi-colored chips and with a self-satisfying grin, made an opening bet of $200,000. To Andrew he said, "I don't know about you, Doc, but I'm getting that feeling of déjà vu all over again."

Andrew met the quip with a polite smile and turned up the corners of his cards. "Yeah, maybe so. But I like where this train is heading. I'm in for the ride." Andrew threw in $200,000 in chips.

If Mr. Van Winkle doesn't go big here, then he doesn't have the full house. And Mr. D? He still has that damn smirk and the light pressure on the chips. He's playing it cool. If Mr. D is drawing towards a straight, he will beat my three of a kind. Mr. Van Winkle is playing with his chips and it looks like he is going to make a play.

Mr. Davidson made eye contact with Mr. Van Winkle as he fingered several $100,000 chips and pointed at him.

"You don't want to do that, son. I mean, I'll take your money, but…"

The stoic Mr. Van Winkle had barely made any facial expressions for most of the night. But now, his eyebrows scrunched together. "I'm *not* your son."

Somebody has some Daddy issues.

Mr. Davidson was taken aback. "Just an expression. I meant nothing by it." Mr. Davidson leaned over the table, and his grin got a little bigger. "I'll tell you what, since I offended you… here, I'll show you a card."

Mr. Davidson flipped over a card, showing the table his eight of diamonds. This move is usually an illegal play in the casinos, but at The Five Iron, the dealer did not raise an issue and let it play out.

Holy shit! That eight of diamonds gives him seven, eight, and nine of diamonds, and with the jack of diamonds on the board, if the other card he's holding is a ten of diamonds, then he has a straight flush. There is still one last remaining card on the river still to go. But I think I'm fucked here.

Mr. Van Winkle barked, "Straight flush?"

Not waiting for a confirmation as Mr. Davidson's face said it all, Mr. Van Winkle closed his eyes, turned his head, and quietly declared, "*Godverdomme.*" He tossed his cards into the muck pile.

Ms. Luveaux didn't give away anything in her facial expressions. She glanced once more at her cards, sat up straight, stopped her gum chewing and said, "Fold." She crossed her arms, pushed up her sunglasses on her nose, and let out a "med" under her breath in creole.

Andrew gave her a look and a slight grin. She peered over her sunglasses as her eyebrows rose and her smooth, shiny forehead wrinkled.

"I spent a summer working at LSU. A lot of Cajun French is spoken there. Learned a few words."

Ms. Luveaux gave a quick smile and shrugged her shoulders.

Mr. Davidson leaned over the table to get a good look at Andrew. "Well, it's just you and me, kid. Here, I'll make it easy on you." He threw in a $100,000 chip.

That's a confident bet. He must have nutted the straight flush. Oh well. But guess what? Here's my chance to help Mr. D out. Make up for yesterday. If I call, the total pot will be $1,050,000. And $410,000 of it is mine. Ah, what the fuck.

Andrew threw in $100,000 in chips and flippantly blurted out, "Oh, come on, Mr. D, no one gets luck like that. I'm gonna call."

The dealer turned the last card, called the "river" card, which revealed a six of diamonds.

7 ♦ J ♦ 7 ♥ 9 ♦ 6 ♦

But Mr. Davidson wasn't looking at the card. He was glaring at Andrew, and a frown replaced his grin.

Mr. Davidson barked, "What do you mean by that?"

"Nothing. I mean, if you got a straight flush on the turn, that's a hell of a hand. I'd like to see luck like that."

"You trying to use some of that reverse psychology on me, huh? You don't think I'm lucky? Is that it?!"

"No?! Mr. D?"

Oh wait, a six of diamonds? I have the six of clubs, so with my three sevens, I have a full house. It doesn't beat his straight flush, but what the fuck is up with him?

"Mr. D, I didn't mean any disrespect. I'm sorry."

Mr. Davidson slammed the remaining chips into the pot. "I'm all-in!"

Mr. Davidson then closed one eye and pointed at Andrew. "Hey kid, last night was your night. Tonight is mine! So why don't you be a good boy, save yourself some money, and just quit. Tonight, you're the loser!"

Andrew's eyes widened as a burst of acidic adrenaline burned through his body. "What did you say?"

14

1993

Ted and a 14-year-old Andrew were on the 18th hole of the Green-wich Country Club. A swoosh and ping sound came from Andrew's driver and the ball as it rocketed off the tee. Andrew's driving was a phenomenon. He could hit a ball as far as most college players. Not that Ted ever acknowledged him for it. But Andrew was inconsistent. Sometimes brilliant, hitting the ball straight as an arrow down the fairway. But some other times he rushed his shots, slicing them into the rough, and he had to work himself out of a jam. Ironically, Andrew's play was very similar to his father's.

It confused him when Ted blew his top at young Andrew for tak-ing big chances. After all, as a professional golfer, Ted was famous for, at critical moments, attempting high-risk shots to clear water haz-ards, or he would blast balls from the rough that often missed the green but found their way into a sand trap. Sometimes after several days of consistent play, his aggression would take him from the top ten on the leaderboard to barely making the cut. Those "go big or go home" shots endeared him to the fans, drove up the TV ratings, but it often cost him and his family tens of thousands of dollars in prize money.

Ted and Andrew walked to their balls. Ted's shot was right down the middle of the fairway. Andrew had hit a monstrous drive by any standard, and his ball was not too far behind Ted's. The only problem was that Andrew's shot was in the rough and almost on the cart path. Ted used this opportunity to blast Andrew as he stood next to his ball that landed neatly in the fairway.

"Wow! You really fucked yourself on that shot, boy! I gave you a 20-stroke lead, and you could have won it on this hole." Ted threw his arms up in the air, club in hand. "But noooo! How many times do I have to tell you?" He pointed his 7 iron at Andrew. "Don't muscle the ball. You overshot the fairway and now you're in the rough. Nice job, dummy."

Andrew seethed in anger and the frenetic energy made him run to the golf cart to grab his 9 iron. His face flushed, and with determination in his eyes, he sized up the red triangular flag on the thin pin in the hole. It had a bright white 18 stamped on it and waved in the summer breeze. He yelled back to his father with a surge and frustration but also confidence in his ability, "I can do it, Dad, I can make the green from here, it's only—"

"No, you can't. Who do you think you are—me? Just lay up. You lost, boy. You had your chance." Ted took a few steps toward Andrew and lowered his tone, "I'll tell you what. If you quit now, we'll say I only won by a stroke, and you only have to do 50 push-ups instead of 100? Deal?"

Andrew took a few steps away from the ball, took one more glance at the pin and declared, "Hmmm, I don't know, Dad. I think I can make the shot."

"Face it, Andrew, you choked! Just quit because that is what losers do; they quit."

Andrew screamed back, "I'm not a loser!"

* * * *

Mr. Davidson's words replayed in Andrew's head, "... So why don't you be a good boy, save yourself some money and just quit. Tonight, you're the loser."

From a deep pit, a white-hot heat consumed Andrew. But when Andrew got this angry, he didn't yell and scream; that was Ted's thing. Andrew got calm. But he also got nasty. He used his words like a sniper's bullet, hitting you with a kill shot before you even knew what happened.

"Well, you know what, Mr. Davidson, there's no way you have that ten of diamonds. You might have a ten, but it's not a ten of diamonds."

Andrew waited for Mr. Davidson's face to drop, and when it did, he added, "Which means you don't have that straight flush. I'm all-in too. Call." Andrew pushed all of his chips into the pot. The total in play was almost $1,300,000.

Andrew could see Mr. Davidson hiding the seething frustration inside him, as he tried not to give any tells at the table. Andrew continued, "And you know why I know that?"

"Why?!" Mr. Davidson snorted.

A darkness enveloped Andrew. He leaned in over the table, lowered his voice in tone but growled out, "Because there is no day on this Earth when I would ever let a sad sack like you let your ordinary straight beat my full house."

Andrew flipped his cards over. Mr. Davidson stared blankly down at Andrew's cards.

The dealer quietly requested for Mr. Davidson to show his cards. He looked dejected and was still staring at Andrew's full house when the dealer announced, "Mr. Davidson, your ten of clubs and eight of diamonds give you a straight, and Dr. Beck, your pair of sixes and three sevens give you a full house. The pot is yours, Dr. Beck."

"You piece of shit! You goddamned piece of shit! That was my pot! Mine!"

Andrew snapped back, "Well, now it's mine, so go fuck off and die, Dad."

"Dad? Dad!? I'd rather father monkeys than a goddamn, mind-fucking Judas like you!"

Andrew didn't know why he said Dad, but he blasted back a retort to shield himself. "I think George will want to see you now."

Mr. Davidson calmed down, stood up, straightened his jacket and tie, and calmly let go of his words. "Yeah, well, I guess it's time to pay the piper. Be seeing ya, kid."

Mr. Davidson threw open the curtain and made his departure in a huff.

Andrew sat leaning over the table, covering the sides of his face as if he was shielding his eyes from bright sunlight. He tried to regain his composure. He ran his fingers through his hair and then put his face in both his hands until he could not control his frustration. He slammed the table with his fist, yelling, "Fuck!"

He sat up and looked around the table. The other players were staring at him. Mr. Chin's normally jovial countenance had turned serious. He leaned over the table and, with a kind smile, said, "Dr. Beck, maybe you should, uh, take a break."

Andrew nodded, apologized to the table for the outburst, and told the dealer he was going to the bar and he could return his marker card to him there. He left the table silently but paused outside the curtains to straighten his jacket and took a deep breath. Inside he heard Ms. Luveaux say in creole accented English, "*Somebody's* got daddy issues."

The other men gave a quiet chuckle, and Andrew could feel his face burn.

15

Andrew was sitting at his desk when there was a knock on his door, and Gina didn't wait for a reply as she peeked her head in the door and announced, "Dr. Beck, Vladimir Poplov is here to see you."

Andrew responded enthusiastically, "Great, show him in."

Gina opened up the door and behind Gina was a large man, six foot two, at least 210 pounds, with closely cropped dirty blonde hair. He was in a polo shirt and jeans. His face was chiseled, yet somber and his eyes were blue and intense. His shoulders were wide, his waist slim and he walked with purpose, almost military in stride. If Andrew didn't know he was a hockey player, he would have assumed he was a soldier.

Andrew got up and extended his hand as Gina made the introductions, "Mr. Poplov, this is Dr. Andrew Beck."

Vladimir's grip was firm, as Andrew expected it would be. Andrew smiled and gestured to Vladimir to sit on the couch as he took his place in his Eames chair. "Nice to meet you, please, have a seat."

As Vladimir sat down, Gina gave him a warm smile and asked, "Mr. Poplov would you like some coffee, tea, or water?"

Vladimir bounced up before his butt hit the couch, like he was doing an explosive squat, and replied to Gina in English, but with a Russian accent, "No, thank you. I'm fine. Please, call me Vlad."

Gina smiled and nodded, "Will do. I was at the Sentinel's versus the Colorado Cougars game when you shut down Alex Vechkiev. You guys were jawing at each other pretty good all game."

Vladimir cracked a smile from his face of granite and shook his head. "Not what you think. We were talking about families in Russia. We trained together on 2004 World Championship Team. We were only teenagers, and I'm two years younger than Lex, but coaches made me mark him during practice. Every time he scored, I did one hundred push-ups."

Vladimir took a moment then looked down at Andrew, who was still seated. "I did lot of pushups." He then looked back to Gina. "But I got to know his moves, so we match up well."

Andrew chimed in, "What's with the hundred-pushup thing? My father made me do a hundred push-ups if I lost a tournament."

Vladimir paused as if he was carefully choosing his words. "Made us stronger, no?"

Gina got excited and turned to her boss. "Andrew, you should've seen it. The Sentinels were up by a goal with a few minutes left. Vechkiev got a pass inside the blue line, the goalie was out of position, and he hit a one-timer, a sure goal! But Vlad came from out of nowhere! He took the puck right in the chest. He saved the win!" She raised one eyebrow above the other and jerked her head back to Vladimir. "Man, that had to hurt, huh?"

Humbly, Vladimir replied, "It was instinct. When we played to-gether, Lex was so good, only way to stop him was throw my body in front of puck. It hurt, but less than 100 push-ups so..." He shrugged his shoulders. But then he looked Gina in the eye and cocked his head to the side, and pointed at her with a relaxed and bent arm, "But you, Gina Perez, are same as me. I saw you play in World Cup. Throwing your body at ball. I have pads when I get hit. You don't. I have helmet and face mask, you...you just use your face to stop ball." He smiled, "Didn't *that* hurt?"

Gina let out a big laugh and nodded her head, then grabbed her nose and shook it from side to side. "Can you believe I never broke my nose?"

Vladimir smiled. "I think you are tougher than me."

Andrew interjected, "Okay guys, we need to get to work. Thanks,

Gina."

Gina waved as she exited the office, "See you outside, Vlad."

Vladimir waved back as he sat, "Da, thank you."

Andrew gave Vladimir a moment to get settled. He sat upright, fighting against the couch's soft cushions, keeping his core tight. Andrew noticed and used a soothing tone to speak, "Thank you for coming in, Vlad. Do you know why you are here?"

"I think so, but why don't you tell me anyway."

"The Sentinels and your GM, Riley Asherton, felt that you might be having some issues at home. And while the Sentinels are all for your aggressive style of play on the ice, at home things have to be, well, different. You know what I mean?"

Vladimir sat back as his hands came together. "My wife, Isrena, we argue. And sometimes we yell…a lot. I'm sorry."

"Your neighbors called the police because they heard furniture smashing."

Andrew kept a sharp watch on Vladimir's body movements and facial expressions, noting that he kept eye contact, but Vlad's eyes moved down and then up to the left, indicating he was searching his mind for facts and data. "Yes, well, Isrena got very mad and threw things at me. But she doesn't have good aim so…"

"Let's talk about that. What got her so mad that she had to throw something at you?"

Vladimir sat up straight and deadpanned Andrew in the eyes. "Hmmmmm. Excuse me, Dr. Beck, but how does this make me better hockey player?"

"I'm sorry?"

"Mr. Asherton said to come here, and you make me better hockey player? What does Isrena have to do with playing hockey better?"

Asherton, you douche! You didn't tell him why he's here. Fuck me.

Andrew took a steadying breath. "Vladimir, yes, I can make you a better hockey player, but first, I need to understand how you think and feel. On and off the ice." Andrew became clinical. "Vladimir, although the NAHL doesn't have a specific domestic violence policy, unlike say baseball and football, they're cracking down. Yaakov Gusev on the Thunder Bay Gold, your fellow countryman and gold medal winner was suspended last season for domestic violence. They're serious about this, Vlad."

"I know, but what husband and wife don't argue?"

"You're a hundred percent right. Every couple argues. But Isrena throwing things at you? And the neighbors calling the police? It doesn't look good for you, and it doesn't look good for the Sentinels. So let's talk. What happened?"

Vladimir took a deep breath, exhaled, and calmly expounded, "She spend lot of money on new diamond bracelet from Tiffany's, diamond necklace from Cartier, and two fur coats. Why she need two more? She already have three. One fur coat is enough for anyone."

"Did that upset you, that she spent the money?"

"No. It's not the money. Sentinels pay me well. We have big Manhattan apartment. It's palace compared to the four rooms I grew up in Chekhov, Russia."

"So what got you angry?"

"She has coats and jewelry she doesn't wear. So why buy new things? Isrena was super-model. Companies gave her all new clothing and jewelry, so she wear them in public. She got everything free. So, no, she has no respect for money."

"Isrena Salenko is your wife?" Andrew tried not to look too surprised as a montage of her sexy ads whipped through his mind's eye. She had mastered the pouty "ice queen" look.

"She did all those Gucci ads right?

"Da."

So, is that what bothers you? The fact that she has no concept of money or respect for money? Or is it that she's spending a lot of it?"

Andrew watched Vladimir's body language as he considered his answer. He slid forward on the couch, hands relaxed but clasped. "I want her to be happy. If just spending, okay, but she brags to people. She post on Instagram, she shows off. I asked her, 'Why? Why you show everyone?' " Vlad shrugged his shoulders and continued, "I get email from my family saying send more money home. She throws it in their faces. That's not right, Dr. Beck."

"So is that what angered you?"

Vladimir became more emphatic. "No. I ask her, but not yell. I ask her, 'Why must you tell whole world?' Then I tell her I have many family members in Russia, and you have family in Russia too. We should help them."

"And then what?"

"She said her family is dead to her. And my family, are…" He looked away as his words drifted off. He clenched his teeth as if he was looking to bite down on his mouthguard.

"Are what, Vlad?"

"козел." Vladimir took a pause, as his eyes squinted as if he had just been slapped.

"Koz-yole?" Beck repeated.

"Goats."

"How did that make you feel?"

"Very angry," Vlad said stoically. "My family is poor, but they work hard. They are good people. If her family is dead to her, fine, but don't hurt my family."

Andrew took a moment to let Vladimir sit with the statement and then gently added, "Vlad, I don't speak Russian, and sometimes words don't mean the same things because of cultural references." He leaned in, expecting an explanation.

Vladimir's tone changed, more technical sounding, as if he was giving instructions. "козел" is very bad insult to say to one person. But to say to whole family? Nyet." He shook his head several times. "Very bad."

Vladimir's tone and body language did not reveal any emotion, despite his words to the contrary. Andrew was amazed at Vlad's emotional discipline. Discipline or disconnectedness, he wasn't sure which. He continued to probe.

"So after you got angry, what happened?"

"Then I started yelling. Call her ungrateful, spoiled little princess." For the first time, Andrew noted some shame as his eyes looked to the floor for a split second as he added, "I shouldn't have said that."

Andrew sat up straight in his chair. "Vlad, answer me honestly here…"

Vladimir seemed to match Andrew and he sat up straight too.

"Da."

"Did you throw anything at Isrena?"

"Nyet. No, but she threw a very expensive and heavy Kosta Boda vase we got as wedding present. I caught it." He paused. "I fake like I going to throw it at her." Vladimir made a feint throwing motion with his right arm as he spoke. "But I didn't. I wouldn't."

"Now Vlad, you're a big guy. You're strong. Do you understand why Isrena might be fearful enough that she'd feel she would have to throw something at you to protect herself?"

"Hmmm, da, I see that."

"Now, I don't condone her throwing vases at you and insulting your family. That's wrong and very upsetting." Andrew let that sit for a second before he continued. "What are some options you might have had at that moment, other than yelling back at her?"

Vladimir took a deep breath and shrugged. "I don't know."

Andrew shifted tactics. "Okay, let's put the same situation in hockey terms. You're on the ice. You're down 3-2 in third period, eight minutes left to play. The Sentinels are trying to get one back to tie up the score. You are in position, and then you catch a high cross-check in the back without the puck. You feel your knees slam the ice and a searing pain in your back. You look up at the refs, but no call."

Vladimir moved forward and held up his index finger to make his point. "He did it on purpose, right? To draw me into fight, yes?"

"Exactly, so how do you respond? Go after the guy? Drop the gloves, fight and take the five-minute penalty and put your team at a further disadvantage or…"

Vladimir instinctively shook his head. "I skate away. I wait for time when guy is in corner and then I smash him against the boards. But no, I don't fight. Not in this situation. Nyet."

Andrew felt a rush of dopamine course through him. "Repeat the first few words you just said, please?"

"I skate away?"

"Exactly. Do you think during your fight with Isrena, you could have *skated away*? Maybe have gone in another room and cooled down?"

"Da, I could have done that."

124

"Great. So, the next time she pisses you off… just skate away." Andrew extended his arm gently like he was showing someone a way through a door.

That garnered a laugh out of Vladimir. "That is good suggestion. I will try, Doctor. Thank you. Is that all? May I go now?"

"Not just yet." Andrew had to fight the instinct to smile at Vlad wanting to stop doing the work. It was natural. His next set of questions would be less affronting. "Outside of hockey, what do you like to do? Any hobbies?"

He thought for a few seconds, then his eyes widened, and half a smile grazed his face. "I like to take apart and build electronics."

"Really? That's amazing. I'm completely mechanically declined."

Vladimir added with some pride in his voice. "I have a degree in electrical engineering. I did all wiring in our apartment." He laughed as he added, "Isrena thought I was too cheap to pay electrician. But I *wanted* to do it myself."

Andrew was taking notes on his iPad, but, genuinely fascinated, he stopped writing and asked, "Why?"

"I like challenge. Problem solving. Although most electrical engineers understand basic circuit theory, most important skill for electrical engineers is ability to think laterally. Same in hockey. So many different angles and play possibilities. You have to calculate, make quick choice where to defend. In electrical engineering if you make mistake with electricity, she teaches you lesson. With pain. Just like in hockey."

Andrew put his pen down, "That's a great analogy. So how did the wiring come out in your apartment?"

"Good, no shocks, no fires." He winked. "Always a good sign."

They both shared a quick laugh and then Andrew took control of the conversation again. "Let's talk about hockey."

"Da."

"Everyone knows you are one of the most feared enforcers on the ice. You lead the league in penalty minutes this year. Sentinels are on their way to the playoffs. And no one has ever gotten the best of you in a fight. You know what they call you, right?"

"Russian Bear."

"How do you feel about that?"

"I don't care what people think, Doctor. People don't know what it is like to be professional hockey player. People don't know how hard we train, how tough eighty-two games a year is. How sore we are. Sore, all the time, playing injured. After game, everything hurts. Especially if I fight. My hands hurt all the time. But every day, we get up, sit in ice bath, put skates on, get on ice. We do it for teammates, for fans, we do it because we love to play hockey."

"What do you love most about the game? Fighting?"

"Nyet! Nyet! I hate fighting! I want to skate, I'm good defender! I made Russian Olympic Team in Vancouver in 2010. I was only 22. I made Olympics again in Sochi. No fighting in Olympics."

Andrew took a beat. "Your family must have been proud of you."

"More proud when I made Olympic team than when drafted by Sentinels. I was, how you say, 'pride and joy' for my family."

"I've seen your films, Vlad. You are an incredible skater and defender. So why fight? Why be an enforcer?"

Vladimir took a second, stared deeply at Andrew—almost right through him—then pointed his finger at him. But it was a different point than the one he'd made at Gina; it was a warning. "Because I won't let *anyone* fuck with my family."

There was a determination and power behind his words. It shook Andrew to his core. He could see that this was deeper than just hockey. His words were a credo. There had to be more behind this. But he had to wait, it had to come from Vlad, and he could see in his eyes he wanted to say something, so Andrew waited.

Vladimir sat back on the couch, he relaxed his hands and his body tension from a few minutes ago drifted like a puck flicked down an endless ice pond. He cocked his head as he broke the silence, "Would you like to hear a story, Doctor?"

"Absolutely." He put down his stylus, sat back in his chair, and crossed his legs.

Vladimir continued, "My brother Nikita and I loved hockey more than anything in world. Nikita was much smaller than me. He took after our mother, Tatiana, who was molecular biologist. I took after father, Sergei. He was Red Army sergeant and after army became police officer. No one could skate like Nikita. Even though tiny for his age, he was fast, could cut, make you cry how good skater he was." A big smile crossed his face. Andrew immediately made a mental note of it and homed in on Vladimir's body language.

"One day, we were playing for school team. I was 15. Nikki was 13. He was smallest on ice. He made move on bigger boy named Konstantin. His father was big in politics. Nikki passed puck to himself by putting it between boy's legs and pick up puck on other side. We all laughed." Vladimir threw up his hands. "But Nikki did that to all of us. It was…how you say, 'his thing,' yes?" Vladimir waited for acknowledgement. Andrew nodded and he continued, "Later in practice, the puck bounce hard off boards, Nikki reached for puck, made nice stick move to control puck and clear it. But when he reach to get puck, he was too extended, defenseless." Vladimir reenacted the play, extending his right arm forward and bent at the side. "Konstantin slammed Nikki into boards. Knocked him out cold." Vladimir's eyes got wider as he continued with the physical reenactment, "When I see this, I…I went mad. I skated to Konstantin, threw him down onto ice and kept punching him as hard as I could." Vladimir started throwing vicious air punches, causing Andrew to move his head back as if the force of the air from his fists was going to hit him in the face. "My teammates tried to pull me off. No one could do it. It took two coaches. I broke Konstantin's nose in three places, broke his occipital bone, fractured his jaw. He missed the rest of the season. I was suspended for five games."

Vladimir composed himself after throwing the air punches. He ran his hand through the top of his hair and sat back deep into the couch. "Konstantin's father was very upset. He wanted me kicked off team. But I wasn't worried about that."

"Oh? What were you worried about?" asked Andrew.

"The beating I was going to get from Papa. Papa had hands of iron. Even when he held our hands to cross street, he would crush them by accident. After first time he spank me on ass, felt like I hit by shovel. After that, I never wanted to get hit by Papa again."

"So, what did you do?"

Vladimir let out another half-smile. "Only smart thing. I begged mother to protect me." The other half of the smile arose. "I'm not stupid."

Both men again shared a laugh, realizing this was a street both men had traveled down precipitously.

"I've used that move myself when my brother and I both wanted to hold my dad's US Open trophy and we fought and broke it. But Mom was always the peacemaker."

The smile left Vladimir's face as he focused back on his story. "Da. So, that night we come home, Nikki has big black eye, split lip, ice pack on head. But that wasn't so unusual. We're boys, we play hockey, things happen. We sit down to dinner. Mama was cooking steak—very unusual. I remember being really mad because if I didn't get beat, I was going to be sent to bed without supper. No supper is brutal punishment after hours of hockey. I was starving." Vladimir shrugged. "But I figured, only being hungry would be getting off easy. At dinner, Papa sits down. Mama puts steak in front of him. Potatoes too. Nikki and I are drooling. Mama, like always, put big piece of steak on Papa's plate. Then Papa looks at me. And he has deep voice." Vladimir lowered his tone to a deep baritone imitating his father. " 'Vladimir, I got call at police station from Konstantin's father, Comrade Bentikoff. You put his boy in hospital, yes?' I tried to make a defense, but as I opened my mouth, he raised his big hand in the air."

Andrew cluttered his words together "That's bad right? That sounds bad."

"It meant, 'Shut up right now, and don't say another word.' I thought I was going to get knocked out right there, but then he told me story…"

Vladimir remembered his 15-year-old self, sitting at the table as his father bore down on him. He heard his father's booming voice in his mind as it further anchored him in the past. "Vladimir, when I was in Red Army, I was stationed way out in Sakha Republic. It was winter, cold, a desolate wasteland of nothing but snow and forest. I was on patrol with two other soldiers. What were we patrolling? Ice and snow? The trees? So, we were bored. Then three bear cubs come out of woods, running and playing. My two comrades start shooting at them. I tell them, 'Hey, you imbeciles, stop that!' But one of them turns to me and says, 'Shut up, Poplov, you don't give orders out here.' I yell back to them, 'You don't fuck with someone's family.' The other soldier yells to me, 'Poplov! They are not someone's family—they're some *bear's* family.' For some reason they thought this was funny joke and they continued firing at little cubs. So I yell to them, 'I'm not going to tell you again. Stop shooting at those bear cubs!' Which they did, but then they pointed their rifles at me, and one said, 'Or what? Tough guy? Maybe we shoot you instead?' They cocked their rifles and aimed them at me."

Vladimir remembered his father pausing at this point and then emphatically raising that giant index finger of his. "Now, I could have rushed them. They were not good shots by the way they were missing the cubs. I think I could have taken them before they shot me. But as I was making my plan of attack, out of the tree line, I saw Mama Bear. She wasn't happy." He paused and looked at both of his two boys quickly. They were fully engaged.

"So, I quietly walked backward, out of her view. And Mama bear did what any mother would do to protect her children."

"I saw the bear charge the two men. They fired shots, but they missed, and then all I heard after that as I drove off was the screaming of those two men as they were torn apart by that bear."

"As I drove off, I fired my weapon twice in the air. When I got back to base, I told commanding officer that my two comrades had been mauled by a bear and taken into the woods. They called me coward for not going in after them. But the men who knew me knew I was no coward. After that, many men were reluctant to go on patrol with me."

Vladimir remembered his father's long, deep, and hard stare. He felt like his brain would melt, but Sergei said, "So, Vladimir, do you know what the moral of my story is?"

Vladimir's flashback ended when he refocused his attention on Andrew and paused, like his father did for maximum effect, extended his index finger again, and said, "Don't fuck with someone's family."

Vladimir's tone changed back to his own. "Then Papa took the big piece of steak off his plate and put it on mine." He brushed his hands off his pants as if he was clearing dust off them. "So why am I enforcer, when I hate fighting, Doctor?" He didn't wait for Andrew's acknowledgement. "My teammates *are* my family. And if you fuck with them, you have to fuck with me." He poked himself in the chest with his thumb several times.

Andrew let it sit for a second and nodded as he responded, "That is some story, Vlad. Thank you for sharing it with me. Andrew scribbled some more notes, but not because he needed to—his memory was excellent—but to create an interlude, a blank passage of time that would allow him to transition to the part of the conversation that was going to be difficult.

"Look, we need to have a few sessions, show the Sentinels and the league you are in counseling when the playoffs start in a few weeks." He searched Vladimir's face for any body language and facial microexpressions that showed resistance. He needed Vladimir to buy into, or at least be open to therapy. He was hard to read, and Andrew sensed some inherent skepticism but not outright resistance. Vladimir was a strong man, smart, and good at heart. But he couldn't be forced into anything. Andrew went with the soft sell.

"I'm sure in a few weeks, we can put this all behind us as a single incident."

"I understand, Doctor."

"Are you willing to commit to therapy and the process?"

"If Mr. Asherton says I have to, then I have to."

"Vlad, therapy doesn't work like that. You have to participate. You have to be honest with me and most of all, yourself. I have to report to Riley and the Sentinels on your progress, and for this process to work, I need your full and willing cooperation." He had to get Vladimir to say the words. Only then could Andrew feel that he could make progress with him. He knew that if he could get through this period with Vladimir, he was positive there were other Sentinels he could work with, and if not them, then there were other hockey players in the league he knew he could help. Hell, if he could make progress with the Russian Bear, he could treat anybody. But first, he had to get Vladimir to commit. "So I ask again, Vlad, are you willing to commit to therapy and this process?"

"Da, I will do my best. I don't want to disappoint my teammates and Mr. Asherton."

"Thank you, Vlad." Andrew was relieved but kept his concerned doctor look intact. Years of high-stakes card playing made Andrew an expert at hiding his true emotions. "I believe you are a sincere person, and you would do your best at anything you tried to do. This process might be difficult, but I know it will not only be helpful in your personal life, but also it *will* make you a better hockey player."

"Thank you, Dr. Beck. I want to be better husband and teammate."

"Okay, Vlad, that's it for today."

He felt the iron grip again, then Vlad headed to the door. But Andrew had one more question. "Oh hey, Vlad, did Nikki play pro hockey too?"

Vlad sighed and said, "Nyet, he died a year later."

"Oh, I'm sorry." He stroked his chin thoughtfully. "We can talk about that another time." Andrew smiled at him and added, "You can book your next time with Gina, and we'll get a schedule for your visits sorted out. And thanks again for the story. Your father sounds like a good man."

Vlad looked Andrew in the eyes and retorted, "Yes, he is. It is easy to see our fathers as heroes when we are boys. In our minds, they are larger than life..."

Andrew matched Vladimir's gaze. "Until they aren't."

"Da."

Vladimir left the office as Andrew took a deep breath and ran his hand through his hair. He could hear Gina calling out to Vladimir, "Hey, Vlad, come on over and we'll get you all set up, I have a few forms..."

Andrew closed the door and sat back at his desk. He opened his Otter.io transcription application on his iPhone and hit record. "Patient Intake Meeting Report for Vladimir Poplov, defenseman, New York Sentinels. Vladimir is very reserved, but I assess a deeply passionate individual. A childhood hockey sensation and product of a difficult circumstance in post-communist Russia, he seems to have grown up in a good home with strict but loving parents. Mother Tatiana, a molecular biologist and Father Sergei, a soldier and policeman. Vlad seems to be a blend of the two. Strong mentally and physically as well as smart. He has a degree in electrical engineering and he's a thinker. The main issue I'm uncovering and working on are his anger issues. Problems at home with wife and former supermodel Isrena Salenko. I am concerned matters could escalate to violence if not monitored closely. Will discuss other methods of deescalating arguments. Major psychological themes: protecting the vulnerable. Vlad sees himself as a protector and guardian on and off the ice. He is one of, if not *the* best fighter in the NAHL. Yet when I questioned if he liked the fighting, he was visibly disturbed. He immediately shifted away from me and clenched his fists, suggesting that his repulsion was genuine. Protecting one's family was a vividly reinforced theme in his childhood, and it seems it has carried on into adulthood and is a trigger for violence when someone threatens or insults his family."

Andrew hit the pause button to gather his thoughts as the Otter application continued transcribing his words.

He hit Record. "Triggers: attacks on family. Vlad is triggered by attacks either verbal or physical on his natural or metaphorical families, for example, teammates and friends. I believe anyone who builds a close relationship with Vlad would classify him as 'family.' Trigger: Isrena, his wife. I believe Isrena provokes him purposely to get his attention and an attempt to control him. She is in danger of domestic violence. I will need to monitor the situation closely. If there is a violent incident with Isrena, the NAHL would most certainly crack down on Vlad and make an example of him. If Vlad were to be suspended during the playoffs, the Sentinels would have trouble getting out of the first round and their run for the Champions Cup would be over."

Andrew added fatefully, "And probably my contract with the Sentinels too."

"Treatment next steps: Vlad seemed responsive to what I called 'skating away' from potential confrontations with Isrena. I will need to exercise and role-play this in future sessions. Additional notes: His younger brother Nikki died young, Vlad seemed very fond of him, and may be another source of his violent tendencies. Need to probe possible physical abuse from father, need to probe relationship with mother to inform choices with other women and Isrena. Treatment Plan: please book one session per week for next three months. Best to book on days when he is playing to give him a clear head, and I can access his mental state before the playoff games. End Patient Intake Meeting Report."

Andrew pressed the stop button and let the application catch up. As he waited, he marveled at seeing the words he spoke a few seconds ago pop up in type. He shook his head and smiled. For the most part, Andrew was an analog kind of guy, but some tech made him marvel. Seeing his words in type as he spoke them not only helped him with client recall, but there was something about him seeing his thoughts in words without him writing them. The smile grew until his cell phone dinged and a text notification popped up on his screen. The ID said "Five."

Andrew read the message from Lorry: "Was notified by Mr. Keegan that you and he were to be at the same table tonight?"

Andrew hesitated. He had to be careful here. He decided less was more.

He sent back a simple, "Yes."

Lorry sent another message: "Keegan said, 'Make sure Beck is at my table. I need to get my money back.' What's he talking about?"

Andrew winced and thought about his reply. "The bet he lost with Fergus. He thinks he can beat me at poker for it. Will be there at 8 p.m."

Andrew tried to cut off the conversation to avoid more suspicion, but he knew Lorry was sharp and had an instinct for spotting trouble brewing. He hoped she wouldn't push it any further. Andrew was relieved when her following text dinged: "Understood."

Andrew took a deep breath. His exhale had more sigh than relief.

That fucker Keegan. He's going to get us both killed.

Andrew's thoughts started clocking at a mile a minute. He needed to make sure Lorry didn't get too nosy about Mr. Keegan's brash boasts. And he didn't even want to speculate what might happen if they got caught. Then he remembered that he hadn't told Sandra he would be out late tonight. He had to think of an alibi so she wouldn't complain—or worse, suspect him of lying about his whereabouts.

16

Andrew texted Sandra to see if they could meet up for dinner at the Park Room Restaurant. At dinner, he would have to come up with another excuse for a late night. Although tonight would be different because he wouldn't have to feign regret—he didn't want to go to The Five Iron. The thought of losing to Mr. Keegan at poker and figuring out a way to do it so Fergus' watchful eyes didn't notice was making him anxious. On the other hand, Sandra was all too happy to meet up as she texted back that she had another rough day with Roxanne.

The restaurant was located in the Park Lane Hotel, overlooking the southern tip of Central Park. The Park Room was another one of Sandra's and Andrew's favorite spots. With twenty-foot floor-to-ceiling windows looking out into dense woods, the elegant furniture, and soft classical music playing in the background, The Park Room was a tranquil place for them, ideal for clearing their heads after a long day of meetings, strategies, treatment plans, team reporting, and scouting out new business.

The two were sitting at the table, enjoying their food, as Sandra vented about work. "We spent hours prepping this client for the press conference and going over all the key points in defending the product recall for the Q&A. So what does he do? No more than a few questions into it, he throws in the towel and says, 'No comment' and walks off the podium."

Sandra took another bite of her food while Andrew processed and asked, "So now the press thinks they're guilty?"

Sandra waited to swallow her food, but not enough time to get a breath of air and she choked out, "Exactly what we didn't want! I wrote the message myself. I worded it perfectly about how they were neither accepting blame nor denying it at this time, and they were conducting a thorough investigation into the matter." Sandra took a beat, and shook her head and added, "Nothing pisses me off more than a client who, in the face of a difficult situation, just *folds.*"

Andrew felt a pang in his stomach, and it was neither the food nor the wine. "Not everyone can handle the pressure the way you can."

Sandra, head down into her food, retorted, "I know, I know, but shit. Have a set of balls!"

The pang turned into a punch, and he sat up and stopped eating. "That's a bit harsh."

"I'm tired, Andrew. I'm tired of being overruled by my mom, dealing with belligerent clients, and being undermined."

Andrew lost his appetite and lowered his tone as he declared, "I have to leave shortly to make it down to TISEC. The Black Knights are playing the LA Bears and—"

"But you never watch Lamar play at the TISEC." Sandra interrupted in an octave higher than her normal voice.

Andrew looked down at his unfinished food and pushed the plate a few inches away from him. "Yeah, I know, but he had me out until two in the morning this week. I told him I'd be there."

"Okay. I just thought we would ride home and watch the game together."

"I know, and I would love that. I need to stay close to Lamar. We had a pretty big breakthrough the other night, and I need to see how he responds on the court. I'm sorry, but I can't say any more than that," he said with a conciliatory smile.

"Okay," she said, poking at her food. But before she could take another bite, her eyes widened as if a notification in her mind's inner calendar just chimed, and she blurted out, "Oh, just to remind you, we have dinner with your parents tomorrow night."

"Ted on a school night. Jeez." Andrew slumped in his chair. But

136

then straightened up and he gave his wife a playful grin. "Hey babe, I'll make you a deal. I'll trade you Ted for Roxanne, and since you're an only child, I'll throw in Brandon too. No future draft picks or anything. It's a sweet deal!"

Sandra laughed and slyly smiled back and added, "Nice try, Dr. Beck, but I'll stick with the devil I know."

Andrew pretended to pound the table with his fist, "Damn." They shared a laugh together.

Still smiling, Sandra nodded as she tapped Andrew's hand gently and said, "It'll be fine."

Andrew stopped laughing and looked at her soulfully. "Sandra, it hasn't been fine with Ted and me since I was five."

17

Andrew did his The Five Iron entrance routine again. The only thing different about today was that he came to The Five Iron to lose for the first time.

The ritual that helped him transform from counselor, husband, son, and friend to mercenary on a mission started at the descent into the steel-doored elevator on Mercer Street. Each moment that went by from the elevator to the concierge desk, to the bar to get his Scotch, to when he sat at the poker table, it felt like he was shedding his skin like a snake—emerging out of his old skin, feeling reborn. But tonight he felt empty. Andrew reveled in the freedom The Five Iron gave him. The freedom to use all his knowledge about poker, people, and the mind to release the dopamine chemical that made him feel in control and invincible. He loved the rush when he won...at anything. Andrew also knew that there is always someone bigger, better, faster, stronger, smarter than you in any endeavor—but especially in sports. And some day, he was going to get his ass kicked. His job was to make sure if an ass-kicking was coming his way, it was going to be minimal.

Although he hated to lose, when he lost to a better player, it was bearable...almost. But to lose on *purpose*, to what Andrew believed was an inferior mind, created a seething pain in him and bothered him to his core. There was only one other time in his life he lost on purpose, but that loss saved his future. Although sometimes he wondered if it was worth it, right now, he had to convince his uber-competitive nature that losing to Keegan was still better than eating a bullet. It was a difficult conversation.

The game still needed to be played correctly, strategically. Andrew knew all too well that sometimes it is harder to lose and make it look like you are trying to win than to win while trying to avoid losing.

The Five Iron had cameras everywhere and they monitored the gaming tables closely. There were rumors about how Fergus handled cheaters. One rumor that Andrew had heard many times was that once two men using their own sign language and clue words, tried to manipulate a game. But the eye-in-the-sky saw through this as George, Lorry and her security crew appeared out of the ether and pulled the men out of their chairs. They were brought to the "interrogation room."

They woke from their beating in a seedy hotel in Newark, New Jersey, tied to chairs. Between them were a card table, a deck of cards, and two pistols, each holding one bullet. Fergus told them that they had to play one hand of cards and the winner could leave. He also said the loser would have to pick up a pistol and shoot himself in the head. The kicker was that as Fergus himself untied the men and lectured them about the errors of their ways, he discreetly handed them each two aces to help boost their hand. Both men read this as it was a signal that Fergus favored them to win, but he could not let the cheating go unpunished. Someone had to die. When both men realized each man tried to cheat the other, they picked up the pistols and fired at each other.

Andrew had an idea what Fergus was capable of, but what choice did he have? He had to watch every move and play carefully and hope that Mr. Keegan, with his oversized ego to match his body, didn't give them away.

About halfway to the Players Room, as two pathways intersected, Andrew saw Lorry, her bright red hair flowing rather than tied up in a French braid. When she moved, she looked like flames had engulfed her head. She had on her trademark Dr. Martens and black pant suit, and Andrew's warm smile was greeted with a fierce stare when he greeted her. "Hello, Lorry."

Her Edinburgh accent made her official sounding voice resonate. "Dr. Beck. Let me take you to your table. Mr. Keegan is expecting you."

Andrew's smile left as he replied with a bit of sarcasm. "I bet he is."

Lorry stopped in her tracks and pulled on Andrew's arm firmly. "Is there something going on between you two?"

"Nothing I can't handle."

Lorry squinted her eyes and shook her head slightly. Andrew changed his tone to put her at ease with a shoulder shrug.

"Lorry, I helped Fergus take two-hundred thousand of Mr. Keegan's money. He can't get it from the big dog, so he's taking his frustrations out on the little dog." He pointed to himself. "Me."

They resumed their walk, but the skepticism didn't leave her tone. "He seems very confident he'll get it back, and he's not a top-tier poker player like you are."

Andrew ignored the comment and craned his neck to look at the people sitting at some of the tables. "Have you seen Mr. Davidson? We ended things a little on the rough side last night."

"No, I haven't seen him, but I wasn't looking for him either."

When they reached the Players Room, Lorry walked him past security, up the carpeted steps, and through the curtain. She directed Andrew to sit but gave him a steely eyed look as she parted without a word.

When Mr. Keegan saw Andrew appear through the drawn curtains, he got up from his chair with a big grin and went up to greet Andrew with wide open arms. "Ah, there he is! It's about fucking time you got here, Beck." Mr. Keegan bear-hugged him. He ignored the pain in his ears caused by the harsh Brooklyn accent and the anger from being manhandled. He whispered in Mr. Keegan's ear, "You need to chill the fuck out. There are cameras everywhere. Lorry is suspicious, and if Fergus finds out what we're doing, he'll have us both killed."

Mr. Keegan didn't let go. He squeezed Andrew harder and returned the whisper. "Well, you let me worry about Fergus. You focus on losing, okay hotshot?"

Mr. Keegan pulled away from Andrew and increased his volume. "Oh yeah? Well, I think I look pretty good in this suit too. You must be trying to butter me up or something!" Then, addressing the table, he boasted, "So I don't take ALL your fucking money, eh, Beck?" This garnered a sporadic laugh at the table, and they sat down to play.

After a couple of hours of poker, the dealer announced that there would be a short break for the players to get up, stretch their legs, go to the restroom, get a drink or some food, and for the dealers to change.

As the players walked out of the Players Room and in different directions, Mr. Keegan caught up to Andrew, grabbed him roughly by the arm, and leaned into him. "What the fuck are you doing, Beck? I said *lose*. You're taking almost half the pots."

Andrew pulled his arm out of Mr. Keegan's grip. "Get the fuck off me. I can't lose every hand. They know me here. Plus, I only owe *you* two hundred thousand. Doesn't mean I can't win against other players."

"Well, I don't want to wait all fucking night!"

Andrew looked around, trying to ensure they were not in the view of any cameras or The Five Iron's security, and then pleaded with Mr. Keegan. "I'm telling you, slow down."

Mr. Keegan gritted his teeth but kept his tone low and leaned into Andrew as if he was about to head-butt him. "I've waited long enough. Give me my fucking money and lose like the cheating son of a bitch you are, or I walk up to Fergus' office right now and tell him you're Palmer's shrink, and you two set me up."

Andrew took a step back but stared hard into Mr. Keegan's eyes. He realized nothing he could say would penetrate the concrete head of his. "Let's get this fucking over with."

"That's more like it."

Mr. Keegan turned and walked away wearing a giant shit-eating grin. Andrew was left shaking his head. He made one last glance in the air to see if there were any cameras pointed at him, then looked around to see if any security personnel saw their interlude. It was busy for a Wednesday night, there was a good crowd, and even Fergus' staff couldn't be everywhere all the time...or so he hoped.

Andrew was back at the tables and before he glanced down at his Rolex Submariner, he covered the face of his watch and guessed the time to himself. "12:30."

He uncovered the watch face, and it was 12:37 a.m. They had been playing for over four hours. In this hand, which Andrew figured would be his last of the evening and his nightmare would be over, it was down to three players: Dr. Beck, Mr. Keegan, and Mr. Benson. Mr. Benson was in his mid-thirties. He dressed well, very hipster-like, and had a sharp mind. He was the CEO of a software development company. As hard as he tried, Benson was still more Bill Gates than Steve Jobs.

People shared some minor details about their work, but never too specific. Of course, everyone can be Googled, which was one of the many reasons why no first names were used, and no phones were allowed past the front desk. Although most players probably did research their opponents once they were on the outside. They had to be careful with the knowledge they gained because patrons prized their privacy at The Five Iron. If anyone seemed like they "knew too much" or was "stalking" another player, they usually ended up in the interrogation room where they had a "discussion" with Lorry and George. That either stopped the behavior, or their membership was revoked. A revoked membership was given with the warning that the club knew where they lived, worked, and where their kids went to school. With threats like these, breaches were rare.

If you were a patron of The Five Iron, it was because you needed to feed the monkey that was on your back. If you had a need: gambling, designer drugs, a sexual fetish—Fergus could fill it. Everyone kept in line since everyone knew this about each other, and Fergus knew this about his patrons. Everyone had their "something," and Fergus provided a world where one's "something" could not only be indulged but celebrated.

At the table, the "community cards" turned face up on the table at the turn were a ten of diamonds, nine of hearts, king of diamonds, and ace of hearts. Andrew hoped this was the final hand so he could get out of there, and at the speeds he drove, he'd be in Greenwich by 1:30 AM.

This play looks like the final hand. I can't believe I have to lose $200K to this schmuck. And I have a frigging ace of spades and king of hearts with the ace of hearts and king of diamonds on the board, that gives me two pair, aces and kings. Keegan is too cocky. He'd be less so if he actually had a playable hand, but he's got nothing. I need to get rid of Mr. Benson here. And make this just between Keegan and me.

Mr. Benson had made a $100,000 bet at the flop, which scared off the other two players. Andrew figured Mr. Benson probably had two pair also. However, Andrew analyzed that even if Mr. Benson had pairs of kings and tens, Andrew's pair of aces and kings would win. Andrew and Mr. Keegan both called, putting the pot at $350,000. Of that, Andrew had $110,000 in the pot.

If Benson makes a play of $50,000, I raise him to $100,000. That gets me over Keegan's $200,000 and I can fold to that bald-headed prick and get out of this mess.

It was Mr. Benson's play. He took a quick peek at his cards. "I bet $50,000." He tossed two chips into the pot.

Yep, Benson has two pair. He has to have tens and nines or tens and kings. Doesn't matter, either way I beat him. Fuck, I can't believe I would win this hand, but have to fork it over to that Mr. Clean-looking motherfucker.

"Your $50,000 and another $50,000." Andrew put his chips in the pot with a kerplunk.

Mr. Keegan had a self-satisfied grin on his face and put in $100,000 in the pot, calling.

Andrew looked over to Mr. Benson. "I think you took this hand as far as you could, Mr. Benson. What do you have, tens and kings at best?"

Mr. Keegan bent over and pointed aggressively at Mr. Benson. "You better watch out, Benson, the Doc over here can read minds and shit. But don't let him fuck with your head. If you got the cards, go all-in, and bring this pot to a cool million."

Mr. Benson looked over his brown, horn-rimmed circular glasses and his eye movement covered both men before he nodded. "Maybe you're right, Dr. Beck. Live to fight another day." He threw his cards towards the dealer and announced, "I fold."

Mr. Keegan sat back in his chair and under his breath, but loud enough for people to hear it, said, "Pussy."

The dealer addressed Mr. Keegan firmly, "Mr. Keegan, I'm giving you a warning on inappropriate language towards another player. Next time it will be a $25,000 fine."

Mr. Keegan shrugged his shoulders and kept the satisfied smile on his face.

The dealer turned over the final card on the river, a queen of spades. At the turn of the card, Mr. Keegan's whole body nodded yes and with that big shit-eating grin of his, barked at Andrew, Brooklyn accent in full effect, "So Beck, you think I got that jack for my straight, or what?"

Andrew didn't make a move and stared at the upturned corner of his cards, not making eye contact, but this didn't deter Mr. Keegan from gloating. "Ah, what the fuck, because I'm a sweetheart of a guy, I'll just tell you...I do."

There is no way he has that jack to complete the straight. I see his shoulders hunch up when he looks at his cards—he's got nothing! He wants to bluff me so he can brag to everyone he made me fold. Goddamn it. I cannot believe I have to lose to this asshole.

With a grimace Andrew said, "Check."

"Come on, Beck, you got nothing. Just fold."

Mr. Keegan looked at Mr. Benson, who was still watching the hand, and then he looked at the dealer before eyeing Andrew. "Admit it. I'm the better man. I'm all-in." He pushed all his chips forward.

Andrew felt his face burn. The thought of this cocky Neanderthal telling him he was the better man when Andrew was losing on purpose was too much to bear. He looked Mr. Keegan in the eye. "Well, Mr. Keegan, now that you put it that way, if you're the better man, you're going to have to prove it."

Andrew reached down to his chip stack and pushed them in the pot. "All-in. Call."

Mr. Keegan's eyes widened. "What!? You mean fold, don't you? I got the straight!" Mr. Keegan took a breath, brushed his hand down his suit, and collected his thoughts. "I think the stress of this game is getting to you, Dr. Beck. And as you, of all people know, stress can be really bad for your health. Sometimes we say things under stress we don't mean. So what you meant to say is you fold, as in you quit, right?"

Andrew nodded his head and altered his tone to a sarcastic one. "You know, you're right Mr. Keegan, this is a stressful game. But health be damned, if you have that straight, that would be a beautiful thing. I gotta see it." Andrew looked at Mr. Keegan with a burning fire in his eyes. "I said…call."

Mr. Keegan slammed the table, threw his cards, and with the force of his standing up, he knocked the chair over and pointed at Andrew and yelled, "You motherfucker!!"

The dealer immediately tried to restore order. "Mr. Keegan! That will be a $25,000 fine. And I will be reporting your behavior to management!" But Keegan was well out of the Players Room before he finished his warning. The curtains flapped like crimson sails on a windy day at his violent exit.

The endorphin release from beating Mr. Keegan and winning another big pot was being tampered with the thought that although he won't get killed by Fergus for cheating, Mr. Keegan will seek revenge. But he would worry about that later. Right now, Andrew was enjoying a cocktail of dopamine and serotonin that sloshed through his nervous system. Andrew gave the dealer a $20,000 tip, smiled, told him he could return his marker card at the bar. He'd worry about the consequences with Keegan later. Right now, he was happier than he had been in a long time.

18

Andrew sat alone on an ornate and comfortably cushioned bar stool. He took the last sip of his mahogany-colored drink. He felt the warm burn of ginger and oak barrel. He quickly got the bartender's attention and ordered another Scotch.

While he was waiting for his refill, Andrew searched for any remaining drops of liquid gold at the bottom of his glass. Lorry approached the bar. She faced perpendicular to Andrew as he looked forward. He could see her reflection in the shelved mirror behind the bar. Her reflection was divided by the glass shelves, and Andrew saw it as a metaphor that she had many levels to get through before he would ever get to see the "real Lorry."

She stuck out her hand with the black metal card. Andrew nodded but faced forward as he continued to search his glass for gold.

She enquired, "You all right?"

He turned his head and answered calmly, with a smile. "Yes, Lorry, everything is fine. Why?"

Lorry shifted her hands to her hips after putting the card on the bar. "There was a report of abusive language by Mr. Keegan. He stormed out of the players' room after you beat him."

"Ah, he's just a sore loser. Nothing to worry about." He stuck the marker card in his jacket breast pocket, which he calculated he had added, after rake and tip, $542,000, bringing his total balance to $3,240,500.

The bartender returned with his Scotch, and he took a sip. He closed his eyes for a second and took a deep breath before speaking. "Nothing better than a good Scotch to savor a moment."

"What's going on, Andrew?" Lorry's eyes were wide, and her jaw was tight. "Look, I know you and he had words. Mr. Keegan left the building in a bit of a huff. Maybe it's best if you slip out the kitchen?"

Andrew shook his head as he went to take another sip. Lorry grabbed his forearm, preventing him from lifting his glass to his lips, and whispered again but firmer, "Andrew, please, he's a dangerous man. Don't be daft."

Andrew then sat up and turned directly to Lorry. He looked her in the eyes and said, "Live to fight another day?"

"What?"

"That's what Mr. Benson said when he folded. He said he would live to fight another day."

"Sound advice, Doctor."

He drained his glass. The burn hit his chest immediately, and he jumped athletically off the bar stool, full of energy. Lorry and Andrew walked hurriedly through the Main Room. As they walked past the Sports Book area, up on the big screen, Real Sport News was replaying the Black Knights and the Los Angeles Bears game. Andrew caught it out of the corner of his eye and came to a dead stop.

"Lorry, wait up a second. I want to see the score."

"Andrew, really, at a time like this? You want to see a bloody basketball game score?!"

Andrew watched the big screen as the announcer called the game. "The Black Knights are leading by 12 in the fourth quarter and Lamar Hayes is playing like a man possessed!"

Another announcer added, "Hayes has totally shut down league scoring leader and three-time MVP Lawrence Brown. Hayes' tough D and thirty-two points are all but ensuring a Black Knights victory tonight and they look like they might take the division this year."

Andrew pumped his fist and let out an exuberant, "Lamar! My man!"

Lorry looked at Andrew, confused. "You know him?"

"Nah, just a big Black Knights fan."

"Happy now?"

"Oh, yes I am." Andrew let out a big grin.

Lorry led Andrew through The Five Iron when Andrew remembered his possessions. "Lorry! What about my keys, phone and wallet?"

Lorry pulled them out of her jacket pocket. "You mean these?"

"How did you…"

Lorry just grinned.

Andrew returned the grin and secured his items as the two passed through the double stainless-steel doors of the kitchen. The kitchen had pure white subway tiles that covered its walls. The tables, the cookware, and the utensils were all made of stainless steel. It looked like an operating room, but the loud chatter between the cooks and servers sounded more like a trading floor on Wall Street, with many of the cross conversations in Spanish.

Lorry and Andrew sped through the room and up a set of stairs, where they came to a darkened end of a long corridor to a large metal door. The exit sign was hanging by a wire and unlit. The door's exit handle was covered in cobwebs. Lorry pulled out a key ring and a penlight. She found the key, inserted it, and turned the deadbolt of the lock. It took some effort to slide the rusted top bolt across to open the door. The metal door creaked loudly, and dust kicked up as it opened into a dimly lit alleyway.

Lorry pointed and held the door open as Andrew walked into the alley. "If you go through here, you'll be on Broadway. You can catch a cab home."

"Good idea. I'll tell my wife I had too much to drink at the game and get my car tomorrow."

Lorry grinned. "I suspect you'll be in the doghouse for that?"

"Better than a coffin."

"Too right." Lorry flung her hand as if she was shooing off a stray dog. "Off with you now. Maybe better to stay away from The Five Iron for a few days, eh?"

Andrew took a deep breath as the events of the night hit him in the chest like a running back's stiff arm. "Probably right. Thanks, Lorry. I… I appreciate it." Andrew knew his eyes said more than his words, as he felt an overwhelming sensation of emotion, realizing the gravity of what she did for him.

Lorry hid a smile behind a long wave of red hair that she let hang and partly covered her face. She gave him a nod. "No problem, you take care."

Andrew's heart pumped, and adrenaline coursed through his veins as he ran down the alleyway. The sounds of a New York City night greeted him as he cleared the alley onto the sidewalk. He took a few steps into the street on Broadway and waved one hand in the air and put his thumb and his index finger of his other hand in his mouth, and blew a piercing whistle as he yelled, "Taxi! Taxi!"

By the time Andrew heard the footsteps behind him, it was too late. Two men surrounded him, and one stuck a gun barrel deep into his rib cage and growled, "Don't move, motherfucker."

"We're going for a ride." The other man added.

A plain white van screeched up to the side of the curb as the side van door slid open.

"Whoa, whoa, I think there's a misunderstanding here," Andrew pleaded.

"Shut the fuck up!" The man yelled at Andrew and pistol-whipped him.

Andrew dropped to the ground with a thud.

19

Andrew felt a splash of water on his face as the smell of pungent sea water filled his nose. His ears filled with the sounds of water hitting the pier and the bell of a buoy dinging as the current moved it from side to side. His brain rebooted.

"What, what the fuck, where am I?" Andrew couldn't move his hands and he felt hard wood underneath him.

"Tied up on a chair on South Street, on a pier on the East River, just like I promised, Beck."

The rough Brooklyn accent gave away who it was before the briny water cleared from his stinging eyes.

"Turn that flashlight on. I can't see a fucking thing," the gruff man ordered.

Andrew's night vision adjusted to the dark shadows around him, and a bright white light blinded him. "You mind getting that light out of my eyes?"

The distinctive voice growled, "Shut the fuck up." He finished his sentence with a punch in Andrew's exposed abdomen. "You think you're pretty smart, huh?"

Andrew coughed and snapped back, "I guess it depends on the company I'm with?" He struggled against the zip ties that restrained his body to get a look around. "So, compared to you knuckleheads, yeah, I'm pretty smart."

Mr. Keegan fumed, "Shut your big fucking mouth." He punched Andrew in the stomach again. Andrew coughed and wheezed. He landed a right cross to his defenseless prisoner, leaving a small red cut mark on Andrew's left cheekbone.

Andrew closed his left eye, as if it would ease the pain on that side of his face, and looked up at Mr. Keegan. "If you want me to shut up, then…" He spat blood onto the boardwalk. "Stop asking me questions."

One of Mr. Keegan's thugs stepped up, cocked his weapon, and pointed it at Andrew. "Boss, let me put a bullet in this fucker's face."

Mr. Keegan put up his thick arm to stop the man from moving towards Andrew. "Wait, you dumb fuck. We need his marker card and the passcode."

The thug groped in Andrew's jacket breast pocket and pulled out his wallet and phone. "Got it. Here you go, Boss."

Andrew looked up to avoid the flashlight. "Now why would I give you the passcode to my marker card when you are going to kill me, anyway?"

Mr. Keegan bent over with a smirk that could reach Staten Island. "Oh, your life is over, Beck! It's fucking over! Now it's just a question of if *her* life is over too."

He showed Andrew the picture on his home screen. It was Andrew's favorite picture of Sandra. She was on Weed Beach in Westport, Connecticut, the calm Long Island Sound in the background. She wore a yellow floppy hat that shielded her from the bright sun and a yellow sundress to match. The sun in the background gave her body a heavenly glow. She was looking down with a big smile as she shifted her toes playfully in the sand. It was his favorite picture of her because she seemed to be content just touching the sand and feeling the warmth of the sun on her body. It was such a rare and beautiful moment. He smiled every time he looked at it.

A thug looked over Andrew's shoulder to get a look. "She's pretty hot, Boss."

Andrew lost his composure. "Hey! Leave her out of this! She's innocent. This is between you and me!"

Mr. Keegan was enjoying being in the power position. "Your marker card code, motherfucker! Then we tap two in your head, toss your Connecticut ass in the East River, and we'll leave her and your family alone."

Andrew looked up at him. Spit more blood. His left eye was swelling, and he closed it. "Scout's honor?"

Mr. Keegan looked out onto the East River, scratched his hairless head with the pistol's handle, and replied, waiving his Glock 19. "Yeah, on my mother. Give me the fucking code!"

Exasperated, Andrew complied, "All right, all right."

"What is it?!" He put the weapon to Andrew's temple.

Andrew saw his watch on Mr. Keegan's wrist. "Is that my fucking watch?"

"Yeah, you won't be needing it. Did that drug addict give it to you?"

Andrew looked away.

Mr. Keegan put the watch to his ear. "Well, I guess it's only fitting then that Palmer pays me as well."

Andrew shook his head in disgust. There was nothing he could do. Just a few days ago, his life was all going to plan, and he was crushing it. *Why the fuck is this happening to me?*

Mr. Keegan continued, "But since it is ruined with this fucking Tides logo on it, I can't be seen wearing this fucking thing." Mr. Keegan unclasped the watch and stuck the face of it in Andrew's face and added, "I'll throw it off one of my Hudson Yards buildings and watch a bunch of union workers fight for it."

The crew laughed, and Mr. Keegan pressed the gun further into Andrew's temple and he shoved the watch into his jacket pocket, saying, "Enough stalling! The code, now! Tell me!"

Andrew looked down. "I don't know the numbers. I spell out the word."

"What fucking word?!"

"I'll give you the letters, and then you can figure it out on the keys."

Mr. Keegan bit his lower lip, cocked his pistol, and then put the barrel on Andrew's knee. "If you're fucking with me, I'm putting a cap in each of your knees. And then I will cut off your fucking toes one by one."

Andrew looked at Mr. Keegan in the eye. "I get it. I'm not fucking with you. You ready?"

Mr. Keegan snapped his fingers and bolted out, "Someone get this down on their phone."

One henchman pulled out their phone ready to type, saying, "I got you, Boss."

Andrew sounded like a schoolteacher who was about to spell a challenging word to his class. "You ready?"

The henchman was looking at his phone, concentrating. "Yeah."

Andrew called out the letters, "F-U-C-K-T-E-D."

Mr. Keegan repeated the word, waving his pistol again. "Fuck Ted? Who the fuck is Ted?"

"I got it!" The henchman yelled out gleefully, "It's three-eight-two-five-eight-three-three."

Mr. Keegan pointed the weapon back at Andrew's face. "Beck, who the fuck is Ted?"

In a calm and confident tone Andrew simply replied, "My father."

The laughter of the entire crew filled the chilly East River air, and Mr. Keegan's laugh sounded like he was doing a Santa Claus impersonation. "Ho, ho, ho, man, you're one fucked up dude."

The henchman behind Andrew, who commented on Sandra, was a sports fan and put two and two together. "Holy shit, your pops is Ted Beck, right? The Masters Champion? He was fucking awesome."

Andrew closed his eyes and shook his head. "Oh fuck."

The man excitedly continued, "Boss, this fucking guy has balls of steel. He would hit crazy fucking shots. Most of the time, they went in the fucking lake, but sometimes…fucking incredible."

Andrew shot Mr. Keegan an irritated glance. "Keegan, can you shoot me now, so I don't have to listen to this shit?"

One of the other henchmen had a device similar to the marker card reader at The Five Iron. He slid the card in, punched in the code 3-8-2-5-8-3-3. The keypad beeped with each pushed button. When he finished and hit the green enter key, the machine beeped again and flashed Andrew's balance. The man whistled to get his boss' attention. "Wow Boss, he's got over three point two million dollars on this thing! Nice score!"

Andrew grinned. "But that is *my* card. How are you going to get the money?"

Mr. Keegan slapped Andrew lightly on the face a few times. "For a fee, I can have someone break into your card and transfer it to mine."

Andrew added, "Fergus is meticulous. He will catch you and hopefully...he will kill you."

"No, he won't. I got a bunch of fucking hackers in a basement in Chinatown. Ah, yeah, they will take 50% but hey, like you said, it's only money."

"You mean, *my* money."

"Your money, my money. Does it really fucking matter right now?"

"Guess not." Andrew shrugged and took a breath as he seemed resigned to his fate.

Mr. Keegan looked around at his men. "Okay, let's get this over with. What do you say, huh?"

The men all cocked their weapons and pointed them at Andrew.

Mr. Keegan threw up his arms excitedly. "Hey, wait! You know what?"

"Now what!?" Andrew yelled.

"I got a better idea."

"Can't wait to hear this."

Mr. Keegan directed the man behind Andrew, pointing his pistol. "Wheel him over to the edge of the dock."

Andrew felt the chair tip back and the man pull him about 100 feet to the edge of the dock. The sound of the water lapping against the wood dock pillars was clearer now.

Mr. Keegan shouted, "How about this, Beck! I will give $100,000 of *your* money to the first man to hit you from 100 feet in the dark. And another $100,000 to the man whose shot knocks your punk ass in the river."

Exasperated, Andrew looked up at the New York City sky. It was gray, shrouded by the lights. He yelled out, "Are you fucking kidding me?" He then looked up into the gray starless sky and he choked out, "Goodbye, Sandra. It would have been a nice life. I'm—I'm sorry."

Mr. Keegan yelled out to his crew, "Okay, first up! Ready! Aim!

Fire!"

A gunshot went off and Andrew heard a "pffft" rip past his ears.

Mr. Keegan cuffed his hands over his mouth to make a megaphone. "You still there, asshole?"

"No! This is my fucking ghost coming back to haunt your bald-headed ass."

"Fuck you, you prick! Next up! Ready! Fire!"

After the next henchman shot, a muzzle flash could be seen and then he heard a yelp of pain.

20

Andrew heard the shot go off but didn't feel anything.

Am I dead? Is it over?

But then he heard one of the thugs yell out, "Ahhh! Boss! I'm hit!"

"What the fuck!" Mr. Keegan yelled.

Still bound and seated, Andrew heard the distinctive sound of automatic weapons firing and bullets pinging when ricocheting off the ground.

Where's this coming from?

The pier was dark, and the dim lights of the buildings' reflections created shadows, making it more difficult to see. A woman's voice in a Scottish accent yelled out. "Drop your fucking weapons! Hands up over your head! Down on your fucking knees, or we open fire."

The pistols hitting the pier with mistimed thuds made Andrew breathe easier. The men, as they got to their knees, called, "All right, all right" and "Don't shoot!"

Andrew yelled out, "Lorry?! Is that you?!"

"You all right, Dr. Beck? You hit?" she asked.

"No, they're about as good at shooting as Keegan is at poker."

Mr. Keegan from his knees joined the conversation uninvited. "You are fucking dead, Beck, you hear me, fucking—"

"Shut the fuck up. Giving me a fucking headache," said a very large black man who hit Mr. Keegan in the side of his bald head with the butt of his AR-15 assault rifle.

Andrew smiled as he recognized the distinctive baritone voice that on some days reminded him of Michael Clarke Duncan, "Is that you, Georgie?"

"Yes sir, Dr. Beck. You good?"

"Ah, you know, another day for a white boy in the big city."

George laughed, "I got you." The other crew members joined in on the humor.

But it all went quiet as another man approached the scene. Andrew could hear the fine leather soles of his shoes grinding and scraping on the rough wooden pier. The wood creaked underneath him until he came to a stop. The only sound Andrew heard was the water lapping up against the pier and dinging of the buoy as it rocked in the rough current of the East River.

Then in a booming Scottish accent, a man said, "Well, well, well. What do we have here? Lorry, fetch Dr. Beck for me, will you? Get up, Mr. Keegan."

As Mr. Keegan held his head and was struggling to get up, Fergus signaled to George. "George, please, tie his hands behind his back. And search him for weapons."

Andrew could hear the heavy Dr. Martens thudding on the pier as her Airdrop M95 bolt action sniper rifle jostled with each quick and powerful step. Andrew called out to her when she was just a few feet away. "Lorry, was that you?"

Lorry emerged from the shadows. "Yeah."

"That was quite a—"

The *shwing* of a six-inch KA-BAR knife leaving its sheath interrupted Andrew's words. Shortly thereafter, the snap of the zip ties binding his legs released the tension in his lower extremities. He felt "pins and needles" as the blood rushed back to his feet.

Although they were away from the group, Lorry whispered to Andrew, "You're not out of the woods yet. Fergus knows you were planning to lose to Keegan on purpose. He's not happy. He doesn't take cheating lightly, and I suggest you speak only when necessary."

Andrew stood and replied with a very compliant, "Understood." He added, "Lorry...my hands?"

Lorry shook her head and guided him like a cop taking a criminal for a perp walk. The pain shifted from his legs to his face as he felt a swelling in the side of his face and a stiffness in his jaw—courtesy of Mr. Keegan's punches.

Fergus addressed Mr. Keegan, who was bound but still standing. "Mr. Keegan, one of your men is wounded. I'm going to allow you to dismiss your men and take him to whatever 'non-hospital' you take your wounded. We should not hold your men accountable for *your* crimes, eh mate?"

Mr. Keegan looked Fergus in the eye firmly. "My crimes? What did—"

Fergus growled, "Answer the fucking question!" He finished with a hard slap across Mr. Keegan's face.

Mr. Keegan's tone immediately changed. "Yeah, let 'em go."

Fergus quieted his voice and glared at him but very politely asked, "Let them go, *what*?"

"What?" Mr. Keegan looked genuinely confused.

Fergus took a step away, took out the pocket square from his jacket, wiped his mouth and hands as if to wipe away the fact that he touched that man.

"Your manners are atrocious, Mr. Keegan," Fergus declared. He then pantomimed as if he was talking to a 5-year-old child. "You say, 'Fergus, let them go…' what?"

Mr. Keegan shook his head and let out, "Please? Let them go, please?"

Fergus slapped Mr. Keegan again, but this time very lightly, and he grinned, "Ah, now you are getting it. Good man."

George then turned to the rest of Mr. Keegan's crew and cocked his AR-15. "You heard the man! Get the fuck outta here."

Mr. Keegan's crew gathered the wounded man and quickly left the scene with him groaning.

Fergus quickly glanced to watch the men gallop away and then turned his attention to Andrew. "You hurt, Dr. Beck?"

"They roughed me up a bit, but nothing broken."

Fergus shot back, "Yes, well, we'll see about that, Dr. Beck. The night is still young."

The brave smirk Andrew was giving Fergus left and was replaced by a deep pang in his stomach. He felt the same every time he saw the red flashing lights when a cop pulled him over going 90 miles per hour. Andrew had talked his way out of tickets by saying he was heading to an emergency patient situation and flashing one of his sports team's medical staff IDs. That usually did the trick. But Fergus wasn't some well-meaning Connecticut State Trooper.

Fergus continued in his rhapsodic brogue, "So then, gentlemen. I have very few rules when it comes to my club. But the few I do have, I take very fucking seriously. And rule number one is no fucking cheating!"

Mr. Keegan pleaded his case, "Fergus, but you both cheated me!"

Fergus frowned and crossed his arms. Mr. Keegan filled in the silence. "Beck's that drug addict Palmer's fucking shrink! The watch he gave him is in my jacket pocket." George searched Mr. Keegan's pocket and handed him the Tides logoed Rolex. As Fergus examined the watch, Mr. Keegan added, "He knew exactly what he was going to do!"

Fergus, who didn't seem to be a man who was easily surprised, cast a glance at Andrew and his chiseled granite face broke with astonishment. His eyebrows rose, but only for an instant as something seemed to click in his mind.

Fergus walked over to Andrew, held up the watch to Andrew's face, and quickly recovered his interrogative manner, looking him in the eyes.

"Is that true, Dr. Beck? Is that boy one of your patients?"

Andrew squirmed. "Fergus, I have confidentiality agreements with my patients—"

"Think carefully, Doctor! Because your life depends on it."

A fierceness in Fergus' eyes penetrated Andrew's soul. Andrew fully understood the gravity of the situation. He pushed his fear deep into his body, made eye contact with Fergus, and confidently declared, "Yes, John is my patient."

"See!" Mr. Keegan protested. "He fucking knew what he was going to do. You both set me up!"

"Oh come off it," Fergus scowled. "Until this moment, I had no idea Dr. Beck was the man's therapist." He put the watch in Andrew's jacket pocket without breaking eye contact with Mr. Keegan and continued, "And besides, if I wanted your money, I'd just fucking take it."

Fergus walked over to Mr. Keegan and tried to smooth out his overstretched jacket. He then straightened Mr. Keegan's tie, the knot done up probably tighter than usual around his thick neck. "But what kind of club would I have if I just took my patron's money whenever I wanted, eh? That's just not sporting now, is it?"

"So then Beck cheated me, and I want my money back."

"You are in no position to be making any demands here, Mr. Keegan," Fergus said, poking Mr. Keegan in the chest.

Fergus turned back to Andrew and asked, "So then it wasn't your 'gut' telling you that he was going to do well. You knew this boy's mind. When was the last time you spoke to him?"

Andrew sighed. "That night."

"Tell me more." Fergus crossed his arms and looked out over Andrew's head into the darkness of the East River.

"I was at the game before I came to The Five Iron. John had a bit of a meltdown on the field, and I went down to the locker room and talked him through it."

"Well done, mate."

Mr. Keegan couldn't help himself. "Yeah, for a coke fiend."

Andrew barked back, "For the last time, you moron, it was amphetamines, not cocaine!"

Fergus seemed to ignore the men's bickering as he was nodding. "You talked to him for how long?"

"Ten, fifteen minutes tops."

"And in that time, you had that big of an impact on his state of mind that you could affect his game play?"

"Their ability is their ability, Fergus. I can't do anything about that. But for athletes at John Palmer's level, there is so little that separates success and failure. Often it's just their confidence that needs a boost. The fear of failure is huge with pro athletes. It's rarely their ability that betrays them, but their own minds."

Fergus was quiet but intently staring at Andrew. He took it as a signal to keep talking.

"For people like you or me, if we have a sense of doubt in our minds for a few moments, it doesn't have that big of an effect on our day. But for these guys even a nanosecond of doubt during a critical moment in a game could be the difference between winning and losing."

Fergus nodded, and Andrew shrugged as he said, "I help them get that doubt out of their heads and focus on their performance."

Mr. Keegan shouted, "See, you knew what he was gonna do!"

"I only knew what he was capable of," Andrew snapped back. "I didn't throw the fucking pitch for him."

"Very interesting, Dr. Beck." Fergus continued his head nod. "So, Mr. Keegan, if you genuinely thought Dr. Beck cheated, why didn't you come to me with this dispute? Why take matters into your own hands?"

"Because that pussy Beck begged me not to."

"I didn't beg—"

Without looking at Andrew, Fergus put up a hand to signal him to stop talking and continued addressing Mr. Keegan, "So you decided that Dr. Beck should lose to you, on purpose, at my tables. That was your master plan, eh mate?"

"Well, yeah, I wanted to punish him—"

Fergus got close enough to Mr. Keegan's face to bite his nose off, "No one! No one punishes anyone in my fucking club but ME!"

Fergus' spittle sprayed onto Mr. Keegan, and he winced as it hit his face. His hands rose to Mr. Keegan's throat and his fingers curled. Then as they got within an inch of Mr. Keegan's throat, Fergus abruptly turned his back and walked a few steps away from the men, his shoulders rising and falling until they stopped. He moved his head side to side, letting out a big crack in his neck. He took a large breath and slowly released it.

He came back to the group and in a calm voice asked, "Dr. Beck, why didn't you pull me aside to tell me that you were this man's therapist."

"Look Fergus, if we are at the poker tables, I'm not going to announce that I have pocket aces. It was a bet. A bet, I might add, that was heavily in Baldy's favor to win. If he didn't think his chances were overwhelmingly favorable to win, his ego, which is somehow even bigger than his body, wouldn't have bet me. He's a bully. Bullies only bet or make threats when they have the advantage."

"Agreed," Fergus conceded.

Andrew continued, "So the bet was fair. The bald eagle of Brooklyn made the bet knowing the odds were in his favor. Did I have, shall we say, 'inside information' on the kid? Yes, but there is no rule in betting that says you must reveal everything you know. We figured that one out as kids on the street corner. Didn't we?"

"Some of us, no doubt." Fergus took a deep breath and exhaled. "Well, then, it is my judgment that Dr. Beck did not have any obligation to tell Mr. Keegan that he was the boy's therapist, and the bet was fair and square."

Mr. Keegan squirmed, "Fine. Can I go now?"

Fergus looked at Mr. Keegan as if he were a child asking something ridiculous. "No, of course not. This doesn't answer for your collusion. You *both* planned to change the outcome of a poker game. That could have seriously compromised the integrity of my tables. We're just getting started, laddies."

Andrew closed his eyes and looked down. A pang worse than Mr. Keegan's punches radiated his whole stomach. His fear came roaring back, and he tried to breathe his way through it.

"Dr. Beck, how did Mr. Keegan approach you to form this unholy alliance? And do not fucking lie to me!"

"Monday night, after Keegan the colossal dolt over here lost—"

"Fuck you!" Mr. Keegan belted out.

Andrew saw what looked like a thin Maglite flashlight pulled out of Fergus' belt area, but then he saw the sharpened blade switch out of its resting place. It was most certainly not a Maglite. Fergus squeezed Mr. Keegan's cheeks together, which smashed his mouth into a deformed oval, forcing Mr. Keegan to groan. Fergus put the blade almost inside his lips. "You interrupt these proceedings one more time and I will cut out your fucking tongue."

Fergus saw the compliance in Mr. Keegan's eyes, and let go of his

163

face. He waved his switchblade like an orchestra conductor. "Continue, Dr. Beck."

"When I left The Five Iron, Mr. Keegan and his men accosted me and threatened to shoot me and dump me in the East River if I didn't lose to him on purpose tonight."

Mr. Keegan was about to protest, but before he uttered a word, the glare from Fergus made him close his mouth.

Fergus continued, "Why didn't you just give him the $200,000 and be done with it?"

Andrew took a breath and sighed. "Because we embarrassed him, Fergus. And Mr. Keegan's narcissistic personality disorder would never allow us, especially me, to get the better of him. He obviously couldn't intimidate you, but he could threaten me. By humiliating me, his damaged ego would be repaired, which frankly, I assess, is more important than the money."

Andrew saw Fergus was listening very carefully, as if every syllable had weight. Andrew concluded, "He said I could either lose to him in poker or lose my life."

Fergus pointed the knife at Andrew as if it were a presentation clicker. "Why didn't you come to me first with this threat, Dr. Beck?"

Andrew shook his head looking at the ground. "I don't know, Fergus. Honestly, I was going to just give him the money and get on with my life."

"But why would you just give him the money?"

"He's a sick man. I took his threat seriously. I can always make back the money. It wasn't worth dying over."

Fergus turned to Mr. Keegan, pointing the knife, moving it rhythmically with every word. "Mr. Keegan, did you threaten Dr. Beck after you lost our bet?"

Mr. Keegan hesitated, "Well…"

"Think carefully, Mr. Keegan." Fergus made a quick nod to one of his men. A man stepped forward, cocked a pistol and pointed at Mr. Keegan. Fergus added matter-of-factly, "If you lie to me, I will shoot you in your fucking face."

"Yeah, yeah! I threatened the little prick." Mr. Keegan said as he looked down away from the gun pointed at him.

Fergus continued his inquisition, "Did you or did you not demand he lose at poker to you on purpose?"

"It's more complicated than that, Fergus…" Mr. Keegan looked directly at Fergus.

Fergus, unhappy with the answer, backhanded Mr. Keegan, giving him matching welts on each side of his cheeks. "No, it's not, Mr. Keegan!" Fergus growled. "It's quite simple! Either you did demand he loses to you on purpose in my establishment, or you didn't demand this. Which is it?!" The sound of two more pistols cocking in unison made a chill ride up Andrew's back. He instinctively moved a step away from Mr. Keegan, but Lorry's strong grip on his arm kept him in place.

"All right, all right!" He moved away from the guns and ducked his head away from the pistols aimed at his head. "Yes, yes, I told the little prick to lose on purpose."

Fergus paused and took a breath. He took a step back and put the knife away. He also wiped his hands with the handkerchief again. Andrew's head bobbed from Fergus to the men pointing guns at Mr. Keegan as if he was watching an intense volley in tennis.

"Mr. Keegan, do you know why people come to The Five Iron rather than Atlantic City, or Mohegan Sun, or the Bahamas? It's not for the food, although it is rather tasty, eh?" Fergus let out a grin, and his men chuckled. Lorry stayed stone-faced.

Fergus continued and put his hand on one of his men's shoulders, which garnered a grin from the man. "They come to The Five Iron because it's a magical world. A world that I created, where you can be who you truly are, without judgment." Fergus let his word linger on the East River wind before he continued. "Whatever vice or depravity you have, I don't care, in fact, I will help you quench your thirst for it. In my world, privacy is paramount. The staff's discretion is unyielding. But most of all, my guests at The Five Iron can be one hundred percent sure that there is never any cheating at my games. And there is one, and only one, punishment for cheating. And that is that you pay with your life!"

All Fergus' men cocked their weapons and aimed them at Mr. Keegan, his voice rose several octaves as he pleaded. "Whoa whoa

whoa! I understand, Fergus, I do! I fucked up! I'm sorry. But in my defense, and with all due respect, we didn't cheat. I *lost* the game. So even though we planned to cheat, we didn't. So technically, I didn't break rule number one."

Andrew quietly chimed in, "He's right, Fergus, I beat him."

Fergus nodded and wagged his index finger in the air. "That's a bloody good point, mate." He addressed his men and moved his arm in a downward motion. "Stand down, gentlemen."

Militarily, the men took a step back and uncocked their weapons in unison as Fergus addressed Andrew. "Dr. Beck, tell me what happened at the table."

"I knew you would not take kindly to us colluding. And I warned bullet-head over here not to push it. That you are always watching, and you would figure us out if we weren't careful."

"Go on, mate."

"I admit, I did fold some hands rather than play them, but players do that all the time to get a feel for the other players. That's not against poker rules. But I also won many hands too, so we wouldn't raise any suspicion. And then the Dimwit of Kings County got impatient. He wanted all his money in the next hand. But I got a Big Slick, Fergus. How can I lay down Big Slick? I did whatever I could to get Mr. Benson out so he didn't get hurt. At a critical moment in the hand, I looked Mr. Benson in the eye, I guessed his hand at the turn, and he folded."

"You guess his hand? Hmm, nicely played, sir."

"Thank you. I also knew shit-for-brains over there was holding nothing and was bluffing."

"How did you know that? Why so certain?"

"When bluffing, you don't deliberately draw that much attention to yourself. The more you say, the easier it is to figure out that you're bluffing. But he wanted to embarrass me. And what better way to show you are the superior player than to beat me on a bluff."

Andrew took a breath and was careful to intentionally look Fergus in the eye. "So yes, I was going to lose and give him back his undeserved $200K and then go the fuck home. But..."

Fergus gave a slight grin again, wagging his index finger. "But you couldn't."

Andrew shook his head. "No, I couldn't. I couldn't lose to this smug bastard."

Fergus shifted his hands to his hips. "Even though you knew he might kill you?"

Andrew closed his left eye as the swelling pulsed. "I guess I got a bit of an attitude problem."

Fergus nodded and looked at him with his icy blue eyes. "Aye mate, I would say you do."

"So I won. Chicken Little lost his shit, and...here we are."

"And here we are," Fergus sang, turning to Mr. Keegan, "Mr. Keegan, is that about right then?"

"Yeah," Mr. Keegan grumbled quietly.

Fergus stepped forward and put his hand behind his ear to pantomime like he needed help hearing. "Come again, mate?"

Louder this time and staring at Andrew, Mr. Keegan declared, "Yeah! The fucking prick double-crossed me." He then jerked his head back to Fergus. "But that means we didn't cheat!"

Fergus replied nonchalantly, "Valid point."

Mr. Keegan pleaded, "I swear Fergus, I—"

Fergus interrupted and boomed, "However! This conspiracy cannot go unpunished."

All the men cocked their guns again and pointed them at Mr. Keegan and Andrew to both of their horror.

Fergus then announced, "Get their marker cards please. All your funds are hereby forfeit!"

George searched Mr. Keegan and pulled his card out of his inside jacket pocket. "Here's Mr. Keegan's marker card, Boss."

Lorry searched Andrew's jacket pockets but came up empty. "Nothing on Dr. Beck."

Andrew pointed with his chin into the shadows as both his hands were bound behind him. "George, mine is over there. They have a device to break into my card."

Fergus jerked his head towards Andrew in shock. "A what!?"

Andrew elaborated, "Yeah, they were going to steal all my money after they killed me. They have some hackers in Chinatown that can break into my card and transfer the money to Mr. Keegan's card."

Lorry let go of Andrew and quickly went to Fergus's side. "That's impossible! The encryption is military grade. I installed it myself."

Andrew shrugged. "I don't know, Lorry. I'm just repeating what the Bald Eagle of Brooklyn said."

Mr. Keegan's eyes bulged and he mumbled a "Fuck" under his breath.

George moved surprisingly quickly for a man of his size and width. He scooped up the machine like he was recovering a fumble and heading for the endzone without missing a step. "Here, Lorry, Dr. Beck's card is still in the reader."

Lorry took the reader looked it over, careful not to dislodge Andrew's marker card. She punched a few buttons. The machine beeped with each touch. Andrew watched her forehead crinkle, and her gaze was stern. The light of the reader lighted up her blue-green eyes. Her fiery red hair was tucked neatly under a black baseball cap. A single French braid stuck out of the hole above the size adjustment strap, and long red strands cascaded the sides of her pronounced cheekbones. It was as if she came right out of central casting for a guest episode on *S.W.A.T.*

Andrew was lost, enjoying Lorry's intensity and her raw beauty. He almost smiled but he came to his senses and looked down to give him a second to wipe the admiration off his face.

Lorry pulled Andrew's card out of the reader and gave Fergus the reader to examine. "Fergus, this isn't one of our readers, but it works."

She then stepped closer to Mr. Keegan. "Where did you get this?"

Mr. Keegan let out a shit-eating grin and wise-assed, "Best Buy, on sale."

Lorry punched him in the diaphragm, knocking his wind out. He doubled over and coughed. Two men roughly propped him back up by the arms.

Lorry repeated, "Where did you get this!" Not waiting for an answer, she delivered a right cross that almost knocked him out. Mr. Keegan's knees buckled, and a gash opened up on his left cheek. The men struggled to hold up Mr. Keegan's thick frame.

Fergus jutted his chin at Mr. Keegan. "Oi, mate! You better answer her. I cannot stop her when she gets like this. She has such an awful temper."

Lorry used a Thai boxing clinch, clasping both of her hands around Mr. Keegan's neck, bending him over as her left knee hit the exact spot in his stomach she had punched. Mr. Keegan dropped to his knees.

He coughed and pleaded, "All right, all right, get this crazy bitch off me."

Lorry slapped the top of his bald head, and it made a noise like a raw steak dropped onto a butcher's block.

Mr. Keegan tried to recover his breath, and after a few beleaguered breaths, he spit out, "I got it from the Haung-Tse."

Lorry turned to face Fergus and lowered her tone. "Fergus, I know them. They're into corporate espionage and racketeering. They also run some gaming, but we've always been on good terms. We don't run in the same circles."

Fergus addressed Mr. Keegan as the men pulled him up by his jacket collar, ripping the seams of his underarms and leaving a big gaping hole. "If this is true, Mr. Keegan, you must have promised them a hefty sum for them to risk their relationship with us?"

Mr. Keegan turned his head, spit and turned back to Fergus, wincing. "Fifty-percent of the card with a minimum of a million bucks."

Fergus said, "Hmmm. Good to know every man has his price."

He put both marker cards in the inside left breast pocket and tapped the outside of his jacket twice, ensuring their safety. "Well, I'll be keeping both of your cards."

Mr. Keegan huffed, "Now are we done?"

Fergus cocked his head, "My dear, Mr. Keegan, that was only the financial reparations. Now comes the next phase. Physical punishment."

Fergus stepped away from the group and motioned for Lorry to follow him. As the two huddled, Fergus looked over his shoulder and loosely pointed at Andrew and Mr. Keegan. "Oh, George, if either one of them moves a muscle, shoot them."

George cocked his weapon and affirmed, "You got it, Boss."

Mr. Keegan strained his neck to try and hear what Fergus and Lorry were talking about as he loudly whispered to Andrew, "What are they saying?"

"I don't know." Clearly annoyed, Andrew quipped, "I'm a mind reader, not a lip reader."

Mr. Keegan's eyes got big. "So you admit it! You *can* read minds! I knew it!"

"Ah, for fuck's sake." Andrew winced.

The conference ended and Lorry and Fergus walked back to the group in step. George stepped aside to let Fergus in close.

"Well, Dr. Beck, looks like Mr. Keegan already gave you a good thrashing and a scare, so you are free to go."

Fergus put an outstretched left arm on Andrew's shoulders. Andrew felt its strength as Fergus wagged a finger in his face. "But if you ever purposely lose a game or cheat in any way in my club, you will regret it. Consider yourself warned."

Andrew nodded in agreement and affirmed, "You're right, Fergus. What I did was wrong. I thought I could deal with this myself. But I should have reported this to you. I apologize."

Fergus nodded his head in a magnanimous manner and gave Andrew a slight smile. "Apology accepted. George, cut Dr. Beck's bindings, please."

The big man complied. "Sure thing, Boss." George pulled out his blade and sliced through the plastic binders.

Andrew whispered over his shoulder, "Psst, George, would you really have shot me?"

"I like you, Dr. Beck, but I don't like you *that* much." The two men shared a laugh.

Andrew rubbed his freed wrists to bring back the circulation. Fergus's face was blank and businesslike. "All right, mate, time for you to bugger off. Lorry, escort Dr. Beck to the street, will you? See to it that he doesn't get into any more trouble, eh?"

Lorry handed her sniper weapon over to George as she nodded in acknowledgement with a low-pitched, "Aye."

Andrew walked away from the group and in a pleasant tone added, "Good night, Fergus, George." Then turned to a bleeding and concerned looking Mr. Keegan and added, "Mr. Clean."

"What about me?" pleaded Mr. Keegan.

Men encircled Fergus and Mr. Keegan as he demanded, "I need to know everything about your dealings with the Haung-Tse. I need names, places, dates. And then we'll talk more about your punishment."

Lorry and Andrew walked swiftly and silently off the pier. Fergus' voice faded quickly and the sounds of the East River lapping against the breaker walls gave way to the familiar sounds of traffic and distant sirens. The streetlights and the lights that shone from the buildings and shops made Andrew's eyes adjust. For the first time in what seemed like a lifetime, he was breathing normally.

They reached the curb on a mostly barren part of South Street with the muffled sounds of cars racing on the FDR sixty feet above their heads. Andrew broke the silence, "Thank you again, Lorry. I..."

Lorry gave him a sideways look. "Saving your arse is beginning to be a full-time job. One I prefer not to have."

Andrew nodded and in an unusually humble tone as the words stumbled out, "I'll be good from now on."

Lorry raised her auburn eyebrows, which were darker than her hair, gave him a half-smile and cracked, "I doubt it."

A black Lincoln Town Car pulled up and the passenger's side window rolled down. Lorry bent over so the driver could see her. "Driver, take him wherever he wants to go."

Andrew opened the back door and got in. He pushed the button to roll down the window, and called out to Lorry as she was walking away, "Lorry!"

She turned. "Yeah?"

"I owe you."

She nodded in agreement and softly added, "Yeah, you do."

Andrew smiled and sat back into the black leather seats as the car pulled away. He was about to tell the driver where to go when he heard a loud bang. It sounded like a car backfiring, but more like a gunshot.

Oh, fuck.

21

Andrew tried to open the door as quietly as possible, turning the key slowly, first opening the deadbolt and then the door lock. It reminded him of when he and Brandon would sneak into the house after a late-night Greenwich party in high school. Andrew sighed a breath of relief when the lock clicked with minimal noise. He slipped off his shoes. Their Brazilian cherry hardwood floors were beautiful but carried sound through the house. But he forgot about the door chime as it announced in a stern female computer voice, "Front door open" and beeped two times. Andrew winced. With his attempt at a silent entry blown, the grandfather clock in the foyer, a match of the one in his parents' house, and a wedding gift from Big Papa Hargrove, struck three times as if he was wagging his finger at him from some other world.

Andrew dropped his shoes to a ker-thump on the wood floors and his keys made a chink-chink sound when he threw them in the blue and gold Berkeley University cereal bowl that was repurposed into a key holder. A shadowy figure jumped off the couch and yelled out, "Andrew! Where have you..." then she noticed the bruising on Andrew's cheek. "Oh my God, what happened?! Were you in an accident?"

Andrew looked at Sandra sheepishly. "I went to a bar with Lamar and some of the Black Knights to celebrate after their win. I guess I got marked, because when I left by myself, I got mugged in the parking lot."

"Are you okay? Did they hurt you?"

"They only got my cash, and beat me up a bit, but I'm all right. Just a little sore." He grabbed his ribcage.

Sandra rubbed his arm and gently pulled him towards the first-floor bathroom. "Let's get you cleaned up."

Andrew resisted. "I'm okay. I want to go to sleep."

Sandra grabbed his arm. "You'll get an infection on that cut. Come on, just a few minutes."

Andrew gave Sandra a soft smile. "All right."

Andrew sat on the toilet inside the comfortable bathroom as Sandra stood straddling his legs and twisted over the sink. Steam rose from the hot water rushing in the dark blue circular glass vessel sink as she poured antiseptic on two cotton balls and mushed them together. As the clear liquid saturated the cotton balls, she turned back to Andrew and warned, "This is going to sting a bit." She surveyed the swelling on his lip and patted the soaked cotton ball on the wound on his cheek as Andrew responded, "Ouch!"

Sandra recoiled but then gave him a sympathetic smile and patted again. "Sorry! But it's better than getting an infection on this pretty face of yours."

The lump in Andrew's throat was bothering him more than the sting of the antiseptic. The night's effect overtook him as he gently looked up at his wife, who was carefully patting away and cleaning his cut. "Sandra."

"Yeah?" she answered, still focused on the task at hand.

Andrew grabbed her free hand, stared at her dark brown eyes as his watered. "I thought I would never see you again. I really thought I was going to die tonight."

Sandra stopped nursing, cradled his head, and kissed its top. "Oh, my baby! I'm so sorry."

Andrew stood up off the toilet. He grabbed Sandra's face with both hands and kissed her as if he hadn't seen her in months. Sandra dropped the cotton balls and returned the kiss with equal passion. Their lips met and foreheads touched as the large space that grew between them in the last few days shrunk down to nothing. They lost their sense of space as they almost stumbled over the toilet into the frosted glass wall of the shower. They giggled, and Sandra forcefully kissed Andrew. He pulled away, laughing and groaning, "Ow, ow, ow. My lip!"

The two laughed together as Andrew rubbed the inside of his cheek with his tongue. He used a finger to check for blood on his lip. There was none.

They took a moment, stared at each other, and Andrew pulled his wife close in an embrace. He stared at her face, noticing every angle and every feature. Overcome with feelings of gratitude, appreciation, and love, he fought back the tear forming in his eye. Sandra returned his adoring look with her gracious smile. Andrew whispered into her ear, "Come on, let's go upstairs."

The two exited the bathroom, hand in hand, until Sandra turned back. "Wait, the water is still running!" Andrew smiled at his wife as she turned off the water and turned out the bathroom light. As she rejoined her husband, Andrew gave her another long stare.

She became uncomfortable. "What?"

Andrew took a breath and touched the soft skin on her face. "You are an amazing woman. Don't you let anyone tell you differently." He kissed Sandra hard, ignoring the pain. The tear he fought back escaped his eye and rolled down his cheek. She smiled back, unable to say anything. Andrew wiped the tear, gave her a playful grin, raised his eyebrows, and pulled Sandra by the arm. Laughing, they ran up the carpeted wood steps in the main hall. The two pounded the steps, racing each other up the stairs. The laughter reverberated in the 40-foot ceilings. They flung the double doors to their bedroom open and then loudly slammed them closed.

22

The suspension cables of the George Washington Bridge's upper level passed Andrew's vision as gray pinstripes lining the clear blue spring sky, just like the ones lining the Tides uniform. Andrew hit the accelerator and crossed two lanes to get around some slower cars. The temperature was rising as a warm spring sun absorbed in his Nightfall Mica exterior, heating the car and forcing him to turn on the AC.

He touched the side of his face, his cheek still a bit swollen and sore. He could feel the round welt on the inside of his cheek with his tongue. He passed a series of cars in the middle lane of the bridge as he turned his head to look up the Hudson River as the early afternoon sun reflected off the sheer cliffs of the Palisades that ran for miles up the western side of the river. The slate color absorbed the golden sunlight, giving them a shiny veneer-like painted glass. The sun reflected onto the water, leaving little diamond sparkles rising and falling with the massive river's current. It was sheer raw beauty, nature at its finest. And when he looked left, he could see the New York City skyline with man's modern marvels, reaching for the sky.

He took one more quick look left and right and let the dichotomy of his two visions course through his mind. It made him think of his life, his double life, and it was his need to reach for the sky that almost made him lose the raw beauty of his life. He was filled with guilt and regret and, at the same time, gratitude that he was alive. He was brought out of his contemplation when about halfway over the bridge, he heard his GPS announce in a feminine voice, "Welcome to

New Jersey."

Andrew's "Road Trip" playlist was on the stereo, and the current song playing was Chumbawamba's "Tubthumping." Andrew used the volume control on his steering wheel to turn up the volume as he smiled and rubbed his sore cheek to the apropos lyrics:

I get knocked down
But I get up again
You're never going to keep me down

He was singing the refrain badly when his phone rang, and the Apple Play screen in his car flashed "Gina."

Andrew hit the answer button on his steering wheel to the outside sound of a car honking as Andrew moved back into the middle lane without using his indicator.

"Hello, Gina."

"Andrew, I thought you were coming into the office before your meeting with the Bulldogs?"

Andrew responded nonchalantly, "No, I got mugged last night, so I slept in a bit."

"Holy shit. You okay?"

Andrew rubbed his cheek again, "Yeah, a few bumps and bruises. They got some cash, but that's it."

"Wow! Glad you're okay." Gina went into logistics mode. "So, after you park, report to the front office, you will meet with the GM Ron Davis, Head Coach Joe McConnell, and Offensive Coordinator Matt Grayson."

"Oh, that's right, Matt is the new OC with the Dogs." Andrew added, "Our families were pretty close at one time."

Gina responded with interest, "Oh yeah?"

Andrew continued, "Uncle Jimmy coached football at Columbia University, and we all played golf together. One time Matt was there, and we played a fathers versus sons match. Matt was around 26, and I was 14."

"How did you do?"

"Ted was in his prime, and he's so fucking competitive he didn't

178

give us any strokes. He wasn't sure how well Uncle Jimmy was going to play."

"I guess you lost?"

"We made a pretty good showing. We only lost by a few strokes. I had a good game, but again, I was 14. And of course, Ted was a total prick. He was busting my chops so much that Uncle Jimmy had to tell him to knock it off."

Gina inquired, "I don't get Ted. In public, he was a media darling, but in private, a complete ass?"

"You have no idea. After the 'dads versus sons' match, Ted ripped me for missing a two-foot putt on the 16th. If I had made it, the score would've been tied. I felt bad, but Matt pulled me aside and said something I'll never forget. He said, 'Andrew, you have amazing talent. You keep practicing hard, and you will get better and better every day. But every day Ted gets older and older. It won't be long before you're better than he is.'" Andrew swallowed the lump building in his throat. "That one bit of encouragement got me through high school."

Gina matched Andrew's reverent tone. "They sound like good people."

"The Grayson's are the best. I'll say this about Ted. He drew some pretty nice people into our lives. The only problem was, they didn't stay long once they got to know him."

Gina abruptly changed gears. It was their familiar dance. "Hey, I sent your key talking points on peak performance by email. Do you want me to drill you on them?"

"Nope, I studied up. I'm good. The Professional Football League draft is only a week away. Who's their top prospect this year?"

"Michael Hubert, quarterback, University of South Carolina."

"Huh, never heard of him."

Gina continued from memory, "South Carolina U upset Virginia University 36-28 in the Orange Bowl. Hubert had a QB sneak for the winning touchdown in the last minute after the Gamecocks were down 28-0 at halftime. Hold on, let me get his stats." Andrew could hear her typing and clicking.

"Hubert had thirty completions on thirty-five attempts with 385 passing yards and 434 total yards. He threw for three touchdowns and one rushing TD, the game winner. The kid had some game."

"Got it. And after the fucking choke the Bulldogs did in the playoffs and Julian Donovan retiring, they'll need a new quarterback."

Gina added with the disappointment of an unsatisfied fan, "Yeah, one who can finish." Gina clicked a few more times, and Andrew could tell she was scanning articles at rapid speed. "It looks like the Bulldogs traded up in the draft to get Hubert in the first round."

Andrew perked up, "Great. I can use that 'expectation pressure' in my pitch."

"You're all set. Good luck."

"Thanks, Gina. Great work on prepping me."

Andrew could feel Gina's smile through the phone as she replied, "Sure thing, Boss. I put the ball on your feet and you put it in the back of the net."

Andrew laughed. "What would we do without our sports analogies?"

"Have boring-ass conversations."

"Ain't that the truth. I'll call you after the meeting."

They both shared a laugh as Andrew hit the gas and smiled as he watched the speedometer climb to 86 as he raced down the New Jersey Turnpike.

23

Andrew entered the glass double door into the reception area of the Bulldogs' front office. He was greeted by the receptionist, who confirmed his appointment with Ron Davis and then led him to the main conference room. As she led Andrew down a corridor, pictures of great moments in Bulldogs football through the ages were on the walls. Andrew focused on the image from 1991 of the Len Barrow 42-yard field goal to beat the Nevada Bandits for the Professional Football League Championship. It stuck in his mind because he remembered Ted, Brandon, and himself yelling and hugging each other, celebrating the Bulldogs' victory. One of the few moments Andrew could remember was when the three Beck men weren't at odds with each other.

They reached the conference room, where Andrew was ushered in through a glass door, and Andrew smiled and thanked her. He paced the room and grabbed a bottle of Fiji water from the counter. He took a few swigs, one a little too fast, but caught the wayward drop on the back of his hand that almost landed on his blue shirt. Andrew began to coach himself as he prepped for his pitch.

Focus on flow, not too many technical terms. Get to the point fast and get them emotionally involved. Find their fear. Find their fear and exploit it.

The door to the conference room swung open loudly as the Bulldogs General Manager and head of Football Operations Ron Davis entered the room. He had played for the Chicago Jazz for three seasons in the mid-eighties as a former defensive back before his knee gave out. Ron Davis still had his lean build and kept himself in good shape. Known as "a players' GM," Davis built the Bulldogs into a powerhouse in the Eastern Division. He was a tough negotiator but was known for being fair in a business where fairness wasn't usually part of the equation.

Davis extended his hand and grabbed Andrew's with a firm grip. "Dr. Beck, sorry to keep you waiting."

Andrew returned the grip with equal pressure. "Mr. Davis. Great to meet you, sir."

"Dr. Beck, please call me Ron."

"Thank you, Ron, and it's Andrew."

Andrew noticed him staring at the pink welt on his cheek and the swelling of his lip. "What happened to your face? Have a bad session with one of your patients?"

Andrew chuckled, "No, I got mugged near the TISEC. But I'm okay."

Ron smiled back, "Well, as long as you're not a Texas Marshalls fan, that probably won't happen at Meadowlands Stadium."

"Nope, I bleed Bulldog blue."

"Good to hear, let's get started."

Andrew shifted in his chair and glanced at the empty chairs at the conference table, "Are coaches McConnell and Grayson joining us?

Ron shook his head. "No, they're prepping for the draft. But Matt speaks highly of you, which is why you're here."

"Ah, that's too bad. I haven't seen Matt in years." Andrew shrugged. "But of course, the draft. You're looking at taking Michael Hubert from South Carolina in the first round, right?"

"That's what the press tells me," Ron said sarcastically.

"You have a big year coming up? Favorites to win the Eastern Division again even with Julian Donovan retiring."

Ron stiffened a little in his chair. "Yes, and the fans are clamoring for a league championship after the choke in the conference finals last year."

"It was very unlucky, Ron."

"Ah, come on now, Andrew. You and I both know there is no such thing as luck. It's skill and preparation."

Andrew leaned in. "Can I speak frankly, sir?"

Ron sat back. "Please do."

"Your team crumbled in the fourth quarter, not because of ability or play calling. You were whipping the Marshalls up and down the field. Up twenty-one points going into the fourth quarter. And if I may, sir?" Andrew took a moment, waiting for a signal of approval to speak frankly, and Ron nodded slightly. "Your team stopped playing to win and started playing *not* to lose."

Ron crossed his arms but didn't break eye contact. Andrew read his body language as either he disagreed or was preparing a defensive response. Andrew wanted to make his point, so he leaned forward, clasped his hands, but he put his two index fingers together and pointed out towards Ron to be more emphatic. "I promise you that from the first time all sixty-three men on your roster could hold a football, they imagined the moment of someday playing in a championship game. They played that daydream over and over in their heads. From peewee to the pros. With a twenty-one-point lead they were only a mere fifteen minutes away from making that childhood dream a reality." Andrew then sat back and swung his hands up in the air, "But all hell broke loose as soon as the Bulldogs predominant thought went from 'let's win' to 'don't lose!'" Andrew banged the table with his fist, not too loudly, but loud enough for Ron to shift in his seat.

Ron shot back, "What's wrong with being conservative and protecting a twenty-one-point lead?"

"Let me try to explain it to you this way: during the game, for three quarters, most of the players were what we call 'in flow.' Flow occurs when brain function becomes heightened, and the slower, energy-expensive system of conscious processing is swapped out for a far faster and more efficient processing of the subconscious. Quite simply, they were acting rather than reacting. It's a much more efficient system for producing on-field results."

Andrew took a moment, but there was no change on Ron's face. "I'll give you an example. On the Marshall's first drive of the game, they were inside the red zone and the receiver was wide open in the endzone. Blown coverage. But then what happened?"

"Billy Bolton had the pick six. Ran it back ninety-three yards, and quick as that, we're up seven to nothing."

"Exactly. Billy seemed to come from nowhere on that play, right?" Andrew pantomimed the play, imitating a player catching the ball. "He plucked that ball out of the air for what should have been an easy touchdown for the Marshalls, right?"

Ron uncrossed his arms and leaned forward placing his arms on the table. "Yep, don't know how he saw that one. The play wasn't his coverage area in the zone. But, in all fairness we drill into these men's heads all the Dallas' tendencies and formations."

"Yes, agreed. But that was an athletic play, not a mental one. You said it yourself, 'he came from nowhere' and he 'wasn't in his zone coverage area.' Billy's brain was trading energy usually used for higher cognitive functions in exchange for heightened attention and awareness. Simply put, his body took over and got him to where he was supposed to be, when he needed to be there. He didn't think…he acted. When players like Billy are in flow, they find the dorsolateral prefrontal cortex, an area of the brain best known for self-monitoring, deactivated. Self-monitoring is the voice of doubt, our inner critic, so to speak. When we are in flow, it is a fluid state where problem solving is nearly automatic. When the dorsolateral prefrontal cortex goes quiet, all second-guessing is cut off at the source."

Andrew paused to let all the data he spilled out settle in. "The result is mental liberation. We act without hesitation. Creativity becomes more free-flowing, risk taking becomes less frightening, our self-confidence soars and we reach peak performance moments. Like Billy did."

Ron sat back again, putting his hands behind his head and supporting his neck, "Okay Doc, that's one man, but how does that explain the entire team's fourth-quarter collapse?"

"Let's take your future Hall of Fame quarterback Julian Donovan. We all knew it was Jules' last season. And what better way to go out than bringing the Bulldogs to the championship game for the third time in his career?"

"I'm with you."

"Julian was picking the Marshalls' defense apart. He had a QB rating of 112 going into the fourth quarter. But at some point, he reactivated his dorsolateral prefrontal cortex. Perhaps he started thinking about his legacy. Going out on top like Bulldogs all-time great Dave Verano. And he started playing *not to lose instead of trying to win*. He started second guessing his decisions, hesitating. It was his hesitation on the play-action on third and long with twelve minutes and fifty-three seconds left in the game that caused the sack and fumble, which was the turning point of the game."

It was Ron's turn to bang the table as he remembered the play. "He held onto the ball too goddamn long!"

Andrew leaned forward with a fist clenched. "Exactly! Then in the next series, he throws an interception, and the Marshalls go down and score."

Andrew added, "Within five minutes, the score goes from twenty-one to zero to twenty-one to fourteen. Then, on your next possession, your all-pro running back Rodney Giles fumbles the handoff on your own thirty-five. The Marshalls recover the ball and score again and now you're tied. Three turnovers, your lead evaporated, confidence shaken, and the Marshalls have the momentum. You go three and out on your next and final possession. The Marshalls get the ball and in three plays get into your territory and hit a forty-yard field goal with twenty seconds left. The collapse…is…complete."

A dejected Ron replied as his tone lowered. "Yes, and the press and fans never let me forget it."

Andrew sat up straight and used his "Clinton thumb" to make his point. "Ron, I can get your team back on track. I can help them understand what happened mentally and emotionally, so they become aware of the times when negativity and self-doubt arise. I have proven techniques to help your team not only be physically strong, but mentally and emotionally strong too. I can help the Bulldogs get to the championship this year."

A few moments of silence passed between the men. Andrew waited calmly and patiently for Ron to talk first, which he did.

"So, who are you working with over at the Sentinels? I know Riley, he's a hard-ass, but he got the Sentinels in the playoffs this year."

"Ron, you know I can't tell you that. Client confidentiality isn't only a medical requirement, and it's rule number one in the sports world."

Ron smirked at him. "All right, all right, I was just testing you."

Andrew smiled back. "As a lifelong Bulldogs fan, I'd be thrilled to work with you and the team. Let's get you a ring on your finger this season!"

Ron nodded. "Yeah, it all sounds good. The draft is next week, and training camp is a few months away. So let's keep talking."

Andrew stood up and walked toward Ron, who stood up and they extended hands. "Great. I'm looking forward to it. Please give my best to Coaches McConnell and Grayson."

Ron released his hand and then snapped his fingers like he remembered something. "Wait a second, Matt said he and his dad Jimmy played golf with Ted Beck and his son. That's you, right?" Ron pointed at Andrew.

"Yeah, we played together a few times."

Ron got a little starstruck. "Ted Beck is your father? Holy crap! Ted was an incredible golfer. A real people's champion."

Andrew looked down and forced a smile. "Thank you. Yeah, he was."

"Man, he had balls of steel."

"Yeah." The feigned smile was disappearing fast.

"Did you play golf, too?"

"Yeah, a little at Berkeley College."

"Your dad still plays, right?"

"Yes, he does. In fact, we are playing this weekend."

"Really? It's 40 degrees out."

Andrew shrugged his shoulders and grinned. "It's a Beck tradition. Dad and I always play the first tee-time of the year at the Greenwich Country Club. You should come and play at the club sometime. Bring the coaches too. Matt already knows the course."

Ron hesitated. "Andrew, uh, you think you could get Ted to play with us?"

Andrew grinned and nodded, "Absolutely."

Ron clapped his hands. "That would be great."

The door to the conference room opened, and the receptionist stuck her head in. "Mr. Davis, Coach McConnell is asking for you."

Ron signaled that he was wrapping up by circling his finger in the air. "Okay, thanks! Sorry to cut this short Andrew, it's big week. We gotta get a new quarterback."

"Yes, you know, it's a lot of pressure moving from a college player to a starter in the pros. I can help with his transition."

Ron patted Andrew on the shoulder as he left the room and shouted back, "I'll keep that in mind."

The glass door closed quickly but Andrew could still hear Ron Davis' muffled yell. "Call me after the draft. And, uh, say hello to your dad for me?"

Andrew gave him a thumbs up. "You got it."

As Ron Davis disappeared out of view, Andrew buried his face in his hands and took a deep breath. Then he looked out the window onto the busy Route 3 highway and watched the cars heading back to Manhattan. He yelped, "Hey Dad, you mind playing golf with me and Ron Davis, the GM for the Bulldogs? It would really help me out."

Andrew imitated Ted in a supportive voice, "Sure son, anything I can do to help. Do you want me to lose on purpose, so they give you the deal?"

Andrew chuckled ruefully. He shook his head and again touched the sore bruise on his cheek. He grabbed the water bottle to take a sip but hit the bottle on his swollen lip and instinctively pulled the bottle away and seethed in pain. Andrew remembered the last time he had a fat lip. He stared out the window and let out a deep sigh.

24

1997

In the middle of the Palm Desert, California, was one of the top golf courses in the country, where the top amateur golfers from around the world gathered for The Palm Desert Invitational. This tournament was broadcast live and carried by the leading sport channel, Real Sports News.

Golf fans would tune in to see who the next up-and-coming players were and if someone were watching on TV, they would have seen the two announcers covering the match.

"Welcome back to Real Sports News for full coverage of the 1997 pro qualifying tournament where the top players will qualify for their entry into Professional Golfers League. I'm Jay Talbot and my co-host is former pro golfer and winner of six major tournaments, Gary Anderson."

Gary Anderson looked over at John Talbot and said, "This is a big day for these young men, and we are at the gorgeous Palm Desert course." The TV panned the course: its curving, manicured fairways, its water hazards, and deep sand trap bunkers. There were trees, but not many compared to Andrew's home course, which was lined with Eastern white pines and sugar maples.

Anderson continued, "Here we are, going into the 17th hole, also known in golfing lore as Alcatraz! Dubbed the PGL tour's most diabolical hole, they call it Alcatraz because it's totally surrounded by water with dangerously jagged rocks circling the green." The TV showed some prerecorded shots of the hole panning in on the rocks to reinforce how difficult the hole was.

Talbot added, "And if that isn't bad enough, the 18th hole is lined by water hazards all the way up the left side of fairway. So even if you're just a little off left, you're in the drink. Many golfing journeys have died a horrible death on these two holes. But let's hope some of these young men experience the thrill of victory…"

Anderson finished his partner's statement: "Rather than the agony of defeat?"

Talbot laughed. "You got it." The leader board then flashed up on the screen and Talbot recapped the standings. "The current amateur leader is Andrew Beck from Greenwich, Connecticut. And if that name sounds familiar, it's because young Andrew is the son of 1988 Master's Champion, Ted Beck!"

Anderson added exuberantly, "And it looks like he's a chip off the old block. This young man has a bright future ahead of him. Andrew is leading by five strokes, so even if he bogeys these next two holes, he's a shoo-in to win the cup and get his professional golfer's card today. He has been strong and steady the entire tournament. I tell you what, I've played numerous times against Ted Beck, and he was one of the toughest competitors I ever played against. And it looks like Andrew inherited that focused look and aggressive attack towards the game."

Talbot added. "The pressure this young man is under is enormous. He's got nerves of steel. Ted has to be a proud papa right about now."

Anderson added factually, "Well, if you remember it was Ted who almost beat Ben Crosby when he was eighteen at that 1972 pro-am in San Antonio before his dad stormed the course. But young Andrew has his dad right by his side."

Talbot excitedly said, "So great to see that father-son connection."

"Yes, so it looks like young Andrew is about to exorcise some of Ted Beck's old demons!"

Talbot started the hole commentary. "So let's go down to the 17th hole. It is a par three and 169 yards. Beck has his five iron out."

Anderson reported the stats, "In the three rounds played so far, Andrew has parred this hole twice, and he birdied it yesterday. So it looks like his escape from Alcatraz will be a clean getaway."

The comment drew a polite laugh from Talbot. "Good one. Andrew lines up his shot. Takes a half swing and punches it…"

The sound of a club slicing the air and the smack of contact with the ball rang out, but the ball made a very high arch off the tee towards the island green.

Anderson spoke out a warning, "Oh no, I don't think it's going to make it!"

The ball hit off one of the large boulders at the front of the island and ricocheted into the water with a loud splunk.

"Whoa! How unlucky!" Talbot reacted.

Anderson said, "It looks like Ted Beck is giving some much-needed advice to his son Andrew."

Ted approached a newly turned 18-year-old Andrew on the golf course and grunted as quietly as he could, "Jesus Christ, Andrew! You hit the green three times in a row. Don't shorten your swing."

Andrew nodded in agreement, "Yeah, thanks."

Ted walked away smiling and waving to some scattered golf clapping.

A young Andrew grabbed his wedge and said under his breath, "Go fuck yourself, old man."

Ted turned and looked quizzically at Andrew. "What?"

Andrew shrugged. "Nothing Dad, just talking to myself, just like you taught me. You know, one shot at a time, right, Dad?"

Ted looked at him disapprovingly. "Yeah, now get the damn ball on the green."

Andrew took a new ball out of his khakis and placed it in a white circle about 85 yards away from the pin. Although significantly closer to the hole, he still had to hit it over the water and avoid the wall of boulders surrounding the green.

For people watching on TV, Talbot continued his commentary, "Let's see how Andrew plays out of the drop zone. With the penalty, Andrew is hitting his third stroke."

Anderson added, "If he makes the green and putts it in, he will score a double bogey, but he will still lead by three strokes."

Talbot commented, "Ted Beck can be seen looking intently on and giving Andrew the encouragement a young man in a tough spot needs."

Talbot described the play. "Andrew Beck, using his wedge, swings, and hits a high lofting ball."

Andrew's swing was textbook. The wedge hit the ball high in the air at a steep arc. The ball reached its zenith of the arc and fell back down towards the ground.

Anderson let out, "Oh no, I think he is going over the green! Either back in the water or the rocks!"

Andrew hit the ball over the pin. As it fell, it hit off one of the back rocks 30 feet past the pin, then ricocheted and hit another rock, which popped the ball in the air. It landed on another rock and jetted right into the water with a loud plunk. The crowd let out a chorus of disappointed "oohs" and "ahhs."

The announcers were shocked at the development of events, and it reflected in their commentary. "Holy Toledo! How about that!" Talbot exclaimed.

Anderson recounted the shot, "It ricocheted off three different rocks and back in the water. Another penalty for young Andrew, and he is quickly seeing his lead evaporate."

Jay Talbot added, "The most diabolical hole in golf. Andrew has his head bowed low and his hands on his hips. He is completely disgusted with himself."

On the course, Ted marched towards Andrew, again keeping his voice low and trying to hide his frustration. "Andrew, what the fuck's wrong with you! You're two over par on this hole as it is!"

Andrew turned the golf club, so the head of the club was on top as he pointed to the wedge head with his gloved hand. "Sorry, Dad. Maybe there is something wrong with the wedge?"

Ted did all he could not to lose it as he grunted under his breath. "It's never the fucking club, boy! It's always the guy holding the club. You're fucking embarrassing me in front of all these people."

Andrew nodded and served up, "Sorry, Dad. I'm doing my best."

Ted shot back, "Do better!" Ted turned and walked away, again smiling at the crowd of onlookers.

Ted wasn't but a few feet away when Andrew mumbled under his breath, "Go fuck yourself, fucking has-been."

Ted turned around. His brow furrowed. "What?"

Andrew shook his head and shrugged. Ted walked back to the edge of the crowd, reassuring the fans his son would make the shot. A few people patted him on the shoulder in a show of support.

Andrew hit the green on his next shot and made his putt, but with the penalties, it gave Andrew a six on hole that was a par three. His opponents, meanwhile, were able to keep pace, parring their holes.

Back up in the TV booth, the commentators were trying to sort out this turn of events. Talbot gave his assessment, "Looks like Ted Beck is once again trying to coach his boy in what could become a devastating defeat."

Anderson added, "As we go to the 18th hole, Beck takes a six on that par three, reducing his lead to only two strokes. But he can bogey this hole and still qualify."

Talbot added, "That's right. Even if Andrew loses the tournament, as long as he comes in under par, he can qualify to play in the Professional Golf League."

The 18th hole at the Palm Desert was a par four, and 440 yards to the pin. On the left of the hole was a long lake, from tee box to green, and on the right was a narrow fairway with sand trap bunkers and trees making it tough for any drive that didn't go straight as an arrow. Andrew's drive, although high and long, hooked to the left and landed in the water. With the penalty, it meant that Andrew was hitting his third stroke. Andrew hit his shot from the penalty area just short of the green. His next shot, his fourth, was a beautiful wedge shot onto the green and the ball rolled within four feet to the pin. So, if he made the putt, it would give him a five for the hole but a one under par altogether. Although he would probably lose the tournament, and he would still qualify to get his professional golfer's card.

On TV, the announcers picked up the live action. The voice of Talbot rang out as the TV panned the 18th hole, "We are back live, at the final hole in what is developing into quite a drama."

Anderson commented, "Yes, Andrew Beck, with just one putt left, if he makes this, he is on his way to becoming a professional golfer. But you never know when the yips are going to come, and you never know when they are going to leave."

Talbot continued, "Now as they move to the green, we go down to our field reporter Ken Howard, who is talking with Ted Beck as Andrew lines up this final shot."

The cameras panned to the reporter clasping his RSN mic and standing next to Ted. The crowd was behind him, and some people were waving and mouthing, "Hi, mom!" Ted had a serious look on his face but forced out a well-rehearsed smile. Howard said, "Thank you, Jay. I'm here with golfing legend Ted Beck, who has watched his son struggle on these last two holes after 70 holes of brilliant play. What do you think Andrew's chances are for qualifying?" He held the microphone under Ted's chin.

Ted confidently mused, "Real good, real good. All golfers have some trouble. God knows I've hit some lousy shots."

Howard quickly pulled the mike to himself and asked, "But you must have prepared him for moments like these, right?"

"Exactly. Andrew is a talented golfer, and he's been in tough situations before. He's a winner, and winners always come through."

Howard looked back to the camera. "All right. Back to you, Jay and Gary."

The camera focused on Andrew. He was crouched behind his ball, eyeing the gradations, the subtle tilts in the grass between his ball and cup. Jay Talbot commented, "Beck lines up his putt. He has been looking up and down the green, measuring the breaks."

Anderson added, "Andrew is about four feet from the hole. His masterful chip onto the green is just what he needed to get his confidence back."

Talbot warned, "Yeah, but it's those four-footers that are the killers. They look so easy, but hit too hard or too soft..."

Anderson added, "Or miss the break?"

"Exactly."

Andrew took a few practice strokes and stepped to his ball.

Anderson said in a hushed tone, "This is it, folks. If he drains the putt, he qualifies."

Talbot matched Anderson's tone. "He looks pretty calm and collected, a testament to the training and guidance he's received from one of the gutsiest golfers of our time, his father, Ted Beck."

Andrew tapped the ball. The little white dimpled ball rolled slowly but directly for the hole. The crowd let out a loud burst of "oohs" as one fan yelled, "Get in the hole!" People started clapping and cheering, sure that the ball was going to fall. But as the ball rolled to the rim of the cup, it stopped. The "oohs" quickly changed to "ahhs" as the clapping stopped and the crowd grew quiet.

Back on the TV Talbot reported, "Well, the crowd said it all."

Anderson said, "Oh, to come so close, and maybe the wind will knock it in. It's right on the edge of the cup!"

Talbot announced dejectedly, "Poor Andrew Beck, ahead by five strokes going into the 17th, but the course swallowed him up."

Anderson added, "Just like in the Summer of '72, when Ted lost at Pine Lake."

Andrew tapped in his final putt, picked up the ball and waved to the fans, who clapped heartedly to give a show of support.

Talbot pointed out, "Here comes Ted, to console his son and give him a hug."

The fans continued their clapping as Ted hugged Andrew.

After they embraced quickly, Andrew, saddened, said, "I'm sorry, Dad. I'm sorry I let you down."

Knowing the cameras were on him, Ted showed a toothy smile. But through this smile he grumbled, "How the fuck could you blow it like that? Jesus Christ. Okay, when we turn around, you smile and wave to the fans and cameras, and I'll go figure out how to fix this fucking fiasco you created. Fucking second place."

Andrew looked down and said, "I know, second place is First Loser."

Ted, still forcing a smile, said, "Just fucking smile, but don't look too happy."

Back in the TV booth, Talbot wrapped up his commentary, "An unfortunate day for the Beck family, and it looks like the ghosts of tournaments past continue to haunt the Becks."

Anderson said, "Well, Andrew is young. I'm sure we will see a lot of him in the future. Let's go back down to the course where Ken Howard is with Ted and Andrew Beck."

Ken Howard shook his head in disbelief. "This one has to be just heartbreaking for you and Andrew, Ted?"

Years of Ted's interviewing clicked in full gear. "Well, golf's a tough game, and this is a very unforgiving course and sometimes you can make the shot and sometimes you can't."

Howard then reached over to Andrew with the mike. "Andrew, this had to be just crushing for you. What do you do now?"

Andrew responded humbly but with surprising assurance, "Well, it's back to practice. I'll watch videos of all my shots and then make the necessary adjustments."

Howard pulled the mike back to himself and said, "That's a great attitude, and I'm sure the coaches at Stanford University will be happy to get a talented young golfer like you."

Andrew shook his head. "I'm not going to Stanford. I was accepted to Berkeley University, where I will be studying psychology in the fall."

Ted was shocked and the mike missed his "What?!" But then he pulled the mike and stated firmly, "No, Andrew's mistaken, he already accepted Stanford." He gave his Ted smile and added, "But thanks for your time. We have to head to the scorer's table and finalize the round." Ted waved to a cheering crowd. "Thanks, everyone!"

Ted and Andrew walked off towards the air-conditioned trailer that housed the course officials.

Howard faced the camera and said, "There you have it folks, Ted and Andrew Beck, the first family of golf."

Andrew finalized his scorecard and as the pair stepped out of the scorer's trailer, a wave of Palm Springs heat hit them like opening an oven door. They were quickly encircled as camera flashes were going off from fans and reporters alike. Ted addressed the crowd, "Okay, thanks everyone for your support, but my son and I need some time together. This was a rough day, so I'm going to ask for a little privacy, okay?"

One of the fans yelled out, "You got it, Ted! You're the best!"

Ted responded with a big smile and pointed straight into the crowd, "No, you're the best!"

Ted continued his smiling and pointing to the crowd. "Thank you everyone! Thank you!" Ted's straight-armed single finger point was his signature move to connect with his crowd, and when he did it, they all clapped, hooted and hollered.

Ted guided Andrew into the clubhouse, and as soon the door was closed, Andrew found a spot to put his golf bag down by the lockers. Ted pounced.

"What the fuck just happened out there?!"

Andrew took a step back, but he was up against the lockers as he tried to explain, "I hit a few bad shots. You said it yourself—they were tough holes."

Ted barked, "I don't give a fuck about your monumental loser performance! I'm talking about Berkeley!"

Andrew looked genuinely surprised, "I thought mom told you?"

Ted snapped back with a weak, effeminate imitation. "No, mom didn't tell me!" Now he growled, "Mom didn't tell me shit! But you're not fucking going to Berkeley. You're going to Stanford like I did." He pointed his thumb at his chest.

Andrew, still backed up against the locker, stood his ground. "No, I'm not, Dad. The psychology department at Berkeley is one of the best in the country. I want to be a psychologist."

Ted fumed, "I don't give a fuck if Sigmund fucking Freud himself teaches there. It's not about that."

Andrew looked at his father and man-splained, "Freud's dead, Dad. Plus, I prefer Jung's theories on archetypes—"

"Shut the fuck up! It doesn't matter what the fuck you are studying because you need to get to the next qualifying tournament, which is next month in Orlando—"

Andrew interrupted, "No."

"No! What do you mean No?"

"I'm done, Dad."

"You're done? What the fuck do you mean you're done? The season is just beginning."

Andrew stared at his father in the eyes. "I don't want to play golf anymore."

Ted lost it. "Are you fucking kidding me?! You lose one fucking tournament, and then you want to be a head shrinker at some nerdy pussy school like Berkeley? And give up golf after all my hard work and sacrifice?"

Andrew crossed his arms and calmly said, "Huh, after *your* hard work and sacrifice?"

Ted's face turned beet red. "You ungrateful son of a bitch!" He grabbed Andrew by his white golf shirt and shoved him up against the locker. Ted's fist was wrapped in Andrew's shirt, and when he shoved him, his fist hit Andrew's bottom lip hard enough to make it bleed.

Andrew yelled back, not breaking eye contact and not showing a shred of fear, "GO AHEAD! HIT ME! I DARE YOU!"

Ted wound up his left hand but stopped and let out a scream in frustration, "Ahhhhhh!"

One of the course officials saw the altercation and rushed over, trying to put himself in between Ted and Andrew. "Hey, hey, Ted! Let the boy go!" The two men looked at each other. The man whose shock and horror filled face tried to reason with a raged-out Ted. "There is a room full of reporters outside."

Ted turned from the official, looked back at Andrew, and screamed, "You have any idea what I went through, boy?! Do you?!"

Blood dripped down onto Andrew's white shirt, and his lip started to swell. Andrew calmly retorted, "It's all about you, right, Dad?"

The official tried to free Ted's grip on Andrew's shirt and tried to wedge his body between the father and son. But Ted wouldn't let go. He spoke in a calm but firm tone. "Ted, let him go."

When Ted still didn't loosen his grip, the man got fed up and raised his voice, "NOW!"

The yell seemed to take Ted out of his rage, and he quickly let Andrew go. He stepped back and drew his hand down his face as if to wipe away his anger. But fury still contorted his face, and he gritted his teeth. As he walked away, he punched one of the lockers, yelling out, "Fuck!"

The official turned his attention to Andrew. "You okay, son?" He pointed to Andrew's face. "Your lip is bleeding."

Andrew curled his swollen and bleeding lip in his mouth and licked the blood. He spit the blood on the carpet and said, "Yeah, I'm okay."

He took a moment and wiped his mouth. He glanced at his hand, which had blood spots on it, and he looked up at the man. Andrew's blue eyes turned a shade of gray. "It's a fair deal." He spat again, the blood splattered on the gray carpet. "A fat lip for a future."

25

The crunching of sandstones under Andrew's feet was a sound that made him feel like he was home. The house on Hawkwood Lane in Greenwich had a long driveway and was covered in yellow, gray, and white sandstones. This was the house Andrew and Brandon grew up in, and one Helena tastefully decorated and did her best to keep sane with two rambunctious boys and a famous husband. The driveway led to a circle with an ornate wrought iron fountain with spouts pouring water in each of the four directions, and in the summer, it was covered in flowers.

Andrew and Sandra walked up the driveway past the fountain towards the front steps of the 6,000-square-foot home on almost two acres of land. Andrew was lost in the crunching sounds in each step. Sandra gently intertwined her forearm into his and touched his hand.

She nodded as she said, "You can do this."

Andrew looked up from the sandstones and gave her a short smile. "Yeah, thanks. Hopefully, Ted isn't in one of his more combative moods."

Sandra responded reassuringly. "Maybe he'll be nicer when he sees that you got mugged?"

Andrew stopped walking and said sarcastically, "Do you know Ted Beck? Empathy to him is a four-letter word."

The two shared a chuckle as they walked up the steps and rang the doorbell to a ding-dong-dong-dong, dong-dong-ding-dong.

Andrew and Sandra heard the click-clack of someone wearing low heels as she approached the door. The big black door opened to the warm smiling face of Helena Beck. Although in her mid-sixties, Helena brought beauty and grace to any room she entered. Her short, cropped blonde hair made her look distinguished with its touches of gray. Her sparkling blue eyes showed the wisdom and intelligence of a woman of the world.

She greeted the couple with a warm smile and a welcome, but the smile quickly left her face when she glanced at the face of her youngest son. "Oh my gosh! Andrew! What happened to you!?" She put her hand underneath his chin and turned his head gently to see the extent of the bruising. Andrew did not resist—what would be the point?

Andrew replied calmly, "I got mugged by some kids outside the TISEC. I'm okay. They got some cash, but I think they were more interested in scaring me."

"What is this world coming to? Well, come in! Dinner is almost ready." She guided Andrew in and hugged Sandra, "Lovely to see you, Sandra dear. You always look so beautiful."

Sandra smiled back. "Thank you, Helena. It's wonderful to see you too."

As they walked through the foyer, Sandra marveled at the wall of framed pictures and stopped to glance. "I love all these family pictures." Her voice went up a few octaves as she smiled at her husband. "And seeing my little Andrew."

Helena chuckled and put her arm in Sandra's as she pointed to some of Andrew's younger pictures. "He was the most adorable little boy. Always getting into something."

Sandra shot back, "Looks like he still is." The two women shared a laugh at Andrew's expense, but he took it well.

"Okay, you two, that's enough," he grinned, shaking his head.

"Oh, we're just getting started. I can't get enough of your boyhood stories."

"I think I'll go back to those kids who mugged me—it'll hurt less."

They all laughed as heavy footsteps approached from the living room. Ted walked into the foyer and stopped, put his hands on his hips and said, "Hey, there you are. We were going to start without you."

202

Sandra walked over to greet him. "Hello, Ted. Great to see you!"

Ted gave her a short pat on the back in his awkward hug. "Sandra, always a pleasure."

Andrew mirrored his father with hands on hips and faced him squarely but still about ten feet away. "Hey, Dad. Sorry, I was in New Jersey for a meeting with the Bulldogs. The GW was a mess."

Ted crossed his arms, "Why didn't you take the Palisades and cross over the Tap?"

"It's called the Mario Cuomo Bridge now."

"Yeah, whatever. The Bulldogs, huh?" Ted took a moment, then noticed the bruising on Andrew's face and pointed at him. "What happened to your face? Did they try *you* out at quarterback or something?"

"No, I uh…" Andrew stammered.

Helena jumped in, rubbing her son's arm. "He got mugged, Ted."

"Mugged? How'd that happen?"

"I got jumped outside the TISEC. They only got some cash."

"Well, glad you're okay."

"Tha… thanks, Dad." Andrew was taken aback at a rare moment of empathy from his father.

"Because for a moment, I thought that the Bulldogs tried you out at quarterback. I mean, they already have one 40-year-old quarterback. Why not have another? And after that choke in the playoffs, what they really need is a foot in the ass, and not some, 'let's all get in touch with our feelings' guy." Ted made a set of jazz hands trying to gesture his opinions on football players with feelings.

Andrew could feel his face burn. "Dad, pro sports is as mental as it is physical. You ought to know that. Golf is one of the most mental games out there."

The women squirmed, Sandra looking down, arms crossed, and Helena slowly wrung her hands. The grandfather clocks chimed as if Big Papa was reaching out to his daughter to warn her about the storm brewing in her foyer.

Ted talked over the first two chimes. "Oh, you're going to tell me about golf being a mentally tough game? It's simple, son—either you believe you can make the shot, or you believe you can't. I didn't need someone patting me on the back every time I did my job." The clock had chimed three more times by the time Ted was done.

Andrew snapped back for the final two chimes, "Oh, so the applause from the fans, wasn't *that* validation?"

Helena put up her hands like a boxing referee, ready to break up a clinch, and in a sing-songy but stressed voice announced, "Dinner's ready! Everyone, please take your seats in the dining room."

The two men walked into the dining room, neither giving ground. Helena rolled her eyes at Sandra, who tried to contain a laugh. She intertwined her arm in Sandra's, and they walked behind the two combatants.

Inside the dining room, they ate their dinner while over the next hour, Ted monopolized the conversation. The grandfather clock in the foyer chimed eight times while Ted added a new conversational thread, "So we got that upfront payment I demanded from Epic Golf. I'm sure Brandon told you all about it."

"No, we haven't spoken in a while," Andrew said.

Ted continued, "Yeah, well Epic is a startup brand of golf clubs and clothing. A so-called 'golf lifestyle brand,' whatever the hell that means."

Sandra interjected, "Yes, I've heard of them. Their PR Firm is Vault PR out of Norwalk. I guess since you're a local celeb, they asked you to be a spokesperson."

Helena reacted, "They're right here in Norwalk? Why doesn't Roxanne work with them?"

Sandra shrugged. "We were invited to pitch them, but Roxanne passed because she didn't know any of their board members."

"Oh, I see," Helena said in a subdued tone.

Andrew read Helena's face and tone and it reinforced his belief that Roxanne's narcissistic behavior would not allow her to lose to anyone, especially in her own backyard. So if it wasn't going to be a sure thing, she didn't want to risk the embarrassment of pitching and then not getting the deal.

Ted flicked his cloth napkin as if giving himself a white flag to proceed lapping the table. "So as I was saying, I got a big upfront payment like I demanded—"

"Dad, sometimes those upfront payments come with some pretty hefty strings attached."

"I know. I know. Brandon handled all the legal stuff."

"Brandon is a good generalist, but this sponsorship work can be tricky. I work with Steve Gotski. I can have him take a look at the contract for you if you want."

Ted looked up towards the upside-down pyramid layered chandelier, "Gotski, Gotski, where do I know that name? Oh yeah, he's one of those 'super agents.' Nah, those guys are sharks."

"Dad, he's Harvard Law," Andrew rebutted. "He looks at sponsorship deals every day for his clients, several of whom are also *my* clients."

Ted shot back, "Brandon is Stanford Law, my alma mater—and it should have been yours too, buddy! Anyway, it has a much better sports law program. Brandon knows what he's doing." Ted dug back into his food.

Andrew shrugged and did the same. "It's your funeral."

Ted, in mid chew, jabbed his fork in Andrew's direction. "I've been in this business since you were in diapers, kid. I can handle a bunch of Texas hillbillies. I got everything I asked for."

"I hope so."

"Helena, I thought Brandon and Jennifer were joining us," Sandra asked, trying to break the tension in the room.

Helena wiped her mouth before responding. "No, today was the first day of Robert's pee-wee soccer practice. He made the travel team. Brandon was so excited and—"

Ted shouted out, "My grandson, the soccer star! Well, we all know the athletic genes skipped a generation there. Hah?!"

"Ted, please!" Helena objected.

"Ah, come on, Brandon is a good lawyer and manager, but an athlete he ain't. So Robert's soccer genes had to come from somewhere. I'm just being honest. Can't blame me for that."

Andrew looked over and smiled at his frowning mother, "Mom, the salmon was amazing."

Sandra added, "Yes, and Helena, the julienne vegetables were a work of art. I almost felt guilty eating them, they were so pretty." The table, except for Ted, chuckled.

Helena smiled gratefully, "Thank you, dears. Sandra, I can show you how I did it. Martha showed me a few tricks in the kitchen."

Sandra inquired, "Martha Stewart?"

Helena replied, "Yes, well, we have some friends in common. Both being Barnard Alumni and all."

Ted clanked his fork on his plate and shifted his arm over the back of the chair, "Hey, Andrew, you remember your Great Aunt Beverly Beck?"

"The one with the gigantic Beach House in Westport?"

"That's the one."

Andrew turned to his wife, "Sandra, most of her backyard was sand, but if you tracked in one little pebble into the house, she threatened to have Gates the butler beat us."

Sandra looked confused. "Why would she have the butler beat you?"

Ted interjected loudly, "Because it was beneath her to do anything physical. Anyway Sandra, the point is, old battle-ax Aunt Bev, she's a teddy bear compared to Martha."

The table except for Helena laughed, but she did bow her chin to cover her grin. Then she added, "Martha's not that bad. You just have to understand where she is coming from."

Andrew let Helena have her moment and then shot her a smile. "Thanks again, Mom. It was wonderful."

Helena returned the smile, "You're welcome, dear. Glad you both could come by."

Sandra got up and collected the dishes. "Let me help, Helena."

"Oh, you're a darling. Andrew, you be good to this girl. She's a keeper."

"Yes, she is!" Andrew blew Sandra a kiss.

In the kitchen, Helena said, "Let me show you how to cut those vegetables."

"That would be great!" Sandra replied.

Helena poked her head back in the dining room. "Oh, and Ted, now that you have some food in your stomach, please take your Zestril."

Ted waved his wife off. "Yeah, yeah."

Andrew looked at his father, concerned. "Zestril, that's an Angio-tensin-Converting Enzyme Inhibitor."

"They're all overreacting, as usual. My doctor just likes having a famous patient. But I have to keep these pills on me in case of an emergency." Ted used air quotes around the word "emergency" and shook the pill bottle so Andrew could hear the pills rattle inside.

"If you're taking an ACE, then are you at risk for a heart attack?"

"Oh, are you a heart doctor now?" Ted snapped.

"They're called cardiologists. I know what an ACE is used for."

Ted looked away from Andrew, breaking eye contact. But in the next moment, he jerked his head, leaned on the table towards Andrew, and gave him a stare down. "So, you ready for your yearly thrashing on Sunday?"

Andrew didn't budge. "I'll be there at 7:30 sharp."

Ted shook his head. "No, 9:30."

Andrew looked incredulous. "I thought the first tee-time was 7:30?"

"Yeah, but they gave it to Davey Redbank. He has a senator and one of her donors coming to play. Can you believe that shit?"

Andrew looked down at the table and grabbed his head with both hands, "Shit! Sandra and I have to meet with Francois at one."

"Who the fuck is Francois?"

"He's an interior decorator. He's really difficult to get an appointment with."

"Why do *you* need to go see an interior decorator? Your mother always handled those things for me."

"Because I'm not you, and Sandra isn't mom. We make decisions together. Anyway, I have to be there at one. It won't be enough time."

Ted flung his hands upward in disgust. "Jesus Christ, you're a pain in the ass."

"I'll call Mr. Donohue, see if I can change the time. Give me a sec."

Ted turned his head away from Andrew and added sarcastically, "Donohue said no, but you go ahead."

Andrew pulled out his phone, pressed the side button, and spoke into the phone, "Siri call Tom Donohue, mobile."

Siri replied, "Calling Tom Donohue, mobile." The phone rang.

Ted jutted his chin out to Andrew and tried to peer at his phone, "Why does your Siri have an English accent?"

Andrew sat up. "Mr. Donohue? It's Andrew Beck."

Ted put his forearm on the table and leaned into it as he eavesdropped on Andrew's conversation. Andrew remarked, "I'm good, thank you. I heard you gave our traditional 7:30 club opening tee time to Davey Redbank and a State Senator?"

Ted peered more closely, watching Andrew for any clues.

"I understand, Mr. Donohue. Which Senator is it? Oh, you don't know? Hold on a second, will you please?" Andrew muted his phone and yelled into the kitchen, "Sandra! Who is our senator that represents Greenwich?"

Sandra shouted back from the kitchen, "Senator Theresa Mann! She's up for re-election in November. I've been trying to convince Mom we should repre—"

Andrew politely interrupted her, "Thank you, darling." Andrew unmuted his phone and continued his conversation. "Mr. Donohue, my lovely wife has just informed me that Theresa Mann is the Senator that Davey is playing with. Did you know she is up for reelection this November?"

Ted shrugged his shoulders as Andrew held up one finger to his dad and winked, "Well, I'll tell you why it matters. What if you tell Davey Redbank that if she arrives at 9:00 for a 9:30 tee time, not only does she get to sleep in, but that you arranged that Ted Beck, Masters Champion, will take a photo with her, Davey, *and* her donor. And let Davey know it was your idea." Andrew grinned. "What do you say?"

Ted barked, "Hey, it's your brother's job to pimp me out, not yours."

Andrew covered the phone, shushed his father, "What do you say, Mr. Donohue? Come on, we will be at the turn by nine and you know that 7:30 am tee time is a Beck tradition…"

Under his breath, Ted said petulantly, "Don't you shush me. I'm your father."

Andrew waited and then rose out of his chair and opened his hand as if ready to make a fist pump. He let out a grin, made the fist pump, and enthusiastically replied, "Great! I'm sure Davey and the Senator won't mind when they get their pic with Masters Champion Ted Beck. Thank you, Mr. Donohue. Remember, this was *your* idea." Grinning, Andrew finished the call. "Great! See you Sunday." Andrew hung up the phone and tossed it on the table looking very self-satisfied.

Ted shook his head and pointed at Andrew, winking one eye, "Man, you are slick. You should have been a used car salesman."

Andrew shrugged. "I got the job done."

"Yeah, by selling me out."

"Ah, come on, you love this publicity stuff. One picture and we get to play at the time we want. It's a good deal."

Ted looked away and shrugged in resolution.

Andrew swallowed hard while Ted wasn't looking and tapped the table lightly. "So anyway, I need a favor from you."

Ted threw his hands up. "Jesus Christ! What else do I got to do for you? Man, you just take and take."

Andrew didn't break eye contact and didn't give in to the shame tactic but stayed quiet until Ted spoke. "What then?"

Andrew sat up straight in his chair and stopped tapping. "Like I said earlier, I met with Ron Davis, the GM of the Bulldogs, and turns out he's…he's a fan of yours."

Ted beamed. "Ha! How about that?"

"Yes, how about that. And I invited him and Matt Grayson to play a round of golf with us."

Ted looked up again at the chandelier, "Oh, yeah, Matt's with the Bulldogs now." Ted suddenly got a big grin on his face and leaned his forearm back on the table, pointing his finger at Andrew. "Did I ever tell you when Coach Jimmy and I played against Jim Brown and OJ Simpson in a celebrity match?" Not waiting for a response, Ted added, "Man, that was fun…"

"Dad! Please focus. Will you play with us after the draft? It would help me out."

Ted tilted his head and leaned back in his chair, "Ah, I don't know, Andrew. I have to check my schedule. Your brother keeps me pretty busy."

There was an uncomfortable silence as Andrew didn't speak and just focused on the ticking of the grandfather clock one tick at a time. He played the waiting game. Ted sat up in his chair and looked at his son, "But if you need me to close this deal for you, son, I'm sure I can ask your brother to move some things around and free up an afternoon. But, hey, lunch and the drinks are on you, buddy boy!"

Andrew forced a smile. "Sure, Dad. Whatever you want. Thanks."

The wonderful meal his mother cooked was now boiling in an acid pit in his stomach. He felt like puking. He focused again on the ticking of the grandfather clock until it seemed to be ticking in rhythm with the thumping of his heart, and it was the only thing he could hear in the room.

26

Ted and Helena stood on the stone stairs outside their red door with Helena waving good-bye to her son and daughter-in-law as they crunched down the sandstone driveway to Andrew's Lexus. "Good night!" Helena called. "Get home safe!"

This made Andrew laugh as he turned to his mother and exclaimed, "Mom, we're two miles away."

Helena retorted, "Well, you know what they say! Most accidents happen within a mile of your home."

"Yes, that's because statistically there is a hundred percent chance of you being within a mile of your house every time you get in your car."

"Hey, don't be a wiseass!" Ted added with genuine annoyance. "Anyway, your mother has seen you drive."

Ted's comment made Sandra grin. In a low voice so only Andrew could hear her, she said, "Gotta point there." She followed it with a short chuckle.

Andrew tried his best not to laugh, and under his breath, he playfully admonished his wife. "Oh, hush you."

Andrew gave a final wave as he clicked his key fob to open the door to a high pitch beep and yelled out to his parents, "Good night!"

Sandra did the same, elevating her voice equally. "Good night, Ted! Good night, Helena. Thank you again! It was wonderful."

Helena gave one final wave as Ted went inside.

Andrew drove slowly down the driveway. He listened to the car's tires crunching the sandstones. The sound brought him almost the same satisfaction as walking on them.

Sandra broke the silence of Andrew's moment in the crunches. "Well, that was pretty painless, wasn't it?"

Andrew looked at his wife and raised an eyebrow. "Up until the point when I had to eat that huge helping of humble pie."

"I heard most of it. What is it with him? Why must he rub your face in the mud?"

Andrew shrugged silently.

"When is he going to forgive you for walking away from golf?"

Andrew shot back, "What?! Forgive me?! Are you fucking kidding me?"

"I'm sorry, I…I didn't mean it like you did something wrong. Poor choice of words…"

"That fucking man tortured me. From the time I was five until I went to college, the only thing in my life was golf! GOLF, GOLF, GOLF! I NEVER HAD A FUCKING CHILDHOOD! FORGIVE ME?!"

"Please stop yelling at me. I said I was sorry."

Andrew rubbed his forehead and took a breath to compose himself. He tapped the steering wheel and looked at the oncoming road. "I apologize for raising my voice. You didn't deserve that. I was triggered, and I overreacted." He looked at his wife. "I'm sorry."

Sandra nodded and touched him gently on the arm. "I'm sorry too. I worded it poorly."

Andrew nodded and forced a smile. "It's been a rough week, sweetheart."

"I know." Sandra let the moment sit for a few seconds and added in an upbeat voice, "Well, tomorrow is Friday, and then we have the whole weekend to look forward to! Right?"

"Yeah. It's a busy sports weekend, but we should have some downtime."

"Hey, with everything that has happened to you, this week can't get any worse, right?"

They both chuckled—an attempt at levity—and shared a smile. Sandra continued to rub Andrew's arm. He increased his speed once he made the turn off Hawkwood Lane and onto North Street.

Their moment was abruptly interrupted by Sandra's phone ringing. Sandra looked down at the number and recognized it. "Oh, you mind if I take this? It's work."

"Not at all," Andrew replied gracefully.

Sandra answered her phone to a beep, "Wells Public Relations, Sandra Wells Speaking."

Andrew focused on the dark road but was eavesdropping on the call out of curiosity.

"Oh hey, Gary, everything okay?" Her face immediately became alarmed, "What?! Arrested? For murder? Okay, okay, I will have Annie from my office call you back in a few minutes. She'll get all the details, and I will be at the Union office first thing in the morning. We'll put together a statement for the press."

The caller continued and Sandra was instinctively nodding as she added, "Well if he's innocent, then that's the position we will take…" The caller interrupted. "…Okay, okay, just remain calm…Yes, I know about the negotiations with Keegan Construction, and while I agree it does give him motive, it's not proof. We'll spin it."

Oh, shit. I hope Keegan is just a popular name.

"Gary, Gary, listen to me. We'll handle it. I'm going to call Annie, and she'll call you right back and walk you through the process. Okay?" Sandra gave Gary a moment, and when she was satisfied, she wrapped up the call. "Great. I'll see you tomorrow."

Sandra didn't waste a second and used her voice activation on the phone to make a call. Andrew was burning with curiosity but asked about her call nonchalantly while Sandra's phone was ringing. Sandra put up a finger.

"Wait one sec, hon. Oh, hi, Annie, sorry to bother you so late." Sandra closed her eyes, and with her free hand, she made a tight fist and controlled her breathing and tone. "Can you call Gary at the Electrical Workers Union office? Anthony Corravallo was just arrested for the murder of Michael Keegan from Keegan Construction."

His first name was Michael. I didn't know that.

After a second for Annie to respond, Sandra added, "Yeah, they were negotiating the final Union contract, and I guess after the stunt he pulled yesterday, it got a little hostile."

Annie replied, which Sandra opened her eyes, released her close fist, and shrugged, "Yeah, no kidding."

Andrew's adrenaline began to pulse. It couldn't be a coincidence. *Fergus, you polished savage, what the fuck did you do?*

Sandra continued her call. "Yeah, get all the deets. I'll meet you at the Union's office tomorrow at nine. It's going to be a long day. And sorry, but our weekends are probably shot too." Sandra winced at her own words. "Ooh, yeah, sorry, poor word choice." She looked up at the night sky through the moonroof, tapped her chin and added, "I keep doing that tonight. Anyway, talk to you later." Sandra hung up.

"So, what was that all about?" Andrew asked, his tone as casual as can be — as he'd only overheard discussion of some mundane matter.

Sandra went into explanation mode, increasing the pace of her speech. "The head guy of the Electrical Workers Union 72 negotiating team, Anthony Corravallo, was arrested on suspicion of murdering this Michael Keegan, the guy who owns the construction company whose crew is working on one of the tower buildings in Hudson Yards overlooking the TISEC"

"What was the motive?"

"Keegan kicked all the union's electrical workers off the job and replaced them with scabs. But Gary says Corravallo didn't murder him."

"Does Corravallo have an alibi?"

"I don't know. The police found Keegan down on the South Street pier bound in a chair and shot through the eye, yuck! The police found the murder weapon caught in some netting just off the pier. It looks like he tried to throw the gun in the water, but the netting caught it. It had Corravallo's prints all over it. It doesn't look good. Corravallo swears he is being framed."

"Wow!"

Sandra added, "But honestly, don't they *all* say that?"

Andrew took a breath and shrugged, "Yeah, it would take some kind of criminal genius to frame someone like that."

"If he were framed, it would have to be by someone who disliked both Corravallo and Keegan. I guess they pissed off the wrong guy."

"Yeah."

Definitely the wrong fucking guy.

Andrew felt his hands shaking. He put them on top of each other so Sandra wouldn't notice. He hit the gas pedal, reaching 63 mph as he passed a white street sign posting the speed limit as 35 mph.

Part 5: Friday, April 12, 2019

27

The muffled sounds of trucks, cars, buses and their horns penetrated the windows in Andrew's office, where he sat in his usual black leather Eames lounge chair, holding his iPad and Apple Pencil, tapping it gently on the screen. Lamar paced back and forth, speaking excitedly and proudly about his performance on Wednesday. But Andrew's mind was switching back and forth from Mr. Keegan to Fergus, replaying the gunshot he had heard over and over in his mind. *It was a gunshot, right? It must have been a gunshot.*

"And I was all over Brown's shit!" Lamar said. There was a swagger in his stride, and he had a way of nodding his head when his confidence was up like he was listening to funky music. Lamar's excited tone brought Andrew back to being present as Lamar added, "Triple double, man. Did you see the numbers I put up?"

"I did."

Lamar continued with a fist pump, "I was in the zone, DB!"

"Yes, you were," Andrew replied robotically. Andrew was able to refocus, but when he looked at Lamar, who had stopped pacing, the stare he was giving Andrew unnerved him. He felt like he just got caught daydreaming at a red light after it just turned green.

"Hey, Doc, you okay?"

Andrew shifted in his seat and craned his neck to look up at his six-foot six patient. "Yeah, why?"

Lamar took a seat, so they were eye-to-eye, and leaned over with his legs in a man-spread. "Well, you got a game face on today. I mean, I know your face is a little fucked up and all, from the beatdown. But usually you're asking me some of that 'feeling stuff' or 'what does that mean for me' shit. You ain't doing that today."

"That's a fair and astute observation, Lamar. It's been a tough week. Please continue, I'm with you."

But he wasn't. As hard as he tried to focus, Andrew was trying to walk the week backward to find out the moment when his life had spun completely out of control. He blinked the thoughts away and tried to refocus.

Lamar sat on the couch and crossed his giant leg, putting his foot just over his knee to make a figure four with his leg. He then spread his long arms across the couch, almost touching both sides with his massive wingspan. He turned his head and looked outside for a moment. "You know, DB, I know what it's like to get beat up."

Andrew decided writing notes wouldn't work as he was fighting his distraction, so he hit the Record button on the Otter.io app, knowing he could listen to the session later.

"I can't imagine anyone beating you up."

Lamar shot him a look. "Fuck, not now, DB. What, you think I was born like this? Damn."

"So as a boy?"

"Yeah, man."

"Who was it? The kids at school?"

"Nah, I had those motherfuckers in my pocket. Basketball got me through a lot of it. Being a good baller made you popular and no one fucked with you. You know what I'm saying?"

"So where, at home?"

Lamar brought his arms back in, uncrossed his legs. His gaze went downward as his voice dropped. "Yeah, my moms...she uh. She was never around, you know? After my pops got killed, she was moving from guy to guy. She let a few bad motherfuckers in that shitty-ass Baltimore apartment." Lamar shifted uncomfortably in his seat and his hands balled into fists. "One of them, Harmon, his street name was 'Arm and Hammer'. He had big fucking arms, and when he hit motherfuckers it was like a hammer."

"Did he ever hit you?"

Lamar had a tough time maintaining eye contact but continued his story. "One time Moms and Arm and Hammer were drunk. Moms drank a lot during those days. She was passed out. I was watching MJ when he played in D.C." Lamar's eyes got big as if he just remembered something very important and looked Andrew dead in the eye. "Did you know that in Michael Jordan's last two seasons he was still averaging over 20 points per game? Fucking amazing, right?" Lamar forgot his place and tried to recall, "Where was I?"

"Your mother was passed out."

"Yeah, so I'm watching the game, and fucking Arm and Hammer says he wants to watch a bootleg boxing video of Lennox Lewis beating Mike Tyson. So I said no, the game is live, and you can watch the tape anytime."

"How did he react?"

Lamar buried his fist in the other hand. "That motherfucker said that the VCR at his house was broke so he wanted to watch it on ours. And what I want doesn't fucking matter because whenever he's here, *he's* the man of the house."

"How did that go over?"

"Not too fucking good. So, I took my 10-year-old body and put it in front of the TV and VCR so he couldn't get the tape in." Lamar spread his arms out, recalling his motion. Lamar brought his arms back, he choked on his words, and closed his eyes for a moment. "So he backhanded me. I knew why they called him Arm and Hammer. You feeling me on this?"

Andrew rubbed his sore jaw and cut cheek. "Yeah, I am." Andrew started recalling the beating he took from Keegan, and the fear he felt when they were shooting at him returned with a vengeance. He skipped a few breaths and took a big inhale, trying not to hyperventilate.

Lamar looked at Andrew with surprise and put his hands up. "It's cool, Doc, it's cool, I'm good. Don't have a heart attack on me. Damn."

Andrew controlled his breathing and gave Lamar a quick nod. Lamar patted his massive legs and looked down at them as he continued his story. "Then I ran to my moms, tried to wake her up. She was still drunk, but then I asked her who was the man of the house, Harmon or me?"

Andrew waited as Lamar hesitated, and then he looked Andrew in the eye. "She didn't answer. All she said was..." Lamar imitated his mom's voice, feminine but low in pitch. "Just let him have it, baby. I'll buy you an ice cream tomorrow."

"Well, that's something, right?" Andrew tried to crack a smile.

Lamar snapped back, "No! I'm fucking lactose-intolerant, man! I couldn't eat no fucking ice cream. Moms knew that!" He looked away and then shrugged. "I don't know. Maybe she didn't. Every time I ate ice cream, I got stomach cramps and fucking farted like nobody's business, man. Fucking sucked, all the kids eating ice cream and all I got was a fucking red, white and blue bomb pop. Always a fucking bomb pop. Hate those fucking things, man. Ice hurt my teeth and gave me a headache. The shit melted all over my clothes and hands into a fucking sticky mess." Lamar hammer fisted the couch. "Hate that shit, man."

Andrew flinched at the hammer fist hitting the couch. He fumbled his iPad but caught it before Lamar noticed. Andrew needed to do something cerebral to get out of his body, so he tried to recap the conversation and focus on cognitive behavioral therapy techniques. "So you get hit, your mother ignores your question about the man of the house and then offers you something that will make you sick. How are you feeling right about now?"

"I was angry, DB, very fucking angry." Lamar clenched his fists.

"How did you deal with your anger?"

"I went to my room and, and laid down on my bed, and uh, I, I don't know." Lamar became visibly uncomfortable and shifted his body.

Andrew caught the shift and immediately called attention to it. "What? What was that, Lamar?"

"Nothing, man." He looked away out the grand floor-to-ceiling windows.

Andrew caught the shift in Lamar's body language and tone. It was as if his mind upshifted from third gear to fifth, leaving his distracting thoughts in a cloud of dust. He was completely focused on Lamar. He pointed his Apple Pencil at him and gave him a serious look and commanded, "No, no, no, you don't get off that easy. What did you do when you went to your room and laid down?"

Lamar continued to fidget, so Andrew shifted in his chair and scooted to its end, forcing his body forward towards Lamar. Andrew shifted his tone and softened his look as he prodded gently, "Come on, you called me out and said I wasn't asking you the hard questions. Now I am. What happened?"

Lamar couldn't keep eye contact. He looked outside at the blue April sky over Central Park and added softly, "Nah, it's embarrassing, man."

Andrew knew he was off his A-game, but he could draw on some well-practiced techniques to get himself mostly out of his head and into Lamar's. "Lamar, this is a safe space for you. Everything you tell me is just between you and me. Come on; you're doing so well."

Andrew saw Lamar's hesitancy as he pursed his lips and looked down and around the room, avoiding eye contact. Andrew tried to add some levity by pointing to his face. "Look at my fucked-up face. Give me some good shit today. It will make this pain go away."

The quip made Lamar laugh and he looked back at Andrew. "That's fucked up, DB. Man, you're one crazy-ass white boy."

"So I've been told."

Lamar paused and added, "I don't know, man."

Andrew sat firm and motionless, not breaking eye contact and Lamar blinked. "All right, fuck it."

Andrew slapped his thigh. "Yeah, give it to me!"

Lamar started talking with his hands again. "I was laying down and I was picturing Michael Jordan and me playing in the game. He was wearing his usual number 23 and I was wearing my number 3. MJ was passing the ball to me, setting up picks for me and I was dribbling and swishing every shot." Lamar's eyes began to water, and he sniffed and took a deep breath and let it out. He looked back at Andrew. "Then as we were running back on defense, I would imagine MJ giving me a fist bump." Lamar rubbed his eyes and his voice cracked, "And, every time, after every basket he would say, 'You're the man Lamar, you're the man.' I scored 32 points in that game...in my head." Lamar took some deep breaths and after wiping his eyes, he stiffened his arms against his knees, forcing his shoulders to shrug.

Andrew let Lamar sit with his feelings, giving him steady nods and keeping eye contact, even though Lamar's eyes darted away. "Thank you for sharing that, Lamar. Really good work. Not having a father at such a young age is hard for a boy. So kids adapt, they improvise, they find a hero like Michael Jordan. Someone to look up to. Harmon not only told you that you weren't important, but he put his hands on you too. By doing this, he reinforced your need for a father-figure, someone to protect you. So as a child you retreated to the only safe place you knew: your imagination. It's a perfectly normal coping strategy. Also, visualization is a common practice we've done together. Remember a few months ago when you were concerned that your rebounds had gone down to less than five per game? What did we do?"

"Oh yeah, I had to close my eyes and picture a shot and me boxing out and getting the rebound. You made me do it for like a fucking hour."

Andrew laughed. "Yeah... and the result?"

"Fucking 18 rebounds against Philly!"

"So let's bring it back to when you were a boy. I'm sure those visualizations helped you become the great player you are today."

Lamar perked up. "Really, that pretend shit made me a better basketball player?"

"One hundred percent, Lamar. But more importantly, you were able to develop a coping strategy as a young boy that helped you create confidence and improved your performance. I bet that same skill can be used today to help you make better decisions on and off the court."

"Wow, pretty cool, DB. So, I was like one of those child prodigies of the mind?"

"It looks like you have *always* been a legend in your own mind."

Andrew and Lamar both shared a laugh.

Andrew shifted in his seat, sitting back, and continued, "So, speaking of better decision making, how did your dinner go with Janice?"

Lamar let out a big grin, "It was great. We were, like, talking and shit. Like, really talking, you know what I mean? We were laughing, having fun. And she was loving Fieri's food. Great call, Doc." Lamar pointed at Andrew.

"Thanks."

"I kept hearing you in my head, "Don't fuck her, don't fuck her." But damn she was fine. You know how hard that shit was? Fuck. But you were right, dawg."

Andrew reached over to Lamar for a fist pound, "I'm proud of you, Lamar."

Lamar obliged the bump and as their two fists connected, Lamar took an unusually humble tone and smiled like when a player gets an attaboy from their coach. "I appreciate that, DB."

The two men sat there for a few seconds enjoying their moment, then Lamar started to rub one hand over a balled fist and leaned in.

"So, DB?"

"Yeah?"

"When can I fuck Janice?"

Andrew flopped back in his chair and grinned. "Ahh, you were so close."

* * * *

As the door to Andrew's office opened, Lamar's figure emerged and in just a few long steps he was at the front desk, where Gina greeted him with an enthusiastic smile and congratulated him on the good game. Gina set up his next few appointments, knowing full-well that Lamar would call Andrew any day at any time of night if he needed someone to talk to. It was part of the process when treating pro athletes whose professional and personal lives were in a pressure-filled goldfish bowl. They didn't work 9 to 5 jobs, and they were all multimillionaires, and when they needed help, they needed it stat.

Lamar hit the bell for the elevator, the door opened right away and as he entered, he threw up his two fingers and shouted out in a much deeper voice than usual. "Peace!"

Andrew closed the door to his office and carried a small briefcase with his iPad and a few other essentials. Gina quickly moved into logistics mode and walked him to the elevator, handing him his helicopter ticket and instructions to the Signature Aviation hangar at Teterboro.

Andrew put the documents in his bag and said, "Thanks, Gina. Let's hope JP has a good game and we start the year at two and oh. Get that ballbuster Rothstein off our backs."

As the elevator dinged and the door opened, Andrew imitated Lamar by throwing up his two fingers. He made his voice sound like Lamar's. "Peace!"

Andrew peeked his head out of the elevator doors before they closed on his head to catch Gina laughing, which made Andrew smile. The elevator opened in the parking lot and Andrew got in the black Town Car waiting for him. The driver turned and said in a rough sounding voice, "Hey, how ya doing?"

Andrew was taken aback at the bald-headed driver. Although he didn't look like Mr. Keegan, between the voice and the neatly shaven head, it was enough for Andrew to grab his chest. The driver's eyes widened at the reaction.

"Relax buddy, I ain't gonna shoot you in the head or nuthin'."

Andrew swallowed hard and laughed uncomfortably. "Yeah, sorry, you looked like someone I knew."

28

The sounds of the helicopter blades whirring were muffled, as was everything else, due to the headset Andrew was wearing. The headset allowed him to communicate with the pilot as well as serve as a protective barrier for the piercing sounds of the helicopter as it flew over the Hudson River to Teterboro Airport in Hasbrouck Heights, New Jersey.

Andrew looked down at the boats in the brown and brackish Hudson River. They looked like toys floating around in a giant bathtub. As they flew over the rising mound that was the Jersey side of the Lincoln Tunnel, the endless lines of cars one after another reminded him of worker ants returning to their nest. He was flying above it all, feeling his wealth, prestige, and life of privilege. He had it all, but what was happening to him? It was all starting to unravel.

Just a few seconds later, he flew over Meadowlands Stadium, and he recalled his pitch to Ron Davis of the Bulldogs and wondered if he would get the work. With each team having 63-man rosters, the Professional Football League hosted the most brutal of American prime-time sports. With such a large number of players on each team, he knew there were all sorts of opportunities. From the quarterback, defensive lineman, running back to even the place kicker, every player experienced performance anxiety. But some players carried real mental health issues too. Depression, anger, addiction to pain killers, and even severe side effects from repeated concussions or Chronic Traumatic Encephalopathy (CTE). These issues would never be professionally addressed by the coaches or the front office. Football was the most profitable of all professional team sports, which meant they had the most to gain by getting their players to perform, and the most to lose if they couldn't. In short, they would do anything to win.

Just like me.

As he was replaying the pitch in his mind, he felt his face burn at having to ask his father to play golf with Ron to help close the deal. All during the week, Ted kept making an appearance in his work, in his life, and even in his near-murder experience on the pier. He wondered if he would ever break free of the choke hold Ted had on him. Walking away from golf wasn't enough. It bought him the time and space to pursue his degree, build his practice and make his own life out of the vast shadow that Ted cast. But somehow, he was back in it.

Andrew was one of the top sports psychologists in the country. He had some of the biggest names in sports working with him, yet Ted always seemed to be lurking somewhere as if Andrew was a quarterback and Ted a free safety blitzing untouched into the backfield and landing a blindside hit on him at full force. The thought made the soreness in his ribs throb.

A few moments later, the helicopter touched down gently onto the tarmac at Teterboro. The man opened the door with one hand holding down the brim of his Captain's hat and yelling over the whirring blades. The pilot, William, pointed to their plane and the two men walked about fifty yards where a Hawker 800 jet awaited them.

Andrew hopped up the four small steps to the plane and made sure to duck his head getting in. When he was on those small steps of a private jet, it was always this moment that it hit him he wasn't flying commercial. Something about how the steps moved slightly underfoot, and how he had to duck his head to get into the cabin sent his synapses firing that this was something different.

Once in the cabin, Andrew had to keep his six-foot frame bent as the cabin height was five feet nine inches high. He turned his body to avoid hitting the other seats as he walked almost sideways down the narrow aisle to one of the plush white leather seats. He sat and strapped his buckle with a neat click. As the pilots were going over their preflight checklist, William spoke over the com system and told Andrew that they needed to get their clearance and runway number, and then they would be wheels up in just a few minutes. William let him know that he should arrive in Miami around 7:40 p.m.

Andrew looked out onto the tarmac, and uneasiness overtook him. In an instinctual response, he took his phone and texted Gina to give him a status about the car pickup in Miami. Although Gina always had the T's crossed, and I's dotted on everything she did, covering logistics was a quick way to get him back in his head and away from the guilt, shame, and anxiety he was feeling about his life right now. However, the fact he was in a $2.2 million jet and flew in a helicopter saving him an hour car ride in bumper-to-bumper rush hour traffic, somehow didn't help his state of mind.

He hit send to a whooping sound on his phone. Three bubbles popped up on Andrew's phone, noting Gina was replying, but then they stopped and instead Gina's caller ID was displayed. He immediately answered the phone, hearing a huffing and hard breathing sound.

Gina spoke first and in rapid succession, "Hey Boss, I'm out for a run, so easier to talk. Got you covered. The car will bring you into the players' entrance. I spoke with Rafael, nice guy. He'll meet you at the VIP entrance and bring you to Darryl Jenkins' seats in the owner's box."

Andrew then heard car tires screech loudly, followed by an extended car horn. Gina screamed, "I'm running here, asshole! Pay the fuck attention!" The driver replied with another long and loud beep, to which Gina shot back, "Oh yeah?! Go fuck your mother!"

The shrill horn caused Andrew to nearly jump out of his seat. "Shit! You okay?"

"Yeah, why?"

Andrew's stomach dropped and he thought the plane had lost altitude, but when he looked out the window, he saw they were still on the ground. He pulled his hair and asked, "Hey, can you pay attention to the Sentinels game tonight? I want to see how Vlad does. Just text me with anything important, like if he gets into a fight, scores a goal, or makes a big defensive play."

Gina replied, "I'm on it. I'll take my little southern belle out for ribs. She loves her some ribs. And she won't mind me peeking up at the game."

Andrew felt the plane rumble as it prepared for takeoff. He felt tense. He had flown private many times, but today he was a jumble of nerves.

"The plane is about to take off."

"Text me when you get to MIA." Gina softened her tone in between huffs. "And take a nap. You need some rest."

"Yeah." Andrew felt his body feel heavy in his seat and then added, "Have a good run and watch out for cars."

He clicked off and felt the plane moving. It was like suddenly, all of his senses had amplified. The jet engine pitch was much higher than a commercial jet and it stung his ears. He could feel the speed of the jet force his body back into his seat, and then in a few seconds, the plane left the ground. He felt the g-force of the aircraft much more, and his stomach rumbled, so he tried to distract himself by staring out the window at the passing Bergen County, New Jersey suburbs. Unfortunately, the speed at which they were passing gave him vertigo, and he thought he might get airsick. He swallowed down whatever was rising from his stomach, closed his eyes to stop the vertigo and put in his Air Pods to play some music. But all he could hear was the aircraft engines as he screeched through a blue sky with a patchwork of puffy white clouds beneath him.

He turned on some of Sandra's spa music that she loaded on his phone and tried to settle into the ride.

Breathe, Andrew, breathe!

He felt his breathing starting to normalize and opened his eyes, and looked outside at the quickly disappearing Jersey shore as the plane made its way out to higher skies over the Atlantic. The vertigo was gone. But his stomach was still a mess. He thought he was hungry, but the thought of eating anything right now made him even more nauseous.

He yelled up to the captain to see if they had any Scotch on board. William said they had a bottle of Johnnie Walker Black on board. Andrew winced and chided himself for not packing his emergency flask of Macallan 18. This was certainly an emergency. Andrew acquiesced to the Scotch, and the copilot brought him a glass. He had put ice cubes in it, which made Andrew grimace. The copilot noticed.

"Is everything okay, Dr. Beck?"

"I usually prefer it neat, but it's okay. This is fine." He forced a smile.

The copilot nodded and went back to his seat. Andrew took a sip, but the burn was not the same, the ice cubes had diluted the Scotch enough to affect the taste and along with it not being his favorite, he put the glass down and pushed it away. He had teased himself, hoping the Scotch would take the edge off, but now there was an 80-proof liquid on a collision course with the nausea in his stomach. This might not be such a good thing.

Andrew closed his eyes, focused on the new-age music, and tried to settle his mind and body. Here he was on a private jet headed for Miami. He would sit with his good friend and hall of fame shortstop legend Daryl Jenkins, be moral support for John Palmer, and hopefully watch him win the game. But these thoughts did nothing to relax him. Even in a plane, he had all to himself.

What is wrong with me? Gina's right; maybe a little nap will help.

Andrew clicked his seat back a few more notches and pulled up the footrest. The Hawker 800 inclined rapidly into the blue April sky, and Andrew's ears became muffled. Instead of trying to equalize the pressure, he found himself ignoring the sitar music playing and listening to his heartbeat. He took a couple of deep breaths and continued to listen to the *ker-thump, ker-thump, ker-thump* as he drifted off into a dream state.

29

Andrew dreamt he was in the Players Room at The Five Iron, replaying his last game with Mr. Davidson.

Mr. Davidson looked at Andrew as he exclaimed, "Well, it's just you and me, kid. Here, I'll make it easy on you."

Mr. Davidson pushed some chips in the pot and called his bet, saying, "A hundred thousand."

Andrew replied, "Ah, come on Mr. D, no one gets luck like that. I'm gonna call."

"What do you mean by that?"

"Nothing, I mean if you got a straight flush right from the turn, that's a hell of a hand. I'd like to see luck like that."

"You trying to use some of that reverse psychology on me, huh? You don't think I'm lucky? Is that it?"

"No, Mr. D, I didn't mean any disrespect. I'm sorry."

"I'm all-in!" Mr. Davison loudly slammed all his chips on the table. He regained his composure and added, "Hey kid, last night was your night. Tonight is mine! So why don't you be a good boy, save yourself some money and just quit. Tonight, you're the loser!"

"What did you say?"

Andrew heard the word repeat, echoing: *Loser…loser…. loser…*

Andrew then saw Ted walk up behind Mr. Davidson, rest his arm on his shoulder, and snap, "Yeah, the old man is right. Just quit, because that's what losers do, they quit. Loser! Loser!"

Andrew yelled back, but he heard his voice not as a man but when he was a 14-year-old. "I'm not a loser!" He cleared his throat, trying to recover his adult voice. It came back. "Well, you know what, Mr. Davidson? There is no way you have that ten of diamonds. Which means you don't have that straight flush. I'm all-in." Andrew pushed all his chips in and glanced at a gloating Ted and angry Mr. Davidson. "And you know why I know that?"

Mr. Davidson shot back, "Why?!"

Ted repeated, "Yeah, why?!"

Andrew leaned over the table and glared. "Because there is no day on this Earth when I would ever let a sad sack like you let your ordinary straight beat my full house." Andrew slammed his cards on the table.

Ted and Mr. Davidson both leaned over to peer at the cards. Mr. Davidson yelled, "You piece of shit! You goddamned piece of shit! That was my pot! Mine!"

Andrew started gathering the chips, which seemed endless. He couldn't grab them all. There were too many, spilling off the table, spilling into his lap, slipping between his fingers. "Well, now it's mine, so go fuck off and die, Dad."

Mr. Davidson looked up at Ted and growled back, "Dad? Dad?! I'd rather father monkeys than a goddamn mind-fucking Judas like you." He then asked Ted, "How come you didn't just put a pillow over his face when he was a baby and get rid of this bad seed?"

Ted looked at Mr. Davidson and wagged his finger. "You know, that would have been a good idea. The biggest disappointment in my life, that little shit over there."

Andrew could feel his anger seething, and he stated in a low but firm voice, "I think George will be wanting to see you now."

Mr. Davidson took a fearful breath as George appeared from out of nowhere, and as he eye-balled Ted, Ted put his hands in a "hand-up" position and retreated in fear. George put his heavy hand on Mr. Davidson's shoulder. Mr. Davidson looked up at the behemoth next to him, then looked back to Andrew, and said, "Yeah, well, I guess it's time to pay the piper. Be seeing ya, kid."

Mr. Davidson disappeared, and Andrew was still struggling to gather the ever-growing pile of chips when he could hear in the distance sounds of punches thrown and landing and Mr. Davidson yelping in pain. But those sounds faded into the sounds of the East River lapping against the South Street Pier. The sound of a buoy bell ringing grew louder and louder.

Andrew could hear not only the buoy bell, the East River crashing against the pier but now his heartbeat as well, beating faster as he felt himself walking at an accelerated pace. He then noticed he was walking next to Lorry as she glared at him and scowled in her Scottish brogue, "Saving your arse is beginning to be a full-time job. One I prefer not to have."

Andrew looked at her and pronounced, "I'll be good from now on."

Lorry returned, "I doubt it." But she gave him a sly smile as the glare disappeared. Lorry leaned into the open window of the black Town Car and said, "Driver, take Dr. Beck wherever he wants to go."

Andrew got in the car, lowered the window, and called out to Lorry as she was walking away, "Lorry!"

She stopped and turned, "Yeah?"

"I love you."

Lorry smiled and looked back at him, "Yeah, you do."

"No, no, I mean I *owe* you," Andrew said shaking his head, trying to correct himself.

The car sped off as Lorry turned and walked towards the pier. Andrew pushed the button to roll up the window and heard the pop of gunfire. The shots then got louder as they repeated—again and again, each shot getting louder and louder until he suddenly heard his phone ringing.

Andrew shook awake and let out a "Fuck!" He glanced down at the phone and saw the ID was John Palmer. He hit the green button to answer it.

"JP?" In the background, Andrew could hear the stadium organs playing and an announcer calling the batting line-up. Andrew figured John was in the bullpen warming up.

John enthusiastically called out, "Hey Doc, you on the plane?"

"Yeah, I was having a wonderful nap too." Andrew rubbed his

eyes and set the leather seat down, so his feet touched the floor of the plane.

"Sorry about that." John sounded sincere.

Andrew shifted, worried about anything that might get John distracted from pitching. "Ah, just busting your chops. How you feeling?"

"I feel good. My control was good in my warm-up pitches and my cutter is moving nicely."

"That's awesome. Stay in the game, not in your head, okay? If things get rough, just go back to playing catch with Wilson like we practiced."

John hesitated for a second and lowered his voice as he asked, "What do I do if I, uh, you know…"

Andrew interjected, "You say your affirmation." He paused. "John, you know ghosts aren't real, right?"

"Yeah, I know."

"Okay then. I'll be there by first pitch."

John hesitated again and then pleaded, "Can you tell Mr. Rothstein how good we're doing?"

Andrew rebuked, "I'm not sitting with the Tides."

That caught John by surprise. "No? Where you sitting?"

"With Darryl Jenkins," Andrew said proudly.

"In the Surf's box? What the fuck, Doc?"

"Relax, Darryl and I go way back. Plus the food is better." Andrew grinned as he said it.

"Okay, but you better make a lot of noise in the box when I strike out their fucking guys."

"I will be a complete pain in the ass. I promise."

This made John laugh and the tension dropped. "Yeah, you will."

"All right, buddy, get your head in the game. I'll be there for you. Okay?"

"Thanks, Doc."

Andrew pulled the phone away from his face to hang up, but he heard John speak. "Oh wait, Doc?"

Andrew put the phone quickly back to his ear. "Yeah?"

"How's the Hawker? Nice, right?"

Andrew let out a small laugh. "Yeah, thanks. But uh, JP, sorry to burst your bubble, but this isn't the first time I've flown private."

John returned the laugh. "No, of course not. Well, see you soon!"

They both hung up and Andrew could hear the Hawker 800 engines revving. He peered out the window, and through the white clouds and the darkening sky, he could barely see the dark blue water beneath him. There was nothing but water for as far as he could see.

Andrew heard the pilot over the intercom, "Dr. Beck, we will be landing in a little less than an hour. Can we get you anything?"

"No thank you, I'm good."

As Andrew continued to stare out at the blacking sky, his phone rang again. It was still in his hand so when he saw it was Gina he hit the green answer button in a quick second, barely enough time for the phone to vibrate a second time. Andrew could hear a loud commotion in the background and between his ears having altitude clog he had to shout. "Hey Gina, what's up?"

Gina shouted over the crowd and sounded concerned. "Andrew! Thank God I got you."

"What happened?"

Gina tried to explain as her voice elevated, "Vlad went ape shit on this guy on the Boston Freedom. I don't know who it was, but it took all four refs to pull him off the guy. They took the poor fucker out on a stretcher. He fucking lost it!"

Andrew's phone started buzzing and he pulled the phone away from his face to see who it was. "Oh fuck, it's Riley Asherton. I gotta take this."

"Good luck."

Andrew clicked over to his other caller. "Hey Riley, I just heard…"

Riley interrupted screaming at Andrew, "Holy fuck, Beck! What did you do? He went fucking mental on Teddy Newsome! I mean, Newsome is a fucking instigator, but holy shit, they carted him out on a fucking stretcher. I hope Poplov didn't kill the guy!"

Andrew pulled the phone away from his ear during the rant and tipped the phone so his mouth was facing the microphone. "Where is Vlad now?"

"In the locker room. They threw him out of the game. The league might suspend him! The playoffs are in two fucking weeks!"

"Riley, calm down. We will get this sorted out..."

"You need to get down here right now and take charge of this fiasco!"

"Riley, I'm on a plane to Miami."

"I don't care if you are on a fucking spaceship to Mars. It's your fucking mess, and you clean it up!"

"My mess!?"

"Well, he meets with you once, you do your whole hokey-pokey, turn-your-mind-around shit and Vlad becomes a murdering psychopath!?"

"That is not how therapy works, Riley. We had a good discussion. Yes, we brought up some of his past violence, which definitely leads to why he is such a good enforcer, but..."

"You know, Beck, I don't really give a fuck. I know you met with Ron Davis of the New Jersey Bulldogs. We're golfing buddies. So unless you get your ass back to New York right now, I will take a giant bulldog crap all over your name. I will make it my mission in life to tell every GM of every PFL Team, every NAHL team, and every fucking minor league hockey team in Saskatchewan, that you are a fucking quack."

"You know Riley, threatening me like that isn't productive, and I have more than enough clients. Thank you very much. So let's get on the same page. I'm not a 22-year-old rookie you can push around."

Riley took a beat and lowered his aggression. "Look Beck, you need to get back here right now. If not for your career, then for Vlad. He's a fucking mess."

Andrew closed his eyes, put his phone against his chest, and banged the back of his head on the headrest three times. Then he picked the phone back up. "Have a helicopter waiting for me at Teterboro. I'll be there in 90 minutes."

Andrew hung up the phone as Riley uttered the word, "Goo—"

Andrew threw his phone on the seat next to him, rubbed his temples, and then unclicked his seatbelt and made his way to the cockpit. Andrew could hear the pilots talking to the tower and knocked on the panel to get their attention.

"Gentlemen!"

William, the pilot, looked surprised as he turned, "Dr. Beck? What can we do for you?"

"I got some bad news. We need to turn around right now and head back to New York as fast as we can."

William inquired, "Why?"

"I have a medical emergency with a patient. Can we do that?"

"Yes, I'll call the towers and alter our flight plans. We will get you back to Teterboro as fast as we can."

Andrew nodded to the pilots. "Thank you."

As Andrew started to walk away, William called out, "Dr. Beck?"

"Yes?"

William's voice was a little unsteady, "I'm sorry, but you'll still have to pay the full price of the round trip to Miami."

Andrew gave him another nod. "Don't worry about it. Just get me back to New York, fast, please."

"Yes, sir."

Andrew heard the pilots calling back to the tower as he made his way back to his seat and buckled the seatbelt. He felt the plane bank hard and left as the pilot made the mid-air U-turn and headed north.

Andrew's frustration got the best of him as he grunted out loud, "I can't get a break this week! Jeez!" He made a hammer fist and hit the armrest several times.

30

Less than two hours later, Andrew walked the corridors of Tomlin Insurance Sports and Entertainment Complex, where it was a basketball court just a few days ago. He could hear the ice hockey game above him. The ceilings weren't as high in the TISEC as in Empire Stadium, so the game sounds above were more easily heard. Andrew could hear a referee's whistle sending the hometown fans into an uproar. It must have been a penalty on the Sentinels.

Andrew made his way to the Sentinels' locker room, where three guards stood outside. Andrew leaned into one of the guards and muttered conspiratorially, "Dr. Beck to see Vladimir Poplov."

The burly guard opened the door but in an equal hushed tone said, "Go right in, Doctor."

Andrew walked into the tan double door, revealing a big green and white with a large Sentinels logo on the floor. The locker room was oval, with tan lockers. The base of the locker also served as a bench where the players sat and changed. The bench also had a drawer underneath—a very efficient use of space, no different than all the other Manhattanites who lived in tiny apartments. You have to make do with the space you have.

Andrew saw Vladimir alone at his locker. He had a towel hanging over his head, his skates and uniform were still on, and his fingers and knuckles were raw and covered in dried blood. Vladimir looked like he had been motionless for some time.

Andrew called out, *"Privyet*, Vladimir."

"Dr. Beck?" Vladimir jerked his head up.

Andrew spread his arms wide in the empty locker room. "The one and only." He paused and corrected himself. "Actually, that's not true. There is a Dr. Andrew Beck in the UK who is one of the leading Cognitive Behavioral Therapists. He wrote an excellent book on treatment for anxiety and depression." He finished with a warm smile.

Vlad stared at him glassy eyed, and then looked back down at the floor. Andrew took a seat at the locker next to Vladimir, turned and softly asked, "What happened, Vlad? They took Teddy Newsome out on a stretcher?"

Vladimir tilted his head left to right a few times and pursed his lips. "A stretcher, eh? Hmm."

"Vlad, this is serious. The NAHL could suspend you for the rest of the year."

Vladimir sighed and bent over. The towel blocked Andrew's view of his face. "Maybe I deserve it."

Andrew put his hand on Vlad's shoulders. He could feel his shoulder pads underneath the sweaty jersey. "Vlad, talk to me. What happened?"

There were a few moments of silence as Vladimir gathered his thoughts. Andrew could hear the sounds of the game much more clearly from the locker room as it led to the team bench. The puck hitting the boards. The violent clacking of stick passing. The shouts of players to their teammates. And most of all, the crash of men slamming into the boards at full force.

Vladimir began to speak slowly and carefully. "Early in first period, we been keeping good pressure on Boston. No hard shots on goal. We were checking hard, playing very tight. They were getting frustrated. I checked Newsome couple of times, clean shots. But twice he hit ice."

"Okay, all part of the game. Then what?"

Vladimir removed the towel off his head and held it around his neck. "A puck got ahead of Freedom center Blaine Doyle. I picked up puck. I saw Chris Kruder on the left wing. After I got puck away from Doyle, I made good skate and stick move and sent pass to Chris for breakaway."

"Yep, I've seen you skate and stick handle—you're great."

Vladimir put up his hand. "No, not great." Then held up his index finger. "Good. But not great. My pass to Chris was behind him." He shook his head and continued. "Bad pass. He turned awkwardly. The puck hit off boards and went back to Freedom."

"Okay, so?" Andrew was struggling to visualize the game and how this set off Vladimir.

"Chris was out of play. But he stretched for puck, he was wide open. Newsome cut across ice and threw his full body into him." Vladimir ripped the towel from behind his neck and snapped it like a whip at the floor while yelling out in anger, "It was dirty play! Chris was defenseless!"

Andrew saw the trigger point—and saw it from Vladimir's perspective. "Vlad, that would anger any player. And as enforcer, your job is to protect your teammates."

Vladimir nodded his head several times and choked out, "Da. Da."

"So even if you dropped the gloves and fought with Newsome, what I saw on the replay video didn't make sense. Newsome didn't see you coming, and you threw him to the ice and pounded him. It took all four refs to pull you off him. You completely lost control. What happened Vlad? Come on, man, talk to me."

Vladimir looked squarely at Andrew as his eyes began to water and his strong deep voice cracked, "I don't know, Dr. Beck. I haven't thought about Nikki in long time. After we talked, so many memories coming back. I don't want to remember those days."

"Why Vlad, what was so bad in those days?"

Vladimir struggled with his English for a moment as he had difficulty processing the memory. "After I put Konstantin Bentikoff in hospital, team only gave me five-day suspension. Comrade Bentikoff was very angry. He used his political power to transfer mother from molecular biology lab to animal testing lab to conduct experiments on them. She loved animals. My father didn't get promotion. He should have been made lieutenant."

Reassuringly, Andrew explained, "Vlad, that's not your fault.

That is a corrupt man abusing power and taking it out on your parents because he couldn't do anything to you."

"That's not worst part, Doctor." Vladimir shot back firmly but at a lower tone.

"What is, then?"

Vladimir pinched his eyes closed with his thumb and index finger, fighting back the emotion. "That winter, Nikki got pneumonia. He got very sick."

Vladimir told how as a teenager he could vividly remember the hospital in Chekhov, Russia, where he was in a dimly lit gray hospital room. He watched from the beside as his younger brother Nikki struggled to breathe even with an oxygen mask. His mother's eyes were red and puffy from crying. The hospital told the Poplovs that they were out of the antibiotics that Nikki needed. They had some on order that would be arriving any day. Several days passed but no medicine and Nikki was getting worse and worse. Every day the Poplovs questioned the doctor, and the doctor's answer was always the same: "Soon, soon it will be here."

A week passed—no medicine. After second week passed, Nikki could barely breathe. He was coughing and spitting up phlegm all day. Then, one morning with a concerned and tearful Poplov family by his bedside, Nikki coughed and spit up blood. Police Sergeant Sergei Poplov had had enough. When the doctor entered the room, he picked him up by the neck with one arm and slammed him up against the wall. Vladimir was stunned to see his father's raw strength and the growl that came from him, Vladimir told Andrew. It made him feel a fear he has never felt since.

Sergei screamed that his son was dying and threatened that he would snap the doctor's neck in two if he didn't get the medicine. The doctor, slowly losing what little oxygen he had, gurgled out there was some red tape and paperwork, and that the shipment was being held until Comrade Bentikoff signed the release forms. Sergei dropped the gasping doctor and without saying a word left the room.

Vladimir sighed deeply and told Andrew that his father went down to Bentikoff's office, put a gun to his head, and told him to sign the papers. Then he drove to the distribution warehouse, flashed his badge and gun, handed them the papers, and took the medicine back to the hospital himself.

Nikki got the medicine he needed, but they brought Sergei before a tribunal. The politburo members humiliated him. They forced him to apologize to Comrade Bentikoff and beg for his job. But they fired him anyway. A tearful Vladimir told Andrew that his father loved being police officer, and then he drifted off.

Andrew was taking it all in, trying to connect the dots on how all this, the injustice, the violence, had shaped Vlad's psyche. But he lacked the key. What had triggered Vlad's rage?

In a monotoned voice, Vladimir said that Nikki survived pneumonia, but his lungs were permanently scarred. He missed the rest of the hockey season, and the next year's also. Hockey was everything for the Poplov boys. So much so, Vladimir explained, that Nikki started practicing in secret when he was supposed to be resting.

Andrew saw Vladimir get visibly emotional, and this time he didn't try to wipe the water forming in his eyes. "He lost so much weight. He was so thin he could slide through bars of gate closing off hockey rink."

A tear gently fell down his left cheek as his voice cracked. "He would practice in middle of the night, then come home. But..." Vladimir struggled to find words.

Andrew waited. He knew that whatever happened to Nikki was the trigger, and he waited patiently, but he could hear the fans and the game was in its final moments. Soon the team would be in the locker room and no doubt Riley would follow, wanting a report. He couldn't rush Vladimir's process. The Russian Bear was opening up to him, but time was against him.

"I knew Nikki was practicing but no one hitting him on the ice. He was only shooting and skating. Shooting and skating. I didn't think much of it so I didn't tell Mama and Papa. I thought, what could happen?"

Vladimir started to breathe more rapidly, and the tears were flowing. "But he was pushing himself too hard. Nikki always pushed so hard to make up for his size. And...and his lung collapsed. He...he

241

died right there on the ice, alone, drowning in his own blood." Vladimir bent over sobbing in his cut-up and blood-covered hands.

Andrew tried to comfort him by putting a gentle hand on his hulking shoulders. "I am so very sorry, Vlad, but it wasn't…"

Vladimir snapped up, the force threw Andrew's arm off him, and his face reddened with rage. Andrew could see a sharp sadness in his deep blue eyes. "It was my fault! I killed him! I killed my Nikita! I was his big brother!"

Vladimir started pounding himself in the chest. The breastplate of the padding took the brunt of the hits. "I was supposed to protect him. I killed him. I beat up Konstantin. I got Papa fired! I got Mama moved to test animals! It's all my fault. I killed Nikki! I KILLED HIM!! Why did you make me remember these things, Dr. Beck!"

Vladimir punched both of his bloodied fists into the air, looked up into the ceiling, and cried out, "I'm sorry, Nikita! I'm so sorry!" And Vladimir continued to sob, his hulking body shaking.

Andrew, for a moment, was shocked at the rage, and when Vladimir started throwing his fists at the sky, he flinched and got up off the bench to get away from Vladimir. Andrew's breathing became rapid, but as Vladimir sobbed in his hands, Andrew's flight response calmed, and he looked for the right words to say. Just then, the final buzzer of the game sounded. He had to get this situation under control, fast! He closed his eyes and went to a place in his mind where he always went when his fear was about to take over. He forced all his emotions down into a deep well, and compartmentalized what he needed to do, and in a snap, he felt back in control again.

He slowly approached Vladimir, putting both hands together as if making prayer hands. "Vlad, I know this hurts now. But this is great progress. I can help you heal these wounds. I can help you, and I will. And I am so very sorry about Nikki, but you didn't kill him." Andrew reverted to making the Clinton thumb again to make his point. "You were a boy, not a doctor, not a grownup. You weren't in the politburo. You were just…a boy."

Vladimir stopped sobbing and looked at Andrew. He shook his head. "What does matter now?"

Andrew moved closer to Vladimir, mirroring Vladimir's hunched posture and trying to impart some gentle hope. "Vlad, you can honor Nikki's memory. You can make the playoffs. You can go and win the North American Hockey Cup. You can do this for your family, for your Nikita."

Vladimir was quiet for a few moments. He stopped sobbing and Andrew waited as the man's chest heaved a few times before he added, "Ya, ya, but like you said, the NAHL will suspend me."

Andrew stood up. "Not if I have anything to do about it." He pointed his thumb at his chest and added, "But Vlad?"

"Da?"

"I need to know, what happened when you saw Chris Kruder get hit?" Andrew sat back down next to Vladimir and looked over his shoulder to see if the players were entering the tunnel to the locker room. Any moment now.

Vladimir shrugged his shoulders. "I went mad, like Papa. I tackled Newsome. Started pounding him. It was like Nikki and Konstantin all over again. It was instinct, and I didn't think. I was like animal. Lost in rage. A sea of red rage."

Vladimir took a deep breath. Andrew saw his eyes, and they were looking right through him. He barely spoke above a whisper and struggled to get the words out. "I wanted to kill him."

Andrew saw the hatred in his eyes and knew if the refs hadn't pulled Vladimir off Newsome, he *would have* killed him. This was new territory for Andrew. It scared the hell out of him, while also fascinated him. The clinical side won out.

"Our talks brought all these emotions back up. When you saw Newsome hit Kruder in the same way as Nikki, you literally saw red. It triggered you and brought up all of your old emotions. And these emotions have so much guilt and shame around Nikki's death, your father and mother's work. The only way to get rid of them in that moment was to kill Newsome."

Vladimir straitened up. "Is Newsome okay?"

"He's alive, but I'm not sure what happened to him." Andrew took a second. "Vlad, you blame yourself for everything. It's this guilt and shame which compels you to send so much money home. And why you fight with Isrena about money. And when she calls them

243

Koz-yole, or goats, not only is she disrespecting your family, but she is also disrespecting all your family's honor, your honor, and your memory of poor Nikita."

Andrew let that settle in. He could see Vladimir was carefully considering what he had said, his chest still heaving. Andrew could hear the rumbling as the players scrambled down the tunnel.

"It's a toxic build-up of guilt and shame," Andrew declared.

"So, you're saying that it's guilt that makes me fight?"

Andrew shook his head fervently. "No, you fight because it's part of what you do in hockey. But when you see red, when you go mad? That's because someone tried to hurt a defenseless teammate intentionally. Like Konstantin did to Nikki. Then all the shame and guilt comes rushing back to you. You get so angry, you could…kill."

Vladimir crossed his arms, sat back into the locker, and tilted his head a few times left to right. "Maybe you're right, Dr. Beck. So what to do now?"

"We need more sessions to get to the bottom of this. Vlad, let me free you from the emotional chains you bind yourself in."

Vladimir's face grew serious. "No, I mean NAHL?"

Andrew sat up, holding himself up with both arms on his knees. "Well, let's see what they come back with. I mean, Newsome had it coming, right? So maybe they will see it as an eye for an eye and give you a slap on the wrist."

"And if slap becomes punch?" asked Vladimir.

"I'll talk to them. I can be pretty convincing when I want to be."

Vladimir kept his frown but gave a nod of his head. Andrew gave him a reassuring look and patted him on the shoulder pads.

Andrew and Vladimir sat as the Sentinels started filing into the locker room with some commotion. As he was in someone's locker, Andrew stood up and shook Vladimir lightly by the shoulder.

"Why don't you hit the showers, Vlad?"

"Da, I don't want teammates to see me like this." His face was flushed and his eyes puffy.

"Vlad, you did really great work today. It is harder to look deep into the pits of our own darkness than it is to ignore or bury it so deep in our minds that we can't find it."

After he said it, there was a pang deep in his stomach, and then his head itched—he scratched it violently.

Vladimir started unlacing his skates quickly and efficiently and had them off in a few seconds. "Maybe," he grunted. "But burying felt better."

"Give it time, Vlad, give it time." But that truth from Vladimir also soothed Andrew like a warm blanket and he felt the fight between his clinical brain. His body and his knees began to shake a little like he was just about to line up a birdie putt to win a tournament. He tried to stay in the clinical brain, bending over with his hands on his knees in hopes that it would stop them from shaking.

"What do ya think, Vlad?"

"Da." He nodded firmly and stood up abruptly in his socks. This forced Andrew to take a step back on his wobbly legs, but he caught himself and Vladimir didn't see him stumble as he was taking off his jersey and shoulder pads. The speed with which he went from a fully armored warrior to a hulking naked man resulted from performing this ritual thousands and thousands of times over his life. Vladimir wrapped a towel around himself and passed his teammates as he disappeared into the bathroom.

Andrew said hello to some of the players as he felt his legs come back underneath him. He headed towards the exit, but his legs didn't want to go as fast as his mind wanted him. He was just a few feet from the turn down the hallway to the exit when he heard a grating voice over the rest of the Sentinels players' crosstalk.

"There you are!"

Andrew turned to a rushing Riley Asherton with a rolled-up lineup in his hands.

Ah fuck, I can't deal with this guy right now.

Riley stood with his hands to his hips in a superman pose. "What the fuck happened? Why did he go berserk like that? I got a fucking earful from the Freedom's Coach Tremblay. He wants Poplov suspended for the rest of the year."

I'm so sick of this fucker.

"Well, Coach Tremblay doesn't make the rules, and it was a fucking dirty hit on Kruder that led to all of this shit. Newsome should get suspended too."

"Well, I'll call Harry Lee at the NAHL and tell him that…"

Andrew interrupted Riley, "No, don't do anything at all. If we seek the NAHL out, especially its president, then it's like we are admitting we did something wrong."

"What are you, a fucking lawyer, too?"

Andrew took a step into Riley's personal space. "A good poker player never shows his cards until he has to. Don't show them our hand…not yet."

Man, I'd love to play poker against him; I'd take every cent off this motherfucker.

Andrew didn't wait for a comment as he turned and pushed open the double doors to the locker room with force, slamming them against the wall. The startled guards outside nearly jumped out of their skins. He didn't answer when one of the beefy guards asked if everything was okay. He had to get out of there. He could hear the sounds of the fans and music as the crowd dispersed from the arena.

Andrew's mind was swirling. He was feeling good about where he left Vlad, but he wanted to punch Riley in the face and then was feeling a Hawker 800 load of guilt for abandoning John Palmer. He had to find out how he pitched. Hopefully, John kept his shit together and had a good game; if Palmer had another meltdown, he could kiss his relationship with John, the Tides, and maybe all of baseball, goodbye.

He pulled out his phone to check the scores, but he was too far underground—he had to get to the street level to get a signal. He never went directly to the street from the team areas; he always went out to the parking garage, so he had no idea where he was going. He was running around like a mouse in a maze, the corridors leading to one dead end after another. He doubled back. He was sweating and looking for a signal on his phone. He saw a food vendor with a tray of hot dogs and asked how to get to the street.

The vendor pointed out some vague directions, but Andrew started running before he finished. He would figure it out himself. He ran up an escalator full of fans when he got stuck behind them and could do nothing but stare at his phone, saying "no service." He was sweating profusely now.

He squeezed past some fans at the top of the steps and followed a path that let him out onto the main rotunda. He was drowning in a sea of screaming fans. It was sensory overload for him, and his head was pounding. He was so focused on getting out he forgot to check that he had five bars on his phone. The line to get out was huge. It would be another fifteen minutes that he didn't have. He smelled a man eating a hotdog with all the fixings and caught a whiff of another man's beer breath and almost vomited.

He saw a door and asked a security guard if he could go out. The guard scowled until he flashed his Sentinels credential—then finally he reached open space. He was out of the TISEC.

The April chill hit him in the face, but the fresh air and loud sounds of cars honking and buses going by somehow grounded him as his mind started to refocus on what he had to do next. He swallowed the upchuck that was rising and looked at his phone, holding on to it with a vice-like grip. The screen was covered in sweat droplets and he wiped it on his jacket.

He put his iPad case between his legs so he could operate his phone with two hands. He opened the Real Sport News app, clicked on the baseball scores, and scrolled to find the Tides' result. But before he could find it, the caller ID appeared. John Palmer.

31

Andrew took a deep breath to settle himself as the ringtone persisted. *Okay, take it easy Andrew, take it easy.*

Andrew answered the phone with feigned enthusiasm, "Hey, JP!"

John sounded cagey, slightly sarcastic. "Some game huh, Doc?"

Andrew had trouble getting a read on him. "Yeah, it was. How do you feel you did?"

"Great, I mean, seven innings pitched, only two earned runs, six strikeouts, and only two walks. It was a good game. Skipper seemed happy."

"That's fantastic, JP. So we're happy, right?"

"Yeah, you know it would've been nice to get..." John was interrupted by one of his teammates yelling, "Nice game, JP!"

John replied to his teammate away from the phone, but John was yelling so Andrew could hear John clearly say, "Hey, thanks bro! Great diving grab in the 4th! You saved a run!" John spoke back to Andrew, "Yeah, you know, but what can you do?"

Andrew tried to be reassuring. "It's okay, John, you did your best. We'll get the win the next time. We're still off to a—"

"What are you talking about?"

Andrew was caught and hesitated. "Uh..."

Now John sounded annoyed. "We were winning three to two when I got pulled in the seventh so, I got the win. I'm two and oh, Doc. Shit, I thought you knew baseball better than that."

"Um, yeah, ah shit, I thought the score was tied when they pulled you. Sorry, JP, it's been a long day."

"Were you watching the game or talking to DJ all night? I didn't fucking fly you down so you could bullshit with him. You said you'd be watching *me*!"

"I was watching you, JP. Come on, now. I brain farted, that's all. I'm sorry."

"Yeah, okay, okay."

A loud set of horns were honking at someone not going when the light was green, and the quiet moment was filled with sounds of New York City.

"You home already?"

"Yeah, we made really good time on the way back. I'm headed back to my car now."

There was pause. Andrew was hoping John wasn't doing the math on the time.

"Cool. Well, thanks again for being there tonight. It really helped knowing you had my back like that."

"No problem. We'll talk next week. Congratulations again."

"Thanks, Doc."

Andrew hung up the phone and shoved it back in his pocket. The April chill hit him, and now that he was cooling down after his slog through the TISEC, he was shivering. He felt an urgency to not only get out of the cold but to go to the one place where he always got a warm feeling inside. He jogged to the street, where he put his two fingers in his mouth and made the "taxi whistle" and yelled out, "Taxi!"

A cab immediately crossed two lanes of traffic, nearly hitting two other cars, to reach the curb and get his fare. Andrew got in and told the driver to take him to Mercer and Grand. "And turn the heat on, would you?" He rubbed his hands together and looked outside as the cab turned from 9th Avenue down Hudson Street. The former brick warehouses were converted into low-rise apartments of four and six floors. A block later, the scenery changed as the line of prewar buildings morphed into newer buildings, reaching higher in the skyline. Then a few blocks later, it shifted again to boutique storefronts with three floors above them—tiny but expensive apartments.

Andrew was starting to feel nauseous from all the travel, the blasting car heat, and the rough stops and starts by the cab. He pushed the button to roll down the window, figuring some fresh air might do him some good. Although it was a beautiful spring day in early April, the temperature dropped precipitously after the sun went down. The sounds of a busy New York City night were amplified with the window down. The air wasn't helping—now he felt cold again *and* nauseous. The cabby missed the light on Broome Street and jammed on the brakes hard enough to tighten his seat belt. If Andrew had had anything in his stomach, he would have thrown it up.

He tried to recall the last time he had eaten something. As he scrolled back through his day, rewinding his internal video. He realized it was lunch and before his session with Lamar. He now wondered if he was car sick or just hungry.

A part of him wanted to go home and go to sleep, but there was a deeper part of him—a drive from deep within his belly that had to sit at that table. He needed it after a day like today and the week he was having. It seemed to be the only thing that might soothe the tsunami of angst inside him. He *needed* to win.

The cab made it to the northeast corner of Mercer Street and Grand Street just past the parking lot where, on most nights, his car would be parked. Andrew pulled out a credit card and swiped it, giving the cabbie a 20 percent tip, despite the heavy braking. He hoofed down Mercer Street, and since there were no parked cars as it was alternate side parking, he walked freely off the curb and on the cobblestone street. The sound of his shoes hitting the cobblestones soothed him. His nausea went away, his pulse slowed, and the day seemed to drift away from him for the moment.

However, Andrew then pulled out his wallet and searched it for the marker card that wasn't there. Fergus had taken his marker card. He pulled out his phone, went onto his banking app, and looked at his accounts. He had his joint account with Sandra, which held a balance of $356,243.67. His commercial bank account for his practice had another $211,896.42, and he had another personal account with $23,105.91 in it. He also had his Bitcoin account, where he held the winnings from his gambling. He checked the balance of his Bitcoin and even if he could find a buyer for all of his coins, it was only just over $100,000. These funds were nowhere near what he needed to fund his table stakes of $500,000. He could gamble at the "regular tables" but he was a "Player" and it was embarrassing enough how he left the last game. He had to win at the Players' Tables. He had to let everyone know *he* was the man. And that the other night, he lost his cool, and it would never happen again. Tonight, he would crush whoever he was playing, get in their heads, dissect their plays, their tells, their very thoughts and dominate. He *had* to win tonight, no matter what.

He clicked on the account transfer feature of his application, he put all the money and set it to transfer to the joint account, which was enough to get him started. His fingers shook as he hovered over the transfer button.

I win tonight and transfer the money back. I can tell Sandra I fat fingered the transfer and when I discovered my error, I put it all back. She won't be any wiser. I can leave just enough in the commercial account for Gina's paycheck to clear. Problem solved!

But right before he hit the transfer button, he thought carefully about the woman he married, how a transfer would get her to start asking question after question after question. He knew Gina checked the accounts every day to handle the books—she would have questions too.

Too many fucking questions. And what if he lost?

He closed his eyes. The burn inside him needed this. He *had* to have it. His shaky finger got closer to the transfer button. A wave of nausea hit him again, and his head started to throb. His breath shortened. He closed his eyes. And they flashed opened, enlivened by a thought. Another way to get the money. It scared him, but at least there would be *no questions.*

He swiped the banking app closed. He was breathing easier, but he could feel his head still throbbing. Once he went down this path, there was no turning back.

The doors to the street level elevator for The Five Iron opened and a few patrons came out. Andrew stepped in and descended to his sanctuary. He followed his usual routine at the concierge's desk, but before he and the concierge could exchange pleasantries, Andrew told him he had to get a new marker card. The concierge didn't hesitate and told him that Mr. Mackenzie had it and requested Andrew see him personally.

Andrew didn't like the way the concierge said *personally*. It had the air of eventuality in it. Andrew could feel the rushing stream of cortisol flowing through his body. He tried to keep a smile on his face and hide the fear running through his body as he took a seat in the waiting area.

The concierge pulled out a radio and pushed the talk button, "This is the front desk. Anyone have eyes on Mr. Mackenzie? I have Dr. Beck at the front."

Andrew heard a woman's voice with a Scottish accent reply. "Mr. Mackenzie is in his office. I'll take Dr. Beck to see him."

"Copy that, Miss James," the concierge replied.

Lorry replied with a curt, "Out."

Andrew felt his knees shake again as he quickly sat on one of the two plush fire-engine red sofas. His nervous fingers traced the ornately carved mahogany armrests. He went to loosen the tie around his neck, but when he reached up, there was no tie. He hadn't worn one in months. His mind was swirling.

Did Fergus want to revisit the other night?

I need money to gamble with, but will I end up like Mr. Davidson?

And what about the gunshot? Did Fergus kill Keegan or was it Corravallo? It must have been Fergus. I heard the pop of the gun? Or did I?

It was all a haze, and Andrew's usual iron trap memory for situational recall was malfunctioning. He was hungry, dehydrated, and nauseous. He knew this was not the best way to visit a polished savage like Fergus, and especially when he had to ask him to borrow money.

The sounds of heavy footsteps approached him, and he recognized the giant figure coming out of the shadows: George. He stopped in front of Andrew, and Andrew rose and wiped the sweat off his hands on his jacked before he shook George's hand.

"Hey, Dr. Beck. You keeping out of trouble?"

"I'm trying my best."

George leaned in to whisper in Andrew's ear. "You must have some serious fucking cat blood in you, brother. Nine lives and shit."

Andrew nodded and forced a smile as George laughed and patted Andrew on the shoulder. It was a pat for George but felt like a wallop to Andrew, and he couldn't help but wince.

Andrew turned to see Lorry marching towards him. She had on her signature Dr. Martens and black pantsuit. Lorry greeted him with a slight nod and asked him to follow her.

The two walked in silence through the main area of people eating, talking, and playing smaller card games. The smells of the food made Andrew so hungry, he was tempted to pick something off a plate, but that would probably end up losing another one of his cat lives.

Lorry and Andrew headed for a red carpeted stairway. At the top of the stairs, the hallway turned right. The right side had a handrail that went the entire length of the hallway. From the elevated floor, he could see the entire club, the eating and lounge area, the smaller gaming tables, the Sports Book with the giant screen TVs, and the Players' Tables in the back of the club. The curtains were closed so he couldn't see who was playing. He would ask Lorry later who he'd be playing against tonight, but now he had to focus on how to ask Fergus to stake him. He wondered what he would want in return. Ten percent? Twenty percent? Fifty percent?

The silence between them created a different pang in his stomach than his hunger.

"Everything okay?" he asked.

Lorry turned over her shoulder and said, "Yeah, why?"

"You're pretty quiet."

Lorry frowned and lowered her tone. "The walls have ears."

Andrew looked around and saw every ten feet of small white half circles with a black lens in the middle. Andrew also responded in a low tone bordering on a whisper, "Gotcha."

"Why is Fergus giving me my marker card personally instead of just leaving it with the concierge?"

Lorry looked up at the cameras, then turned around and walked backward, whispering, "He's playing chess, not checkers." She quickly spun around to continue walking forward.

Andrew wasn't sure he heard her right, but if he did, it didn't answer his question and it didn't make sense.

What kind of chess game would Fergus be playing with me? Was he still pissed off about the card game? Was he going to kill me too? No, if he asked to meet me in a seedy hotel in Newark, well…but he wouldn't do anything to me in his office. Would he?

The end of the hallway turned left, but before the left was a large red wooden door. It looked like it was taken from a manor home in Scotland. Andrew wondered if it was from Fergus' house. The polished brass doorknob had an ornate round knocker, and a matching brass mail slot in the middle of the door, except the lettering said "Post" instead of "Mail." Lorry used the knocker and hit it three times. The ring of brass on brass had a sound that unnerved Andrew. It sounded like a knock on the gates of hell.

From behind the door, Andrew heard a booming Scottish voice. "Enter!"

Lorry opened the door and signaled with an outstretched arm for Andrew to proceed in the room. But Andrew stayed beyond the threshold a moment. She looked intently at him, her face was serious, and she swallowed hard. If he didn't know better, her blue-green eyes had a look of deep concern and care. They were glistening. She blinked as she reacted to how hard he was staring at her, and she looked away. Lorry never looked away…from anything. Andrew felt his heart thump. She had never looked at him like that, ever. The look stunned him after all their games of cat and mouse, his playful and harmless flirting, and her determination not to respond. Andrew read that she cared about him. And she was *scared.*

Andrew stepped into Fergus' office as Lorry announced, "Dr. Beck is here."

Fergus looked up from his large mahogany desk. It was lit by only a green banker's lamp as there were a few short piles of paper neatly stacked that he was going through. "Ah, great. Have a seat, Dr. Beck." Fergus gestured for Andrew to take the seat in front of him.

Lorry asked, "Will that be all?"

Fergus gave her a smile and a nod. "Aye love, cheers."

Fergus smiled at Andrew. "Take a seat, give me a minute to finish some of this paperwork, eh, mate?"

Andrew smiled back. "Take your time."

The heavy wood door closed, and Andrew's stomach jumped. He tried to make himself comfortable in the seat and looked around Fergus' office. There was a large white marble fireplace behind Fergus, it was unlit, but it had wood in the fireplace. Andrew assumed it was just for decoration. On the large office walls were oil paintings depicting various outdoor, hunting, and nature scenes. Andrew could only assume that the rising triangular hills depicted in them were the Scottish Highlands. The male figures wore traditional Clan Mackenzie blue and green tartan kilts with leather sporrans and wool Tam o' Shanters that flopped over the right side of the wearer's face below the ear. The office was spartan, neatly furnished, and nothing looked out of place. Above the marble fireplace was a mounted golf club. It was an antique with a wooden shaft and the silver iron had turned blackish with age, and possibly use. Andrew couldn't place exactly what club it was, but since the club's name was The Five Iron, he had a pretty good idea which club it was.

Andrew was listening to the sound of Fergus' pen on the paper and knew it had to be a fountain pen. Andrew sat up very straight to get a look at Fergus' pen. He was using a beautiful black and platinum coated Mont Blanc Meisterstück fountain pen. Andrew had a similar one he used only for contract signing. The sound of Fergus' nub scraping on paper, leaving a valley to fill with ink, was soothing to Andrew. It helped him clear the thoughts of Lorry and the money he would need. But there was one burning question inside him still. He had to know what happened that night. He needed to be careful to ask and not accuse, as this would surely ruin his chances of borrowing money from Fergus. He was about to play the most important hand of poker he would play tonight. He decided to come out strong preflop.

"Did you hear they found Mr. Keegan murdered down on South Street yesterday?"

Fergus stopped writing, put his pen down carefully, sat back in his chair and folded his hands on his desk. "Yes, well, that was quite unfortunate."

"Unfortunate?" Andrew was intrigued by Fergus' choice of words. "So, what happened after I left?"

"We roughed him up a bit more to make sure he would promise to leave you alone. And true, I wasn't very happy about him using another card reader to break into your card. But he willingly and without much coaxing gave us all the information about his hacker chums in Chinatown, the Haung-Tse. We'll deal with them too." Fergus leaned in. "But I assure you, Dr. Beck, when we left him, he was very much alive." Fergus waited a moment and relaxed in his chair. "But, as we were leaving, we did see another crew going his way. But we thought it was his own men coming to collect him. I thought nothing of it at the time. I guess it was Corravallo and his men."

Andrew searched Fergus' face and eyes for clues that he was lying. But it was an impenetrable visage, nothing but cold, clinical detachment, and bold assurance. Andrew's angst could have been getting the better of him.

Fergus added, "And I believe they found Corravallo's prints on the gun?"

Andrew nodded; Sandra had told him that too.

Fergus shrugged. "Well, one way or another, I guess justice was served."

"Justice?"

Fergus unclasped his hands and folded his arms, "Well, Mr. Keegan won't be bothering you again, will he, Doctor?"

Andrew felt a surprising relief rise in his chest. "No." He paused reflectively. "I guess he won't."

Andrew was more relieved than he cared to admit. Fergus raised his preflop bet. It was time to call and see what the turn would give him. He pivoted the conversation to something more congenial that gave him a moment to get his emotional bearings. "That's a nice pen, Fergus."

"Oh, this? Yeah, I'm a bit old school. I like the feel of a pen rather than typing. It takes a little longer, but I find it keeps my mind focused."

"Yes, I agree." Andrew went into his safe place by pontificating, "sometimes the connection between a physical object and the task allows our mind to focus. Also, handwriting activates parts of your brain involved in thinking and working memory, allowing you to store and manage information. The movement associated with the pen, especially when using a fountain pen, due to the feel of the nib on paper and the weight in your hand, can help you encode and retain information long-term."

"Oh, so is that what I owe my ability to remember facts and figures?"

"Maybe, every mind is unique."

"Agreed." Fergus's tone became deeper and more resolved. "You seem to have a unique mind, Doctor."

Shit, he came out strong at the turn.

"Oh, how so?"

"Your ability to read people, athletes in particular, you can tell if they will succeed or fail."

Andrew squirmed a bit in his seat. *Gotta raise that shit.*

"I can read an athlete's body language. I can read their facial movements, which helps me decipher what's going on in their minds."

"Can you only do this with your patients?"

"With my patients it's at a deeper level because I know their issues. So I know exactly what to look for. But for the most part, I can watch any athlete and between all the data available and their body language, the way they're warming up, shooting or pitching, I can tell if they're going to have a good game or not."

"Quite a skill, Doctor. So, how do you know athletes so well?"

"Ah, well, I was a competitive golfer when I was young." Andrew laughed to hide the burn he was feeling in his face.

"Golf. I see, just like your father?"

Andrew's eyes grew big, and his mouth opened, but no words came out. *Shit, he reraised me. What's he holding, pocket kings?*

"The famous Masters Champion, Ted Beck. Yes, I know. There is very little I don't know about my patrons, Dr. Beck. Your connection with Ted Beck wasn't hard to find."

Fergus stared intensely at Andrew. Andrew tried to hide any emotional tell. He couldn't help feeling like he was Batman, and the Joker just pulled his mask off, revealing he was Bruce Wayne.

He tried to downplay it. "Yeah, he's my dad. I played competitively as a youth and in college, but I gave it up to pursue psychology."

"He must have been disappointed?"

"Yeah, but I wanted to help athletes, not be one. Less of a toll on the body, and a lot longer career span." Andrew tried to use his disarming smile, but Fergus was motionless.

Andrew didn't want to bring Ted into his sanctuary. The pot was getting bigger and bigger. Fergus was good at changing the conversation and getting Andrew to talk about himself, a basic conversational control method. He needed to retake charge of the conversation. He had to see if the next card on the river would improve his hand. Andrew looked above Fergus's head at the golf club hanging on the wall.

"That's a beautiful club hanging on your wall. Looks like an antique," Andrew said with a charming smile.

Fergus didn't budge, only nodded, staring right through Andrew. "Aye. That five iron has been in my family for three generations."

"Ever use it?" Andrew asked with a curious smile.

"Aye. I beat my dad to death with it." The smile left Andrew's face.

"My father was the meanest son-of-a-bitch that ever lived. He was a drunk. Well, one night he came home late, and his supper was cold. Somehow this was me mum's fault. So he squared off and punched her in the face. I'll never forget the sound of the thud when she hit the ground. The fucker kept punching her." Fergus' face was contorted as he made a short punching motion with his fist.

Andrew did his best not to flinch. Fergus was far away enough, and he resisted his urge as Fergus continued his tale.

"Me wee brother and I jumped in front of the fucking maniac, to protect me mum. But then he took off his belt and whipped us until we were bloody. Me brother was sobbing, and I said, 'Don't let that bastard see you cry, otherwise he'll keep beating us.' I pulled him close, and I could feel the warm blood from his back run down my hand."

Fergus paused, took a breath, but never broke eye contact with Andrew. "The bastard exhausted himself and passed out on the floor. Me brother asked me if he had killed mum? I said, 'No... not this time.'" Fergus put up a finger. "But this had to end." He took a breath and wiped a hand across his desk as if he was getting rid of some dust. "So I took the first club I could out of the old man's golf bag and whacked his head as hard as I could with that five iron until his brains were scattered all over the floor."

Andrew felt a pang in his stomach as he saw no remorse in Fergus' eyes.

"He never bothered us again." Fergus ended the story with a short shoulder shrug and a quick side nod.

Fergus' face then had a look of almost surprise as he added, "Hmm. I've never told anyone that story."

Andrew searched his brain for something to say but, his mind was blank. The two sat for a moment in utter silence.

Andrew opened his mouth to talk, say something, *anything*, but Fergus beat him to the punch. "Down to business."

Caught off guard by the abrupt change, Andrew sat back in his chair. Fergus opened a drawer and slid a black graphite card across his desk. "Here is your new marker card. We had to destroy the other since it had been compromised."

The metal scraping on wood brought Andrew out of his haze as his clinical brain started spinning on what killing your father with a 5 iron must do to a boy. He had a million questions but now was neither the time nor the place. His amygdala hit the Red Alert button and shut down the myriad of clinical questions and possible diagnoses of Fergus' personality. His fight or flight response was acting like a fire station when an alarm goes off. His adrenaline was sliding down the firepole, and if it could talk, it would have been saying, "Let's go, let's go!"

He resisted his flight mode. It was time to fight. He had to make his play. He felt his burn, his itch, and he had to get to the card table. Now was the time. Fergus shared something with him, a deep truth, an opening—now was the perfect time to ask.

Andrew picked up the card off the desk, put it in his jacket pocket, and smiled politely. "Fergus, I had all my, shall we say, play money on that card. And I accept the fact I had to forfeit the money for breaking your rules. And I appreciate you saving my life from Mr. Keegan's firing squad, but I don't have enough Bitcoin or free cash to make the $500,000 I need. What terms would you charge on staking me tonight?"

Fergus sat back in his chair, hands folded. "There is nothing more I appreciate in this world than a gentleman. You have handled this situation gracefully. But the reason why I called you up here was not to hand you an empty marker card, nor was it to put you in my debt, which by the way, is the last place you want to be. Trust me."

Andrew's relief was short-lived and he could feel his chest tighten.

"I have a business proposition I want to discuss with you, Doctor."

Andrew's stomach tightened, and he felt his legs wanting to bob, but he controlled them.

"In exchange for returning your winnings of over $3 million, and for saving your life, as you most humbly added, I would like some information from you."

"What kind of information?" Another knot in his stomach tightened.

"For starters, who are the other athletes you are treating?" Fergus said bluntly.

"Why do you want to know that?" Andrew deflected.

"So you can tell me how I should bet on their teams when they are playing, of course."

Andrew's amygdala was in full panic mode, but his limbic cortex pushed it aside like a soldier moving a shell-shocked civilian out of the way before they became collateral damage.

"I can't do that, Fergus."

He's got a full house and I got two pair. How do I bluff my way through this?

"Why not?"

"Because it's unethical. I could lose my license and—"

"Oh, don't you think we are a bit past that now, mate?"

There was silence between them. Andrew was resolved not to speak first. He had always promised himself that under no circumstances would he ever bet on sports. It was not only a sure way for him to never work in sports again and lose his license, but it was how he justified his gambling. He wasn't harming anyone, as long as he didn't bet on sports. He didn't bet on a score, not an over-under, no side bets, not even on a strike or ball. He wouldn't even join a fantasy football league. It was the line he would not cross. Sports was his temple, his place of purity, solace, and non-compromise. Whatever demons he had running through him, they would not enter his work, his passion. He was a sports psychologist, for fuck's sake! There had to be one place where the world was right in his mind. Even if the world of pro sports was fucked up, his world was right. What Fergus was asking him to do would tear him apart. But what choice did he have?

"Fergus can't I just borrow $500,000 and we forget about this?"

Fergus ignored his request. "What sports are your patients in? No harm in telling me that, eh?"

The knots in his stomach spread to his intestines. It was as if they were forming their own knots and tying them tight. He looked around the room—he was surrounded by Scottish men armed with pikes and muskets, and all of them seemed to be in foul spirits as if a cold, wet wind had rushed up their kilts.

The words seemed to resist coming out of his mouth. "Baseball, as you know. Basketball... ice hockey... and tennis."

"See, that wasn't so hard now, was it?"

Andrew frowned and took a deep breath and let it out. *I can't go all in. I don't have the cards.*

"And the teams they play for, Doctor?"

"Ah, come on, Fergus!" The fear and knots were gone, and anger and shame took up their mantle, leaving a burning in his chest.

"Here are your choices, Doctor: tell me the teams your patients play for and continue being a gentleman, and you get your $3 million back, or you insult all I have done for you, our friendship ends, and you leave my club... FOREVER!" Fergus pounded his desk.

The thump rattled Andrew, and he jumped. Fergus's stare penetrated Andrew's brain, and he felt naked, vulnerable. The thought of not being able to gamble, to scratch his itch—the thought of that tore him apart at a level even Andrew couldn't fathom.

Why is this happening to me? Anything but sports. Why? Why? Why?

"I will not ask again! The teams. Name them!"

"The Tides, The Black Knights, the Sentinels, and tennis doesn't have any teams. It's a solo sport." Andrew looked at the 5 iron on the mantle, wishing Fergus' father had made different choices in his life. "Are we done?"

"I saved your life! Isn't that worth just a bit of information that I can profit on?"

Andrew looked away.

"Oh, I see, you want your cake and eat it too."

"How do you figure?" The anger was a five-alarm fire in Andrew's chest.

"Do your patients know you come here to gamble? Does your *wife* know you come here?"

Andrew gave away his answer with his look.

"That's what I thought." Fergus shook his head. "So here you are all high and mighty, about ethics and such, and you lie to your wife, you're gambling at an illegal casino, you almost lost your life to a corrupt gangster, and all this posturing just to protect that little world inside your head where you think you are in control? Hmmm."

Andrew felt as if he were in a dream. He couldn't think straight. He felt as if the Scotsmen on the walls had closed in around him, he was the wounded deer, unable to run any further, and they all had their shotguns pointed at him for the kill shot.

"I think I should go now, Fergus."

Andrew got up and walked towards the door. He only got a few steps before Fergus calmly called out, "Where are you going to go, Doctor?"

Andrew stopped and turned around to look at Fergus, who had risen to his feet.

"Where will you go?" Fergus shrugged his shoulders. "Mohegan Sun?" He put his hands in his pockets and stepped away from his desk. "Play poker with your friends in their basements for a few hundred dollars? You think that will satiate you?" A grin started to graze Fergus' face. The grin when you know you have the winning hand.

"Oh, I know, maybe you can try online poker, eh?" Fergus paused and then shook his head. "But you'll just be looking at a screen where you can't see and read the tells of your opponents. Where's the sport in that, eh?"

Fergus took several steps toward Andrew, closing the distance between them. Andrew felt the flames of his burning rage doused by gallons of shame. Fergus continued his verbal onslaught, each word ripping apart the foundation of Andrew's mental facade. "Where will you go where you can gamble freely, play the way you want, and your privacy is maintained, so there is no risk of losing your career?"

"Maybe it's time I quit gambling."

"Do you even know why you gamble?" Fergus approached him, getting within a few feet of him. "Let me tell you." Fergus leaned close, and his icy blue eyes pierced Andrew's soul. "You do it because you *have* to win. You use all your psychological assessment skills to figure everyone out and therefore beat them before they even know what's happened. Every hand you win proves to yourself that you are the smartest man in the room."

Fergus took a step back and pointed an outstretched finger at Andrew as he paced. "You may have quit competitive golf, Doctor, but you never have, not for an instant stopped competing. Because you can't. You have to win, win at any cost, even if it means...*dying*."

Andrew knew he had to get out of Fergus' office. But his legs wouldn't respond. His arms couldn't move either. They all seemed like they were rusted shut like he was the Tin Man in *The Wizard of Oz*. He was defenseless. His brain was cross-firing messages, but the one making the loudest call was, *You need this!*

Andrew looked down, blinked, and asked, "What do I have to do?"

"I want you to tell me the mind states of your athletes before they play. I want to know if you think their performance will positively affect the outcome of the match, or game, or whatever. When you do, and I win, I'll release $250,000 on your marker card. If your information pays off, it shouldn't take long before I earn the cash I need for the camera upgrades. The faster I earn, the quicker I'll release the rest of your money. But if you are inaccurate on your predictions, or you try to double-cross me, like you did to our unfortunate Mr. Keegan, then I guess you will be giving me information about your athletes for quite a while."

"Why do you need these upgrades?"

"Obviously, I need better audio—otherwise I would have caught yours and Mr. Keegan's corruption at the start, and we wouldn't be in this whole bloody mess now, would we?"

Andrew didn't answer. Fergus asked again more firmly, requiring compliance. "Would we?"

"No, we wouldn't." Andrew looked disgusted.

"Don't look at me like that, Doctor. Your actions put you in this situation, not mine. You have done very well here. Don't look at me like I'm the one in the wrong. You could have compromised my gaming business and cost me millions of dollars. You think I'm being unreasonable here? I'm the one who has been wronged in all this."

Fergus closed the distance once again between him and Andrew and lowered his tone. "Perhaps I should have let Mr. Keegan just kill you." He looked Andrew up and down. "And then Corravallo would have killed Keegan, and the whole thing would've been a page three story in *The Post* and I'd be done with all of you."

Andrew had nothing to say. Andrew was caught, he was on fire and Fergus had the hose, but he wouldn't turn it on. His mind was racing through the events of the week at a warp speed. He was looking for where it all went sideways. He was in the middle of a car crash, wondering if it was happening or not. But the jolt to his body was real, the throbbing in his head was real, the only way he could fight this was go with it. Fergus had all the cards, and the chips. Andrew had to fold this hand and save whatever chips he had for the next hand. Fergus had won.

Andrew looked down, closed his eyes briefly, and then looked up and said, "$250,000 isn't enough to stake in the Players Room."

"I guess you better be right twice in a row then." Fergus walked back to his chair, sat, and folded his hands on his desk. He looked up at Andrew with an expression of compassionate concern. "You don't look so good, mate. Perhaps you should get something to eat, eh?"

"Yeah. I think I will." But Andrew couldn't eat even if he wanted to. There was nothing but a pit of molten lava turning over and over in his belly. He took a deep breath and left Fergus' office, each step causing his throbbing head to ache more. He had to get out of there and get out now.

32

The brass knocker of the big red door reverberated a few times as Andrew left Fergus' office. It sounded more like a gavel that pounded after a sentence was given by a fire and brimstone judge than the homey ring to a welcoming manor house.

As Fergus had suggested, Andrew felt nauseous, and the thought of eating something was the last thing on his mind. He descended the red carpeted steps from the second floor slowly. Each step was one step closer to his new reality. About halfway down the steps, Andrew spotted Lorry, arms crossed, eyeing him as he took each step. She closed her eyes, and a hand quickly went to her eyes as she shook her head.

Was that a tear she wiped away?

And for the second time in as many years as he knew her, he could read her face, and the emotion behind it: disappointment and sadness. She cared about him—she really cared. It didn't help his nausea.

She tried to warn me! She knew what Fergus would ask. And by the looks of her face, she knew I would give in. Fuck me!

When he reached the bottom step, he made eye contact with her. He shrugged his shoulders in defeat. Lorry walked away in a hurry, her head still shaking.

Andrew thought that maybe a good game of cards would get his mojo back. He took a deep breath and then summoned up some energy to power walk and shake off the guilt and shame that flooded his mind and body. In a few short minutes, Andrew was at the steps to the Players' Tables. He gave a quick smile to the security guards, they opened the velvet rope for him, and he bounced up the four small steps to the platform. He reached for his marker card and felt the hard, cold graphite. But as he did, he was hit with what felt like an electric shock as he remembered he only had $250,000 on the card. He needed $500,000. Rather than risk further embarrassment, he stuck the card back in his breast jacket pocket and turned around. The guards gave him a questioning look, and he told them he would be right back; he wanted to get a drink. A guard called that someone could get it for him, but he waved the man off and headed towards the bar.

He walked silently through the main room, and the noise surrounding him, of people playing cards, eating, and drinking, and talking, became white noise. His head pulsed. He was about 50 feet from the bar when he saw a figure with salt and pepper hair hunched over the bar.

"Mr. Davidson?" he said out loud but only to himself. Andrew's heartbeat rapidly, and he felt the pulse in his brain rush, forcing his body to walk quicker than normal. When he was about six feet away from the bar, Andrew called out excitedly. "Mr. Davidson!" Then, reaching the man, he gently repeated, "Mr. Davidson?"

The bartender immediately approached and asked, "A Macallan 18 for you, Dr. Beck?"

Andrew politely waved him off, "No thank you, buddy." Mr. Davidson was zoned out, ignoring Andrew.

Andrew asked, "Are you okay?"

Mr. Davidson looked at him with a raised eyebrow and snapped, "Of course I'm okay. What kind of question is that? And furthermore, why do you even give a fuck?" He had now turned so they were face to face. Andrew searched his face for marks or bruises, but there weren't any, but there was deep anger.

"It looks like you're the one who got a beatdown! Who'd you lose to?"

Andrew tried to get the words out but struggled, "Mr. Davidson, I'm, I'm…"

Mr. Davidson turned back to the bar and gritted, "Ah, save it for someone who gives a shit."

Mr. Davidson finished his drink, slammed his glass down, and walked away. When he was about three steps away, he turned and snapped, "Judas!" Then he slipped into the crowd of patrons.

An overwhelming sadness overtook Andrew. He ran his hand through his hair and walked away from the bar. He walked past the Sports Book area, went in, and took a seat. The baseball games on the West Coast were still live, and the Phoenix Falcons were playing the Austin Wings in Phoenix. Andrew watched the Falcons right-handed relief pitcher Davey Rizzo facing off against the Wings' second baseman and bottom-of-the-lineup hitter Jerry Barnes. Rizzo was a good pitcher with an ERA of 2.78. With a batting average of .208 last year, Barnes was paid for his defensive skills, not his bat. All glove, no stick.

Andrew watched Rizzo's pitching motion, facial expressions, and body movements while also looking at Barnes' stance, face, and how he waggled the bat. Andrew assessed Rizzo had a clear advantage over Barnes statistically. But there was something about the look on Barnes' face— like he knew something Rizzo didn't.

The couches were scattered with a few men watching the games with various levels of interest. In an off-blue Tom Ford suit, red Louis Phillippe tie, and silver and blue Ray-Ban glasses, one well-dressed man was also studying the players carefully.

"This poor guy doesn't have a chance against Rizzo," he said as he looked over at Andrew.

Andrew shook his head. "I don't know. He might surprise you."

"I'll bet you $100,000 he doesn't even get the ball out of the infield. Hit or no hit, the best thing this kid will get is a foul ball." The well-dressed man threw his marker card down on the table with a thump.

Andrew's knee-jerk reply came out, "I don't..." But he stopped himself. A repulsion shot through Andrew's body, and anger and resentment grew from deep inside him. He directed it towards the man to avoid going to the person it was meant for...himself. Without another word, nor eye contact, he reached in his jacket pocket and tossed his card on the table as well.

The two men sat silently, staring up at the big screen. Rizzo's first pitch was low, a ball. He looked strong on the mound, and the pitch was a fastball, clearly wanting to overpower Barnes. The next pitch, a curveball, went inside. Rizzo was trying to brush back the right-handed batter, but it didn't faze Barnes. He still had a determined, confident look on his face. The next pitch was right down the middle, a fastball, and Barnes took a wicked cut but missed it. The man smirked briefly. The count was two balls and one strike.

The next pitch was a curveball, and Barnes ripped it down the third base line, but it was in foul territory. This made the man sit up. It was Andrew's turn to smirk. But the two men didn't engage. The count was two balls and two strikes. One more strike and Andrew would lose the bet.

Andrew watched Barnes settle in. The cameras focused on his face, and there was sheer determination and fearlessness there. When the cameras focused on Rizzo, Andrew saw him push out a deep breath and pull his lips in as if he was refraining from cursing.

Andrew turned to the man and said, "This pitch, he'll hit it."

The man scoffed, "Bullshit."

"Double it then."

The man agreed and scooted to the end of the couch cushion. Andrew sat back and crossed his arms. He felt his heart burn, and the anger inside him was rising to the surface. He gritted his teeth to keep it at bay.

Rizzo's next pitch tried to overpower Barnes, throwing a hard fastball, but Barnes swung quickly and smoothly, like he knew it was coming, and the ball sailed high and long. The fans roared as the Falcons' outfielder raced to the left field wall. He ran hard and put one foot on the wall where the giant lettering of 384 was painted, meaning how many feet the left field fence was from home plate, and leaped in the air, extending his glove high enough to reach over the wall. He snatched the ball, saving the ball from going over the fence. Even though Barnes was out, the cameras showed he had a satisfied grin on his face. It was the farthest ball he hit in quite a while.

The man looked at Andrew, took a breath, raised his eyebrows and said, "Well, he definitely hit it out of the infield. I guess I owe you $200,000, Mister...."

Andrew got up, picked up his marker card off the table, put it inside his jacket pocket, buttoned his navy cashmere sport coat, and looked down at the seated man peering over his Ray-Bans. "It's Doctor. Dr. Beck. And forget it. I don't want your fucking money."

The man looked surprised and taken aback by Andrew cursing at him. Andrew walked away, pointing at the screen, "They both played at UCLA in college! Barnes knew Rizzo's fucking pitches. Why else would a shitty hitter like him have that confident look on his face?!"

As Andrew left the Sports Book area, he didn't feel the relief he always felt when he won. Instead, he was fuming inside. He needed that $200,000 to gamble, but he couldn't get it *that way*. His body was feasting on a stew of guilt, shame, frustration, and anger. He was looking for something or someone to direct it at. But there was no one. No one but himself. And that was the greatest burn of all.

Andrew retrieved his belongings and asked the concierge to call a car service to take him to his car, as it was still at his office. He was exhausted and wanted to get home as soon as possible. As The Five Iron elevator doors opened to Mercer Street, he felt a blast of April chill. He shivered as the sport coat wasn't doing the trick. He hoped the car would arrive fast as he tried to block the biting wind with his small briefcase. His internal stew was still boiling, and now his head was throbbing from the cold too. He stepped into the cobblestone street and paced back and forth to keep himself warm, hoping the sounds of his shoes on stone would soothe his frayed nerves.

Andrew turned on his phone, saw he had three messages from Sandra, and he scrolled through them.

"Hi honey, are you okay? Kiss emoji."

"Please text me when you land, okay?"

"Heading to bed, I hope you had a good night. Sleeping emoji."

Andrew wrote back, "Hi Babe, sorry, no service on the plane, heading home now. See you in the morning, kisses."

Andrew sent the message and he tasted guilt the most from his emotional stew right now. He wished he had headed right home after seeing Vlad. He stared back at the nondescript stainless-steel elevators and cursed them and the hold The Five Iron had on him. He wanted nothing more right now than to be lying next to his wife, just to be still, a moment where he didn't have to juggle any more balls, to not feel regret for what he had done and dread for what he had still to do. He shivered so hard he fumbled his phone, but he caught it before it fell to the ground. At least his reflexes were still working.

A black car pulled up and Andrew got in and instructed the driver to take him to his office.

The car heat was on, which helped him warm up, but his head was still throbbing. He put his head back on the black leather Town Car seats, a significant upgrade from tonight's yellow cab experience. He closed his eyes, not so much because he was going to sleep, but looking at buildings and streets whizzing by only exacerbated his nausea and headache.

Andrew drifted off into that state where you aren't asleep, but you are not fully conscious either. He was in limbo, stuck between the conscious and unconscious, not dreaming but not in reality either. It was a state of mind that he tolerated. He needed to get a quick nap in so he could make the trip to Connecticut without falling asleep behind the wheel.

About 15 minutes into his ride, he was in the tunnel under the Madison Avenue Bridge when Andrew's phone rang. The caller ID said Riley Asherton. Andrew hit the answer button and said, "Hello?"

"Beck? This is Riley." For once he wasn't using his dickish voice.

"It's very late, Riley. What do you want?" But Andrew used his.

"Vlad is going to have to go before a panel of NAHL brass. He could be suspended for the rest of the year. If he misses the playoffs, I swear I—"

Andrew interrupted the rant. "What time is the hearing?"

"Tomorrow at 1 p.m."

"Tomorrow?!"

"Why, is that going to ruin your weekend playing crochet or whatever you people in Greenwich do with each other?" His civility couldn't last.

"Cut the crap, Riley. I'll be there."

"The address is 1185 Avenue of…"

"The Americas, or as real New Yorkers call it: 6th Avenue."

"We'll be on the 15th floor. And you fucking better—"

Andrew hung up. He had enough of Riley's attitude. He had enough of all of it. But he was stuck, caught in a trap that had no way out. Fergus had him, but he was not going to give in. He *couldn't* give in. He would never let another man like Ted control his life ever again. That was the promise he made to himself all those years ago, the last time he felt he wasn't in control of his life. But that was an 18-year-old breaking away from his father's iron grip. This scenario was different—this was life and death. He was going to be playing a dangerous game. His frustration grew at the position he had gotten himself into, but now wasn't the time to feel sorry for himself. He had to come up with a plan—a plan to beat Fergus at his own game. And the only way out…was all-in.

Although beating Fergus weighed heavily on his mind, he first needed to get Vladimir out of trouble with NAHL brass. His tired brain started working overtime. He had to find their weakness. Just as Fergus had found his—he just needed a moment. A moment when these arrogant ex-hockey players and coaches would reveal their hand, and then he would force *them* to fold.

Part 6: Saturday, April 13, 2019

33

Andrew was sound asleep. His breathing was deep as he exhaled through his mouth. The door to the bedroom opened, and Sandra walked in casually. Andrew heard the door open and woke up but didn't open his eyes. In fact, he rolled over and buried his face in his pillow.

Sandra playfully said, "Good morning, sleepyhead. You want to get up now?"

With his face still in the pillow Andrew mumbled, "What time is it?"

Sandra sat on the bed in an oversized white T-shirt that went down just past her hips, looked at her Pink Sand iWatch, and replied, "Almost noon."

Andrew shot up as if he was jolted with electricity. "NOON! Fuck! I have to be at the NAHL office at one! Why did you let me sleep so late?!" He leaped out of bed and headed towards the bathroom.

"You were so exhausted and..."

Andrew's voice echoed from inside the bathroom as he spat out, "Fuck, fuck, fuck, fuck!"

A few seconds later, a dripping wet and toweled Andrew raced to the closet. Sandra, running her hands through her disheveled hair, sat on the bed looking down and wringing her hands.

"I'm sorry, I didn't know..." she choked out.

Andrew was rustling in the closet and barked out, "Forget about it."

The hangers were being roughly moved on the metal closet bar creating an unnerving scraping sound. "Where the fuck is my Canali blue linen shirt?" Andrew felt as if the walls of time were closing in on him.

Sandra said in a shaken voice, "We have date night tonight at the club."

Andrew found his shirt and exclaimed, "Ah, there it is." But he didn't quite hear what Sandra said. He yelled, "What?"

Sandra repeated louder, "We have date night tonight."

"I know," he replied sharply.

"Okay, well, good luck. I'll see you later." Sandra quickly exited the room. The door closed behind her quietly. Andrew could hear the rubber of her Oofos sandals on the hardwood floor fade as she walked towards the stairs.

Andrew stopped buttoning his shirt and ran his hands through his unbrushed hair.

Shit. What the fuck is wrong with me? It wasn't her fault. You're such an asshole.

Andrew drove 70 mph on the Henry Hudson Parkway, weaving in and out of traffic. His adrenaline was pumping as he yelled at a car in front of him that changed lanes at the same time he did. He rode up near the car's bumper, blasted his horn and flashed his high beams.

"Get the fuck out of the way!"

He maneuvered back into the middle lane and hit the accelerator as he pushed the command button on his steering wheel to activate his phone. He told Siri to call Gina Perez. On the third ring, Gina picked up. "Yeah, Boss? You at the NAHL Office?"

"No, I fucking overslept. GPS has me there at 1:06."

"You want me to call Riley?"

"No, I'll deal with him when I get there. I have dinner with Sandra at the club tonight." Andrew took a second, wincing as he uttered, "I think I need some 'get me out of the doghouse' flowers at our table. Can you handle that?"

Gina replied supportively, "Yeah Boss, no problem."

Andrew then had another car cut in front of him, moving at least 15 miles an hour slower than him. He hit the brakes and slammed on the horn. "Motherfucker! What are you doing?!"

"Talking to you, and that's Miss Motherfucker to you, mister," Gina replied sarcastically.

"Not you, an asshole in a Beemer cut me off."

"Yeah, but it's not his fault," Gina explained.

"What?!"

"Yeah, BMW drivers can't help cutting people off because in a Beemer, the default factory setting is always on douche bag mode."

Andrew laughed, "Oh god, I needed that. Thank you, Gina." He continued to laugh quietly.

Gina replied with a lighthearted tone, "All in a day's work, Boss."

Andrew sincerely said, "What would I do without you?"

"You'd be a sorry-assed, hopeless headshrinker forced to listen to Connecticut white people talk about the soulful torture of having to decide between summering in the Hamptons or Martha's Vineyard."

Andrew laughed even harder. "Oh, shoot me now." Then he stopped laughing abruptly as a flash of Wednesday night ran through his brain in a microsecond.

"Maybe I should stop saying that," he added.

Gina was confused at the comment and asked, "What?"

"Nothing."

Gina switched gears into logistics mode. "Do you need to prep anything for Vlad's defense?"

"I think I'm pretty good. Vlad and I made some breakthroughs this week, but he's a complicated person."

"Aren't we all? But you'll get him through this!" Gina reassured him.

"Thanks. Really Gina, I don't know what I would do without you. Thank you."

Gina was quiet for a moment, and then her tone turned serious, "Andrew, you know why I work with you, don't you?"

"I thought it was the six-figure paycheck and the amazing coffee at the office."

"First of all, I buy the coffee, so you're welcome. And secondly, yeah, the money is good, but you're a total pain in the ass, and you call me late at night and on Saturday mornings! But no, it's not the money either."

Andrew knew that for Gina, leaving the US Women's National Team was the hardest decision she ever had to make. She was partying too much, and she told him in some of their after-work conversations that she was with so many different women, she couldn't keep track. It was all so easy. But she was miserable. She had been playing soccer since she was six. And even though she and her team won two World Cups and played professional soccer, the league paid peanuts, and she struggled financially. When she took her annual two-week vacation in July from Andrew's practice, she didn't go to Cabo or the Caribbean, but she went to coach at elite soccer camps. The irony was that she made more money during her vacation than she did in a half a season playing professional soccer. The disparity between men's and women's salaries in professional sports, except tennis, is crazy.

Gina's fall from grace occurred when a poorly timed picture was taken at a party with a 19-year-old fan named Amber Mangelli. The picture showed them both with drinks in their hands. Their eyes and facial expressions showed they were both drunk. Gina's hand inadvertently slipped down around Amber's behind, and the young woman posted the pic on all her social media accounts. The post went viral, and consequently, Gina lost her sponsors, the USWNT stripped her of her co-captain title, the league suspended her, and she was utterly crucified in the media.

Gina told Andrew that the two weeks she spent in her Atlanta apartment waiting out an official investigation and her suspension, isolated, avoiding the press, friends, and family, was the lowest time in her life. She considered killing herself. All the shit she had gone through in coming out, her estrangement with her mother, and the Catholic family members who tried to "cure" her of who she was. The suspension and negative attention destroyed her love of the game. What was left worth living for? She still loved her teammates, winning and being recognized on the national stage. The fame was great— before it became infamy.

Gina turned to booze to not only kill the pain in her aching legs, knees, and hips, but to kill the voice in her head that screamed at her, "Without soccer, you're worthless." Then one morning, she woke up hungover and covered in her vomit and she decided it was time to quit partying, quit soccer, and get her life in order.

So here she was, 28, and out of pro soccer, and she didn't have one marketable skill. She wanted to coach. However, even when the league exonerated Gina of any formal "moral clause" issues in her contract, colleges don't give coaching positions to women accused of fondling an under-age drunk girl. The press never spends the same amount of time promoting the truth as they do sensationalizing the rumors.

She would often tell Andrew that he was one of the lucky ones. He got his masters and his PhD. He left sports intact...mostly. Gina, however, was a mess. She went from two-time World Cup co-captain and hero to pariah in the second it takes to upload a post online.

Andrew met Gina when he made a presentation on how to achieve peak performance through positive self-talk and visualizations to Hofstra's women's soccer team. He complained to their Head Coach that he needed someone to organize and manage his business affairs. The coach, who side-stepped protocol to have Gina on staff for the summer camps, knew he could not keep her on when the season officially started in the fall, recommended her to Andrew. From their time together Andrew knew how dedicated, smart, and capable Gina was. Gina was as green as the grass of a soccer pitch when it came to business, but she had potential, and Andrew saw it. Right away, Gina and Andrew connected. He knew her combination of a 'no-shit' attitude and penchant for detail which made her a top defender would also be transferrable to his practice and would be good for him and his patients.

Gina hesitated and her voice choked a bit. "No offense, but it's not about you. It's about the athletes. When I see Lamar and John Palmer, and even Robbie Owen, who hits on me every fucking appointment, I am still connected to that world. That world of professional sports. I miss it. I miss it every damn day. But when I see them after their appointment, and I get a few minutes to connect and talk to them about their latest game and what's happening in their lives, I'm back in the locker room just shooting the shit. I'm home again."

Andrew took a second and let the moment sit. "You know Robbie hits on everyone, right? Men, women...plants. Doesn't matter with her."

Gina laughed. "Yeah, she's a pisser, but it's all an act. Come on now, Andrew, be a hundred percent honest with me."

"About what?"

"Don't you miss competitive golf? The fucking butterflies, getting your best shot of the day? Making the winning putt? You must."

"Gina, competitive golf is so far behind me. It dominated so much of my childhood that no, I don't miss it at all."

"Really? At eighteen, you were the top-ranked amateur golfer in the country. You don't get there on just ability. You gotta have the drive. You gotta have a love of the game, the thrill of competition."

"Yeah, I do love competition, but I find other, more healthy outlets for myself. Something that isn't so...damaging."

"Like what?"

Andrew took a second. "I guess that's why I like pitching new business. When I step into the boardroom or even the living room for that matter, it's like stepping onto the green to make that birdie putt—that same rush. And seeing people like John Palmer go from drug addict and on his way out of baseball to the ace starter of the Tides. That's where I get my thrills."

Gina wasn't convinced. "I dunno. That's real meta stuff. For me, there was nothing like getting the ball away from a striker, knocking her to the ground and clearing the ball. Letting them know there was no way they were ever going to get a shot off today. No offense, but golf is a pretty passive sport." She added, "How did you get the physical intensity out?"

Andrew shot back, "It wasn't passive according to the Ted Beck School of Kamikaze Golf. There wasn't a single moment when you weren't visualizing your next shot or getting in your opponent's head. I was taught a 'take no prisoners' approach to the game." He squeezed the wheel, his hands ground the leather and his voice intensified, "Whatever I had to do to win, I did. I did many things I wasn't proud of."

"My point exactly, so now where is your outlet? Look, you can fool some people, but I know you, Andrew. You must have an outlet for that need for competition. It wouldn't be—and as a gay woman, I hate this word—but *normal* if you didn't."

"Okay, you got me. I do have one outlet where I can totally let my competitive side go nuts."

"Oh yeah? Doing what?"

Andrew paused and then let out a grin. "Driving!" He bought the car to a screeching halt in front of the 1185 Avenue of the Americas.

Gina chuckled. "Yeah, you are a bit of a wild man behind the wheel. But you know, I still don't buy it. Come on, it's me. Level with me."

"I'm here and it's 1:03pm. I gotta go."

Andrew hung up the phone and bolted out of the car. He had parked in a no-parking zone, but with his "PSY" license plates and his hazard lights flashing he hoped he wouldn't get a ticket. He raced through the glass doors into the building.

34

Andrew was ushered to a conference room on the 15th floor, where seated on one side of a long conference room table was Riley Asherton, General Manager of the New York Sentinels hockey team. On the other side of the table were several older men, board members of the North American Hockey League. Most of the men were ex-hockey players and coaches. They munched on continental breakfasts. Andrew remained standing and said, "Sorry I'm late, gentlemen, traffic was brutal on the Henry Hudson."

Riley remained seated but pointed to Andrew and did his best impression of an introduction. "I think you all know Dr. Andrew Beck; he's the Sentinels' sports psychologist, and he is currently treating Vladimir Poplov."

The man seated in the middle of the table spoke up. He was an older gentleman, mid-sixties, white-haired, and although he had the broad shoulders of a hockey player, his belly showed the years in between the last time he had put on skates. "I'm Orrin Gates, head of the Disciplinary Actions Subcommittee for the NAHL. And yes, Dr. Beck, I read your article on using meditations and visualizations to invoke peak performance in any sport. Very interesting."

"Thank you, Mr. Gates. Glad you liked it."

Gates continued, "Dr. Beck, we have all reviewed the video of Poplov's fight with Teddy Newsome. Mr. Asherton tells me you have some insight into this overreaction and why Poplov should not be suspended for the rest of the season. Please explain."

Riley looked at Andrew and signaled for him to come down so

Riley could whisper to him, "Don't you fuck this up, Beck, or I will have your head."

Andrew wasn't fazed and stood up and smiled at Riley. "Thank you, Riley. Yes, I'll make sure to mention that."

Gates inquired. "Dr. Beck?"

"Yes, thank you, Mr. Gates, and the rest of you gentlemen for coming in on a Saturday. On behalf of the New York Sentinels and Vladimir Poplov, I appreciate having the opportunity to show you the extenuating circumstances and psychological triggers that resulted in an excess of violence by Vladimir Poplov."

Gates rolled his hands at Andrew. "Yes, yes, that's all well and good. Please proceed, Dr. Beck."

Andrew spoke with his hands in a controlled rhythmic manner, "Vladimir Poplov was a product of post-communist Russia. Life was very difficult for him and his family. As we all know, the collapse of the former Soviet Union's economy had a devastating effect on its people. Hockey was the one positive outlet for the Poplov family that both Vlad and his younger brother Nikita, or Nikki, relied upon. Vladimir Poplov is a four-time all-star and two-time Russian Olympian. He's one of the top defensemen in the NAHL. The reason why the Sentinels leads the NAHL in goals scored and are in first place in the Eastern Division is that Sentinels forwards have his protection."

Andrew began to pace the length of the table, making eye contact with the various members around the table. "When the 'Russian Bear,' as Vlad is known by, is on the ice, his forwards know there won't be any cheap shots. And they can play the kind of hockey they want to play. Good, clean, hockey."

Gates was getting annoyed. "We get it, Dr. Beck. Please tell us what, as you call it, 'triggered' Poplov to beat a man senseless."

"Mr. Gates, the harsh realities of the collapse of the Soviet Union created familial bonds that were iron clad. Vlad's father, Sergei Poplov, was adamant that under no circumstances was anyone ever allowed to harm a family member. One time, a bigger boy hit Vlad's younger brother Nikki, who was younger and much smaller than the other boy, with a cheap shot. And Nikki didn't inherit his father's strength and size, as Vlad did. Nikki was boarded and knocked unconscious. Vlad went after the other boy, as any big brother would do and gave that boy a beating he would not soon forget. But unfortunately, the boy Vlad attacked was the son of someone important in the politburo. And the retribution from the attacker's father was fast and furious. And Vlad's brother ended up dead as a result."

Gates did his best impression of someone who cared. "I'm sorry, Dr. Beck, but regardless of how tragic a story this is, what does this have to do with Newsome?"

"I'm getting to that, sir. These memories have been repressed for years. However, during our therapy session, they surfaced, and they had a profound effect on Vlad."

Andrew continued his pacing, stopping every so often to make eye contact with the various members. "Often, the release of repressed emotions can be more intense in the present than it ever was in the past. So getting back to the game, Vlad saw his teammate and leading goal scorer, Chris Kruder, reaching for a bad pass from Vlad. The puck hit off the boards. He was out of the play and defenseless. And then, out of nowhere, comes Teddy Newsome. Attacking a defenseless Kruder, with an illegal hit that was premeditated, dangerous, and intended to cause harm. Then add to that the fact that the refs missed the hit, and there was no call for interference." Andrew slapped the table. "This is hockey! A retaliation was begged for!"

Gates rebutted, "The Freedom claim Newsome's forward momentum could not be stopped. That it was not intentional."

Andrew folded his arms across his chest and leaned up against the windowsill of the conference room window that looked out towards eastern Manhattan. There was a clear view of the top of the Chrysler Building. Andrew said, "I disagree, as do the Sentinels, and the approximately 30,000 fans in the TISEC who saw it for the cheap shot it was. The fact that *Newsome* is not being brought up for suspension is beyond me, but that is me as a fan, not a NAHL front-office man."

Gates sat back in his chair and crossed his arms too as he responded sarcastically, "And we appreciate you acknowledging you are *not* a professional in the NAHL."

Andrew took a more conciliatory tone. "Sir, Newsome boarded a player who was not able to defend himself. It was a cheap hit that triggered the remembrance of an extremely traumatic event in Vlad's life. As I work with him to purge this guilt and shame, I assure you, he will not have an outburst like this again. This was a 'perfect storm' of events that brought up two decades of repressed feelings, not a flagrant abuse of the rules of hockey."

Andrew let the moment settle, then uncrossed his arms and added, "But don't take my word for it. Look at the data. How many fights has Vlad been in? He has led the league in penalty minutes for two years in a row, but never once did he do anything like this. I've studied hours and hours of video to get to know what makes a person like Vladimir Poplov be the Ice Guardian he is." Andrew saw a few head nods and continued. "And in several fights, he has gone so far as to help up his opponent, checking to make sure he was okay. Like it or not, hockey has kept fighting as part of the game. Is fighting necessary for the game to protect the players? Does it bring in more fans as hockey has to stay competitive? I don't know. But what I do know is the violence committed by Vladimir Poplov was not premeditated. It was almost an uncontrollable response."

Gates shot back, "Okay Dr. Beck, thank you for that. So let's assume that it was, as you say, a 'perfect storm,' and he was reliving some kind of psychological trauma. What's to say he won't do this again? How do we know he won't be triggered again? That he won't become some, some raging lunatic?"

"First of all Mr. Gates, I resent you calling Vladimir Poplov a lunatic." He emphatically added, "That is not medically correct, nor is it socially acceptable, and I want my objection noted for the record that Mr. Gates' remarks are pejorative and prejudicial."

Gates backpedaled. "All right, all right, Dr. Beck. I withdraw my statement and apologize."

Andrew pounced, "Regardless, Mr. Gates, Vladimir won't have another reaction like the one he had because we have processed it. He is aware of the dark place where the outburst came from, and once a patient is aware of these traumas, they begin the healing process. They almost never resurface again in the same way."

Andrew clasped his hands in front of him, "Fans adore Vladimir.

He is a loyal teammate who gives everything to them and to the game he has played since he was a little boy." Andrew paced back to the front of the room and added, "Newsome can play with a broken nose; almost every player in the NAHL has." Andrew grinned when one of the panel members pointed at his nose and silently held up four fingers. His pitch was working. Andrew continued, "Vlad was ejected from the game. Kruder missed the rest of the game with bruised ribs. If Boston is looking for an eye-for-an-eye, they got it, sir. That, and then some."

Gates got a tap on the arm from the man next to him and they huddled quietly. Two of the other men wheeled their chairs over as they seemed to all have something important to say to Gates. They were whispering, and though Andrew strained to hear them, he couldn't make out what they were saying.

Gates wheeled his chair back to his position, straightened out his sport coat, cleared his throat, and said, "Thank you, Dr. Beck, for your testimony. I think we have heard enough. We will let the Sentinels know our decision shortly."

Andrew nodded and politely said, "Thank you."

The men stood up, and Riley went to shake the committee members' hands, and then Riley and Andrew exited the conference room.

Outside the building, Andrew was relieved to see there was no ticket on his windshield. Maybe his doctor plates had some influence. Either that or New York City's finest were busy ticketing somewhere else. Either way, Andrew was grateful for the bit of luck. Andrew leaned his back against his Lexus and crossed his arms in satisfaction. The blue in his shirt contrasted nicely with the Nightfall Blue of his car. "I think that went well," Andrew said.

Riley crossed his arms and spat out. "You better hope so, for your sake."

Andrew used his hips to vault him from the car and got close enough to Riley's face to headbutt him. "Cut it out, Riley. What do you want from me, huh? I defended Vlad and made a good case."

"We have to have Vlad for the playoffs!" Riley said as he spread his arms out and backed away. He stuffed his hands in his pockets as if to signal his pistols were holstered and asked, "Is all that shit true about Vlad?"

"Yes, it is. He's in a tough spot. You put him in a role he excels in, but it's not the role he wants."

"What are you talking about? He's never complained about his role. He gets ice time—he's on the first line."

"Yeah, but he spends most of his time in the penalty box. He's happy to be a part of the team—especially this team. You're having a great season, and he knows he's a part of that. He'll never complain because a weakness like that would never be a part of his Russian character. But he also feels it's a true honor to protect his teammates. That's what drives him, not the violence, but family! *His hockey family!*"

The perplexed look on Riley's face disgusted Andrew. Until now, he thought most of Riley's posturing and tough guy schtick was just that, an act. But it turned out he played with athletes as if they were chess pieces. They were to be played and sacrificed for the good of the team, for the good of the team's owners, and the good of Riley's climb up the sports management ladder.

Andrew took a deep breath, but his frustration was getting the best of him. "Violence takes a toll on a man's mind, even someone as solid as Vlad. What—you think they go out, beat the crap out of another human being because it's their fucking job, and then just get on with their lives? Jesus Christ, Riley!"

Andrew composed himself, took a beat, then lowered his tone and spoke with his hands making calm but distinct movements. "Look, when Gates fucked up with that lunatic remark, I knew he made his mistake, and I pounced on it." Andrew made a fist like he squished a bug. "If Vlad gets suspended, throw your lawyers at Gates *personally*. Sue the shit out of him *and* the NAHL. Seeking treatment for mental health issues does not make you a lunatic; it makes you a strong person. It's okay to say you're not okay. The press would have a field day with this."

In contrast to Andrew's gesticulations, Riley was still. "Yeah, I caught that," Riley said calmly. "But will it work?"

Andrew was past his point of no return, and he lost his professorial tone. "Of course it will, Riley! I know what the fuck I'm doing. I read Gates' tells. I know you and the rest of those men have a base macho-man bias against therapy—like it's a weakness to be in therapy. Instead of dealing with traumas, you should just 'be a man' and 'rub some fucking dirt in it.'" Andrew rubbed his arms, pantomiming like rubbing dirt on a scrape. Andrew closed the distance between him and Riley and held up a finger. "And I knew if I pontificated long enough with the sad story of Vladimir Poplov, Gates the mental Neanderthal would get bored. Then his giant ego would force him to interject. I was banking on him saying one thing where that macho bullshit would come out. I knew that the wrong word, in the wrong context, would set us up for a lawsuit if the committee didn't rule in our favor."

"You figured all that out?"

"Yeah, Riley. Everything in life is poker. You play the man, not the cards."

Riley looked a little out of sorts, so Andrew explained further.

"I knew Gates had the stronger hand, but like Vlad fights for you, I fought for him." Andrew pounded his chest and then mumbled to himself. "God knows you'd be no fucking help."

Riley either didn't hear the comment or let it go, because surprisingly he didn't react. He stood staring at Andrew, entranced.

"I knew all I had to do was tilt him into making a bad decision and say something stupid, which he did. Now they are forced to fold." Andrew spread his arms out and exclaimed, "Vlad will be in uniform, or we sue."

Riley nodded his head and said, "Remind me never to play poker with you."

35

Andrew raced back to Greenwich. At one point, he was doing 78 mph on the Merritt Parkway. The narrow two lanes made it a challenge to maintain his speed, especially as traffic increased on a warm April Saturday afternoon. He took exit 31 off the Merritt, onto North Street, and hit the accelerator, now hitting 60 mph in a 35-mph zone. Andrew enjoyed this part of the ride because there was a point where North Street and his street, Sprain Road, met, and there was a triangle where he had to make a hard left, and he liked to take it screaming fast, downshifting with the paddles on his steering wheel, then gunning it to keep from fishtailing. It was something that gave him a rush. Today would be no different, and as he approached the triangle, he slowed down to 34 mph and then made the hard left. He spun the leather steering wheel, but he went too far and the rear end of the car kicked out. Andrew smiled and slapped the steering wheel and laughed out loud to himself. "Too much on the turn, damn. Next time."

His house was only a few hundred feet away, but that didn't stop Andrew from accelerating until he reached the wide birth of his circular driveway. He skidded to a stop at his front porch rather than parking in the garage around the west side of the house. Andrew leaped out of the car and launched himself into the house, calling out Sandra's name. But despite his calls, there was no response.

Andrew walked hurriedly into the kitchen, but no Sandra. He threw his keys and car fob on the kitchen table, walked into the living room, and called again for his wife. But again, no answer.

Andrew approached the thick sliding glass door to the back patio and saw Sandra sipping coffee and reading *The New York Times*. He smiled as he watched her for a moment, fully engrossed in what she was reading. Her ability to focus on something as if it was the only thing in the world but yet be very aware of what was happening around her was something he admired about her. She had on her purple North Face fleece to stave off the April chill while the deep purple pulled in the heat from the afternoon sun that lit up the entire backyard. She looked radiant in the sunlight, similar to the picture on his phone. He could only smile, and he thought for a second that he didn't want to interrupt her moment of Zen. However, the excitement that had built up inside him had to be shared, or he would bust wide open.

Andrew slid the glass door and stepped outside. The warm sunlight greeted him, as did the chirping birds, and there was a slight breeze. It couldn't be a more perfect New England spring day.

Andrew grinned as he called gently out to Sandra, "There you are."

Sandra looked over her shoulder, "Hey, you're back. How'd it go?" she said in a subdued tone.

Andrew kissed her on the cheek and sat down. Sandra put down the paper, pulled up her legs into the chair, wrapped her arms around them, and leaned her chin on her knee.

"He might be suspended for a game or two, but the Sentinels will have him for the playoffs."

"That's good," she said in a subdued tone.

Andrew took a moment and then humbly said, "Hey babe. Sorry I snapped at you this morning."

Sandra sprung out of her ball, firmly planted her feet on the patio, sharpened her tone. "Yeah, let's unpack that a bit."

"It wasn't your fault and…"

"You're damn right it wasn't my fault. I know you have been under a lot of stress and your mugging must have been really scary, but these angry outbursts? Not cool. Not cool at all."

Andrew pleaded, "You're right. I'm sorry. Every step I took this week seemed like I was stepping on a landmine."

"That's no excuse for treating me like shit. Or not coming home or staying out all hours of the night without calling me."

"I explained why, and I apologized." Andrew sat back in his chair. "What more do you want from me?"

Sandra shook her head and looked intently into Andrew's eyes, but her tone was quieter. "I want you to treat me like someone you love."

Andrew sighed and his words were lost. He looked out into the large back yard.

"Maybe you should talk to someone," Sandra suggested.

Andrew raised an eyebrow and said, "So you're saying the psychologist needs to see a psychologist?"

Sandra leaned forward and became very sincere as the anger drifted away. "Maybe the mugging is triggering some of the trauma Ted put you through. Or maybe you're repeating Ted's pattern of rarely being around, and then being in an awful mood when you are." Sandra took a beat and then as if something hit her for the first time. "You know, you're starting to act and sound an awful lot like him."

"Sandra! Don't ever compare me to that man! I told you what happened this week, and I've apologized! That son-of-a-bitch never apologized for anything he did to me, to Mom, or Brandon."

Sandra spread her arms out and retorted in a louder tone, "Look at yourself! I just mention his name, and you're raising your voice at me again!"

Andrew grabbed the armrests of the cushioned chair with both hands and took a deep breath. "Yeah. He's a trigger. Sandra, you have to understand—he is the antithesis of everything I want to be."

"I get it, but look at what you're doing to yourself, look at what you're doing to me."

Andrew rubbed his head and let out a heavy sigh. Sandra extended her arms, pointing at the house and everything around them and said, "Andrew, look at me. Is all of this, the house, the country club, the offices, the cars…is it all worth it?" She swept her arm from the yard to the house. "Is it worth forcing you to be out so late that you come home beat up, or you're forced to sleep on a couch in your office? Is it worth it that you're so stressed and anxious that you're getting mad at the one person who is always on your side?"

"Sandra, it's been a hell of a week. Things will change. It's just a bump. That's all." He hung his head and rubbed his neck.

Sandra shook her head. "When does it end, Andrew?"

Andrew jerked up. "What'd you say?"

"When does it end?"

Andrew looked away again to the backyard and shook his head, "Jesus Christ, we sound like my...parents!"

Sandra leaned over and softly stated, "That's what I'm talking about. That's why this has to end."

Andrew peered off into the trees. "Once, Dad got into a screaming match with my Grandpa Samuel Beck because he wouldn't attend Dad's 'Member of the Year' ceremony at the country club. It was 1991. He had won the US Open and the PGL Championship that year—he was on a roll. I was twelve, Brandon was fourteen. We were sitting on the steps when we heard the whole thing go down."

He was picturing his young self, sitting next to Brandon. They had a bird's-eye view from the top of the stairs as they watched Ted slam the phone and call out Helena. They could hear the big grandfather clock ticking in the foyer. It seemed to be ticking faster than normal, that somehow that clock always seemed to follow the rhythm of whatever was going on in the house.

"That son-of-a-bitch. He won't come!" yelled Ted.

Helena tried to calm him down. "Oh dear, I'm sorry. Did he say why?"

Ted barked, "Because that selfish bastard can't stand to share the limelight with me!" He added with sarcasm, "He always has to be the big kahuna!"

Helena pleaded, "Yes, but what reason did he give?"

"He has a finance committee meeting for his company. And, get this, he doesn't want to drive across town at rush hour. Can you believe that guy? It's Greenwich, not Manhattan!"

Helena tried to find some middle ground. "His health isn't good. Maybe sitting in a car is difficult for his sciatica?"

"No! That's not it. What's difficult for that asshole is the fact that my 'stupid game of golf' has made me wealthy, successful, and famous! And that more people at the club love me than him. He hates it when I'm the center of attention!"

"Oh darling, I'm sure he's proud of you in his own way."

Ted spoke in a denigrating tone, "Helena, he's still pissed at me for the summer of '72, when we told him we were going to visit all the National Parks between Greenwich and Palo Alto on my way to college. But instead, I played in tournaments to gain points to become a pro golfer."

Helena disputed him, "Oh Ted, come on now, do you really think he's holding a grudge from a little fib made by an eighteen-year-old boy?"

"No one holds a grudge like Samuel Beck. But it wasn't the lie as much as how he found out about the lie. Remember that?"

Helena gasped. "How can I forget? In front of all those people, too."

"How dare he!" Ted expounded. "I should be the one pissed *at him*! He should be on his hands and knees begging for *my* forgiveness after that event." Ted stood steaming with his hands on his hips as he quipped, "Miserable bastard. Well, fuck him. Fuck Samuel Beck and his miserable fucking Transatlantic Industries."

Helena was aghast. "Ted, your language! The boys! They'll hear you."

Ted yelled out, "Good!" Then he peered up the stairs at a seated and shocked Andrew and Brandon. "Hey, boys! Your grandfather is biggest son-of-a-bitch that ever lived! Consider yourself lucky you only have to see him at Christmas, Easter, and your birthdays!"

Helena threw her arms out in disgust, "Oh, Ted Beck, sometimes you are an insufferable man. When does this end, Ted? When does it end?"

Andrew remembered hearing his mom walk away, the click-clack of her heals in sync with the ticking of the grandfather clock. Ted just shook his head and headed into the living room.

Andrew gave her an impish grin. "Brandon and I had to look up 'insufferable' in the dictionary." He laughed out loud as he added, "We were hoping it was a curse word. We had no idea because Mom never cursed."

Sandra stayed on point. "I get it, Andrew. I didn't grow up with the healthiest family either. But I don't like what is happening to you…to us.

"What do you want me to do? I can't just quit!"

"I'm not asking you to quit. I'm asking you to look at your priorities. Look at our life. Maybe we don't need all of this…this stress and aggravation."

"I worked really hard to get where I am. There are maybe a hundred other psychologists that work with as many athletes I do. I've broken into hockey this week, and football is next. It's taken me years to get here—I can't just stop."

Sandra crossed her arms and looked away into the newly leafed maple trees lining their back yard.

"Okay, I have to tell you something, and maybe it will explain some of my behavior this week."

Sandra jerked her head, and her eyes became wide. She leaned in and was attentive to every word.

"I got fired from the Tides on Monday. I got pissed at that asshole Rothstein and threatened to treat John privately, and he didn't blink."

Sandra reached across the chair, put a hand on Andrew's forearm, and rubbed it consolingly. "I'm sorry. That must have been hard." Her compassionate face faded as she asked, "If you weren't working with John, then why did you fly down to Miami?"

"I *am* working with John. I convinced him to work with me privately, but I was pretty nervous he wouldn't, truth be told. Addicts always find a way to avoid therapy and dealing with their addiction."

"So, then what's the problem?"

"Well…on the flight down, Vlad attacked Newsome, and I had to turn the plane around. I never made it to…"

Sandra gasped. "Oh Andrew! Did you tell John what happened? I'm sure he would understand."

"Sandra, he's a 23-year-old kid, he has no family, he's still processing his father's death and his drug addiction. No, I didn't tell him. I felt it might devastate him."

Sandra grimaced.

"Riley threatened to fire me and badmouth me to the Bulldogs, and everyone else he knew. I just got John on board. I didn't want to lose him again, so I made a call. Maybe it was a bad call, but I had a gun in my face." The words made his body convulse, but he caught it, and put both his hands behind his head and leaned back.

Sandra was shaking her head. The blonde curls at the end of her hair swung with the shake. "Where does it end, Andrew? Where does it end?"

Andrew pulled at his hair and looked off into the blue sky. He felt deflated again. Every win this week was countered by a bigger loss. What he did was wrong—he knew it.

"I'll call him on Monday. I'll come clean. You're right. He deserves that."

Sandra smiled. "And your conscience will feel much better." She took a broader grin and yelled out triumphantly, "The truth will set you free!" She ended with a self-satisfied giggle.

Andrew forced a smile. He didn't know if he even knew the *truth* anymore.

36

Inside the Greenwich Country Club, the tables were filled with club members and their guests having dinner and drinks. Soft music played in the background, and people were enjoying a happy Saturday night out.

The dress code for Saturdays required a jacket for men and boys, but ties were optional. Andrew had on his Canali blue linen shirt with a tan linen blazer. It was a little light for April, but he wanted to invite summer to get here faster after wearing dark clothes all week. Sandra had on a pink and black houndstooth dress cut two inches above the knee. Beneath the dress, she wore a black turtleneck shirt and a silver chain with a diamond charm in a teardrop shape around her neck. Sandra's sense of style was always something Andrew appreciated about her. She could be casual or formal, but she was always classy.

Andrew and Sandra were led to their table by the hostess, and when they arrived there was a bouquet of white roses in a clear glass vase on the table. Sandra looked at her husband and smiled.

"Those are for you, my dearest. I've been out of sorts all week. And you were right, I directed my frustration at you several times this week and it was undeserved, unwarranted, and I am very sorry."

Sandra took a seat, put her face near the roses, closed her eyes, and gave a deep inhale. She took a moment to take it in and then opened her eyes and looked across the table at Andrew. "They smell beautiful. Thank you, and apology accepted."

Andrew smiled and reached across to grab Sandra's hand. He

squeezed it affectionately with a warm smile.

As Sandra and Andrew were getting settled and looking at the menus, the waiter approached and said, "Good evening, Dr. Beck and Ms. Wells."

Sandra replied, "Hello, Adam. Good to see you again."

Adam smiled graciously. "Good to see you too, Ms. Wells. Can I get you anything to drink to start?"

"I'd love a glass of chardonnay, the Rusack Vineyards if you have it?"

Adam nodded and smiled as he looked over to Andrew for his order.

Andrew asked, "Did you get that case of Macallan 18 that I asked for?"

The waiter responded, "We certainly did, and I carried it down to the cellar myself."

"I'll have a glass, thank you." Adam nodded and turned to get their order when Andrew added, "And may I have it neat, please." Not wanting to repeat his flight experience. Adam acknowledged the specificity and headed towards the bar.

When Adam was a safe distance away from the table, Andrew leaned in and lowered his voice. "How you keep all their names straight is amazing."

Sandra smiled. "It's not that hard. I use word association around the first letter of someone's name. For example, Adam is tall and lean like an antelope, so 'Adam Antelope.' That sticks and is easy to recall."

Andrew was impressed. "You made a mnemonic device—great cognitive strategy. I'm always forgetting people's names. I remember their faces but forget their names."

"You should try it then."

"I will."

While Sandra glanced through the menu, she multitasked by leaning her nose over the bouquet to get a smell every so often, which made Andrew smile. As he scanned the menu, he was far more interested in the Keegan-Corravallo case than anything new that might have appeared on the menu. He was watching his wife, looking for the right moment to ask the question burning in him. As she glanced away from the menu and looked Andrew in the eye with a smile, Andrew took it as now was the right moment. But as he was about to ask, Adam returned with their drinks, interrupting the moment.

Adam set down a tray and two glasses and said, "Your chardonnay, Ms. Wells." He placed the wine glass holding the light golden liquid on the table. He then placed the highball glass with a caramel-colored liquid before Andrew. "And your Macallan 18, Dr. Beck."

Andrew looked up and smiled. "Thank you, Adam. I appreciate it."

Adam nodded, smiled and said, "You're welcome, sir. Enjoy."

The two put in their orders and Sandra waited until Adam was a few feet away before leaning over the table and in a low tone with a big smile saying, "Hey, you remembered his name. Nice!"

Andrew laughed. "Yeah, even a blind squirrel finds a nut every once in a while." They laughed and smiled at each other.

Now was a better moment. "I've been meaning to ask you. What happened with the Corravallo case?"

Sandra's eyes lit up. She rushed to get her words out, almost choking on the sip of wine. "Oh, yes! He was arraigned on first-degree murder charges, and bail was set at $1.5 million. The union is working on it now."

"Did you speak to him?"

"To Anthony Corravallo? No. Just to Gary at the Electrical Workers Union." She continued, "Last I heard, they couldn't establish Corravallo's alibi. He was last seen leaving his Lower Manhattan apartment around 10 p.m. and traffic cameras had him walking near Mercer Street around 10:23 p.m."

Andrew nodded. "Mercer Street, huh?"

That can't be a coincidence. Fergus had something to do with this! I know it!

As Andrew pretended to scan his menu, he threw out, "But the murder happened at South Street, right?"

Sandra smiled. "Yes!" She tapped him affectionately on the hand. "Corravallo said he was meeting a business associate at the Mercer Kitchen, he had a drink, waited for about thirty minutes, made some

301

calls from his cell, but the person never showed. The lawyers are going through the evidence trying to figure it all out."

"What about the cameras at Mercer Kitchen? Did they confirm his alibi?"

"The union's lawyers subpoenaed the footage. They should get it next week, and they said they would share it with us if there was anything to be used to calm the media storm against him."

I've got to get my hands on that video. Was he supposed to meet Keegan there? Maybe to hash out the union issues, and then when he didn't show...? Or was he supposed to meet Fergus there and he was too busy saving my sorry ass. If I could just see Corravallo's facial expressions, I...

Sandra sat up straight and smiled with her big brown eyes as much as her mouth. "Thanks for asking."

The pleasantness in her voice and sincerity in her face took Andrew out of his detective thoughts, and he smiled back at her as a wave of guilt smacked him in the chest: he was a good listener, it's what made him a good psychologist, but he had ulterior motives. He did well to control his facial features in a happy smile to maintain the bluff.

Sandra then inquired, "You hear anything more about Vlad?"

Andrew shook his head. "No, not yet. I was told the NAHL will make the decision today about his suspension. I'm surprised Riley hasn't called to harass me."

Sandra exhaled and grunted, "What a punk."

"You're not kidding."

Sandra raised her glass. "Cheers! Here's to date night."

Andrew smiled at her. "To date night." He raised his glass too. They clinked their glasses and took a sip.

Over dinner of salmon for Sandra and a lamb chop for Andrew, they covered a variety of light subjects from sports to business, to politics. It was ironic how Senator Mann seemed to disrupt both of their lives when it came to politics: on Tuesday, Sandra's race to the community center and her almost taking his and Ted's golfing spot on Sunday. Sandra told him that she and Senator Mann only got a few moments to talk, so she didn't get a chance to pitch her. Then, she only half-jokingly blurted out if she should stalk her on the golf course. Andrew, trying to hold back a laugh, raised an eyebrow and said, "Yeah, don't do that. She has trained bodyguards."

The two laughed together, continued talking, and finished their meal. It was a good night: the harsh feelings of the day had disappeared in the smell of the roses; the crackle of the fireplace in the dining area charmed them and the warm food in their bellies pleased them.

Sandra glanced over her shoulder to see who else was at the club tonight and then turned back fast after looking at the bar. She looked at Andrew and with a frown stated, "Oh God, Mom is holding court again at the bar."

Andrew pursed his lips for a second. "I noticed. I didn't want to say anything. I can see her from here, and she's throwing back the G and T's pretty hard."

Sandra looked over again, as did Andrew, and although she was fifty feet away, Roxanne Wells' booming voice carried. Roxanne was in her mid-sixties, dressed up in a navy pinstripe Gucci Double G chain dress with a white blouse underneath. She had a crowd of hedge fund babies in their twenties and thirties around her. She was telling stories of the "Mad Men" days of Madison Avenue in the 1970's. Roxanne definitely had a few too many in her and was talking loudly. "...And then I said, Mr. Warhol, if they keep paying you to paint soup cans, you keep fucking painting them!" The men around her laughed as Roxanne added, "True story! True fucking story. What a little pain in the ass he was..."

Sandra rolled her eyes and shook her head in disgust as she declared to Andrew, "Oh crap, that story comes out after G and T number five."

Andrew reached over to grab her hand and gently patted it. "Hey, babe. Don't let her ruin our night. We had a hard week. Let her do her thing, and we'll do ours, okay?"

Sandra nodded. "You're right, you're right. Let's enjoy the evening."

Andrew suddenly started to laugh, and Sandra inquired, "What's so funny?"

Andrew leaned over the table. "It reminds me of the time you and

I had our first *real* conversation. I had seen you around the club for a while, said hi to you a few times, but you didn't engage. Then one night, your mom was doing the same thing, holding court at the bar, except I was in the crowd of young men."

Sandra affirmed, "She always likes a circle of men when she's telling her 70's and 80's stories."

Andrew pointed out, "Yeah, but you were there too."

37

Andrew pictured the scene as he described it to Sandra. It was 2010, and Andrew was at the bar with a group of other men as Roxanne was telling her favorite story. Rihanna's "Only Girl (In the World)" was playing in the background and Andrew was eavesdropping on the conversation. But he was focused on the woman standing next to Roxanne: a young woman with short cropped blonde hair, wearing a red Dolce & Gabbana cotton minidress. Although she was stunning, it was the look of complete annoyance that grabbed Andrew's attention while all other onlookers were captivated by Roxanne's tales.

Andrew was distracted by the young woman's face as he could see her ready to burst, but then he heard Roxanne bellow out, "…And then I said, Mr. Warhol, if they keep paying you to paint soup cans, you keep fucking painting them."

All the men started laughing as she added to her ending, "True story, true fucking story."

With frustration, the young woman said, "Mom, don't be crass."

Roxanne shrugged her shoulders and snapped, "What? Just one of the boys. Right, fellas?"

A chorus of young men agreed with her, and one twentysomething held up his Heineken and yelled, "Yeah, you go, Roxy!"

"Oh, please. Mom, I've been hearing that story for years. What you don't understand about Andy Warhol is that he was making a statement about the relationship between art and commercial images. And rather than giving in to the critics' predictions that art would, as one critic stated, 'suffocate under the weight of a consumerist culture,' Warhol explored the very nature of consumerism and art by combining the two."

The bar became silent, and Roxanne blinked several times before she belted out, "Pumpkin, I didn't understand a word you just said. I guess that arty-farty degree from Vassar I bought you did its job." The men howled again.

Sandra's eyes squinted slightly, her lips pursed, and her face turned red. She was a stick of dynamite, and the fuse was lit.

"Oh, Pumpkin! Look at that face! It was just a joke."

"You're the joke, Mother, not me." Sandra marched off.

Roxanne put her hand by her mouth and drunk-whispered loudly, "She's really sensitive."

"You know, Mrs. Wells," Andrew interjected, "you should be proud to have a daughter like her. It's my professional opinion that you are threatened by the fact that your daughter is smarter, more cultured, and more eloquent than you are. So you gaslight her in public."

Roxanne turned, and her smirk was replaced with shock, as Andrew continued, "As well, you take advantage of your role as mother and boss to reinforce your dominant position." Andrew shrugged his shoulders, took a sip from his glass, then turned to Roxanne and added, "It's textbook narcissism."

Roxanne put her hands on her hips, squeezed into a dress that was a size or two too small, and barked, "Who the hell are you, kid?"

"Dr. Andrew Beck." He gave her a wily grin.

Roxanne started to think out loud, "Beck, Beck, Beck? Ted and Helena Beck's son? I thought they just had their lawyer son, Brendan."

"It's Brandon. And I've been out west for a while."

Roxanne wasn't ready to give up the fight. "You said Dr. Beck. What in God's name are you a doctor of, kid?"

Andrew stared into her eyes and responded confidently, "Psychology. And perhaps you should come and see me for a few sessions. You could use it."

"How dare you, you little weasel!"

Andrew reached into his Brooks Brothers suit jacket pocket, pulled out a white business card and added, "Name calling, very mature. I guess we all know who got the brains in the family. But we can discuss this at my office. Call me." Andrew put the business card on the bar, tapped it twice, and walked away, following Sandra's path.

Roxanne fumed, "I'll tell you what I think of you." Roxanne ripped up the card into pieces and threw it on the ground, but Andrew didn't see it; he just smiled and laughed to himself. He walked to the beat of "Only Girl" feeling very self-satisfied.

Andrew walked through the club lounge and exited the door, which led to an outside porch that wrapped around the club dining and bar area and overlooked the ninth hole and a putting green. It was a warm summer evening and still light out as Andrew heard the familiar sound of sprinklers spraying water on the greens in a repeating pattern.

Sandra was peering over the white railing on the porch, looking out onto the carefully manicured golf course.

Andrew called out, "Sandra?"

Sandra turned. Her eyes were watery, and she gave a quick sniff as she said, "Yes."

Andrew stuck out his hand. "Hi, I'm Andrew Beck. I've seen you around the club and wanted to introduce myself."

Sandra blinked for a second and declared, "You were…were one of the guys at the bar with my mom, right?"

Andrew nodded and kept his hand out. "I was. And I thought what you said was brilliant."

Sandra extended her hand and shook his while she stumbled on her words, "Tha…thank you."

The two shook and let go as Andrew leaned on the railing and pointed inside the club with his thumb. "Your mom is drunk and just trying to impress the boys."

Sandra was frustrated. "But why does she have to do it at my expense?" She threw her hands out at the empty putting green of the ninth hole.

Andrew shrugged. "You threaten her."

"I threaten *her*?!?!"

"Yes, you're twice as smart as she is. You are refined and cultured. And she resents the fact that you are at ease in a place like this and she is not."

Sandra was taken aback, but she smiled. "Thanks, I, I appreciate that."

Andrew added, "Which is why she needs a bunch of gin in her and a crowd of sycophants around her just to get through the night."

The two smiled at each other and were having a nice moment when a young man slammed open the door to the porch and double-timed it where Andrew and Sandra were standing. He stumbled a little, and it was clear he had a few in him. Andrew recognized the man as one of his golfing buddies and old high school classmate, Tad Bartley.

Tad called out to Andrew, "Hey, Beck, man, you really pissed her off."

Sandra inquired, "Pissed who off?"

Tad looked at Sandra and blurted out, "Your mom!" He then turned to Andrew and added, "Andrew, man, she was cursing you out. Mouth like a drunken sailor."

Sandra grabbed Andrew gently by the arm. "Andrew, what did you say to her?"

Andrew smiled and shrugged. "Nothing but the truth."

Tad chimed in, "Bro, you called the CEO of Wells Public Relations a narcissist to her face!"

Sandra burst out laughing. "You did *what*?"

Tad looked at Sandra, talking wildly with his hands. "And he told your mom that you threaten her."

Sandra continued to laugh. "Really?"

Andrew looked back at Sandra and nonchalantly exclaimed, "Like I said, it's the truth."

Tad grabbed Andrew's shoulder to make a point but also for support. "Bro, when you told her she should come see you for a session, she ripped your card up at the bar."

Andrew moved away, which almost sent Tad over the railing. Andrew looked at Sandra. "I knew she would. I put it there intentionally just to piss her off."

Tad added, "Dude, you have always been the king of the mind-fucks."

"What?" The comment took Sandra by surprise. Andrew shot Tad a "shut the fuck up" look.

Andrew tried to reassure her. "Sandra, I'm a psychologist. I know how to get into someone's head if I want to."

Sandra crossed her arms. "So, *Doctor* Beck, you trying to get into *my* head?"

Andrew looked sincerely into her eyes. "No, Sandra, but I'd love to get a drink with you."

Tad was smiling and hovering. Andrew took a step towards Sandra, and Tad braced himself on the porch railing, all of a sudden not looking so good. Andrew held out his arm and asked, "Why don't we go somewhere else?"

Sandra put her arm in his and said, "Yeah, the walls in this place have eyes, ears, and lots and lots of opinions."

"Well, you know what they taught me in my doctorate program at Berkeley about the medical qualities of opinions?" Andrew asked as her chocolate brown eyes enamored him.

Sandra shook her head earnestly. "No, what?"

"Opinions are like assholes; everyone has one, and they all stink."

Sandra laughed and rebutted, "Oh, is that what they taught you at Berkeley?"

Andrew then imitated Roxanne, making his voice sound pretty close to hers: "True story, true fucking story."

Sandra laughed harder. "Let's get out of here."

As the two walked down the back steps and crossed the putting green, watching their timing to avoid getting sprayed by the sprinklers, Sandra added, "Nicely done, by the way."

Andrew quipped, "Thank you, I'll be here all week."

Sandra laughed again. When she laughed, her whole face lit up. The waves in her cropped hair reverberated, and in the setting sun, they shined like waves of gold. He was smitten. The two laughed together as the sprinklers continued squirting rhythmically and the sun disappeared behind the pine trees of the golf course.

38

Back in the present, Andrew and Sandra sat at their table smiling at each other, and Sandra once again raised her glass. "To good times."

Andrew smiled and returned the toast. "To good times." The two clinked glasses, sipped, and took in the moment with a smile. But their moment didn't last long as a drunk Roxanne walked like she was on uneven ground towards their table.

Andrew could see her approach as Sandra's back was to her. Andrew shot out a warning, "Oh, shit. Here comes Roxanne."

Sandra fidgeted but resisted the urge to turn. "Really?"

Andrew spoke fast while trying to keep cool. "Yeah, just keep calm. She's drunk, don't let her trigger you."

Sandra took a few deep breaths and chanted, "Okay, okay, okay."

Roxanne approached Sandra and used a high-pitched voice as if she were talking to a little girl. "Why hello, my dear little Pumpkin." She bent down and kissed her daughter on the cheek and put her heavy arm on her shoulders.

Sandra recoiled and slid away from her mother's arm, almost knocking her off-balance. "Phew, mom, had a few tonight?"

Roxanne caught herself on the back of Sandra's chair and waved her hand, admonishing her. "Oh hush. It's Saturday."

Andrew tried to break up the conversation. "How ya doing, Roxanne?"

Roxanne looked up at Andrew. "I'm good, Andrew. I saw your mom earlier but not Ted. Is he here? He's so entertaining."

Andrew responded with a hint of sarcasm in his voice. "I'm not sure, Roxanne."

Roxanne added, "I can never get enough of that Master's story and how he came back to win it. He's got guts, your father."

Andrew cranked up the sarcasm. "Yeah, he was the best."

Roxanne bent over and pointed a shaky finger at Andrew. "Is, buddy. IS the best. He's still living, you know."

Andrew huffed, "Did you just come over to say hello, or was there something you wanted?"

Roxanne then pointed to the sky. "Ah, yes, I remember now. San-dra!"

Sandra winced. "I'm right here, Mom. You don't need to yell."

"This place is so fucking loud I can't hear myself think."

Sandra shot back, "No, that would be the six gin and tonics."

Roxanne ignored the comment and retorted, "I didn't see the final presentation for the Robbins account—did you finish it?"

Sandra snapped, "No, Mother, of course not. We've been all hands on deck on the Corravallo case. Three-quarters of the staff have been dealing with social media, the press, and crafting statements for the union on Corravallo's innocence."

Roxanne demanded, "Well, I need it tomorrow."

Sandra rebuked, "Tomorrow's Sunday, and Andrew and I have plans."

Roxanne increased the volume and tapped the table with each word she spoke. "What could be more important than this?"

Sandra stepped into the trap. "We have an appointment with Francois, the decorator." Andrew tried not to wince; he knew this was a thorny path.

Roxanne replied sarcastically, "*You* got an appointment with Francois?"

Sandra replied, "Yes. And there is nothing on the Robbin's account happening that cannot wait until Monday."

Roxanne closed her eyes and waved her hand indignantly. "That's okay. I'll give it to Betty to finish."

Sandra shot back, "Betty?! Betty's a receptionist. She doesn't know anything about strategy. Hell, she screws up my lunch order almost every day!"

Roxanne put her hands on her hips and barked, "Well, excuse me, but I've got a company to run. I need this report." Roxanne turned to Andrew, holding out an open hand. "Andrew, you know what it's like to be the boss. When you need something in your company, you need it, right?"

"Roxanne, 'my company' is only Gina and me. And she handles all the hard stuff. I just treat my patients."

Roxanne added, "Oh, I know what you mean. I'd be lost without Betty. If it weren't for her, the place would fall apart."

Andrew saw Sandra's jaw clench and her eyes squint, which is what his wife did when she was seething mad. He had seen it a few times before; luckily, it was directed at him only once in the last nine years.

Andrew braced for impact as Sandra lashed out, "As opposed to the person who handles all your major accounts? All the strategy sessions? And the emergency calls at all hours of the night?! You mean *that* person?!" She pointed emphatically at the table with every statement.

Roxanne quickly shifted into passive aggressive mode. "Oh Pumpkin, if you need some reassurance of your importance in the office, just ask for it."

"I don't need your reassurance, Mother. I know I do a damn good job. But your appreciation every once in a while, *that* would be nice."

"Oh, come off it, Sandra!" Roxanne barked back. "You think being the only female PR CEO in the eighties was a picnic? Huh?! I never got so much as a thank you from my clients, and they treated me like a fucking secretary." She looked away. "Sexist bastards."

"So then you understand how it feels to be underappreciated, right?" Sandra said.

Andrew covered his mouth to hide the pride he felt for his wife's debating skills. Considering how pissed off she was at Roxanne's goading and gaslighting, her emotional control was outstanding.

Roxanne wagged her finger. "Don't turn the conversation around on me, Miss Smarty Pants!"

Roxanne's reaction confirmed Sandra had taken control of the conversation. Andrew's proud smile broadened.

Andrew's cell phone vibrated. Normally cell phones were forbidden in the club, but doctors and doctors with famous patients who liked to play golf and sign autographs for club members got special privileges. He looked at the caller ID, then looked at Sandra. "Shit, it's Riley."

Sandra pleaded, "Andrew, no. Not now."

Andrew began to get up from the table, holding a finger aloft. "I'll just be a minute, I promise."

"Please," Sandra pleaded.

Andrew set his cloth napkin on his chair. "One minute."

Roxanne gestured at Andrew. "See, *he* has his priorities straight."

Andrew answered the phone as he walked away from the dining area into the lounge with soft cream couches and matching cushioned chairs, and a blazing fireplace that warmed the room. He looked for a quiet place to talk, but an elegantly dressed woman was playing soft classical music on the baby grand piano.

Riley asked, "Hey Beck? Can you hear me? It's really loud."

"Yeah, I'm at dinner."

"What? I can't hear you."

"Hold on." Andrew quickly walked through a door to the outside porch that had a fresh new coat of white paint for the season's opening. Andrew's nose was filled with the smell of paint as the sprinklers were sputtering water in a circular motion over the green. It was dark, and the cold April air had taken the place of the warm spring day from that afternoon.

Andrew called out, "Riley, can you hear me now?"

"Yes, finally," Riley exclaimed.

Andrew inquired, "What did the NAHL say?"

Riley launched in, "Well, you slick son-of-a-bitch, Vlad and Newsome each got a one-game suspension. I can't believe they fell for that bullshit."

Andrew got pissed. "It wasn't bullshit, Riley. Like I keep trying to tell you, Vlad has had a pretty tragic life and—"

Riley cut Andrew off, "Yeah, yeah, boo fucking hoo. He makes $7 million a year playing professional fucking hockey."

Andrew shot back, "Jesus, Riley, you're a piece of work."

"Whatever. We play the Colorado Big Horns next. They are in last place in their division so we can beat them without Vlad. We're resting Kruder too. So it looks like Vlad will be ready for the playoffs, as long as you don't turn him into a fucking lunatic in the next few weeks." Riley added a cynical laugh, trying to get at Andrew.

Andrew didn't take the bait. "I'll talk to you next week. I gotta get back to dinner." Andrew hung up and rushed back inside to his table.

When Andrew got back to the table, Roxanne was gone. He plopped down in his chair and said excitedly, "Sorry about that, but Vlad only got a one-game suspension! We won!"

Sandra was livid. "How could you do that?!"

"What? It was just for a minute."

"How could you leave me with her drunk and demeaning me!" Sandra's eyes were watering, and her face was flushed.

"You were handling her. You seemed fine."

"No, I wasn't fine, Andrew!" Sandra looked away as a single tear fell down her cheek and she quickly whisked it away.

"I'm sorry! But you know how Riley is."

Sandra snapped, "You could have called him back!"

Andrew stopped. He closed his eyes and let out a deep sigh. "You're right. I could have... I'm sorry."

Sandra's brown eyes were on fire. "You know what?" She pointed at him. "I'm tired of me being right and you being sorry! I guess you *do* have your priorities in order!"

Sandra got up from the table and stormed away. Andrew called out to her, but she bolted through the lounge, which led toward the club's front exit. She almost bumped into a couple walking in as she pardoned herself and made haste.

Andrew sat there for a minute pulling at his hair. This was another time this week when all was going well and then turned to shit. After another fast rewind of the past few hours, a message in his brain said, "Well, go get her, asshole!"

Andrew ran through the lounge, making a hard left toward the club entrance. He dodged customers like he was returning a kickoff. Even at 40, he still kept some of his athletic prowess. He received a scornful look from the Dining Manager, but he flew open the front door to a dark front entrance anyway. His eyes adjusted to the dark, and he saw Sandra at the bottom of the circular driveway where cars valeted.

His heart was racing, he felt a deep fear inside him, and he was hoping he could talk his way out of this one. He ran up to her, the sprinklers still spurting water as Andrew called out, "Sandra! Come on!"

Sandra spun around and shouted, "What! What can you possibly say, Andrew?"

Andrew looked around as a few patrons getting out of their cars, dressed nicely for the evening, gave very unsettled looks. People didn't air their dirty laundry in public in Greenwich, especially here.

"Come on, not here," Andrew pleaded.

"Why, why not here? Why do you give a fuck about what these elitist shitheads think?" One woman covered her mouth in surprise while her gray-haired husband shook his head in disgust and ushered his offended wife away into the club.

"Sandra, I'm sorry. You're right. It was insensitive. I've been waiting for that call all night and—"

"I've been waiting all week for you to *show up*."

"That's harsh."

"Is it?" Sandra's angry tone changed to a questioning one as she took two steps closer to him. "Is it really?"

Andrew was at a loss for words. His wife's eyes were piercing through him. Sandra took a step back. "I need some time to think." She looked away quickly and then right back at Andrew. "I'm going to the city to stay at the Plaza Hotel. I have an Uber coming to take me to the train station. I will meet you and Francois tomorrow at one."

Andrew was dumbfounded and couldn't find words. But Sandra could as she shook her head and peered directly into his eyes. "Right now, I'm remembering the advice you once gave me about my mother. You said that I could either accept Roxanne for who she is or change the way I deal with her. Well, I will no longer accept this behavior from you. One of us has to change."

Andrew felt a pang deep in his stomach like he had just been punched. He couldn't form words. It was as if his brain had hit a pause button.

Sandra continued, "And if you won't change, then the only change I will be making is my address."

A Toyota Prius pulled up to the front entrance, and the driver rolled down the passenger side window and asked, "Sandra Wells?"

Sandra bent down and said politely, "That's me. Give me a moment, please." The driver nodded and rolled back up the window.

Andrew felt the pang in his stomach go deeper and he couldn't find a way to restart his brain.

Sandra shrugged her shoulders and shook her head. "Is all of this really worth it?"

Andrew extended his arm, but he got nothing but air as the "play button" in his brain was finally hit and he called out, "Sandra, wait!"

But Sandra got in the back seat of the Prius and slammed the door. The high-pitched hybrid battery rang out as it quietly pulled away from the curb and went around the circle and out the club's exit.

Andrew stood watching, his heart beating fast and his stomach tightening. He looked around at the dark sky, and a cold, wet wind whipped up the open golf course, sending a shiver down his spine. The sound of the spurting sprinkler filled his ears and became deafening.

39

Andrew sat on his living room couch, looking around. The silence was deafening. He could not remember the last time he was alone in his house. From the couch, he peered around the room, and his eye caught one of the many pictures that captured Sandra's and his idyllic life. It was a picture Sandra had taken of him on the golf course at Sandy Lane in Barbados. Sandra captured not only his perfect post-swing posture but the smile on his face that said he had just hit a monstrous drive. Andrew looked at his face. He looked happy and content — a feeling he didn't remember often experiencing on the golf course. Golf had given him so much pain, but there were also moments of joy when he could go out and play his way. He wondered if maybe he made a mistake walking away from the game at 18. Perhaps he could just cash in his marker card, quit his practice, and focus on becoming a pro golfer.

The fantasy disappeared like a puffy white cloud on a breezy day when the frontal lobe of his brain admonished him: *Yeah, because there are always 40-year-old rookies in the Professional Golf League.*

Andrew let out a deep sigh at his foolish thought. At the end of his breath, he felt his phone vibrate, and he looked at the caller ID. It said "Five." He quickly answered, "Hey, so glad you called, I…"

Although the voice on the line was Scottish, it wasn't the female voice he wanted. "Aww, that's sweet of you, mate. I was beginning to think our relationship had become strained."

Andrew's eyes closed with dread and disappointment.

Fergus continued, "This evening's games are about to start, and as

319

we agreed, I wanted to know how the Black Knights and the Sentinels will do?"

Andrew couldn't get the words out; he found the Play button he had lost during his argument with Sandra, but now it was as if someone hit Mute on his voice. Speaking the answer Fergus wanted seemed to amount to a kind of apostasy.

Angrily, Fergus said, "Listen mate, I need this information before the games start. So let's hear it!"

Andrew pushed his emotions down into a deep hole within him and replied almost robotically. "The Sentinels will win. I spoke to their General Manager. The Colorado Big Horns are in last place, with nothing to play for, so I wouldn't expect a big effort from them. Their enforcer, Vladimir Poplov, got a one-game suspension and isn't playing, but they're also resting their star player, Chris Kruder. That should lower the odds for the Sentinels, but they'll still be heavily favored to win, which they'll do."

"And the Black Knights? How will they fare against...let's see, ah, yes, the Durham Devils?"

"I haven't spoken to Lamar, but they're not a very good team and—"

"Well, mate, the game goes on in less than twenty minutes. Call him!" he said emphatically. "I'll call you back in exactly ten minutes." He hung up the phone before Andrew could say anything.

Andrew's emotions tried to escape from their hole, but he pushed them back in. His finger quaked looking for Lamar's contact info. He found it, closed his eyes, let out a long exhale and hit the Call option. The phone rang, and he was having a tug-o-war with his thoughts—one that wanted Lamar to pick up and the other hoping he let it go to voicemail.

Andrew heard the loud background noise of what could only have been the Black Knights' locker room.

"Lamar!"

"Yo, what up, DB?"

"Hey, I just wanted to check in with you and see how you're feeling tonight."

"You never did that before."

"Yeah, well you had such a huge breakthrough this week, and… and I wanted you to know how proud I am of you, and I'm really happy that things are going well with you and Janice."

"Appreciate that, DB. Yeah, man. I'm good." He paused. "I got to get ready so…"

"Of course, yeah." He stumbled over his words. "Just one more thing…"

"What's that?"

"You're the man, Lamar. You're the man."

Andrew could hear Lamar get choked up over the phone, "I'm gonna score forty tonight for you, DB!"

Somehow, the emotions escaped their hole and flooded Andrew as tears rushed down his face.

Lamar added before he hung up, "Peace, brother."

Andrew's chest began to heave as the tears flowed freely now, and he could feel an itch under his nose as mucus ran out both his nostrils. He quickly wiped the snot with his sleeve, not even attempting to reach for his handkerchief. A silent sob reverberated through his body, and he fell over into the couch and buried his face in a pillow. He could feel the salty tears mix with his mucus, trapping it on his face. He didn't care. He sobbed for a few more minutes when his phone vibrated again. This time, the caller ID said, "Unknown Number." But Andrew knew who it was. He took out his handkerchief, wiped his face and blew his nose. He took a couple of quick breaths, sat up, and answered.

"Fergus?"

"What did you find out?"

"Lamar is good, the Black Knights will win, and I would bet the over-under on Lamar scoring more than 30 points."

"Mmmm. Good lad. See, it's not such a big deal." Andrew was quiet as he felt his shame move to anger.

There was an uncomfortable silence. Andrew wanted to get off the phone as he thought he might vomit the stormy sea of bile churning in his stomach.

"Look mate, if your information pans out, I'll have made the money I need to pay for my security upgrades fairly quickly and we can put this to rest and you can go back to playing poker whenever you want."

Andrew was a swirling bowl of discursive emotions: embarrassment, fear, guilt, and shame. He wanted to crawl into a hole. "If there's nothing else, I'm gonna go."

"All good, mate. Have a good night."

Andrew clicked off the phone. He put his hand over his mouth, not sure if he was going to vomit or not. Thinking he might need both hands to hold the vomit in, he tossed his phone onto a cushioned chair across the room. It bounced off the seat cushion, hit the back cushion, and somersaulted to the edge of the seat, but it didn't fall over. Andrew hustled to the foyer bathroom and opened the lid. A wave of vomit came out of his mouth and splattered all over the toilet. Most of it landed in the bowl but not all. He fell to his knees. He was sweating profusely, and he felt another heave from his stomach, but this time nothing came out. He grabbed his ribs as the retching aggravated his injury again. He was lightheaded and after the vomitless retch, he placed his face on the side of the bowl and felt its cool, smooth porcelain surface.

Andrew washed his face and rinsed out his mouth. He walked back gingerly into the living room as he tried to comfort the searing pain in his ribs by wrapping both arms around his rib cage. It was as if he was trying to prevent his innards from bursting out like an alien baby. He plopped himself on the couch and let out a deep sigh, trying to ignore the nausea and pain. He focused his mind on figuring out what his next move would be. How could he find out who really killed Mr. Keegan? And if it was Fergus, could he get proof and use it to set him free from Fergus' chokehold?

As he was deep in thought, his phone vibrated, and Andrew quickly got up and caught the phone before the vibration forced it off the seat. The pain in his ribs reminded him that he moved too fast, and he winced and gritted his teeth. When he opened his eyes to see who was calling, his sight was blurry and he needed a second for his eyes to refocus. He could only make out a series of letters and numbers on the caller ID—an alpha-numeric scramble. He cautiously answered, "Hello?"

"Andrew, it's Lorry."

"Hey, what's this number?"

"It's an encrypted line. Look, we don't have much time. I know what's going on between you and Fergus. You need to be very careful."

"Thanks, I will, I promise." He paused, and then a smile cracked his face. "Maybe I should just move to LA, set up practice there. It's only a three-hour drive to Vegas." He ended with a chuckle.

Lorry snapped back, "It's three hours and forty-nine minutes."

"Not the way I drive—"

"This isn't a fucking game, Andrew!" He'd never heard her swear at him before and was shaken out of his comedic deflection.

"Wherever you go, Fergus will get to you. And if not to you, he can make life difficult for everyone you care about!"

Andrew felt a pang in his stomach. "What do you mean, *difficult*?"

"Fergus has his ways. He has powerful people in his pocket. Cops, judges, businesspeople, politicians. Even a senator."

"Oh, which one? From New York, New Jersey, Connecticut?

"They don't wear a badge or anything when they are here. It's a woman, that's all I know.

Could it be that Senator Mann who is playing at the Club on Sunday? The one Sandra has been trying to land as a client?

While Andrew was thinking, Lorry spouted, "But it doesn't matter because you can't win, Andrew."

Andrew was roughly taken out of his connect the dots moment around Senator Mann, "Win?" I only have to make him enough money to pay for the upgrades to his security cameras. He said it should just only be a few weeks."

Lorry was quiet on the other side, and then her tone softened. "Andrew, we upgraded our entire system in January."

Andrew said, "I was with John Palmer almost all of January…getting him through rehab."

Lorry said, "We closed The Five Iron for a week and worked 24/7 to get them operational."

Andrew felt as if he had just swallowed a rock when Lorry said, "Why do you think I turned and faced you and walked backward when I told you 'he's playing chess, not checkers.' I didn't want the audio to pick it up or the cameras to see my face where our software could figure out what I said."

"Your cameras can read lips?"

"Our system is military grade, Russian technology. Yes, it has an algorithm that will give us the most likely readout."

"So you heard Mr. Keegan's and my conversations? You and Fergus knew all along."

"Yes. Fergus' greatest asset is information. The information creates vulnerabilities in people with weaknesses. Like drugs, sexual fetishes, or..."

"Gambling?" Andrew finished her sentence like he was predicting her cards.

There was a silence between them, each not knowing what to say. This was the hand he was dealt. He only had one option. "Then my only way out is all-in!" Andrew said emphatically.

Lorry was subdued. "Afraid so."

"Lorry, what really happened with Mr. Keegan?"

"I was with you, Andrew. By the time I got back to the pier, Mr. Keegan was gone. I assumed Fergus let him go."

"But didn't you hear the—"

"Ah, you bawheid! I gotta go." She clicked off.

Andrew sat with his mind swirling. The tick-tock of the grandfather clock echoed in his ears. He *had* been playing checkers while Fergus was playing chess. He felt his face burn that he was trapped so easily. The burn of embarrassment transformed into resolve as he stood and yelled to the room right as the clock struck eight. "If he wants to play mind games, so can I!"

40

Andrew woke up at 4:30, well before his alarm was scheduled to go off at 6:30 am. He stared up at the ceiling for a while before he looked over to the empty spot that Sandra usually occupied, the blanket still neatly made. He closed his eyes, not out of sleepiness but in hopes that it might stop the gallons of angst and regret that were filling his chest.

It felt like an hour of agonizing pain had gone by, but when his phone rang he saw it was only eight minutes later. The caller ID had yet another Unknown number. He cursed to himself and waited a few rings to take a calming breath before he warily answered.

A synthetic voice over the phone said, "Listen to me carefully, Dr. Beck. There is a package outside your door. Go and get it please."

Andrew's brain started racing. "Who is this?" he said, trying to find his mental footing.

"An ally. You may call me Master Huang. I know you are being blackmailed by Fergus Mackenzie. I'd like to help you."

Andrew couldn't make out if the voice was a man or woman because the synthesizer effectively neutralized any distinguishing male or female tones. Still in his boxers, Andrew shuffled down the steps searching his brain for who this could be. The sun hadn't come up yet. He opened the door into the dark and on his doorstep was a box wrapped in brown paper.

"Mr. Keegan mentioned that the Huang-Tse were the ones who were going to break into my marker card. Is that you Master Huang?"

"Yes."

"Why do you want to help me?"

"At this juncture in time, let's just say that our interests are aligned. Fergus is blackmailing you, and he threatened me. And I don't take kindly to threats."

Andrew picked up the box. "I have it. Now what?"

"Now you open it. I thought that would be obvious, Doctor."

Andrew shook the box and heard something rattle inside.

The caller heard and let out a huff in disappointment and annoyance. "It's a phone, Dr. Beck. Please open it. If I wanted to blow you up, I would have done it already."

Andrew couldn't tell if the cold shiver that ran up his spine was from standing on his doorstep in his boxers or if somehow he had gotten mixed up with yet another gangster. Andrew went back inside and closed the door, and he ripped open the brown paper as he walked into the living room and sat on his couch. He opened the box and in it was a Samsung phone and it was on.

"Okay, I have the phone. What now?"

"Click on WhatsApp. You will see there is a video link. Watch the video. I think you will find it fascinating." He heard a click, then silence.

Andrew sat on his couch and clicked on WhatsApp and there was a video. He played it. It had a greenish background: the recording was using 'night-vision" technology. The video looked like it was recorded on a flat roof, thirty feet in the air. The image zoomed in. A shock wave of adrenaline coursed through Andrew's body as he saw the images of himself, Mr. Keegan, Fergus and Fergus' crew standing on the pier, the East River's waves lapping behind them. There was no sound. The video started at the point where Mr. Keegan was pleading to Fergus, Fergus' body convulsed, and the men pointed their weapons at Andrew and Mr. Keegan. Andrew looked at his own face, the genuine look of horror on it as his body jerked slightly backward and he tucked his head as his hands were bound behind his back. Andrew could see Fergus in an aggressive posture. George's hulking frame entered the view, and he was seen getting Mr. Keegan's marker card and handing it over to Fergus. Lorry searched Andrew's pocket, and he watched his face look at her hair while she searched him. He then saw himself pointing his chin out of the frame and saw George walk out of the frame in the direction he pointed. He watched as Lorry looked over the card reader and discussed with Fergus, she was barely in the frame, and only half of Fergus' body was. The camera shifted view to capture them both and zoomed on the reader for a moment. Then the camera zoomed in on Andrew, who was staring at Lorry. Andrew watched himself lost in Lorry's beauty. Just a few moments before, he thought he might get shot, and now he saw his face relaxed as if he was in the Louvre admiring the Mona Lisa. Andrew shook his head in bewilderment and continued watching.

He watched Lorry beat on Mr. Keegan when he refused to give her answers. The beatings stopped when Mr. Keegan spoke, and Andrew recalled this is where he first heard the words, Huang-Tse. They were in Chinatown, Andrew recalled. Andrew saw Fergus stick both marker cards in his pocket and tap it twice. Fergus and Lorry stepped out of the frame, and then he saw Fergus' arm reach back in the frame, moving left to right, pointing loosely to the men. Andrew's stomach tightened when he recalled the words Fergus said, "Oh, George, if either one of them moves a muscle, shoot them."

Andrew looked at his face, the unadulterated fear that slapped him like a wet blanket. For the third time that night, he saw in his body language that he might die. He watched George cock his assault rifle, and Andrew's mouth got dry and he swallowed hard. He almost put down the phone, but his rational brain told him, "Nothing happened, remember?"

Andrew watched Mr. Keegan and himself in a soundless exchange where Mr. Keegan asked what Lorry and Fergus discussed. He didn't get Andrew's sarcasm when he said, "I'm a mind reader, not a lip reader."

Andrew let out a slight chuckle as he saw his head tilt back and close his eyes, and he read his own lips, "Ah, for fuck's sake."

I guess I can read lips, just only my own.

Fergus and Lorry came back into the frame, and he saw Fergus put an outstretched arm on Andrew's shoulder and wagged a finger in his face. He saw his head bow a little as he made his apology. The experience sincerely humbled him. He watched George cut his bindings, and his head turned to whisper to George and the smile they shared at George's comment, "I like you, but I don't like you *that* much."

He watched himself exit the frame with Lorry, and Andrew caught himself also feeling the same relief. It was as if he was having a dissociative flashback, but this wasn't memory recall. He was watching the event again. His clinical brain switched on, and he acknowledged that this series of events had left him with post-traumatic stress.

He terminated his clinical self-observation, 'time upping' himself. The session was over. He had to focus on what happened next, as this would be new information. The camera stayed trained on Fergus and Mr. Keegan. For the next few minutes, Fergus could be seen questioning Mr. Keegan and he was talking, no doubt giving all the information about the Huang-Tse and what they were going to do with Andrew's marker card. Fergus signaled to his men to take Mr. Keegan away. A minute later, Lorry and Fergus and George stood alone on the pier and the three were seen having a conversation. Lorry and George exited, and Fergus stood there for a while staring out into the East River.

A few moments later, the men walked back with Mr. Keegan, sat him in a chair and tied him to it. Andrew could see Mr. Keegan protesting vehemently. Fergus nodded to one of his crew members and the man produced a sealed bag. Fergus pulled out surgical gloves from his inside jacket pocket, put them on, and then pulled a pistol out of the bag. Mr. Keegan looked like he was trying to reason with Fergus, but he took aim and shot Mr. Keegan in the eye without a word. He then pulled out a small leather case from his other inside jacket pocket and in it several pieces of what looked like strips of clear plastic. Fergus meticulously adhered the plastic to the pistol and then slowly pulled the strips. He then walked over to the side of the pier and was seen lying flat on his belly and moving his arm. When he stood up and brushed himself off, the weapon was no longer in his hands. The video stopped a few seconds later.

Andrew's mind was racing. He had the proof he needed. He was free. Who was this ally that just saved his life? How did he know to be at the exact pier where this was happening? Why did Fergus threaten this…person? Andrew went to forward the video to his own phone. He clicked on the arrow to forward the video to himself and sent it to his number. When he went to his phone, there was a blank dialog box. The video didn't forward. Andrew quickly picked up the Samsung phone, but the video was gone. It had erased itself after he watched it.

His heart sunk into his stomach. He shook the phone and closed and restarted the app several times, but the video was gone. The Samsung phone rang. It was the same synthetic voice.

"Did you like what you saw, Doctor?"

"What do you want?"

"I know you had quite a lot of money on your marker card. You have 72 hours to get me three million dollars and the video is yours."

"Fergus froze my funds. I can't get the funds off the card."

"That doesn't sound like Fergus. He must want something from you."

"He does."

"What?"

Andrew hesitated. He was scared, angry, frustrated, but he took a breath and let out. "Information."

"Well, then you better give it to him fast, because in 72 hours, this deal is off the table."

"How can I trust you'll keep your word."

The caller snickered. "You can't. But what other choice do you have?"

The chill left Andrew's body replaced with a burn of anxiety and frustration.

"When I get the money, how do I contact you?"

"In the contacts, there is one phone number. Call it and someone will give you instructions."

Andrew started to ask a question, but the words didn't come out.

Master Huang would not have heard them even if they had because the line was dead.

* * * *

The hot water spurted from his rainfall showerhead and pummeled his head. It sent streams of water down his face so abundant that he had to tuck his chin to prevent waterboarding himself.

He stood bracing himself against the wall, figuring how he was going to break free. He had no choice but to trust the ally. It seemed like he had no options anymore, just compliance. He was angry at how his life had taken a wrong exit ramp into the bad part of town. His life, career, and marriage all threatened to end horribly this week. The one he focused on right now was his marriage, perhaps the one thing he could fix.

* * * *

As the water pounded on his head, he heard Sandra's voice echoing in his head, "Right now, I'm remembering the advice you once gave me about my mother. You said that I could either accept Roxanne for who she is or change the way I deal with her. Well, I will no longer accept this behavior. One of us has to change. And if you won't change, then the only change I will be making is my address."

The replay of her words stung just as bad as they had the previous night. And "Is all of this really worth it?" kept ringing out over and over in his head.

The shame parade continued as he recalled his conversation with Fergus and Lamar. The thought of Lamar going out to score forty points for *him*. Did he say the things he said because he believed in Lamar, or just get him to a place where he would play better, ensuring a win for Fergus... and himself. He was disgusted with his thoughts and yelled out, "What the fuck am I doing?" His cries echoed in the shower.

The frustration and hurt sent his brain reeling. The week was re-winding with all the greatest hits playing voices in his head loud and clear. Ted yelling at him, "You're a loser!" And Mr. Davidson's parting shot, "Judas!"

Then Mr. Keegan's goad at the card table, "Come on, Beck, you got nothing! Just fold. Admit it—I'm the better man."

Lorry's warning, "He's playing chess, not checkers."

These disembodied voices replayed over and over in his head, each time speeding up faster and faster.

You're a loser.

Judas!

Admit it. I'm the better man

He's playing chess, not checkers.

The disembodied voices cycled at a speed so fast that eventually they layered atop each other like a horrible shame mix in Andrew's mind. Then they suddenly all went silent, and only Sandra's voice remained in the mind-fuck party with her parting words, "Is all of this really worth it?"

Andrew roughly turned off the water and sank to the bottom of the shower, where he sat naked, dripping, pounding the tile floor. He let out a primal scream—a scream from a dark place in the depth of his being. He buried his face in his hands, and sobs and gasps shuddered his body.

* * * *

Andrew went into the garage and panicked as he couldn't find his golf clubs and only saw his shoes. Then his brain reloaded, and he recalled leaving them yesterday at the club to be cleaned.

I should have just cleaned them myself and taken Sandra to Polpo.

He analyzed the chain of events like a CSI detective, from changing the tee time to dropping off the clubs at the country club, to the "date night" dinner that went sideways. He now had video proof that Fergus killed Mr. Keegan, but he couldn't access the money that was locked up on his marker card. Just like everything else this week, every time he thought he had a winning hand, fate had a better one. But Monday, he would get Lorry to find five other players. He would take all their money and then buy his way out of Fergus' steel trap.

Andrew checked his watch. He was running late. He raced down North Street in his car, passing a runner who barked, "Slow down, asshole! Kids play here!"

Andrew's phone rang and "Mom" flashed up on the caller ID in his car. Despite his despondence, he answered her pleasantly, "Hello, Mom."

"Hello, dear. You on your way to the country club? Your father left 15 minutes ago."

"Yes, I'll be there in five minutes."

"Well, I called to ask you if you could please make sure your father has his heart medication on him." She cleared her throat as if something was stuck in it. "He's been bad about taking it lately. He thinks it makes him weak."

Andrew heard the unease in his mother's voice. He thought of a way to comfort her and then a playful grin came to his face. "Hey mom, you want me to force a few pills down his throat?"

Helena laughed good-naturedly. "Oh you!"

Andrew continued the ruse. "I mean, I will. I *am* a doctor you know, and the patient must take his medicine. I can think of several ways..."

Helena was full-on laughing but composed herself to say, "Andrew, that's enough." But one more giggle escaped.

"Okay, Mom," Andrew said.

Helena became serious. "Andrew?"

"Yeah, Mom?"

"Please don't antagonize him."

"I'll be good. I promise."

Andrew hung up the phone as another car honked at him. One more person objecting to his speed.

41

The Greenwich Country Club men's locker room had long wooden lockers and a Kelly-green carpet. There were various pictures on the wall depicting all-time great golfers and photos of the golf course over the years dating back to the 1950s.

As usual, when Ted Beck was in the locker room, he drew a crowd of middle-aged men more than happy to relive his glory days. Ted was in the middle of one story as Andrew walked in the locker room, where he was greeted by his father's distinctively overconfident voice, "So on the 15th, I hit my seven iron off the tee. It's only 165 yards but I sent it airmail, and I thought, 'Damn it, I flew the green.' As I'm walking, I'm thinking, 'Yeah, I can probably save par.' But then I'm looking all over, and I can't find my damn ball. I even asked the guys on the thirteenth hole if they saw my ball. They said that nothing came through. I knew I didn't overshoot it that badly. So I start walking to Golf Club Road thinking, 'This is the worst fucking shot of my life.' But then I hear from Bobby over there. Bobby, tell them what you said."

One of Ted's long-time local golfing buddies, Bobby Spencer, was the CEO of a Greenwich hedge fund, was a frequent tag-along on Ted's outings. When Ted was a pro, Bobby was a dedicated roadie, and he used his Leer 31A to fly Ted to all his tournaments. Bobby laughed. "I said, 'Hey Ted, you playing a Titleist ProV1?'"

Ted then explained, "Then I say, 'Yeah, you know I always play a fucking Titleist ProV1.' Then what you'd say, Spence?"

"I said, 'Ted! It's in the fucking hole!'" Spencer said exuberantly.

Ted threw his arms out in satisfaction. "Fucking hole in one, boys."

Spencer added, "I didn't see it roll, so we looked, and the ball made a small dent in the green a few inches from the cup. He almost swished it, like a fucking basketball." Spencer pantomimed shooting a basketball.

Ted did the same thing as he called out, "Yeah, that's right! Swish!"

The group of middle-aged men started clapping and laughing. Spencer added seriously, "Greatest fucking shot I never saw." He exploded into laughter and the other men joined in.

Andrew waited for the laughter to subdue before greeting his father. "Hey, Dad."

Spencer walked over to Andrew and shook his hand. "Hey, it's Andrew, the boy wonder!"

Ted pointed correctively at Spencer. "That's Dr. Beck to you, Spence."

Spencer corrected himself, "Oh yeah, that's right, Dr. Beck! Sorry! Hey, your boy Palmer's having a hell of a year. Two and oh. Go Tides!"

Andrew replied surprised, "What?" He shot a look at his father.

Spencer turned to Ted, "What do you say about that, Ted? Andrew got the kid off drugs and now he's their next pitching ace."

"How do you know that, Spence?"

Ted confessed, "Hey, I was so shocked that shit actually worked. I told a few of the guys."

"Jesus Christ, Dad!" Andrew grabbed his forehead, trying not to start the day with a fight.

"Hey, Andrew," Spencer pleaded, "It's just *us*. It's not like we're posting locker room talk on Instagram."

Andrew was fuming, but he was about to let it go when Ted had to get in the last word.

"Anyway, it won't matter much if the kid can't hold up in October when the playoff pressure is on."

Andrew defended his client. "He's a solid pitcher, Dad. Anyone can go through some trouble and pull themselves out of it."

Spencer added, "Yeah, Ted, give the kid a break. I mean, he's had some real tough luck. His mom dies as a teenager from a drug over-dose, and then the kid finds his dad dead in a chair watching *his* game films. Shit, I think I'd have some issues too."

Ted poked back, "You already got issues, and her name is Hei-neken. Look at that Buddha belly! Jesus Christ!" Ted patted Spencer's heaving belly.

All the men started laughing again, including Spencer, who was rubbing his belly gently in circular motions. "Hey, this took years of hard work!" The men were howling with laughter.

The Starter and Club Manager, Tom Donohue, walked through the crowd, maneuvering in between the men with his clipboard in hand. "Hey, Ted and Andrew Beck!" he barked. "Let's go! You're up! I got Senator Mann coming in behind you, and her secret service guys are giving me shit, so get a move on, huh?"

Ted waved a reassuring hand Donohue's way. "Okay Tom, we're coming."

Donohue cautioned, "Hey, Ted, just remember, the only way I got Davey to change the time was to get that photo op with Senator Mann, you and Andrew at the turn."

Andrew replied, "Yep, you got it, Mr. Donohue." He patted him on the shoulder.

Ted turned to Andrew and said, "So, we playing the usual twenty bucks a hole, right?"

"Whatever you want, Dad."

"No strokes, we play even up!"

Donohue lowered his tone, "Hey Ted, not so fucking loud. You know it's against club rules to gamble on the course. Jesus Christ, you *trying* to get me fired?"

"Come on, Tom, everyone fucking gambles." Ted didn't lower his tone.

"Just keep it quiet, will ya?" Donohue lowered his even more.

"Yeah, yeah," Ted replied sarcastically, and then turned to An-drew, saying, "You ready for your annual ass-kicking, boy?"

Andrew shot back, "Bring it on. Let's see what you got, old man."

"Old man?!" Ted threw up his hands and turned to his crowd.

"No respect, these kids nowadays. Hey wise ass, Arnold Palmer played competitively until he was my age, 65."

Andrew shot back with a grin, "Good thing I'm not playing Arnold Palmer."

Ted looked over to Donohue for support. "Tommy, your kids speak to you this way?"

Donohue, busy writing on his clipboard, said without looking, "Hey, don't get me involved, Ted. You two are like oil and water." Then he picked his head up and looked at both Ted and Andrew, pointing his pencil at the both of them. "And don't you start arguing like the last time."

Ted pleaded, "He moved his fucking ball."

Andrew barked back, "I told you, it was on the cart path! Rule 24-2b, Immovable obstruction. If your ball lies on or near the cart path or when the obstruction interferes with your stance or the area of intended swing, you may take free relief. Read the rule book sometime. You made me memorize the damn thing."

Donohue rolled his eyes at the ceiling. "Jesus, Mary and Joseph, all right, all right, forget about it. Just please get to the first tee. It's 7:30."

The men filed towards the exit with their golf cleats noisily raking the carpet. Each wooden locker had a brass tag number. As they approached locker #2193 Ted banged on that locker door twice and yelled out, "Let the ass-kickin' begin!"

As the two men emerged outside on the sunny April morning, Ted pulled out his white golf glove out of his back pocket and put it on. Andrew walked up to his father and inquired, "Hey Dad, I've been meaning to ask you, why do you do that?"

"Do what?"

"Bang on locker #2193. You always bang on that locker before we go out like it's that Notre Dame 'Play Like a Champion Today' sign."

"Oh, do I? Huh, well it's my lucky locker." Ted said nonchalantly.

Andrew continued to push the issue, "Why is that?"

Ted explained, "I hit that locker the day I got that hole in one Spence was talking about, and I've done it ever since."

"Really? I didn't know you were superstitious."

"I'm not." Ted pointed to a golf cart and added abruptly, "My cart is over there. I'll see you at the first hole."

As Ted walked off, Andrew realized Ted would never concede an inch to him in anything. For Ted, admitting he was superstitious would be an admission of defeat to Andrew. It didn't matter what it was. Ted would never acknowledge Andrew was right, nor would he ever admit he was wrong. Andrew shook his head at the realization. As he did, Donohue pulled Andrew aside gently by the arm and whispered, "Hey, Andrew."

"Yeah, Mr. Donohue?"

"Twenty-one ninety-three was your dad's locker when he was a kid. He used to have to hide his clubs and shoes in there so your grandfather wouldn't know he was playing golf. I was pretty new then, working as a caddy, and I remember we had to secretly remove the top shelf of the locker so his clubs would fit. No one uses that locker anymore. It's like a shrine to him."

Andrew smiled, "Huh. How about that? Thanks, Mr. Donohue."

Donohue patted him on the shoulder and gave him a wink. He smiled at Andrew and recited the golfer's prayer as he drove away in his golf cart. "Hit 'em high, hit 'em long!"

Andrew jogged over to his father and called out, "Hey, Dad!"

Ted looked up, "Yeah?" Ted was opening up a new box of balls, Titleist Pro V1s, no doubt.

Andrew called out, "Mom wanted me to ask you if you have your pills."

Ted scowled, scanned around to see if anyone was nearby, then produced a little orange pill bottle from his pants pocket. He rattled it several times with a "don't test me" raise of the eyebrows and got in his cart. "Nag, nag, nag. You're worse than your mother." He stomped the pedal, the electric motor whirring, leaving Andrew, again, shaking his head.

42

Ted and Andrew finished the first hole without incident. Ted hit for par, and a rusty Andrew bogeyed the hole. After each made their drives from the tee box on the second hole, they drove their respective golf carts on the path up the neatly trimmed fairway. A wall of green pine trees lined the pathway like soldiers standing at attention. There was a chorus of sparrows chirping and a chill in the air that early sunny April morning.

Their carts split up around 170 yards down the fairway. Andrew was more right as Ted's tee-shot landed almost in the middle of the fairway and he yelled out, "Look at that, a perfect lie."

Andrew returned the call, "Yep, nice one. I see mine up ahead. If you get to yours first, just hit. Ready-golf, okay?"

Ted, offended, barked back, "You're not that far ahead of me."

Andrew tried to backtrack, "That's not what I meant..." But mid-explanation, a ring came from his phone that was sitting in the golf cart cupholder. Andrew grumbled softly, "Shit." The caller ID showed "Unknown number," and his stomach sank.

Ted's critical glare shot across the width of the fairway Andrew picked up. Ted yelled, "No phones on the course, boy!"

Andrew waved a hand to him and yelled, "Just hit your ball." Into the phone, Andrew blurted out, "Hey, can't talk, I'm on the golf course—"

A deep Scottish voice replied, "Ah, my favorite sport!"

Andrew said what he was thinking out loud by mistake. "Well, I think you play the game a bit differently."

Fergus replied, "That's funny, mate. But believe it or not, I do swing a club the *normal* way sometimes."

"Great, we can play for my debt. Double or nothing," Andrew said confidently.

Fergus replied sharply, "I never said I was any good at the game."

Andrew tried to lighten the tension he created. "Only sport in the world where it takes years and years and years of dedicated practice just to be awful." The two shared a short and forced chuckle.

"I'm shite, mate. You on the other hand..."

Andrew questioned, "What makes you think I'm any good?"

"The acorn doesn't fall far from the tree, eh?"

Andrew tried not to let the burning feeling take over because he needed to get his plan into action. He quickly turned on his Otter.io app to record the call. "What can I do for you, Fergus?"

"Well, I thought I'd just get your voicemail, and I was calling to say the information you gave me was excellent. At this rate, it won't take long to pay for those cameras."

Andrew let a few seconds pass. "Fergus, I have to ask you something. It's been bugging me. Would you have really shot me that night?"

Fergus replied sincerely, "Doctor, you are one of the few I admire of all the people in my club. You are a very skilled poker player, you dress well, and you hold yourself as a man of class."

"Nice of you to say, Fergus." Andrew was still skeptical.

"Well, that's why I was so angry and disappointed to hear your integrity could be cheapened by Mr. Keegan's corruption. Yes, I was very angry with you, Doctor, but would I have killed you over it?" He paused. "No."

"But you told George to shoot us if we moved," Andrew questioned.

"Oh, come off it, Doctor. What was I going to do, give you a big 'wink wink' to let you know I was only making a threat to get Keegan in line?"

"Okay, so you were just threatening Mr. Keegan?"

Fergus continued, "You watch too many movies, Doctor. Not only was Keegan stealing $3.4 million from you and about to murder you, but he was going to use you as fucking target practice! Then dump you in the East River, never to be found again."

Andrew pulled his 7 iron out of his bag and walked towards the cart path, getting as far away from Ted as possible. He let his club rest on his shoulder, tapping the shaft of his club to his trapezius muscle, helping relieve some tension. He watched his father set up his shot; he only had a few more seconds before Ted would rage at him.

"Look Doctor, I gave very specific instructions to Lorry, who could put a bullet between your eyes at 200 yards in the wind, *not* to kill anyone. Forgive me for the theatrics, Doctor, but you of all people know that the *threat* of imminent bodily harm can be a far more effective tool for obtaining compliance than the actual harm itself."

Andrew let his silence confirm the correctness of Fergus' statement.

Fergus continued. "It's not my fault that Mr. Keegan has enemies. He fired over a hundred union electrical workers in Hudson Yards, replacing them with scabs. The unions don't take too kindly to that."

Andrew stayed quiet, praying Fergus would say something incriminating.

"Look, Doctor, I know I'm no choir boy, but neither is Corravallo. He's been brought up on racketeering charges before."

"Do you know him?" Andrew broke his silence.

"Only by reputation."

"Well, he says he's being framed."

"If I was a suspect, don't you think the police would have questioned me by now?"

Andrew had to switch the subject as he needed another $250,000 to gamble on Monday—his clock was ticking.

"Fergus, I wanted to play some poker on Monday, you only gave me $250,000 so I need another $250,000. The Sentinels and Black Knights are off today but play again on Monday. John Palmer only pitches once every four or five games. Could you advance me the money?"

"Tell me where their heads are at Monday evening, and I'll release the funds so you can play. If you're wrong, we'll deal with that later."

Andrew felt the cocktail of disgrace and satisfaction swirling together. It tasted acidic in his mouth and his stomach burned. He got what he wanted, but he'd need to turn that $500,000 into $3 million. He hated himself right now, but soon he would be free, and that bastard Fergus would be behind bars, never to threaten him again.

In the distance, Andrew heard the whoosh of a club swing followed by the distinctive ping of a club head meeting golf ball. Andrew heard Ted yell out, "Yeah baby, got all of that one!" Andrew turned and acknowledged Ted's shot with a weak smile. Ted cupped his hands around his mouth to make a mini-megaphone, "Put down the fucking phone and play!" Ted added mockingly in a high-pitched voice, "I thought you had to be somewhere at one?!"

Fergus couldn't help but hear Ted's admonishments. "Ah, sorry, mate. Poor golf etiquette taking a call. See you next week."

Fergus hung up abruptly and Andrew put the phone back in his cup holder. He felt the frustration of not getting anything he could use. But if Fergus was lying about the cameras, he was sure he was lying about Corravallo and Mr. Keegan.

With a 7 iron in hand, Andrew studied the path to the pin. Then he opted for a 5 iron instead. As he approached his ball, the irony of his club choice wasn't lost. He ruefully shook his head.

Fucking crazy Scotsman.

He was about 175 yards away. He was about 40 yards ahead of Ted's ball before hitting it, but his ball was much further right and Ted had a clearer line to the pin. Because he was a little off right, Andrew chose the bigger club and figured he would take something off his swing.

He took a few practice swings, approached the tee, settled his feet, and swung at the ball. His backswing was slow up and quick down as he torqued his body and hit the ball cleanly. The ping of the ball off the iron sounded great, but Andrew knew he put too much into his swing as the ball took a high arc and sailed like a rocket into the blue sky.

Andrew yelled at the ball, "Oh shit! Sit down, sit, sit!"

Ted swung his cart in an arc close enough to Andrew so he could comment on his shot. "You hit it too goddamned high! You're in the sand trap!"

In frustration, Andrew swung his club one-handed, slicing through the grass like a sickle sending little green nubs of grass in the air. "Yeah, that's exactly where I am. In a fucking sand trap."

They played the next six holes cordially…for them, with just a few digs at each other but nothing to start an argument. On the ninth hole, Andrew made the green in two strokes, but his stroke putting was out of practice, and he three-putted the par 4 hole, bogeying another hole. Ted let him know it.

"Drive for show, putt for dough! Pay up! Twenty bucks! Those three putts will kill you, boy."

Andrew reached in his pocket and handed Ted a $20 bill. "Here you go. Lots of golf left to play, Dad."

Ted was marking his scorecard and noted, "Another hole for me, that makes it six holes to three. You're going to have to have a hell of a back nine."

Andrew shot back, "I always get stronger as the game goes on."

Ted pointed at Andrew with his pencil. "Yeah, like how you played at the Pro-Am in Palm Desert?"

Andrew became annoyed. "Oh, give it a rest, Dad. That was over twenty years ago."

Ted shot back, "Twenty years ago to you, buddy boy. It was like yesterday to me."

Andrew leaned on his putter with one hand and put his other on his hip and looked down at the short cut grass on the green and shook his head, "What do you want me to say, Dad? I was a kid. It was a tough course."

Ted fumed, "Don't give me that tough course bullshit. You choked! You couldn't handle the pressure, so you did what losers do. You quit!"

Andrew yelled back, "I'm not a loser!" Andrew dropped his putter, took two steps toward his father with clenched fists.

43

Andrew pushed the studs of his golf shoes into the soft green to stop himself as he fought the urge to pop Ted in the mouth. Ted had a look of concern for a moment, like that moment when a father first realizes his kid can take him. But when Andrew stopped walking, Ted regained his confidence that Andrew wasn't going to swing at him and shifted back to being angry and frustrated. When it came to their standoffs, Andrew usually took the higher road and tried to keep the peace, but he had had enough today.

Andrew unclenched his fist and instead ripped the Velcro fastener on his snug golf glove to loosen it. He glared at his father. "You know what? I've had a fucking hell of a week, and I don't need to take this shit from you."

Andrew turned and walked away. He picked up his putter and pinched the shaft under his armpit as he pulled his glove off with his other hand.

Ted yelled to Andrew's back, "Where the fuck are you going?"

Andrew went to the back of his cart, shoved the putter in his bag, and yelled, "I'm done with you and your attitude!"

Incensed, Ted strode over. "No, goddamn it. You don't get to walk away. You finish the round. You *always* finish the round."

Andrew looked at his seething father and calmly said, "Well, not today."

Ted squinted his eyes, glaring at his son, and then his eyes got big as if something popped in his head as he threatened, "You walk away, and I won't play with you and Ron Davis and Matt Grayson!

345

You can kiss your Bulldogs contract goodbye!"

Andrew huffed, "So it's like that, huh, Dad?" Andrew crossed his arms tightly in the hope that the rage building in his belly would be trapped there.

Ted growled, "You always finish the round."

As the two entered into their stare-down contest like two MMA fighters, a strong but feminine voice called out, "Mister Ted Beck!"

Andrew and Ted turned their heads simultaneously to acknowledge the voice. They saw a crew of people approaching the green on the ninth hole. There were bodyguards complete with dark glasses and earwigs, a young woman furiously checking her phone while giving instructions to a man carrying an absurdly large camera. Next to her was Mr. Donohue, Davey Redbank, Mr. Westbrook the club president, and Edward R. Collinsbury IV, a Greenwich blue blood and political donor whose family came over on the *Mayflower*. They all flanked Senator Theresa Mann in a semicircle as she took confident steps towards the Beck men.

Senator Mann was a full-bodied woman in her early sixties and fully dubbed up, head to toe in Epic Golf gear. She had on mauve golf slacks, pure white golf shoes, and a white logoed golf shirt covered by a matching mauve golf vest to stave off the morning chill. Whether she could play golf or not was a mystery, but she certainly dressed the part.

Ted went into "fan-greeting" mode and was ear-to-ear smiles as Mr. Westbrook made the introductions to the Senator and Collinsbury. Ted shook hands and said hello to fellow club member Redbank. Andrew hung back and marveled at Ted and the senator.

Ted and Senator Mann had both mastered the game of smile, handshake, and maintaining eye-contact while not giving a shit about the person in front of them. Oh, they would listen, and nod in the affirmative, but it was mainly so they could interject their own narrative.

Andrew saw Ted pointing at Redbank and with his other hand Ted gave Redbank his version of the Vulcan nerve pinch as he jested to the senator how Redbank almost stole the traditional Beck opening day tee time. Ted was able to poke fun at him while ingratiating himself to the senator and assuming the "alpha" position in the dogpile with verbal and physical dominance. Ted used an unassuming voice so masterfully that he was able to disguise an emasculating dig as a good-natured ribbing. It made him the terror of the PGL. When other golfers got paired with Ted Beck, they knew they were in for a long day with Ted's belittling comments disguised as helpful advice from a Masters Champion. And no other golfer talked bad about Ted in public because the fans, reporters, and sponsors adored him.

But the senator was no rookie. She knew exactly what was going on and spun the situation. "Oh Ted, don't get mad at Davey. It was really all my fault." She looked soulfully into Ted's eyes, closed the distance between them, place both hands on her chest, which was bursting through her vest. "But I just had to meet Ted Beck in the place where he began his road to greatness: the Greenwich Country Club." She extended her arms to the golf course and twisted from left to right for maximum effect, which garnered smiles and golf claps all around.

In one soundbite and body movement the senator scored points and saved face for all the powerful men surrounding her. This was how she survived, and thrived, in the full-contact, male-dominated sport of politics. She knew how to get what she wanted while not damaging the frail male egos that controlled her world.

Andrew looked down at his shoes, slapping his hand with his golf glove in a rhythmic fashion and tried not to shake his head at the level of patronizing going on when he heard, "And who is this handsome young man?" from Senator Mann.

"Andrew, come over and meet the senator." Ted motioned for Andrew to join the dogpile.

Andrew knew the drill; he had been doing it since he was a boy. Stand up straight, smile, maintain eye contact, firm handshake, don't look directly into the camera, and most importantly remember the lines:

"I love watching my dad play, he's the best!"

"I'm going to be a pro golfer just like my dad. I only hope I can make him proud."

"I work hard and practice every day. I'm really lucky to have him not only as my dad, but my golf coach too!"

Andrew took a deep breath, pushed the charm button in his brain, and walked into the maelstrom. After a few more minutes of small talk and chatting, the photographer tried to organize the unruly party into a group photo. It was herding cats as he directed the overprotective security guards to step out of the picture and he assured them that at 9:18 a.m. on a Sunday morning in April, on the ninth hole of the Greenwich Country Club the chances of finding any assassins or Democrats were slim and none.

When the photographer completed his mission impossible, another round of handshakes and bro hugs ensued. A young woman offered a basket of pastries, bagels, and muffins to the group. Andrew smiled politely at the young woman and declined anything from the breakfast basket.

Andrew's phone rang again; Ted shot him a dirty look as he stepped away from the crowd.

The caller ID said John Palmer. He answered the phone and used an upbeat tone, saying, "Hey JP! What's up? You're up early."

John replied dryly, "Yeah, well I couldn't sleep, so I was catching up on some emails and I got the strangest email from William, the pilot over at Signature Aviation."

"Oh?" Andrew felt his stomach tighten.

"Yeah, he said that he understood that my guest had to handle a medical emergency, but the airline and the FAA frown upon mid-flight course changes." John's matter-of-fact tone changed to anger, "So you never even made it to Miami! What the fuck, Doc!"

"JP, JP, I'm sorry. You're right. I had a medical emergency. A client was in serious trouble, and I had to go back to New York."

John was incensed, "You lied to me. You promised you'd be there for me. That you'd be watching me..." John became emotional.

Andrew pleaded, "John, I have no excuse. I'm really sorry. I'll pay for the flight."

John shot back, "I don't give a fuck about the money, Doc!" He sniffed. "How, how, how could..."

Andrew knew he was in hot water and declared, "Okay, I fucked up, I'm sorry." He could hear John taking some deep breaths, but he didn't answer for a few seconds. Andrew called out to him gently, "John? John, you there?"

John sniffed and his voice cracked, "Yeah, I'm here."

Andrew pleaded again, "Let's talk about this next week when we are face to face, not over the phone. Come on, John, I'm sorry."

John snapped, "Yeah, you said that. Look, I gotta go."

"John, come in next week, let's talk…" But John hung up. Andrew squeezed his phone and clenched his fist as he looked up to the clear blue sky and shouted, "Fuck!"

The crowd of people turned their heads briefly but then went back to their conversations as Ted took a big bite out of an uncut bagel and his eyes shot daggers at his son.

Sandra was right. He should have called John right away to come clean. Just one more misstep, one more bad decision, one more instance where Fate was calling *his* cards at the poker table, and beating him over, and over, and over again.

Pulling at his hair, he plopped into the seat of the golf cart. He was glad the cart didn't have a rearview mirror because the last thing he wanted to see right now was his face. Ted left the group, got in his cart, rode up next to Andrew and mumbled, "You ready?" He swallowed the big chunk of bagel, took a swig of Coca-Cola, and pointed at Andrew's phone. "And turn that fucking thing off, no more phone calls! And watch your language, you fucking embarrassed me in front of the Senator."

Andrew put his phone on silent mode and put it back in the cupholder. He took a sip of some red Gatorade, lifted the brake, hit the accelerator pedal, and passed Ted's cart as he said in a sarcastic tone, "Yeah, yeah, yeah."

The two men were civil over the next three holes, especially because Andrew got focused and upped his game. Much like he said he would do, Andrew got better as the game went on, and perhaps with Andrew getting pissed, it also focused him. As well, Andrew could tell Ted was getting fatigued. Andrew beat Ted on the 10th, 12th and 13th holes, taking three out of the first four holes. The 14th hole was a par 4, 468 yards.

Andrew felt confident and, in a groove, as they whirred their golf carts up to the white tee box. "Hey Dad, we're coming up to my favorite hole, number fourteen. I won the last three of four holes, so it's now seven holes to six. Looking to tie it up here."

Ted snapped back, "Don't gloat."

Ted quickly grabbed his new Epic Golf driver. It had a long shaft with an oversized titanium head. This was one of the few clubs Ted liked from his newly sponsored brand.

Ted marched up to the tee box, teed up his ball, and announced, "I'm teeing off."

Andrew pulled out his Ping Driver and disputed Ted's call, "But I won the last hole. It's my honor."

Ted snapped back, "Well, I'm here and it's ready-golf, remember."

Andrew shook his head and quipped, "Be my guest."

Ted took a few practice swings and waggled his club a few times as he addressed his ball. The birds in the nearby pines were happily chirping away, but it didn't affect Ted as he was focused. Ted took a long back swing and came down smoothly and swiftly and the ball had a high-pitched ping as it shot off the club and straight down the fairway. Ted lingered as he watched his ball land over 270 yards with a generous roll.

Andrew had cooled down and threw a bone to his father, "Nice shot, Dad." He hoped maybe they could keep the civility.

Ted was gleeful, "Yep! Looks like Pebble Beach '98. I kicked Jack's ass up and down the course at that Open."

Andrew quipped back, "What was he? 70?"

Ted grumbled, "No wise ass, 58." Ted swung his club in perfect form. "Did you see how fluid my backswing was? You just muscle the crap out of the ball."

Andrew nodded as he pushed the ball in with the tee to set it up. Andrew looked back at Ted, then looked down the fairway and without taking any practice swings or wagging the club at the ball. Andrew corkscrewed his body and smashed it. The ball hissed off the tee and sailed through the air, well past Ted's ball, and then hit the fairway and rolled even further. Another 300-plus-yard drive.

Andrew turned to his father and sarcastically said, "Wow, look how far past your ball that went." He then winced and feigned disappointment, "I guess I muscled it again. Sorry, Dad."

Ted didn't do a good job of hiding his anger that Andrew got to him. He was losing his ability to hide behind his chiseled face. He took off in his cart and wiped his face with his sleeve. Andrew grinned with satisfaction as he watched the back of Ted's cart whizz down the cart path.

Andrew made the green on his next shot and drained a 14-foot putt for birdie. Ted parred the hole, so now it was seven holes to seven. The 15th hole was Ted's hole-in-one hole and he felt confident he would take the lead. The hole was a par 3, 167 yards. Each man pulled out their 7 irons and approached the hole.

Ted was playing mind games, trying to get in Andrew's head by continuing to usurp Andrew's honor to tee off first. But Andrew knew all of Ted's kamikaze tactics. So he didn't react or call him out; he let him have it.

However, Andrew wasn't going to let him take his honors without getting his own dig in. "All tied up, Dad. Seven holes to seven." And then he added to make his point, "I told you I get better as the game goes on."

Not to be undone, Ted shot back, "Oh yeah? Fourteen may be your hole, but I own the fifteenth. Fifty bucks says I pitch this within two feet of the hole."

Andrew nodded. "I'll take that bet." As Ted teed up, he added, "And hey, I'll even let you hit first."

Ted wasn't amused as he looked down the fairway to the pin. He had to hit the ball almost exactly 165 yards to win the bet. Ted was feeling good and had originally picked his Epic Golf 7 iron out of the bag but then he saw his 7 iron from Taylormade. Ted still kept a few clubs from his playing days and the Taylormade 7 iron was one of his favorites. This was the club he had made the hole in one with.

Ted took his time with a few well-timed practice swings that cut the air with a whoosh. He addressed his ball and took a healthy swing. He took a nice sized but not too chunky divot. The ball left the tee box and shot almost straight up. The arc was a thing of beauty and it landed on the green and took a short roll heading to the left of the hole. Ted couldn't contain his excitement, "Look at that, buddy boy! That might make it to the hole!"

The two men raced down the fairway and circled the water hazard from different sides but they met at the top to get a better look, "Oh yeah!" Ted exclaimed.

Andrew couldn't help but grin, "Nice shot, Dad! Just rolled past the hole, but you're definitely within two feet. Fifty-bucks, here you go." Andrew pulled a $50 dollar bill out of his billfold and handed it to his father.

Ted continued to bask in his shot as Andrew set up his ball. "You remember when I sank that chip on sixteen at the US Open to clinch it?"

Andrew was taking a practice swing and replied, "No. I don't."

Ted got annoyed, "You should. That shot bought the house you grew up in."

Andrew glared over at his father as he kept his golf stance, "Wonderful. Can I hit my ball now?"

Ted threw his hand at Andrew in acquiescence.

Andrew took a nice swing and hit the ball solid with his 7 iron. The ball pitched on a high arc. When it landed on the front of the green, it had some spin on it, and the ball took off towards the front of the hole. The ball's momentum stopped just a couple of feet away from the pin and hole.

Andrew announced, "Not as close to the hole as yours, but I'm good."

Ted, still steaming, shoved a finger in Andrew's direction. "You know what your trouble is? You take everything for granted. My old man never even saw me swing a club."

Andrew was fed up and moaned, "Jesus Christ. Don't start."

As Andrew left the tee box to put his 7 iron back in his bag, Ted followed him and continued his rant. "I was there for you at every tournament. Even the fucking rec league matches. It was torture watching those little bastards rip up my course. But I was there. I was traveling over 150 days a year on the PGL Tour, going up against the toughest competitors in the world. But I always found time for you."

After shoving his club in his bag, Andrew turned and pointed back at his father. "You found time for my tournaments. Don't confuse the two."

Ted was exasperated. "Everything I did, I did for you. I turned you into a champion!" He pointed back at Andrew.

The two men were face to face at the back of Andrew's cart. Andrew then questioned, "So you making me a champion, that makes you a good father?"

Ted thew his hand down emphatically. "Goddamn, right it does!"

Andrew shot back, "Brandon's not a champion. Were you a good father to him?"

Ted was speechless and turned around and got in his cart and sped off to the green. Andrew followed.

The two men reached the green in silence. Ted was about a foot and a half away from the cup and Andrew was about four feet. Since Andrew was "away" he hit first. He lined up his putt and hit it nicely, but it was just short of the cup. He looked up at Ted, who looked away from him but nodded, in essence permitting him to putt again. Andrew lightly tapped the ball and it fell in the hole, scoring a three or par for the hole.

Ted lined up his putt. If he drained it he would win the hole and put himself back in the lead. Ted took his time. He hit the ball lightly but somehow, he missed the break and the ball went right and missed the hole, putting him about four inches away from the cup. Ted was incensed at his miss and muttered, "Goddamn it, son-of-a-bitch!"

Andrew started walking away and tossed out, "You're good. Pick it up." Meaning Ted didn't have to hit the ball in the hole and Andrew conceded that Ted would make it. However, the concession did not get the reaction Andrew expected.

Ted barked at Andrew, "Don't placate me, boy."

Andrew flippantly threw out, "Dad, it's just a game."

Ted was incensed as he pointed his putter at Andrew. "You owe everything to this game. And—"

Andrew interrupted and shot back, "And *you*? That's what you were going to say, right? That I owe everything to this game and *you*?"

Ted slammed his putter in the ground, putting a dent in the beautifully manicured green. "You're fucking-A right. But you flushed it down the toilet. We should have been the first father-son Masters Champions! And you fucking stole that from me!"

"I *what?*" Andrew questioned with shock.

Ted yelled, "You fucking quit!" Then added with a sarcastic and demeaning tone, "And why? Because I pushed you too hard?"

Andrew didn't react and pushed back, "That's not why I quit." Andrew made his way back to the green and added, "I quit because I didn't want to be anything like you."

Ted started to make a beeline for his cart, but Andrew cut him off and stood in front of him, blocking his path. Ted got in his face, "Get the fuck out of my way!"

Andrew didn't budge. "Or what? No lockers to shove me up against out here!"

Ted shot back, "What the fuck are you talking about?"

"Remember in the locker room in Palm Desert. After I quit golf?"

"Oh, come on. I barely touched you."

Andrew disagreed. "A guy from the locker room had to force you off me." He added, "You gave me a fat lip!"

Ted poked Andrew in the chest. "You choked—I was pissed! I went on national TV saying you were a winner and then you quit! All my hard work! Gone."

Andrew poked his dad back, albeit lightly, but multiple times. He lowered his voice to say, "I'll let you in on little secret."

"What's that?"

"I didn't choke."

"The score says different, pal!"

"On the seventeenth, I aimed for those rocks. Got them twice. Pretty masterful shots, if you ask me."

"Bullshit! That is some lame-ass, cover-up bullshit!"

Andrew continued not reacting. "Then on the eighteenth, I sunk that tee shot into the drink, but then, just to give you some hope, I hit that beauty of a chip shot onto the green."

Ted's face was a ball of confusion. "You did what!?" He started breathing hard.

"And then, after that wonderful fatherly pep talk you gave me, I tried to hit that ball as close to the hole without going in. Another fucking masterful shot, if you ask me." Andrew nodded his head as he announced with some sarcasm, "That might have been my best shot ever."

Ted's breath was raspy and his mouth gaped open as he tried to draw in more air. As he started to stumble away, his face was flushed and his words jumbled together. "On purpose?" He started to stutter, "Why, why, why the fuck would anyone do that?!"

Andrew lashed out, "You stole my childhood because you didn't have one. Your father didn't give a shit about you. He cared more about making money than spending time with you."

Ted got a breath in, but the anger from Andrew's remark sent him into a rage as he rushed his son. "You little son-of-a-bitch! I'll kill you!"

Ted threw a wild haymaker at Andrew, which he easily slipped. The force of the missed punch sent Ted tumbling to the ground.

Andrew bent over, putting his hands on his knees and taunted his father, "Missed me by a mile. Look at you!" Andrew paced the green like a boxer in the ring, taunting his opponent. He motioned to his father and barked, "Get up, old man!"

Ted put one leg up so he was kneeling on one knee and pushed himself off the ground. The pill bottle fell out of his pocket and rolled across the green. The Zestril tablets inside rattled with each turn of the bottle.

Andrew continued to taunt his father as years of anguish and anger surfaced. "Your father didn't love you, so you turned to the only people who would— your fans."

Ted staggered to his feet as he grappled with what Andrew had just said. He mumbled, "No...no, I'm a good father."

"You fucked me up. You made Brandon a basket case. You drove Mom into a lonely depression. You ruined all our lives so you could hear the applause. But I don't hear it now." Andrew put his hand to his ear as if he was straining to hear something. "Where is it?"

Staggering, Ted forced out, "People...people love me."

Andrew held his father by his shirt with two hands and glared into his eyes. "That's because they don't *know* you."

Ted's eyes rolled backward in his head as he fell to the ground out of Andrew's grasp. Ted hit the ground with a thump as Andrew was taken by surprise. Ted reached for the pill bottle, but it was a good two feet beyond his grasp. Ted coughed. "My...pills, I can't reach..."

Andrew raced and got the bottle, then pulled Ted onto his lap. "Dad! I got them. Hold on!" He looked into his father's eyes, and the anger and vengefulness he felt inside turned to horror as he saw his father's eyes roll backward in his head. Andrew fumbled with the child safety cap of the pill bottle.

Ted managed to choke out a call to his son, "Andrew..."

"Yeah, I'm here. Hold on."

Andrew was fumbling and trying to open the bottle. The panic in his brain was sending emergency messages to his hands and they were malfunctioning.

"Andrew, look at me." Ted pushed his words out with a huff.

Ted was looking up at him, his face was losing color, his voice was weak, but he managed to open his mouth, then close it as if the words decided to go back down his throat, he opened again and said, "You're, you're...my greatest...disappointment."

Andrew sat in shock. That couldn't have been what he said. That's not what a father's last words to his son are! He looked down at his father, a wave of confusion and sadness took him over, and he waited for his father to correct his words. He didn't.

Ted closed his eyes and his head fell away onto Andrew's thigh.

"Dad! Dad! No, no, no! Help! Help! Someone!"

He looked around at the pine trees blowing in the breeze, their fine needles moving ever so gently. The birds squawked, and the sounds filled the air for a while and then went silent. The red and white lettered 15th hole flag was lying on the ground where he had placed it when they were putting. The flag no longer flapped in the spring breeze. It laid flat on the soft green, motionless, just like his father.

His eyesight was limited, tunnel vision and all he could see was a little white ball, four inches away from a small black hole. He sat there. He didn't know how long. He felt a man's body on his lap until he felt the weight of a hand on his shoulder, and he felt Ted being pulled off his lap and out of his clenched grasp.

He felt two arms grab him underneath his armpits and he was lifted away. He saw a man in a blue jumpsuit performing compressions on Ted's chest and an oxygen mask over his face. He felt disconnected from his body and being led away from the green. He felt like he was floating in a current of a river.

The people sat him inside of a big red vehicle. There was a light shining in his eye and a woman was talking to him, but her voice was muffled too as if he was underwater.

He peered around the woman and saw the man in the blue jumpsuit rip Ted's golf shirt open, exposing his chest. Then the man took two bright yellow paddles and for the first time words became decipherable as he heard "Clear!" The man in the blue jumpsuit quickly placed the paddles on Ted's chest, and his body convulsed, then dropped back on the soft low-cut grass of the green. "Again!" A rising whirring pitch, and another yell of "Clear!" and Andrew saw Ted's body flop for the second time, and for the second time, it fell back. The woman in front of him left Andrew to go to the other two men around Ted. His view of Ted was blocked.

Andrew felt something held tightly in his hand. He looked down and it was as if his fingers were in a permanent fist, and they refused to respond to what his brain was telling them to do. He looked at his hand again, intently, and slowly his fingers began to respond. In it was a small amber pill bottle. The cap firmly closed.

Andrew was confused, his mind racing but going nowhere. He couldn't string cohesive thoughts together. Every thought was interrupted with an electric pulse. He was trying not to fall out of the back of the vehicle he was in. He was leaning up against the hard metal door. He felt something round and solid grinding against his thigh. He reached in his pocket, and now instead of holding a small plastic cylinder, he held a pure white dimpled golf ball.

He began to shiver convulsively. He dropped the ball and watched it roll away. As the ball rolled on the green Andrew became dizzy and his view went from a bird's eye to being directly in line with the ball on the ground. He felt the soft cool grass on his face.

Beyond the ball, which looked much bigger now due to the closeness to his eye, Ted's face lunar eclipsed the white ball. It was as if Ted's little head was connected to a big white ball, he looked like a snowman. Andrew could see his father's face clearly, eyes closed restfully, as if he was taking an afternoon nap. Andrew felt a sleepiness too, and he closed his eyes. As he did, he heard his own heartbeat. The sound comforted him.

Right before he slipped into unconsciousness, he heard the man in the blue jumpsuit with the yellow paddles say, "He's gone."

44

Andrew woke up in the back of the ambulance. An oxygen mask covered his face. He slowly sat up. He heard the woman say, "Hey, take it easy. You fainted." He sat up. He took the mask off and grumbled, "I'm fine."

He pitched his legs off the stretcher and onto the metal floor. He rose slowly and the woman grabbed his forearm for support. With her help, he climbed out of the ambulance only to see paramedics, police, Tom Donohue, and other club staffers moving en masse. The paramedics moved a white sheet shaped like an inert Ted Beck. A paramedic rushed over to Andrew, and he waved him off.

The stretcher rolled across the green, leaving two rows of wheel tracks on the sensitive grass. "Is that my dad? He's dead?"

The paramedic mournfully replied, "Yes, your father had a massive heart attack. We tried to revive him, but he didn't respond. I'm sorry."

Mr. Donohue and Bobby Spencer rushed to Andrew, each red-faced and eyes glistening. They group-hugged a dazed Andrew. Bobby tried to speak, his mouth moved, but no words came out, just sadness in his eyes. Andrew found his legs and his brain rebooted. It was like he woke up from a dream—a dream that was now happening.

Andrew watched them load Ted's body in the back of another ambulance. He looked around the course at the various people working the scene. In the distance, he saw another golf cart racing up the fairway, not on the cart path, making deep grooves in the fresh and damp fairway. Andrew's first cognitive thought hit him.

The greenskeepers won't be happy about that.

As the cart drew close, he saw Mr. Westbrook and next to him was his mother, Helena.

The golf cart stopped short of the green. Ripping up the fairway was one thing, but even the death of an all-time great like Ted Beck was not an occasion for sacrificing a green. Helena hopped out of the cart and ran across the grass towards the ambulance with Ted's body. Andrew watched his mother run and a second thought hit him.

I've never seen my mother run before.

The paramedics stopped her as she drew close to the ambulance. Andrew freed himself from Mr. Donohue's and Bobby's grasp and went to her. He gently held his mother, whispering in her ear, "I'm sorry, Mom."

She pulled away enough to look him in the eye. When he stared into her bright green eyes, Andrew saw confusion and sadness, but he was taken aback when he saw what looked like a hint of relief on her face.

Mother and son remained locked in a mutually therapeutic embrace. They watched the ambulance pull off slowly onto the cart path–flashing lights on, wailing sirens off.

Andrew sat with his mother in the empty restaurant at the country club while tears flowed down her cheeks. Andrew's scabbed laceration on his lip had opened again when he fainted. His right hand held a 2 x 2 gauze pad as he applied pressure to stop the bleeding. While doing so, he never loosened the warm and comforting clasp of his mother's hand with his other hand. Meanwhile, a group of men and women from the country club stood out of ear's reach, commenting on the sad scene. Andrew read their body language. Torn between the equally compelling urges to give the Becks their space and wanting to approach to express their sympathy, they shifted their hips and shoulders in uncomfortable gestures.

Helena's futile attempts at suppressing her emotions did not go unnoticed. Peering again into his mother's eyes, Andrew caught her shuddering as she breathed. She was determined to avoid creating a dramatic scene. She straightened her posture, took a few slow deep breaths, and gracefully wiped the stubborn tears from her eyes. Subconsciously, she pulled at her short blonde hair, a gesture that jolted Andrew into a flash of heartwarming insight:

Ahhh…So that's where I got it from!

The door to the restaurant slammed open as Sandra ran into the room wearing the same clothes from the previous night. She yelled out her husband's name and rushed to him. He stood up, dropping the gauze, and gently let go of his mother's hand.

Sandra and Andrew embraced as she whispered gently, "I'm sorry, I'm sorry."

Andrew pulled her tight, "No, I'm sorry. It's my fault. I'll change. I promise."

The couple looked into each other's eyes, and uncontrollable tears flowed down their cheeks. They embraced again and then Andrew pulled up Helena to join the group embrace.

The sound of more commotion drew their attention as the MIB looking bodyguards cleared a path for Senator Mann while her assistant, still with her phone out, looked a little freaked out.

The woman came to Helena and grabbed Helena's hands with hers. "Mrs. Beck, I'm Senator Theresa Mann. I am so very sorry. This must be a terrible shock."

Andrew jerked his head, wanting to look at the Senator, he didn't know what expression he was looking for, but he intently watched her, nonetheless.

Helena graciously nodded her head and forced a polite, "Thank you, Senator. Very kind of you."

The senator looked around and saw a face she recognized. "Hello, weren't you at the ribbon cutting this week?"

Sandra wiped the tears away with her left and extended her right. "Yes, Senator. I'm Sandra Wells, from Wells PR. We put on the event."

"You did a wonderful job." She nodded her head, and her assistant also nodded in unison. Senator Mann then turned her attention back to Helena. "Mrs. Beck—"

"Helena, please, Senator."

Senator Mann smiled at her, "Helena…if there is anything my office can do for you in your time of need, please reach out to us." The assistant tried to get around the Senator with a business card but couldn't find an angle to Helena. Andrew reached with his hand out and nodded. The woman politely gave him the card with a soft smile.

Senator Mann saw this out of her peripheral vision and turned to Andrew. Helena said, "This is my son, Andrew."

"Yes, we met earlier today." The Senator didn't break eye contact with Andrew. Her whole face and body seemed to emanate an aura of sympathy and concern. But Andrew saw it, in her eyes: it was sympathy and not empathy. Senator Mann, a life-long politician, had 20 years of rehearsed moments like these, and she had the concerned look down pat.

"I'm so sorry, Andrew." She shook his hand with both hands clasped around his.

"Thank you, Senator. I appreciate it." Andrew replied, still searching her face and eyes for micro-expressions that would give her true intent away. But she was good.

Nice poker face.

She added, "A great man was lost today. One of Greenwich's finest."

Andrew winced and he saw the Senator's eyebrow raise when he did. He broke contact to look at his mother. A slow tear rolled down her flushed cheek. She caught the wince too.

Mr. Westbrook came over, and Senator Mann's secret service detail asked if they could move to a less public spot as the Sunday morning breakfast crowd was starting to form outside the restaurant.

Mr. Westbrook offered to take Helena personally to Greenwich Hospital, where she would have the unfortunate task of filling out the death certificate and claiming Ted's personal effects.

Sandra was driving Andrew's car as he sat in the passenger seat. Things always look different from the passenger seat. Andrew noticed things on the short drive home he had never seen before, like the beautiful statues at the front of one house's gates: two angels, hands in prayer. And another house had a perfectly manicured lawn. He thought it would be a great place to play a touch football game.

After a few minutes of studying these strange new sights, he asked, "Are you taking a different route home? Because it seems much longer."

Sandra raised an eyebrow at him as she said, "No, we're on North Road. This is how long it takes when you drive the speed limit."

"Oh, that makes sense." They both shared a well-needed chuckle, and Sandra reached out for Andrew's hand. He gladly took it, kissed it and said, "Thank you."

Sandra nodded her head, but she was too choked up to reply.

"Oh, shit!" Andrew exclaimed.

Sandra panicked, clutching the wheel with both hands as if she was about to hit something, "What?! What?!"

Andrew shook his head and frowned, "I guess we're not going to make our appointment with Francois."

Sandra put a hand on her chest. "Oh, that!" She let out a deep exhale. "Don't worry about it, hon."

Andrew looked sincerely at his wife. "I'm really sorry, Sandra."

"Andrew, don't worry about it. I'll find another decorator."

"No, not that. I mean, I'm sorry for everything I put you through this week."

"It's okay." She choked up and nodded.

"Look, I'm going to get through this."

Sandra looked at him quizzically. "Is there something else going on that I should know about?"

"I got it under control. I'm gonna fix this. I promise."

Sandra looked at the road and back at Andrew as if she was watching a tennis match. But Andrew didn't make eye contact. He looked down the winding bucolic street and nodded to himself. However sad, angry, and confused he felt about the one man who controlled his youth, who was now under a white sheet, he forced those feelings deep into his gut. He put all his focus on the man who was trying to control him now. He pictured himself winning the poker game and getting the video to his phone with 24 hours to spare from his ally's deadline. He would show the police and see Fergus hauled out of that stainless steel elevator to hell in handcuffs. Andrew wanted to see his smug, confident face traded for a face that was smacked by defeat, knowing who it was that defeated him.

He would play the poker game of his life on Monday, and when he won, he would be free. No one would ever control him again, ever.

His only way out was all-in.

ACKNOWLEDGEMENTS

I have always envisioned my writing as a team sport. True to this vision, there have been a core group of people who helped me to get *Headcase* across the goal line. As this is my debut novel, I do feel compelled to acknowledge many of those people. So please bear with me.

First, I will start off with my oldest and biggest supporter, my best friend, Mike Bothwell. Mike and I have been best friends since college. Mike cheered me on as I pursued my dream to be a writer after the sale of my company in late June 2019. My last day as the Chief Financial Officer of the company I co-founded in 2009 was January 31st, 2020. With almost no time to adjust to my "new life" the pandemic hit in March 2020.

From those early days in March, a big part of my day was Mike's and my daily 9 am call. Mike would get my latest updates and struggles of what was going on with my novel as I made the switch from analyzing financial statements and living in Excel spreadsheets, to writing a grammatically correct narrative and living in Microsoft Word. Mike has seen so many different versions of *Headcase* I'm always amazed how he could keep the current plot and character arcs straight in his head. He always had good feedback from a reader's perspective and was always constructive in how he made his points. He didn't sugar coat things when they needed to be said, and he gave ample praise when it was deserved. Mike has been the rock in my life, and he has been on this journey with me every step of the way. Thank you, Mike, I could not have done it without you!

Next, I have to thank my editors Ben Obler and Jill Tomlin.

Ben is a talented writer, editor, and teacher. I met Ben in April 2021 over a zoom introduction. We hit it off immediately. He was a tennis player and liked sports, but to my unbelievable luck, he was also a poker player—and a good one at that. I learned how to play poker by downloading a video game on my phone and watching Daniel Negreanu's Master Class. Ben was not only able to help me with the story, and character development, and teach me specific narration and dialogue techniques, but he helped me learn the nuances of poker so I could reflect that in my story. Ben has been a significant part of my development as a writer during this period and I've learned so much from him. He was patient with my mistakes, and he was an excellent soundboard for pitching ideas. He helped me apply techniques to my raw storytelling and gave me a set of writer's tools that I use every day. I'm so thankful for his mentorship and friendship.

My other editor was Jill Tomlin, and if that name sounds familiar, that's because it is the name of the fictional arena in *Headcase: The Tomlin Insurance Sports and Entertainment Complex* aka the TISEC.

Jill's husband Michael and his brother John are close friends of mine. John and Michael were born and raised in Barbados, and John is my attorney in New York. When I spent Christmas of 2019 in Barbados, I met Michael and Jill. Jill is originally from Trinidad, and I love her "Trini" accent. When I moved to Barbados in September 2020, the entire Tomlin family took me in as one of their own, and we have been close ever since.

Michael has an insurance brokerage firm that is spreading through the Caribbean like wildfire. We share a love of the sea, sports, and entrepreneurship. I thought having an arena named after him would be fun but also a nod to a fellow entrepreneur with a great future.

Jill really helped me acclimate to Barbados in my early days by helping me find things I needed for my house. She also drove me around to the shops until I got the hang of driving on the left side of the road and in a car with the steering wheel on the right.

As if that wasn't enough, when I got severely ill with Dengue Fever at Christmas 2020, Jill checked in on me, and because I was delirious with fever and forgot to eat, she made me lunch and made sure I was taking care of myself. But not only is Jill an angel of a human being, but she is also an English teacher and an editor. I now refer to her as "Jill the Grammarian." Jill really helped me tighten the language, improve my grammar, and worked with me on my repetitive tendency to write comma-spliced sentences. She was patient with me and meticulous about the little things that mattered. As an accountant by trade, I love it when people are detail-oriented, and Jill explained some of the grammar technicalities behind the edits she made in great detail. She explained the techniques so my visual-kinesthetic learning style could grasp and implement them immediately. I guess years of teaching High Schoolers came in handy there.

Between Ben and Jill, I had the perfect editing team. They both have that rare combination of being incredibly technically proficient and great communicators, teachers, and mentors. They delivered their rebukes with a smile, as they both knew my objective was not to save my ego but to make *Headcase* the best it could be.

"Edit without mercy" is my writing mantra, and Ben and Jill took me to task. They challenged me, pushed me, and made me a better writer. I still have a lot of growing to do as a writer, but I feel confident my writing will get better and better with Ben and Jill in my corner. If *Headcase* reads easily and smoothly, then it's all due to Ben and Jill's work.

Perhaps something that is a little unusual for most writers is that a big part of the imagery of the characters is not just in my head, but I have actual pictures of the characters. You can see the images on my website *www.chriskjones.com/meet-the-characters* and the book's back cover.

The original artwork of my characters was created by a talented illustrator, Chelsea Dunlap, who worked for me at one of my companies. Back in 2017, I sent Chelsea a few scenes and the descriptions of the characters. From this limited amount of information, Chelsea captured my characters' essences using minimalist art (featureless faces). Chelsea took the pictures out of my mind and brought them to life.

When it came time to come up with the uniform colors for my sports characters, I worked with my web designer, Dave Bixler, and we came up with the color scheme and fonts for their uniforms. Dave took Chelsea's art and designed the uniforms with the colors and fonts I wanted. He did a fantastic job, and it was so cool to see my characters decked out in their uniforms.

I first came up with the idea for *Headcase* in 2016. I envisioned it as a TV show, but I did not know anything about writing a TV pilot. While working 60 hours a week running a hyper-growth company, I had no time to go to film school. So I hired GiGi New, an experienced TV writer and instructor, to teach me one-on-one. GiGi and I worked together for several years to develop a pilot script. Every Tuesday night, I'd race home from work and flick a switch in my brain, and from 6:00 pm to 8:00 pm, the CFO went away so the artist could play. GiGi taught me the fundamentals of character arc, dialogue, story, and most of all, to stop "pulling my punches" with characters and not shy away from making their lives incredibly difficult. I have a hard time seeing these characters that I care about suffer, however, the only way to have them grow is through the hardships they experience due to their poor choices. Although I ultimately decided to make *Headcase* into a novel, GiGi's time with me laid the groundwork for *Headcase* to be what it is today.

And lastly, I have to thank the one companion that had been with me since the start of my writing *Headcase* in novel form, and that is the Republic of Barbados. I had been going to the island since 2012, but I never stayed more than two weeks. In late July 2020, John Tomlin told me about the one-year visa Barbados was granting to remote workers, and I jumped at the opportunity. I figured Barbados would be the perfect place to "hunker down" and write my first novel.

From the moment I arrived on September 23rd, 2020 under the Welcome Stamp Program, Barbados greeted me with a warm hug. I rented a wonderful beach house on the South Coast. I found it impossible to give myself any excuses for not writing every day when all I needed for inspiration was to look up and see the sun's reflection on the turquoise sea just a few steps away from my desk. Barbados has always been my go-to place to heal and recover from my high-

stressed entrepreneurial life. Now, Barbados was my den of creativity, and I lived my lifelong dream of becoming a writer. Every day I tried to show my gratitude by not getting too distracted by the sun, sand, and surf and by writing a novel that would make the people of my adopted nation proud.

Writing is the loneliest profession in the world. I spent countless hours with just my thoughts, and it felt like I was on an island… well yeah, I know I was on an island, but you know what I mean. Anyway, I was so fortunate to be surrounded by such good friends, mentors, and advisors who cared enough about me to share their wisdom and support for my work. I hope you have as much fun reading *Headcase* as I did writing it.

ABOUT THE AUTHOR

Chris K. Jones is a former competitive athlete and coach. His experiences in his youth with professional athletes shaped his interest in understanding the minds of athletes. Trying to mimic his heroes, he ignored the messages his body was sending him. After a series of broken bones, an eating disorder, and mental health issues, he knew he had to change. Chris turned to Judo, translated as the "gentle way," Buddhism, meditation, and intensive self-reflection to begin his journey to healing. This served as a pathway to understanding who he was, on and off the mat, and how to turn failure into success. Chris uses his imagination and suspenseful storytelling to raise awareness about generational trauma and mental health in sports. Chris splits his time between Tarrytown, NY and Barbados.

Made in the USA
Monee, IL
12 September 2022